Keri Arthur won the *Romantic Times* Career Achievement Award for Urban Fantasy and has been nominated in the B... Contemporary Paranormal category of the *Romantic* ... Reviewers' Choice Awards. She's a dessert and f... cook by trade, and lives with her daughter in M... urne, Australia.

Visi... er website at www.keriarthur.com

Darkness Devours

A DARK ANGELS NOVEL

KERI ARTHUR

piatkus

PIATKUS

First published in the US in 2012 by Signet Select
an imprint of New American Library
a division of Penguin Group (USA) Inc.
First published in Great Britain as a paperback original
in 2012 by Piatkus

A CIP catalogue record for this book
is available from the British Library.

ISBN 978-0-7499-5765-0

Printed and bound by CPI Group (UK) Ltd, Croydon, CR0 4YY

Papers used by Piatkus are from well-managed forests
and other responsible sources.

MIX
Paper from
responsible sources
FSC® C104740

Piatkus
An imprint of
Little, Brown Book Group
100 Victoria Embankment
London EC4Y 0DY

An Hachette UK Company
www.hachette.co.uk

www.piatkus.co.uk

I'd like to thank my editor, Danielle Perez,
and everyone else at NAL, for making me feel so
welcome. May we work on many books together.

This book is dedicated to my agent, Miriam;
thanks for the advice, the hand-holding,
and the friendship.

DARKNESS
DEVOURS

Chapter 1

We do what we have to do—we track these people down by whatever means necessary.

The words weren't mine, but they ran through my brain nevertheless, going around and around, chased by echoes of pain and heartbreak as I stood on the footpath and stared up at the multistory building in Southbank.

I'd never been inside but I'd driven past it many a time. And, more than once, I'd stopped here at the curbside, sharing a lingering kiss, reluctant to let what we'd experienced the night before come to an end.

I'd been so in love. Stupidly, foolishly in love. And it had all been a lie. Not on my part, but his.

Jak Talbott—the werewolf I thought I'd spend the rest of my life with—had wanted nothing more than a good story. And he'd got that, mixing lies with reality so deftly it was hard to pick them apart. Mom had sued both him and the paper over the story, but in the end had settled out of court rather than have her name—and possibly mine—dragged endlessly through the gossip mags while the court case was ongoing. But mud tends to stick, even if it isn't true, and she lost several lucrative TV spots because of it. Not that *that* had particularly worried her. She'd been more concerned about the effect of Jak's actions on me.

And my reaction had been fairly intense. Even now, two years later, I avoided anything resembling a deep or lasting relationship, preferring the fun but emotionally sterile liaison with my Aedh lover, Lucian.

Meeting Jak Talbott again was the last thing I ever wanted to do.

I crossed my arms and rubbed them lightly. The midday sun held plenty of warmth, but it didn't chase the chill away from my flesh.

We do what we have to do—we track these people down by whatever means necessary.

Fine words, but did I have the courage to actually follow them through? After standing here in front of this building for the last five minutes, I wasn't so sure that I did.

I glanced at my watch and saw it was a few minutes past twelve. If I was going to run, I'd better do it now . . .

Awareness tingled across my senses and I looked up the steps to the building's entrance—straight into the intense black gaze of Jak Talbott.

I can't do this, I thought, as all the old pain and hurt rose, threatening to drown me all over again. *I just can't.*

But even as that thought crossed my mind, the inherently stubborn part of my nature rose, as well. I straightened my spine. Clenched my fists. I could do this. I *needed* to do this. Not only for the sake of my heart and any future relationships I might have, but also because saving the world from the hordes of hell might well depend on what happened here with Jak.

I watched him walk toward me, his strides long and lithe, graceful in an almost feline sort of way. He wasn't a classically handsome man, but his rough-hewn features were easy on the eyes and his body was well toned without being too muscular. His hair, like his skin, was a rich black, although these days there seemed to be a fair amount of silver glinting through the shaggy thickness of it.

He stopped several feet in front of me, his gaze briefly skimming me before resting on the fists clenched at my sides.

"I hope you're not going to aim those at me, Risa."

"You've already had one good story out of my family," I said, amazed that my voice actually sounded civil. "I'm not about to give you another one."

"Really?" The black depths of his eyes were wary, watchful. "Then what do you want?"

"Coffee." Although, in all honesty, several large bottles of alcohol—the stronger, the better—would probably have been more suitable right then. I might have the constitution of a werewolf, which meant it was damnably hard for me to get drunk, but several bottles would at least soften the haunting sense of loss.

Jak raised an eyebrow, but waved a hand toward the small café not far up the road. "They make fairly good coffee."

"Then let's go."

I strode forward, the heels of my sandals clicking on the concrete, a tattoo of sound as fast as my heart. He walked beside me, his familiar woodsmoke scent washing over me, raising memories of lazy evenings spent in front of the old log fire in his house, our bodies entwined . . .

Damn it, he used you, I reminded myself fiercely. *Remember that, and only that.*

The automatic fly-screen door swished open as we neared the café. Inside was shadowed, the air a mix of rich coffee, fried food, and sweaty humanity. The air-conditioning obviously wasn't doing a great job at this end of the room.

I wove through the tables, heading for one near the back, close to the overhead vent. The rush of cold air had goose bumps racing across my bare arms, but at least it was free of the more unpleasant smells in the space.

"So," Jak said, pulling out a chair and sitting down opposite me, "what is this all about?"

Instead of immediately answering, I asked, "What would you like to drink?"

His smile held a wry edge. "Forgotten already?"

"It's been a few years, Jak. People and tastes change." And I wish *my* tastes had changed. Wished I could honestly say I no longer found him so damnably attractive.

"I haven't changed. Not when it comes to coffee, anyway."

Meaning he'd changed in other ways? Somehow I doubted it. I punched in an order of coffee and cake for us both and swiped my credit card through the slot to pay for it. Then I faced him again. "I want a favor."

He leaned back in his chair and crossed his arms. "I

would have thought I'd be the last person on earth you'd ask a favor of."

"You are," I snapped, then mentally clawed back the escaping anger. "But you're the only reporter I know, and you happen to specialize in paranormal and occult news and investigations."

"I do." He studied me for several moments, his gaze still wary. As if *he'd* been the injured party in the whole sordid mess. "And what do I get in return for granting this favor?"

"A story that could blow anything else you've written out of the water."

Excitement flared briefly in his dark eyes before he managed to control it. But I'd expected nothing less. For a man like Jak, the story was all.

"Does this favor involve doing anything illegal?"

"I doubt it." I paused, but couldn't help adding, "Although we both know that wouldn't exactly faze you."

Amusement teased his lips and an ache stuttered through my heart. *Not over him*. Not by a long shot. Or rather, not over the memory of what we'd once shared. Even the hurt of his deception couldn't erase all that had once been good. And that sucked.

"You and I both know the childhood your mother presented to the world was a lie," he said evenly. "I had sworn statements that proved it, and your mother never did refute them."

I gave him a somewhat bitter smile. "The people who mattered knew the truth about my mother's past. No one else needed to. Not then, not now."

"What about the public she was defrauding?"

A waitress approached with our coffees and cakes. I gave her a smile of thanks and waited until she left before saying, "My mother's psychic powers were real, and they helped a lot of people. Shame you didn't do a story about *that* rather than besmirching her name."

He reached for his coffee. "I don't do good-news stories. I prefer the dark and dirty underbelly of things."

"Which is exactly why I'm here." I wrapped my hands around my coffee and hoped like hell I was making the right decision to confide in him. But even if I wasn't, I still had to chance it. It wasn't like I had a whole lot of options right now. "How much do you know about witchcraft and ley lines?"

He frowned. "I know some people think the lines and their intersections resonate with a special psychic or mystical energy, but the jury is out as to whether there's any truth to it."

"What if I told you they're not only more powerful than you could ever imagine, but there's a major leyline intersection here in Melbourne?"

"I'd have to say, so?"

"So, a consortium has used extreme force in an effort to gain control of the area around that intersection."

His gaze searched mine for a moment. "Why say 'has used' rather than 'is using'? No one is interested in old news."

"It's not old news if only two of the three men have been captured. The Directorate are pushing resources behind the hunt for the third man, but so far they have been unable to locate him. The man is a ghost, existing only on paper."

Of course, the Directorate—or Directorate of Other

Races, as they were officially known—also had bigger problems on their hands. They were, after all, responsible for going after all non-humans who crossed the line and killed.

He studied me for a moment, one finger tapping the table lightly. A sure sign I'd snagged his interest. "For the Directorate to be pushing all resources behind such a hunt, these men had to have done something pretty bad."

"They raised a soul stealer and set it after the relatives or friends of anyone who wouldn't sell them the properties that surrounded the intersection. One of those who died was a little girl." A little girl whose soul would never move on, never be reborn. Hers was a life lost to the world forever.

"You always were a sucker when it came to children." His voice hinted at the warmth of old. "Is that what this is about? Revenge for a little girl?"

"Both the thing responsible for the little girl's death and the witch who raised it have been dealt with." And both of them were dead, sent to the fiery realms of hell itself—although who actually knew if hell *was* fiery. "*This* is about finding the third member of that consortium."

He sipped his coffee for several moments, his expression giving little away. But I knew from past experience that behind the neutral expression there was a clever mind going at full tilt, chewing over information, working out possible angles. "Why does this consortium controlling the intersection worry you so much? You're not a witch. You aren't even as psychically powerful as your mother."

"I have different gifts than my mom had, but that doesn't make them any less powerful." Although admittedly, being able to walk the gray fields—the unseen lands that divide this world from the next—talk to souls, and see the reapers who guided the souls on to the next life weren't exactly the most usable psychic gifts in a normal, everyday life. But my life of late was as far from normal and everyday as you could get.

And those were far from the *only* gifts I had.

Jak raised an eyebrow. "Meaning you can use the ley lines?"

"I can't even see them."

"So why is it so important to *you* that the consortium be stopped?"

I picked up a spoon and scooped up some chocolate cake. It was a little dry, but I needed the sugary energy right then. The air-conditioning might be blasting every other scent away, but it didn't seem to be doing a whole lot to erase *his*. And every intake of breath had the past stirring within me.

"These people attacked friends of mine. I want to find them."

His gaze scanned mine again and a smile tugged at his lips. "The truth, but not the whole truth."

I acknowledged that with a slight nod. "But the whole truth is a little out there."

"I'm a reporter who investigates all things paranormal and occult, remember?" Sarcasm edged his voice. "You'd be surprised at just how 'out there' I'm willing to go."

I was betting even *he* wouldn't believe the real truth—that the intersection might well be tied up in a desperate scramble by at least four different parties to find the keys that would unlock the portals of heaven and hell. That one of those keys not only had been recently found, but had been used to open the first of the portals that protected our world from the hordes of hell.

I'd held that key in my hand. Held it, and lost it.

I didn't want that to happen with the next two keys, and that meant finding out as much as we could about *all* the players involved in this race. Which meant digging up as much information about John Nadler—the consortium's elusive third man—as we could get.

But computers could go only so far. Sometimes the only way to find out anything useful was to hit the streets. But the sort of people who would hold the information we needed weren't likely to talk to someone like me, even if I could find them. They would talk to Jak, though. They always had. He had a talent for putting you at ease.

Or at least he did when he wasn't sitting opposite the woman whose heart he'd shattered.

"An intersection as powerful as this one," I said, "can be used to manipulate time, reality, or fate. If someone succeeds in controlling such an intersection, he could wreak havoc on the very fabric of our world."

He briefly looked surprised. "The intersection is really that powerful?"

"Yes."

"Well, then, I guess finding the third man *is* something of a priority." He leaned forward a little. "But why are you involved? And why come to me? Why not just leave it all to the Directorate? It seems to be more their line of business than yours or mine."

"I'd leave it to the Directorate if I could, but that's not an option."

"Leading me to the next obvious question—why not?"

"Because I'm being blackmailed into the hunt." Which was the truth—it just didn't actually apply to the intersection.

Amusement flirted briefly with his mouth and something deep inside me twisted. It was a stupid and illogical response, and it made me want to scream at my inability to just forget what might have been.

"Did someone dig up some more dirty laundry on you or your family?" he said.

His article had been more than dirty laundry—he'd accused her of lying about her past. Which she *had*, but not for the reasons he'd suggested. There were no nefarious crimes or shady dealings, just her creation in a madman's laboratory—a fact that she kept well guarded, and for good reason. Her extraordinary abilities had caused many to treat her as a freak—it would have been far worse if they'd learned the true nature of her birth. "No, they didn't. They're threatening my friends."

That the man behind the threats was both an Aedh— who were creatures of light and shadows, an energy so fierce that their mere presence burned the very air around them—*and* my father was something I wasn't about to explain.

Jak frowned. "If that's the case, involving the Directorate seems even more logical."

"They *are* involved, but their investigation is going nowhere and they can't protect my friends forever."

They weren't even trying, in fact, simply because they didn't know about the threats. There was no point in telling them when they could never, ever protect us from the force that was my father.

"So why do you think I'll succeed where the Directorate are failing?" Jak asked.

"Because you not only have a knack for getting people to talk to you, but you seem able to uncover those who would rather remain hidden."

The half smile appeared again. "That was almost a compliment."

"It's the truth," I said flatly. "Nothing more, nothing less."

"Huh." He finished his coffee, then leaned back in his chair again. "How do you expect me to find someone the Directorate—with all its resources—cannot? They have some of the strongest telepaths in Melbourne in their employ. What could I get that they can't?"

"They're tackling the situation from a criminal angle. I have people tackling it from a computer angle. What we need is someone on the street." I paused, and my smile held only the slightest trace of bitterness. "And we both know just how much you love digging the dirt in the street."

"You should do that more often," he said. "It suits you."

I stared at him for a heartbeat, totally confused. "Do what?"

"Smile."

Something twisted inside again. Old pain, old love, churning together, one fighting the other. *Bastard*, I thought. It was hard enough fighting the memories without him muddying the water by throwing compliments.

"I may want your help, Jak, but I don't want anything else from you. I don't like the way you treat your lovers."

He shrugged. "It was only a comment, not a flirtation."

"Well, keep such comments to yourself. I don't need them. I just need your help."

"Which I can't give if I don't actually have a starting point—other than the name of a man no one can find."

I reached into my purse and pulled out my phone. "You still have the same number?" When he nodded, I attached a file and sent it to him. His phone beeped from the depths of his pockets. "That's all the information we have, on both the consortium and the three men."

"What about the people they were threatening?"

"Also there." I hesitated. "If you talk to Fay and Steven Kingston—the parents of the little girl—don't mention the soul stealer. They don't know the truth about their daughter's death. They don't know that the threats and Hanna's death are connected."

"Really?"

His gaze seemed to intensify, as if he were trying to get inside my head. Which he had no chance of doing, thanks to the super-strong nano microcells that had been inserted into my earlobe and heel. Nanowires—the predecessor of the microcells—were powered by body heat, but for the wires to be active, both ends had to be connected so that a circuit was formed. Microcells were also powered by body heat, but they were contradictory forces that didn't need a physical connection. Once fully activated, the push-pull of their interaction provided a shield that was ten times stronger than any wire yet created.

With them in place, no one was getting inside my head. Well, *almost* no one. The reaper who'd been assigned by the powers above him—powers he refused to name—to follow me around seemed to have no problem accessing my thoughts, and neither did Lucian, although at least Lucian was hit-and-miss.

The one test the microcells hadn't yet passed was Madeline Hunter, who was not only one of the strongest vampire telepaths around and the woman in charge of the Directorate, but also—technically—my boss. Which wasn't a situation I was happy about, but then, that's what I got for agreeing to work for the high vampire council.

Of course, working for them and actually *helping* them find the keys—which they wanted not only so they could maintain power, but also so they could use hell itself as some sort of prison—were two entirely different things. But it was a precarious balancing act, simply because half of the high council thought it would be better to kill me than use me. All that stood between me and them was Hunter herself. Which meant that, like it or not, I would do what I had to do to keep her happy.

Jak blinked, suggesting that he'd given up attempting to squirrel into my thoughts. "So why didn't you tell them the truth about their daughter's death?"

"It was bad enough that their little girl died. They

didn't need to know that it wasn't just her flesh that had passed." I eyed him warily. "And if you tell them, I shall beat you to a pulp."

He laughed softly. The sound shivered down my spine, warm and tingly. "You've gotten a little aggressive since we parted. Hope it's not my fault."

I snorted. "Don't give yourself any credit, Jak. I've had far worse traumas in my life than you using me to get a story on my mother."

And given that she'd been torn apart by an unknown assailant, that was the understatement of the year, to say the least.

Jak didn't say the obvious—*Sorry about your mother's death*—and I was glad. I might just have given in to the temptation to hit him if he had.

"So, I track down any and all information about this consortium and the man no one else can find—then what?"

"You give me progress reports, and you let me see everything you have before you print said story."

"Since this story looms so large on the Directorate's radar, will I actually be allowed to print it?"

"They can't stop it if they don't know about it," I said. "All you need to do is keep your head down."

"Yeah, that's going to be easy given what I'm investigating." His gaze moved down again, narrowing slightly when it came to rest on my left arm. "Interesting tat."

"Yeah," I said dismissively, not even glancing down at the wingless lilac dragon that twined its way up my arm from my fingertips. I certainly *wasn't* about to explain that it wasn't actually a tattoo, but something far more deadly—a Dušan, a spirit guardian that came to life on the gray fields to protect me. "Have we got a deal?"

"Maybe. Let me dig around a little, just to see if there really is a worthwhile story in all this."

"Just don't take too long to decide, because we haven't got a whole lot of time left."

He nodded, finished his coffee in one long gulp, then rose. "I'll let you know, one way or another, by tomorrow."

He walked out. I tried to resist the urge to watch, but my gaze still flicked that way. The man sure could move nicely . . . Something fluttered at the outer reaches of my vision. It was almost ghostlike, a wisp of silver that was quickly shredded by the sunlight streaming in through the window. I frowned, scanning the front of the shop, intuition tingling. Whatever it was, it didn't reappear.

Jak left the café and the door whooshed shut behind him. I sighed in relief and ordered a second cup of coffee. My damn hands were shaking so bad it took several attempts to swipe the credit card through.

"You should not have met him if his presence affects you so."

The words came out of the emptiness behind Jak's chair even as the heat of Azriel's presence caressed my skin. Reapers, like the Aedh, were beings of energy rather than true flesh and blood, but they could attain that form if they wished to.

Which was how I'd come about. My father had spent one night in flesh form with my mother and, in the process, had given life to me—a half-breed mix of werewolf and Aedh who was lucky enough to get most of the best bits of each and few of the downsides.

"You're the one that said we had to do everything possible to stop the remaining portals from being opened. No matter what I might think or feel about Jak, he *is* good at digging up forgotten information." I stabbed my spoon into my cake for another bite. "If it's out there to be found, he'll find it."

Azriel formed substance on the other side of the table and sat down in Jak's recently vacated chair. While reapers were basically shape-shifters, able to take on any form that would comfort the dying on their final journey, they did possess one "true" shape. Usually I just saw whatever form they used to claim the soul they were meant to escort, but for some weird reason, I always saw Azriel's real form rather than the shape he decided to take on. Even he had no idea why this happened—or if he did, he wasn't telling me.

Which wasn't exactly a bad thing, because his real form was rather stunning. His face was chiseled, almost classical in its beauty and yet possessing the hard edge of a man who'd won more than his fair share of battles. He was shirtless, his skin a warm, suntanned brown and his abs well defined. The worn leather strap that held his sword in place seemed to emphasize the width of his shoulders, just as the dark jeans that clung to his legs hinted at the lean strength of them. A stylized black tat that resembled the left half of a wing swept around his ribs from underneath his arm, the tips brushing across the left side of his neck.

Only it wasn't a tat. It too was a Dušan—a darker,

more stylized brother to the one that now resided on my left arm.

Azriel's gaze met mine, and his blue eyes—one as vivid and as bright as a sapphire, the other the color of a storm-held sea—hinted at sympathy.

"Couldn't you have just asked him all this on the phone?"

I grimaced. "Jak's the sort of person who prefers face-to-face meetings."

"Because of his gifts."

"Yes." I gave the waitress another smile of thanks as she delivered my second cup of coffee. She didn't even blink at the half-naked, sword-carrying man sitting opposite me.

But that wasn't entirely surprising. The same ability that allowed reapers to see what form a soul would most likely accept in their guide allowed Azriel to take on an outer skin that would raise no eyebrows, no matter where he was. The waitress probably saw him as just another man in a suit.

"Actually," he said, "she still thinks Jak sits at the table."

"Well, I'm glad he isn't," I muttered around a mouthful of cake.

"Odd words, since your thoughts suggest otherwise."

"As you have previously noted, human thoughts are not always rational."

"But you are not human."

"And right now, I'm not exactly rational." I finished the last of my cake, then pushed the plate away and reached for Jak's. Never let it be said that I let chocolate cake go to waste, even if it wasn't the best I'd ever tasted. "So, what's next?"

He shrugged. "Until your father contacts us with details of the next key's location, we are basically at a standstill."

"Well, if he wasn't the one who stole the first key from us, maybe he won't." And if he *wasn't* the one who'd stolen it, I was more than happy for him to remain far, far away. If only because I'd seen him angry—and, despite the fact that I'm part werewolf, it had taken days for the bruises to fade. "Maybe he'll consider us too great a risk to use us again."

He raised an eyebrow. "Do you honestly believe that?"

He knew I didn't. He could read every thought, after all. I threw the spoon onto the plate, but it bounced and clattered over the edge of the table. Azriel caught it casually in one hand and gave it back to me.

"Finish the cake," he said softly. "You need the sustenance."

I scowled at him. "Stop mothering me. Besides, cake isn't sustenance."

"It is impossible for me to mother you when I am male," he replied evenly, but there was a hint of humor glinting in the depths of his eyes, and, as usual, it did strange things to my pulse rate—which only emphasized just how irrational I really was. He added, "And is not chocolate one of the five essential food groups?"

I rolled my eyes. "You, reaper, need to stop believing everything you read in my thoughts."

He merely raised an eyebrow. "If it is not essential, why do you have it so often?"

I studied him for a moment, wondering if he was still teasing me or not. "Because it's like love and sex— it's just something a woman has to have." I paused, but couldn't resist asking, "What about you? Is there anything in your life that you'd consider essential?"

"Valdis," he said immediately.

"Valdis is your sword." A demon-forged sword with a whole lot of power and a voice and mind of her own, granted, but still a sword. I had a similar one sitting at my back, but Amaya was shadow-wreathed, and no one would ever see her—not until her black blade pierced their flesh, anyway. "Swords don't count."

"Then it would be duty," he said.

I snorted. "It's a sad statement about the reaper community that duty is considered a far higher priority than love and laughter."

"It is natural our priorities are different considering our beings are completely different in design."

I frowned. "Aren't you even curious as to why we humans consider love, sex, and chocolate so vital to our existence?"

"No." He paused. "Which does not preclude the possibility that I have experienced at least *one* of those options."

"I wasn't talking about the reaper version of love and sex."

"Neither was I," he said, amusement teasing his lips.

I stared at him for several seconds, completely dumbstruck. No, he surely couldn't mean . . .

He'd shown no interest in eating in the time I'd known him, so I had to think chocolate was out. And it was hard to imagine him falling in love with a human, given his often harsh opinions of humanity as a whole. But that left only sex and I really couldn't imagine . . .

"Why not?" he asked softly. "If I can find death in this form, why would you think me incapable of finding other emotions?"

"Death isn't an emotion. Neither is sex." I said this in total disbelief. I was still trying to get my head around the fact that Azriel had had *sex*. In *human* form.

"On the contrary, death is a time of great sadness. And does not sex bring joy and completeness?"

"Yeah, for us. You're not us."

"Why can you believe it possible for the Aedh to enjoy the benefits of flesh, but not a reaper?"

The Aedh he was referring to was Lucian. Despite all the help Lucian had given to us recently, Azriel both disliked and distrusted him, to the point where he refused to call him by name—even if he was in the same room with him.

"I believe it because I've seen the joy Lucian gets out of sex. Besides, reapers are soul guides and it seems to me that you all treat that role with great respect and utmost devotion. I would have thought fraternizing with us would be banned." Hell, there seemed to be rules forbidding almost everything else in the reaper world.

"Ah, but it is," he said, and there was an almost bitter twist in his brief smile.

I blinked. "Okay, now you're just confusing me."

He studied me for a few moments, his gaze more intense than usual, as if he were judging me. Which was odd, because he was connected to my chi and probably knew me better than I knew myself.

"You remember I mentioned the friend that died?"

"Yes."

"He was sent to retrieve a soul, but found a trap instead. Ten more reapers found their deaths before I tracked down the person responsible." Azriel paused, and regret touched the air. *But over what it had cost him,* I thought, *not what he'd done.* "I was not a dark angel—not a Mijai—at the time, but I did what I had to do to uncover the killer."

Which was what he'd advised me to do not so long ago, and the only reason I'd come here to see Jak today. "And doing what you had to do involved sex with a human?"

"Yes. Seducing the killer's former mistress was the only way I could uncover his location."

I raised my eyebrows. "Why couldn't you have simply read her mind, or even waited until he came to see her again?"

"As I said, she was his *former* mistress. Apparently he'd stopped seeing her just before the killings began. And though it is extremely rare, there are minds reapers cannot read—that is why you sometimes see the classic gray shroud form of reaper." He shrugged. "Violence was out—I would not desecrate my position as a soul guide that badly—so my only option was seduction. It took two weeks to gain her trust and get the information. That time was . . . enlightening."

I bet. "So you became a Mijai because you seduced a woman?"

"And scattered the soul of my friend's killer to the four winds, never to be reborn."

Holy shit . . . He really *had* got his vengeance. "How the hell are you even still alive?"

I might not know a whole lot about the reaper world, but I *did* know that sort of action was out of bounds unless it was ordered by whoever was in charge of the Mijai. Or dark angels, as they sometimes called themselves.

"It was a close decision," he said softly. "And I am still paying for my actions, even as a Mijai."

"So your becoming a Mijai, and then being assigned to follow me, is part of that punishment?"

"Yes."

No wonder he'd been so hostile at the beginning of all this. "So when this assignment is over, will you be forgiven?"

"I doubt it. My sin was great. My penance will be a long one."

I eyed him for a moment, suspecting there was more to his punishment than what he was admitting. "And you don't care, do you?"

"I care that I will never again be a guide. Beyond that, no."

Because he'd avenged his friend. And to think I'd once thought this reaper wasn't capable of emotion.

I lifted my cup, then paused, the coffee washing warmth across my lips. There was another odd glimmer in the shadows behind Azriel. It definitely wasn't smoke from the deep fryers or anything like that, because it was stationary under the vents. Steam would have been sucked out.

What? His voice slipped into my mind as smoothly as dark silk.

I think we have company.

Where? He didn't move, but blue fire began to flicker

across Valdis's sharp edges, a sure sign that sword and master were ready for action.

It's behind you.

His eyes narrowed a little, and power slithered through the air. His, not that of whatever it was behind him. *It is neither a ghost nor a day walker—although there is one in the room.*

I raised my eyebrows. *Day walker?*

The spirit of one who has left his living body to roam this world.

Ah. An astral traveler. *So what about those shimmers of silver I keep seeing?*

Those, he said, his mind voice flat, *are Ania.*

I had no idea what that was—other than that it wasn't of this world—but right now there was a more important question. *Why didn't you sense them before I did?*

He hesitated. *My concentration was wholly on you rather than on our surrounds. It is a mistake I shall endeavor not to repeat.*

Considering all the mistakes I'd made over the past few weeks, I could hardly grumble at his one brief lapse in concentration—and it was oddly gratifying that I was the cause of it. I frowned at the shimmer still standing in the shadows behind him. *What is an Ania?*

The ancient Greeks gave them the name—it means, literally, the female personification of trouble.

Which doesn't exactly tell me what they are. Or why they'd be here in this café, closing in on us.

Ania are demons. They can be summoned to perform a number of tasks, including harassment, assault, and murder. He paused. *It is unusual to see them in great numbers. They are normally solitary beings.*

Two is hardly what I'd term great numbers. And given the size of the shimmers I'd seen, as demons went, they seemed to be on the small side.

There are at least six here, and size is not an indicator of dangerousness when it comes to demons, he chided softly. *Ania are rarely seen outside the dark realm. They are hard to summon and harder to control.*

So they're not the type of demon that breaks through the portals of their own accord?

No. His expression was grim as it met mine. *Whoever summoned them has been able to do so simply because the strength of the portals has been weakened.*

Because there were now only two portals protecting us from the hordes of hell rather than three. And *that* was entirely my fault.

Losing the first key is a blame that lies on us both.

Considering he'd been busy protecting me, and all I'd had to do was hold on to the key, that wasn't exactly true. But it was pointless getting into an argument over it—no amount of arguing or remorse was going to change what had happened. *So the Ania are here to kill us?*

If killing was their intent, they would have attacked immediately.

Then what the hell do they want?

That I cannot say until they actually act. He hesitated. *But Amaya and Valdis are well equipped to handle Ania.*

That I knew. Valdis practically glowed with the blue of her fire and Amaya's hissing rolled across the edges of my mind, filled with eagerness and the need to rent and tear.

It wasn't the swords I was worried about. Or Azriel.

It was me. I'd proven woefully inadequate when it came to protecting myself against the more dangerous elements that kept coming at us.

You are alive, Risa. Given what we have been through, that in itself speaks volumes about your ability to survive.

Surviving and fighting were two entirely different things. *So what do we do?*

We attack.

I glanced around. There were at least half a dozen people eating and drinking in the café, not to mention the five staff members. *Not with all these people in here, we won't.*

He raised an eyebrow. Power slid through the air and, as one, everyone got up and walked out.

I blinked. I guess that solved one problem.

But it caused an even bigger one.

Because the minute the people left, the Ania attacked.

Chapter 2

I scrambled out of my seat and pressed back against the café's rear wall as I drew Amaya. Lilac fire fell from her blade, spilling across the floor in a ribbon. It was almost as if she was marking a line in the sand.

The Ania crossed it.

I swept my sword from left to right. She hissed and spat, the sound becoming oddly satisfied as her sharp point tore through one of the approaching wisps. The Ania moaned—a sound abruptly cut off as her fragments were swept up in Amaya's trailing fire and burned to a crisp.

Two more Ania came at me. I swept the sword around again. This time they ducked, but as the blade whooshed over their heads, they lunged forward, one seizing my sword arm, the other my legs. Their ethereal fingers sank into my skin like talons, drawing blood.

I tried to shake the thing from my arm, but even as I did, the one on my legs heaved, and suddenly I was on my butt and being dragged forward. Toward what, I had no idea, but the sensation of power suddenly surged and the air near the café's door started to waver oddly.

Fingers began clawing at my hand—a third Ania trying to break my grip on Amaya. The sword hissed furiously, her black blade ablaze and spitting fire all around us, setting the wooden furniture alight. The flames leapt upward with unnatural speed, filling the room with smoke and setting off the alarms. Sprinklers came on, soaking me in an instant, but they failed to quench the thirst of the fire.

As the flames crawled along the roof, I threw myself sideways, rolling in an effort to squish the Ania clinging to me. Their ghostly forms briefly scattered, and I quickly switched the sword from my bloodied right hand to my left and stabbed sideways across my body. The sharp edge of the blade ran across my belly, becoming ethereal where demon-forged steel met my flesh, leaving me unharmed as she slid deep into the wispy heart of an Ania. Purple fire wrapped around the creature, capturing it, drawing it back into the sword. Feeding on it.

Chills crept down my spine, but I had no time to think about a sword that fed on fellow demons. The Ania had latched onto my legs again and were dragging me forward. This time I knew what they were trying to do. The surge of power I'd sensed before had been a doorway forming. A dark and decidedly creepy-looking door to god knew where.

I dragged in a breath that was all smoke and swung Amaya again, her lilac fire like a comet's tail as she bit through the air. The Ania dropped my legs and scattered, then suddenly Azriel was standing in front of me, Valdis screaming her fury as she sliced through the two retreating Ania. They exploded and a second later the doorway was gone, sucked back into whatever realm it had come from.

I scrambled to my feet. Flames were crawling down the walls, consuming everything in their path. The whole place was alight, and yet there was no heat, just smoke. Lots and lots of smoke.

I sheathed a still-hissing Amaya. She felt heavier on my back, as if the weight of the Ania she'd consumed had somehow increased the mass of her steel. I shivered at the thought, then grabbed my bag from underneath the table and slung it over my shoulder.

Azriel clasped my elbow, his blue eyes as fierce as the fire that swarmed Valdis's side. "We need to get out of here."

"What about the fire? Can you stop it?" The words came out wheezy. The fire might not hold any heat, but the smoke was thick and it clung to the back of my throat, making it hard to breathe, let alone talk.

"The fire is not mine, so no, I cannot." His grip slipped down to my fingers, his palm warm against mine as he tugged me toward the rear exit. The smoke was so bad I could barely even see the emergency exit sign.

"Meaning I can?"

"Maybe."

He pushed the doorway open. Beyond lay a small lane bathed in sunshine, but the sudden rush of fresh air seemed to send my lungs into a spasm and for the next few minutes I could do nothing but cough.

"Do you need a drink?" Azriel asked.

I shook my head and made a motion back toward the café. Smoke was funneling out of the open door and the purple flames were licking at the frame. It was almost as if they were following us.

"Amaya is their source," Azriel said. "They follow where she leads."

"Then how do I put it out? And why didn't the café at Werribee mansion"—which was where we'd found, and lost, the first of the keys—"go up like this when Amaya set that alight last week?"

"Because her lust was fully sated and the flames could gain no hold. I suspect that's not the case now."

She was still hissing away merrily, so he was right in his presumption. "Then how do I calm her?"

He tugged me forward again, taking us farther down the lane, away from the front of the café and the approaching fire engines. "Every sword is different. What works for one will not work for the other."

Which was a fat lot of help. I frowned, and tried sending calming thoughts her way. Her hissing only increased, and it felt oddly like she was telling me to get fucked. It would be just my luck to get a sword with attitude.

So I did the next best thing—I mentally promised her plenty of blood in the near future. She made several hissy, grumbling-type sounds, then quietened. A glance over my shoulder revealed that the flames were similarly calming.

Now all I had to do was hope I could keep the promise.

"Given that this attack was probably little more than a first foray," Azriel said grimly, "I have no doubt that you will."

We came out on Southbank Promenade and turned toward the underground parking at the arts center. He finally released his grip on my hand, but the warmth of his touch lingered.

"Who the hell would be sending Ania against us?" I glanced around to see if anyone was watching, then hitched up my dress and squeezed as much water from it as I could.

"They weren't sent against us," he said grimly. "They were sent to retrieve *you*."

"That's not what I asked." I smoothed the dress back down, but it continued to drip.

Azriel acknowledged my point with a slight nod. He hadn't put Valdis away yet, and the sword still glowed with angry-looking blue fire. I very much suspected it was a reaction to his emotions rather than any sense of lurking danger.

"It could be your father, it could be the Raziq, it could even be whoever stole the first key." He shrugged and finally sheathed Valdis.

"My father has so far preferred to do his own dirty work, and the Raziq have always sent their Razan." Razan were basically the long-lived human slaves of the Raziq, the secret group of Aedh priests who were apparently dedicated to finding a way to permanently close the portals between this world and the next. And, in the process, possibly destroy us all.

After all, if no souls could move on, then no souls could be reborn. And if there was no soul, then there could be no spark of life. The thought of babies being little more than lumps of meat, without inner life or any sort of hope, made me shudder.

It was the Raziq who had developed the keys, but my father had arranged for them to be stolen before the

Raziq could put their plan into action—but whatever *he'd* intended had also gone awry, because the people who'd stolen the keys had died before they could tell anyone the exact location of them.

Why, exactly, my father had the keys stolen when he showed as little consideration for humanity as the Raziq did was something I'd yet to figure out. Especially when he kept saying he wanted me to find and destroy the keys, and yet had gotten dangerously annoyed when I'd suggested that leaving the damn things hidden was probably safer for everyone.

"I did mind-read one of the Ania during the attack," Azriel said. "The creature did not know who summoned it."

"So how did those things find us? You said the Raziq probably wouldn't be able to locate me once I was away from either my apartment or the café."

"It may not be the Raziq."

"Let's just forget the *who* for the moment." Annoyance edged my voice. "How did the Ania find me?"

"The Ania work along the lines of bloodhounds, only they are visual rather than scent hounds. Show them a picture and they will scour the earth until they find that person."

"How could someone show them a picture of me without becoming visible themselves?"

"If it *is* the Raziq, then they have Razan. The only time the Raziq ever acquire flesh to do a task is when they cannot use the Razan to interact with this world— such as the time of conceiving. And even then, it is only the shortage of Aedh females that drives some of them into the arms of humanity."

Well, that was one thing I wasn't going to complain about, considering it had given me life. "And if it wasn't the Raziq?"

He shrugged. "Whoever stole the key from us and opened the first portal would be clever enough to conceal their identity from any low-level demons they'd summoned."

I pushed open the side door into the parking lot and walked down the stairs. My footsteps echoed in the concrete void, but Azriel was as silent as a ghost.

"So what do we do, given that they'll probably hit us again?"

"We attempt subterfuge." He paused, suddenly appearing just ahead of me to hold open the fourth-floor door. "How long can you hold a change?"

I frowned. While I was part werewolf, I couldn't actually attain a wolf shape. In fact, the moon held no sway over me at all, and I was neither afflicted by the moon heat—although I did have a healthy sexual appetite—nor forced to change shape on the night of the full moon.

However, Mom hadn't been just an ordinary werewolf. She'd been a helki werewolf, and one refined in the labs of a madman. Helkis were face-shifters. They could literally alter the shape of their face, hair, and eyes—although, oddly, the eyes were the most difficult to keep altered over long periods of time. I'd inherited that ability from her, but it wasn't something I used very often, so it took a whole lot more out of me than it had Mom.

"That depends on just how much of a change we're talking about."

He stopped the door from slamming shut with his fingertips, then fell in step beside me. The heat of him washed over me, warm and comforting. "The Ania are somewhat rigid bloodhounds. Show them an image and that is precisely what they search for. I would think a simple change of hair color would suffice for now."

I grimaced. I actually loved my coloring. Silvery hair and lilac eyes were a startling—and somewhat rare—combination, and I liked the attention they sometimes gave me.

"Black hair and lilac eyes would be no less startling," he commented. "And as your skin is not pale, it would look very suitable on you."

"Suitable?" I said, amused. "God, Azriel, surely even you can come up with a better compliment than that."

He raised his eyebrows at me. "Why is 'suitable' not an adequate compliment?"

I studied him for a moment, not sure if he was teasing me or not. "Because I guess it sounds so . . . average."

"Which you are obviously not." His expression was still totally serious and yet, if he'd had an affair with a human woman, he surely couldn't be as obtuse about human—or non-human—vanity as he was making out. "So, would the word 'stunning' be considered more appropriate?"

I rolled my eyes. Why was I even bothering to fish for compliments from him? "This conversation is insane. Let's just forget about it."

"As you wish. You have not, however, answered my original question."

It took me a couple of seconds to actually *remember* his original question. "I've never actually held either a full or a partial change for any great length of time. I could probably hold a hair color change for three or four days if it's continuous, but it'll wear me out physically. If I simply revert back to my natural color once I'm home, it might be a little more sustainable."

"Then do it."

"What? Now?"

"There are no cameras in this immediate area, and no one nearby. And it is infinitely better to be safe than sorry."

I nodded a little reluctantly. Face-shifting wasn't as easy as shifting into an alternate form. From what I'd been told, donning your wolf form—or whatever other form of animal you might be—involved little more than reaching into that place inside where the beast roamed and releasing the shackles that bound her. Face-shifting was a little more complicated. Not only did you have to fully imagine all the minute details of the face you wanted to copy, but you had to hold it firm in your thoughts while the magic swirled around and through your body. Easier said than done when the magic was designed to sweep away sensation *and* thought.

Of course, I was only changing my hair color, but given how little I face-shifted, even that wasn't a walk in the park.

I flexed my fingers, then closed my eyes and pictured my own face—from the lilac of my eyes, the slight up tilt of my nose, and my defined cheekbones, to the fullness of my lips. But instead of shoulder-length silver hair, I imagined it black and with a pixie cut. A black so rich that it shone dark purple in the sunlight.

Then, freezing that image in my mind, I reached for the magic. It exploded around me, thick and fierce, as if it had been contained for far too long. It swept through me like a gale, making my muscles tremble and the image waver. I frowned, holding it fiercely against the storm of power. The energy began to pulsate, burn, and change me. My skin rippled without altering, but my hair suddenly felt shorter and somehow finer. As the magic faded, I staggered a little, my knees suddenly weak.

Azriel caught my arm and steadied me. "Does it always affect you like that?"

"It's usually worse." I shrugged, locked my knees in place, then gently pulled away from the strength of his touch. "I'm told it gets easier with use, but I just don't use it often enough."

"So it will become easier as the weeks pass?"

"I don't really know." I eyed him for a moment. "Do you really think I'll need to hold it that long?"

"Until we know who is behind the attack—and why—then, yes, I think it very likely."

"Fabulous." *Not.* I ran a hand through my hair—my now *short* hair. It was an almost surreal sensation, but one I'd have to get used to on a semipermanent basis, apparently. "Will changing my hair work if I'm still riding the same bike and working in the same place?"

"As I said, the Ania are precise hunters. A motorbike is not a unique object, and it could be anyone under the helmet. Sending them after a particular facial image is far safer." He shrugged. "But we'll know soon enough."

I grimaced. "Hopefully, Jak will come up with something interesting tomorrow, because I really don't want to be sitting around waiting for either my father to contact me or to be attacked."

"We have little other choice." Frustration briefly edged his voice. "Where do you go now? To the café?"

I shook my head. "I'm not scheduled until tonight. I thought I'd go see how Tao is faring."

"He still lives."

I grimaced. "Being in a semi-coma and living a fully functioning life are two very different things."

And right now, Tao was still doing the former rather than the latter. He could swallow food and water, but there was little response to stimuli, and no sense that he was aware of our presence. No one knew when—or if— he was ever going to come out of it. Even the witches at the Brindle—the place that was now the home of all witch knowledge, ancient or new—could find no mention of anyone ever consuming a fire elemental before Tao had done precisely that—and there was no spell or potion to reverse what had been done. We were all playing the waiting game and hoping like hell that he'd come back to us.

"The witches do not appreciate my presence in their sacred place, so I shall meet you there but will wait outside." He winked out of existence, but wasn't entirely gone, because he added, "The black hair *is* truly stunning, but your natural color is more beautiful."

Then the heat of his presence faded completely, leaving me grinning like an idiot. An obviously *insane* idiot, because Azriel and I were about as viable as Lucian and I when it came to anything resembling a relationship. But at least I could enjoy sex with Lucian.

Of course, Azriel *had* explored the intimate delights of flesh, but that didn't mean he'd actually enjoyed it. The term "enlightening" could have meant *anything*.

And I really, *really* needed to steer well away from this line of thinking. Azriel's presence might not burn the air, but that didn't mean he wasn't somewhere nearby and following every wayward thought.

I reached into my purse and retrieved the keys to my motorbike. She sat alone in the designated bike parking area, her sleek silver body gleaming brightly in the shadowy confines of the lot. The Ducati was one of the first things I'd bought when our café finally started making a profit, and even though her hydrogen engine was more than a little outdated these days, she was still a joy to ride.

I pulled out my helmet, leather jacket and pants, and Kevlar boots from the seat storage, then deposited my purse. Once I'd donned my bike gear, I climbed onto the Ducati and started her up. Unlike regular motorbikes, hydrogen bikes run relatively silent, with only the lit-up light-screen dashboard and the slight vibration running through the frame to tell you they've started. In fact, when they were first developed, our nanny-inclined government had forced manufacturers to add a fake engine noise so that pedestrians could hear them coming. These days, that rule was pretty much defunct, as pedestrians had far greater worries— namely the air blades, which were basically jet-powered skateboards. Those things really *were* dangerous—a fact I knew because I'd tried them recently. Not only had I almost decapitated Lucian, but I'd spent more time on the ground than I had on the damn blade.

I drove out of the parking lot and headed back into the city. The traffic was light, so it didn't take me too long to get there. I swung onto Lansdowne Street, then into Treasury Place. The Brindle was a white, four-story building that had once been a part of the Old Treasury complex. It looked innocuous until you neared it—that was when the tingling caress of energy burned across your skin. This place was protected by a veil of power, and it didn't suffer fools—or evil—gladly.

I stopped in the parking bays along the edge of a park that had once held the premier's office. After I'd stripped off the leathers and retrieved my purse, I locked the bike and helmet in place and headed into the Brindle. I climbed the steps and walked through the huge wood and wrought-iron doors into the shadowy interior. Even though I came here at least a couple of times a week, a sense of awe still struck me. This place—these halls—was almost as old as Melbourne itself, but it was so immersed in power that mini comets of energy shot through the air at any sort of movement.

The foyer wasn't exactly inviting, but the rich gold of the painted brickwork added a warmth that the somewhat austere entrance lacked. I walked on, my footsteps echoing in the stillness and little explosions of fire following in my wake. A woman appeared out of one of the rooms farther down the hall, then stopped, her hands clasped together in front of her tunic-clad body.

Her gaze rose to my hair, but all she said was, "It is good to see you again, Risa."

"And you, Margo." I stopped and made the expected tithe at the discreetly placed urn near the reception room's entrance. For normal dealings with the witches of the Brindle, it wasn't required, but Tao's situation was far from normal, and they'd been throwing a whole lot of resources behind the effort to make him whole again.

I hated to think just what it was going to end up costing Ilianna. Tithes or not, it was only thanks to her—and the promises she'd made to the Brindle that she wouldn't tell me about—that the witches had agreed to take him in.

The only thing she *had* said about the promises she'd made to get him treated scared the hell out of me. *He saved my life at the cost of changing his very being. I can do no less for him.*

This whole key mess was changing the very fabric of our lives, and there was virtually nothing any of us could do to stop it. I'd asked them both many a time to walk away, but they wouldn't. And while part of me was relieved, mostly I was just scared. For Ilianna and Tao, for what the ultimate cost to them might be.

They were my childhood friends, my best friends, and we not only shared a home, but owned and ran a café together. I didn't want to lose either of them.

I followed Margo down to the far end of the hall and through a small, ornately carved door. The hall beyond was smaller, its walls a soothing green. The air was a riot of indefinable scents that had my nose twitching even though it wasn't exactly unpleasant. We passed several rooms, including the one Tao had been in a few days ago.

"He's been moved?" I asked, as we continued on. "Why?"

"Elementals need a heat source to survive. We suspect the shadowed room could have been the reason for his failure to improve."

Tao was a werewolf rather than an elemental, but it was possible that consuming the elemental had changed his physiology enough that the lack of sunlight would affect him. "So the new room is sunnier?"

"Yes." She stopped at a doorway near the far end of the hall and motioned me to enter.

I took a deep breath, fearing what I might find, then stepped inside the small, sunlit room. Tao lay on a bed in the middle of the room, his lower body covered by a sheet—more for modesty, I suspected, than any real need for a cover. Even from here I could feel the heat radiating off him.

Ilianna sat in a chair beside the bed and did something of a double take as I entered. Dark smudges dulled her green eyes and her normally lustrous blond mane hung limp and lifeless.

I frowned. "You really need to go home and get some rest."

"I will. Soon." She half shrugged, but the worried look in her eyes said "soon" wasn't going to be anytime in the near future. It also suggested that nothing I could do or say would move her, and I couldn't use force in a place like this. The building—or the magic that guarded it—would not appreciate it.

Not that *that* would stop me from trying if it came down to it. The last thing I wanted was her falling sick, as well.

She scanned me from head to toe. "The new hairdo is startling, but I'm thinking there's something a little more than the need for a change behind it."

"Someone sent demon bloodhounds after us. Azriel thinks this will throw them off the track for the moment."

"Let's hope he's right."

He usually was. Annoyingly so. "How is Tao today?" He actually looked a little better. His face—although covered in a wiry brown beard that was growing thicker by the day—had lost some of its gauntness, and his breathing was less labored.

"He's doing okay," she replied, touching his hand lightly. "We actually managed to get a decent amount of gruel into him today and he kept it down."

The so-called gruel they were feeding him was a revolting mess of herbs, vitamins, protein, and carbs, designed to bolster his body and strength. Up until recently he hadn't been able to keep much of it down and I can't say that I was entirely surprised. If there was any spark of consciousness inside him, he sure as hell wouldn't have been happy about being force-fed the smelly muck.

But at least he *did* have some basic motor capabilities. If he'd required intravenous feeding, then he would have landed in hospital. The Brindle witches weren't legally allowed to perform that sort of procedure, even if some of them knew more about the body and medicines than many fully trained professionals.

"Has there been any sign of consciousness returning?" It was a rather inane question, because if there *had* been, Ilianna would have been straight on the phone to let me know.

She shook her head. "But his muscle responses seem to be improving, so that's a good sign."

"And the heat?"

Her gaze swept down his length. "His core temperature has come down a little and he's not sweating as much, but he's still radiating massive amounts of heat."

No surprise given that he'd consumed a creature that was little more than a furnace on legs. That he'd done it to save Ilianna only made her feelings of guilt an even heavier cross to bear. I pulled up another chair and sat down. "Why don't you go get something to eat? I'll sit here with him until you return."

She frowned. "I really don't think—"

"Ilianna," I said, gently but firmly, "Tao would be the first person to tell you off for running yourself into the ground for him. Besides, he's going to need lots of care when he wakes up, and you know I suck at providing any sort of long-term sympathy or patience when it comes to tending to the sick."

A smile briefly lifted the tiredness from her eyes. "Your bedside manner is robust, to say the least."

"Which is why *you* don't want to get sick, either, because then you'll be at my not-so-tender mercy."

"As threats go, that's one of the best, but—"

"Ilianna, please, just go."

She studied me dubiously for a moment, then sighed and grabbed her purse from beside the bed. "I'll be as quick as I can."

"Take your time and get something decent to eat. I'll ring you if anything happens."

She hesitated, obviously about to argue, then nodded. "Just make sure you do ring."

"I will, I will. Now *go*."

She went. I reached out for Tao's hand, wincing a

little at the heat of his fingers. How it wasn't actually killing him I had no idea.

I spent the next hour simply talking to him—updating him on the restaurant and everything that was going on with the keys and our search for the mysterious third man behind the consortium. Maybe he heard, maybe he didn't, but in the end that really wasn't important. He was in there somewhere, and I just wanted him to hear my voice and know that we were near, waiting for him.

Ilianna returned just after two o'clock. She looked flushed and happy, and I very much suspected she'd gone home to see Mirri, her partner. Her apartment was only fifteen minutes away, if that.

"Feeling better?" I asked, amusement teasing my lips.

"Totally," she said, dumping her purse beside her chair before sitting. "I'm so glad you forced me to go eat."

"I hope you actually *did* remember to eat," I said dryly. "Otherwise I'm going to tell Mirri off."

She briefly looked startled, then chuckled softly. "I should have known a little afternoon delight would not escape the attention of a werewolf."

"Not when you're wearing such a satisfied smile. How's Mirri doing?"

"Good." She made a face. "But she's on nights all this week."

I frowned. "I thought there was some rule against giving mares too many night shifts?" Apparently because mares—which, like their animal counterparts, was what female horse-shifters were called—coped worse than most shifters when it came to nights. Something to do with their being more day balanced than night—whatever the hell that meant. Certainly Ilianna coped well enough with night shifts at the café, but then I guess she never did more than two nights in a row, since we rationed them out among the three of us. Or had, until Tao's incident with the fire elemental. These days, it was mostly me, with trusted staff filling in for both Ilianna and Tao.

"There is, but with the ongoing strike, they're running on skeleton staff to cover essential areas, and Mirri's number came up." She shrugged. "It's only for five days, then she's got five off. She'll be fine."

"Hopefully the strike will end before then." The government surely couldn't keep cutting nursing numbers and expect the hospitals to keep providing the same level of care. But there again, this *was* the government we were talking about. I was sure none of our elected officials actually lived in the real world.

"What are your plans for the rest of the day?" Ilianna asked.

"I'm working tonight, so I might just go home and grab some sleep."

She raised an eyebrow. "What, Lucian kept you up all night again, did he?"

"Up, down, in, out, and sideways," I replied with a grin.

She laughed. "If you could package and sell that man's stamina, we'd make a fortune."

Considering he put most werewolves to shame, we certainly would. My vid-phone rang, the sound sharp in the hushed confines of the small room. I reached into my purse and pulled it out. And my stomach sank.

It wasn't just anyone calling me. It was Madeline Hunter. I was tempted to let it go to voice mail, but that would only result in pissing her off. Never a good thing to do when you were talking about one of the most powerful vampires in Australia.

I pressed the ANSWER button, and her image flashed onto the small screen. "Madeline, how lovely to hear from you."

"Oh, I'm sure it is," she said, her green eyes as cool as her voice. "But this is not a social call."

"I didn't think it was."

"I imagine not." She shifted, revealing the panoramic view out the window behind her. Surprise rippled through me. She was ringing from her office at the Directorate, so something serious must have happened, given that I was working for the vampire council, not the Directorate. If Uncle Rhoan—who was one of the Directorate's top guardians and also something of a whiz at sniffing out unusual occurrences—got the slightest idea that I was, in any way, connected to Hunter or the Directorate, there'd be hell to pay. I had no doubt that both he and Aunt Riley—who was a consultant rather than an actual guardian these days—would even go as far as threatening Hunter herself. When it came to the safety of their pack—and they considered me one of theirs even if I wasn't by birth—nothing and no one with any sense got in their way.

Of course, being in the employ of the vampire council was actually far worse than the Directorate ever could be. At least the Directorate was governed by rules and regulations. For all intents and purposes, the council was not. It was a shadowy organization at the best of times, and a rule unto itself at the worst.

Hunter added, "A problem has come to my attention that I believe might benefit from your expertise."

"If it's a Directorate investigation, why would you think you'd need my help?" Hell, they had witches on the payroll who'd probably forgotten more than I actually knew about the gray fields.

"This will not become a full Directorate investigation, although guardians have performed discreet preliminary inquiries."

It wasn't like I had a choice about getting involved, but still, curiosity stirred. "Why restrict the Directorate like that? Does it involve the council again?"

"No. But it does involve a certain aspect of the vampire world that we have no wish to make more generally known."

"So vamps have secret lives? Who'd have guessed that?" I said, a tad more sarcastically than was wise.

Anger flashed across her expression, and something within me chilled. *Don't poke the bear*, I reminded myself fiercely. *Not if you want to avoid being executed by the high council.*

"Vampires are hardly alone in keeping secrets," she said, her voice crisp, holding little of the fire I'd seen only a heartbeat ago. That I'd even seen it suggested that whatever the problem was, it was big. Or at the very least, annoying. "And you would do well to remember that, considering how well your mother kept her own secrets."

"My mother's secrets were little more than an unorthodox birth and upbringing, and it'd be of little use to anyone now to reveal it." As Jak would say, she was old news. "Speaking of my mother, just what is happening with the hunt for her killer? You did promise to put full resources behind the investigation if I helped you and the council."

She paused, considering me for a moment, reminding me very much of a cat studying its prey and wondering whether to eat it or play with it. "The hunt is currently at a standstill."

That much I'd gathered. "Why?"

"Because there are no leads. Whoever killed your mother did so without leaving *any* sort of trace evidence."

"Given her battered state—" I paused, swallowing heavily as I tried to ignore the memories that rose. "How could the killer have left no evidence whatsoever? Even if he was wearing a full DNA containment suit, there must have at least been footprint smudges."

There'd been too much of her blood, too much of her flesh and body parts, splattered around. No killer, no matter how careful, should have been able to get out of that kitchen without leaving *some* trace of himself. Unless he could fly. But even then, there should have been DNA evidence of a shape-shift—even if it was only feather fluff lost in the change.

"The Directorate is at a loss to explain it, and neither they nor the Cazadors have had any luck uncovering anyone who might have wanted your mother dead."

So she *had* kept her word and thrown the resources of the council behind the hunt. She'd ordered a Cazador—who were basically the vampire council's leashed killers—to look into it. It was actually more than I'd thought she would do, even though she had made the promise.

"So we're looking for a ghost?"

"Or an Aedh."

Her words hit like ice, chilling me to the bone. An Aedh *could* get in and out unseen, and they certainly had the capability to tear a body apart without leaving any trace of themselves behind. Hell, *I* could do it if I wanted to. It was the nastier side of my Aedh heritage, one I'd been reluctantly taught by Quinn, Riley's vampire lover and a man who'd once trained to be an Aedh priest.

"But why would an Aedh want to tear my mom apart like that?"

I didn't realize I'd said it out loud until Hunter answered. "For information, perhaps. Maybe they thought she had knowledge of the keys."

I frowned. "Mom didn't know much about the gray fields and, despite spending a night with an Aedh, she knew even less about them. Killing her for information about either makes no sense."

"But neither does your mother's death. It was brutal and deliberate, as if it were some kind of message."

A message no one could understand. I rubbed my eyes for a moment, then said, "What is the problem you want me to investigate?"

"A number of murders have occurred, and the only link we can find, besides the manner of their death, is Dark Earth, a vampire establishment in Brunswick."

I frowned. I knew Brunswick fairly well since Tao, Ilianna, and I had lived there for a few years during our university years, and I certainly couldn't recall a place called Dark Earth. "I gather it's new?"

"No, old," she said crisply. "But it's one that only vampires know about."

"Ah, an underground club." There'd been talk about such clubs existing over the years, but no evidence had ever been uncovered and the vamps certainly weren't forthcoming with any information.

"Figuratively and physically," Hunter said. "If it sat at street level, humanity would be aware of its existence and that could be dangerous for everyone."

Which only made me wonder what the hell went on in the place—although I had a bad feeling that I was going to get a firsthand answer to *that* one.

"In the last week," she continued, "there have been five deaths. All were low-level vampires, as Dark Earth caters to a particular type of clientele."

A type she clearly wasn't going to tell me about right now—and that only made me more nervous about going to the damn club. "That doesn't explain why you want me to investigate rather than the Directorate."

"The Directorate is brilliant at what it does, but it is too large an organization to guarantee the utter discretion this investigation requires."

"In other words, I'm to shut my mouth about what I find and report only to you?"

"That goes without saying." She paused, and her expression intensified. Trepidation shivered down my spine. "And if you breathe a word of this to that reporter you talked to this morning, he will discover a whole lot more about the dark edges of this world than he might wish to."

The chill got deeper. "How do you know I talked to a reporter this morning?"

Her sudden smile was anything but pleasant. "I did warn you that we intended to keep track of your every move."

But how? Cazadors were vampires, and no vampire, no matter how old, could stand the sun between noon and one o'clock. Although some—like Uncle Quinn and Hunter herself—could walk around at any other time, thanks to their age.

And if a Cazador had been following me, why hadn't I sensed it? At the very least, I should have been able to smell his presence, even in the human-drenched confines of the café.

Unless . . . Could the dream walker Azriel had mentioned have been a Cazador? There *were* Cazadors capable of astral travel—Hunter herself had told me that. And an astral-traveling vampire would *not* be restricted by the noonday sun, because it was only their flesh that burned. Their spirit—soul—did not.

Shit. We were going to have to be very careful about what we said when that traveler was near. Especially if we wanted to ensure that the keys *didn't* fall into the council's hands.

"If you know anything about my history with the reporter I talked to, then you'll realize I wouldn't want to tell him anything I didn't have to."

Her smile lightened. The same could not be said for the look in her eyes. "Yes, he did gain himself something of a reputation after the rather nice story he did on your mother. I must admit to some surprise that you'd even meet with him again."

To call it a "nice story" was something of a misnomer, given that it had become a staple for gossip mags for several weeks. "If you know about the meeting, then you'll undoubtedly know the reasons behind it. Can we get back to the reason for this call?"

She did so. "As I've mentioned, we can find no real connection between the victims besides the club and the manner of their deaths, no apparent motive for the murders, and no trace evidence to suggest who or what might be behind them."

A chill ran through me as images of Mom's murder ran through my mind again. My mouth dry, I asked, "And just how were they killed?"

"They were eaten."

Eaten? Good lord, I did *not* want to go after something that would eat vampire flesh. "I can't imagine a vampire sitting around letting someone munch on him."

"They didn't. Whatever this thing is, it scratched them first. We found traces of venom in the wounds and further analysis revealed that it contained powerful inhibitors."

I frowned. "But vampires don't actually need to breathe." It was more an instinctive reflex left over from the time before they'd been turned. "And I've never heard of a poison capable of killing a vamp."

"The venom wasn't what killed them," she replied, neatly skirting the issue of poisons and vampires. Which to me suggested there *were* poisons capable of doing just that. "The inhibitor prevented reaction, and the killer simply ate them."

While they were alive? Oh god, this was getting worse and worse. "If it scratched them, surely there was some DNA evidence left in the wounds?"

"None, other than the venom, which we have not been able to trace to any source so far."

I released a somewhat shaky breath. "This really does sound more like Directorate business than anything I could help with."

She gave me *that* face. The one that said I'd better do what she wanted or die. And yet I don't think her muscles even twitched—it was more an odd sort of darkness that crept into her eyes.

"We believe this creature—whatever it is—might have come through when the first gate was opened. The timing is suspicious."

I shoved away the useless surge of guilt. There was nothing I could do now except get to the other two keys and prevent them from being used. Because if they were, then it really would be hell on earth.

"So where are the bodies?"

"The first four victims have already undergone their final deaths via sunlight, as was their wish. The fifth, however, still lies in state at his home."

Meaning vampires made wills, like the rest of us did? That was something I hadn't realized, but I guess it did make sense. Even vampires didn't live forever— though I guess they could, if they were lucky enough. Or unlucky enough, as the case might be. "When was he murdered?"

"He was found an hour ago." She paused, studying me. "Why?"

"Because if the thing that killed him did come from hell, then it might have left behind some sort of resonance that we could use to track it down." According to Azriel, most demons and whatnot that broke through the hell portal left such a trail. I added, "But it would dissipate with time."

"Then you'll need to get there ASAP. But I would advise you to go to Dark Earth immediately and talk to the manager, Brett Marshall."

Which wasn't a very vampire-sounding name, but then, the newer vamps tended to have regular monikers. "Why so urgent?"

"Because he is a friend, and I wish you to talk to him first."

"And?" There had to be another explanation, because I wasn't buying the first one at all. From what I'd seen, Hunter wasn't the type to have friends. And even if I was totally wrong, she didn't seem the type who did favors for them. She was more of a "what's in it for me" type of vampire.

"And because," she said, "Dark Earth is no place for a non-vampire to be after dark."

Fear quickstepped into my veins. "Meaning?"

"Meaning," she said softly, "that even the presence of your dark angel could not guarantee that you'd walk out of that club alive."

Chapter 3

The sick sensation of fear settled deep in my stomach. "So how is going to this club in the daylight any safer?"

"The bar will be almost empty, and Brett is powerful enough to control the few who are there. He has guaranteed your safety this afternoon."

Which didn't mean I *would* be safe. Not if the place was as dangerous as Hunter was making it out to be. "What about viewing the body?"

"I'll send you his name and address. He lived alone, so you can choose your own time to go there. He will lie in state until his maker arrives to officiate his final death in a few days."

Makers officiated the final deaths? That was something I hadn't known. "Have autopsies been done on all five victims?"

"On what remained, yes. Results will be slow to come, though, as we need to keep this private."

Which suggested the autopsy was being done in-house via high council resources rather than through the Directorate. "And what, exactly, do you expect me to find at this bar?"

She shrugged—an oddly elegant movement. "Talk

to Brett. Look around the bar. You may see or sense something that the Cazadors—who don't have your psychic skills or your knowledge when it comes to the gray fields—wouldn't be capable of."

Given that they had Cazadors capable of astral travel, I actually doubted they'd have any less knowledge of the gray fields than I did. Although I guess astral travelers were restricted to *this* plane and weren't able to travel on the fields themselves. "I'll give you a call once I've gone there." *And* gotten out alive.

"Be sure that you do."

It was on the tip of my tongue to retort that it really didn't matter if I did or not because she'd get the report from the Cazador who'd been assigned to follow me around anyway. But I resisted the urge. Right now, it was better if Hunter didn't know I knew about my follower.

I signed off without bothering to say good-bye and shoved my phone back into my purse.

"There goes your afternoon nap," Ilianna commented darkly. She'd expressed her opinion about my working for Hunter more than once, but had finally stopped harassing me about it. She knew, like I did, that there was no real choice given that half the council currently wanted me dead.

I grimaced and stood. "Yeah. But there's not a lot I can do about it."

"No. And I haven't got holy water or even a stake in my purse to give you."

"You said that like they're everyday items one finds in a purse," I said wryly.

She snorted softly. "Given the way Hunter is dragging

you further and further into her web, they should be. At least then when the spider calls to the fly, the fly will be better armed."

"Ilianna—"

She held up a hand, stopping me. "I know, I know. But the fact remains, you want revenge more than you want out of any deal with Hunter."

Well, *that* was certainly true. "If this whole key business blows up in our faces, we might yet need Hunter and her Cazadors on our side."

"If this whole key business blows up in our faces, we're *all* going to be ass-deep in demons and fighting for our lives. I think Hunter and her council cronies will be too busy saving their own skins to worry about the rest of us."

That was also probably more true than not. And Hunter was an unreliable ally. She may have convinced the council to give her more time to prove my worth, but that didn't mean she—or they—couldn't change their minds. And considering that they'd already thrown one test at me, I wouldn't be surprised if this was yet another one.

I sighed and rubbed my tired eyes wearily. "I've arranged for Sara to come in and do your shift at the café. I want you to go home tonight and get some sleep."

She wrinkled her nose. "Sara couldn't pour a decent drink to save her life."

"Which is why I'll be pouring drinks and she'll be tending tables." I raised a hand against her objections and added, "No more arguments. Just go home and rest."

"Okay, okay," she muttered. "I promise."

Which meant she would. In this place, you didn't break promises made. "I'll see you sometime tomorrow, then."

She nodded. I dropped a kiss on Tao's fiery cheek, then left. The day seemed even hotter after the cool darkness of the Brindle. I squinted up at the sky, looking for the storms they'd been predicting for later this afternoon but seeing only endless blue. This was Melbourne, though; weather could—and often did—change in a blink of an eye.

As I neared my bike, Azriel appeared. "I do not like the sound of this bar."

"Neither do I." I unlocked the Ducati, then pulled on my leathers. And immediately began to sweat. Having to wear heavy protection on a hot day was one of the few bad points of bike riding—although it was better than falling off and skinning my body down to bone on the tarmac. "Which is why I wouldn't mind you appearing as something fearsome."

He raised an eyebrow. "I would think a reaper is fearsome enough, even for a vampire."

I wrinkled my nose. "I guess that depends on what you expect death to look like. If they envision him as a scantily clad, nubile young woman, I rather suspect that's not going to be much of a deterrent."

"I am not female, so I can hardly give them the visage of a young woman."

Amusement ran through his words and a smile tugged at my lips. "So they'll see the scythe-bearing shroud instead?"

"Yes. And that is often scarier than anything I could draw from their minds."

Having seen such reapers myself, I could certainly attest to that. Even knowing that they weren't coming for me didn't erase the tendrils of fear. That vision of death was too locked into literature and film to produce anything else.

I checked my phone and discovered that Hunter had followed through with her promise and sent me the address—not that I'd expected anything else. Dark Earth was located on Barkley Street, either near or in the Barkley Square shopping center. It didn't seem an ideal area for an underground vampire bar, but maybe that was the whole point.

I shoved the phone away and met Azriel's gaze. "Shall I meet you there?"

He nodded and disappeared. I climbed onto the bike, fired her up, and zoomed out of the parking lot. The traffic was heavier than before, the roads filled with people undoubtedly escaping the office to enjoy the afternoon sunshine, so it took me a little longer to get across to Brunswick, even though it wasn't that far away.

Once I'd parked and secured the bike, I walked down Barkley Street. According to Hunter's instructions, the entrance to Dark Earth was located between Coles and the Kmart loading bay, in a small shopping-trolley collection nook.

I found the nook easily enough, but there sure as hell wasn't any entrance.

Azriel appeared behind me, his heat fiercer than the day itself, but a whole lot more welcome. "It wouldn't be evident given that the vampires have no desire for humanity to know its existence."

"Logic is not what I need right now." I ran my hand over the sunbaked apricot-colored concrete wall. It was rough and grimy under my hands, and there were vague stains lower down that smelled faintly of urine.

"Then may I suggest that you press what looks to be a piece of chewing gum on the upper part of the left rear wall?"

"Seriously?" I studied the gum a little distastefully, then stepped forward and did as he bid.

Nothing happened. Not immediately, anyway. I stepped back and frowned at the wall. As I did so, there was a faint crackle. "And you would be Risa Jones, I'm guessing," a deep, somewhat dry voice said. "Hunter is nothing if not efficient with her people."

"I'm hardly her people," I retorted, my gaze searching the top of the wall for some sign of the camera that had to be there, with little success. Whoever had installed them had done a damn fine job.

"If you work for her," the voice said, "then you're hers. There is no escaping her web once she has spun it around you."

A comment that echoed Ilianna's fears, and not something I wanted to hear. "Look, I'm here to see Brett Marshall. If you're him, let me in. If not, tell him I'm here."

"My, we are an impatient one, aren't we?"

"The sooner I check this place out, the quicker we may be able to track down the killer." And the sooner I could get away from it. I might not have been inside yet, but Hunter's words loomed large in the back of my mind. I did *not* want to be here any longer than necessary.

"Then by all means, come in."

As he said the words, the wall gently slid to one side, revealing a long, steep staircase that led down into darkness. Trepidation flicked through me and I hesitated.

"I will lead if you'd like," Azriel said softly.

I frowned as I glanced over my shoulder and met his gaze. "You can see in that ink?"

He withdrew Valdis. Her fire flickered across the dull concrete walls and danced through the darkness. "I will sense more than see if anyone nears."

I stepped to one side and waved him through. No one could ever accuse me of letting valor get the better of sanity—at least not when it came to stepping into dark vampire pits.

He moved into the stairwell, his steps barely audible on the concrete. I followed, keeping close, my fingers itching with the need to reach out and touch him—to keep a physical connection between us as the door silently closed and the shadows pressed close.

The walk down seemed to take forever, but in reality it was only a few minutes before the stairs gave way to a long corridor. The air here was cool and musty, and surprisingly free of the scent of vampire. Black tiles lined the walls and the floor was covered by a dark red rubber matting that swallowed all sound.

Valdis's bright flame lifted the darkness, revealing the doorway at the far end of the corridor. It was metal and extremely solid. Not something that would be broken down in any great hurry.

I glanced behind me, wondering if our astral-traveling Cazador was still following us.

No, Azriel said. *He awaits on the street.*

Wonder why?

Azriel shrugged. *Maybe Hunter fears that one of the vampires in this place will sense him and give warning.*

Maybe. And it was good to know that we weren't going to be shadowed absolutely everywhere.

The door opened as we approached. The room beyond was small and somewhat intimate in its feel. While the black and red theme continued here, electric wall sconces gave the room a muted warmth and the combination of blackwood furniture and well-padded sofas lent it a feeling of casual elegance. A small desk hugged the right side rear of the room, and behind it sat a woman. Like the room itself, she was black, from the tips of her hair to the leather pumps that were evident underneath the desk.

"Brett Marshall waits for you in the main room, Ms. Jones," she said in a smoky sort of voice. "Please go in."

Two doors—which I hadn't actually noticed until that point—slid silently open at her words, revealing a larger, darker room. The air that wafted out was filled with the aromas of vampire, blood, and hunger. A shiver ran through me as Amaya's hissing began to filter across the back of my thoughts.

I glanced at Azriel. *How many people are there?*

A dozen vampires, and at least twenty humans. Distaste ran through his thoughts. *They are thralls, and yet not.*

I frowned as I walked warily into the darkened room, wondering how someone could be a thrall and yet not. But the question went unanswered. Either Azriel didn't know or he wasn't saying.

The former, he said, voice full of censure. *You really need to start trusting me more, Risa.*

I do trust you—to watch my back and keep me alive. What I don't trust is that you're ever going to be completely honest with me.

I have never been dishonest with you.

No. But you never tell me everything you know, either.

Sometimes it is better that way.

And that is why I trust you to keep me safe but not to keep me informed.

A shadow loomed in front of us, forming into a long stick of vampire. He had carrot red hair and the eyebrows and beard to match, and his eyes were a merry blue. He smelled faintly of lilac and soap, which was a damn sight more than could be said about the other vampires in the room. It seemed they were upholding Aunt Riley's pet peeve about certain sections of the vampire community—or the great unwashed, as she tended to call them. They were usually younger in vampire years, although—again according to Aunt Riley—there were a few guardians who apparently had an aversion to cleanliness, too.

"Risa Jones," the vampire said, stopping in front of us and holding out his hand. "I'm Brett Marshall. Pleasure to make your acquaintance."

"I'd love to say the same," I replied, noticing that his flesh was cool and his grip without real strength. Maybe Hunter hadn't told him that I was half werewolf, so he was adjusting the handshake accordingly. I had certainly expected someone capable of curtailing any wayward actions of the better part of a dozen vampires to hold more physical strength than what he'd just shown. Maybe Hunter had meant something other than physical strength. "But that would be a total lie."

He laughed. It was a pleasant sound, but sat oddly against the tense, almost needy atmosphere in the room. "I would have questioned your sanity if you'd said anything else." His gaze flicked over my shoulder. "I see you have brought along a rather impressive guard."

"His name is Azriel," I said, "and can you blame me?"

"Certainly not. Please, follow me."

He turned and walked down some steps. The darkness seemed even deeper here, a blanket that was lifted only by the flickering of Valdis's fire. It was hard to see anything, but I could smell booze and blood under the stink of vampire. Another shiver ran down my spine and my pulse rate jumped a little—never a good thing in a room filled with needy vampires.

I followed Marshall across the room. Tables and chairs gradually became visible as my eyes adjusted to the darkness, but the vampires remained curiously out of sight. They had to be shadowing, because the scent that surrounded us indicated that some of them were quite close.

Marshall opened a door at the far end of the room, and faint amber light fanned out across the nearby shadows, briefly lifting them. To the right of the door stood a vampire who was little more than skin and bones. His face was gaunt—sunken-cheeked and pop-eyed—and he reminded me very much of someone on the edge of starvation. But given the underlying aroma of blood in the room, that surely could not be the case.

I stepped into the room and looked around. Like the foyer, it was comfortably furnished, with an office set up at one end and a sofa and chairs at the other. A percolator burbled away in one corner, the rich aroma thankfully overwhelming the smells coming in from the larger room.

"Please," Marshall said, "help yourself to coffee."

I glanced at the percolator, but—mindful of my somewhat uneasy stomach—opted not to take him up on his offer. I perched on the edge of one of the chairs instead. Azriel stopped behind me, the heat of his presence swirling around me, a blanket I wanted to wrap close to chase away the increasing sense of trepidation. And I wasn't sure whether it was this place, Hunter's warning, or something I sensed but had yet to uncover.

Marshall walked past us and took a seat on the sofa opposite us, one arm stretched across the back of it. If he was worried about the deaths linked to his club, he wasn't showing it.

"So tell me," he said pleasantly, "why you?"

I shrugged. "I have more experience roaming the gray fields, so Hunter thinks I may spot something the Cazadors would miss."

He raised an eyebrow. "And did Hunter give you the nanowire you're wearing?"

I hadn't felt him attempting to read my mind, but then, with the best telepaths, you didn't. "No. That's something I thought might be handy considering who I'm often dealing with."

"It's not one I've come across before."

"Because it's not actually on the market yet." I'd gotten it from Tao's cousin, Stane, who had some very well-placed fingers in the black-market pie. "I haven't come here to discuss nano implants. Hunter tells me the five victims were all regulars of your club."

He crossed his legs and plucked at lint on his pants—

that addiction wasn't fed—would only fan the flames of that suspicion and make it spread.

"I would have thought it'd be illegal for clubs like this to use what are basically drugged-up humans as a constant food source."

He shrugged. "It is. But where there is a need, a way will always be found. The whores are here willingly. They are well fed, in well-maintained, generous-sized accommodations, and on rotation, so that they are never overdosed on sensation."

But also never allowed to experience life outside these walls, by the sound of it. I wondered where in the hell the families of the whores were. Or had they simply given up, knowing that the addiction was so strong it was something they could never cure?

"So, slaves," I muttered, not quite able to keep the distaste out of my voice.

He shrugged again. "They are not slaves, because slaves, by definition, are owned, and have no right to freedom or property."

But they were slaves to their addiction—an addiction that the vampires were readily fueling in order to cater to their own addicted. It was an almost incestuous relationship, one addiction feeding the other, a wheel in constant motion that no one could escape.

You are not here to judge, Azriel reminded me softly. *And the sooner you question him about the dead, the sooner we can be gone from this place.*

Good point. "Could one of the blood whores be a connection point between the men who died?"

"No. We thought of that possibility—that perhaps

someone close to a whore might be taking a bit of retal-
iatory action—but the five men had different tastes
when it came to their preferred source."

I frowned. "And there was no obvious connection
between the men themselves?"

He shook his head. "None that we could uncover."

Which meant I was totally out of ideas. Some inves-
tigator I was. I hesitated, then asked, "Where do the
feeds happen? Out in the main bar?"

"No. Watching another vampire feed can be an
erotic experience, especially for one of the addicted. We
keep the feedings in one-on-one soundproofed rooms.
There is less chance of a frenzy being created that way."

And that, I thought with a chill, was his first real lie.
There was too much desperation—and the scent of
blood was too strong—in this place for the feedings to
be entirely separated.

"Where are these rooms?" I asked.

"Downstairs."

"And the whores' living quarters?"

"Also downstairs, but on a separate level."

Living underground, never to see the light of day or
breathe fresh air. It was a hell of a high price to pay for
ecstasy.

"Can we see the feeding rooms? And talk to a couple
of the whores?"

"Sure. But they have already been interviewed."

"And Hunter sent me here to do it all again."

He smiled. "And if one values life, one does not go
against Hunter's orders."

"Precisely."

He rose and headed for the door. I followed, Azriel

at my back. As we headed left across the club floor, I noted that the scent of vampire and need seemed thicker than before. I edged a little closer to Marshall and said, "What time does this place start getting busy?"

"Usually not until the sun sets. Most of our clients are lower-rung vampires and, as such, cannot handle much sunlight."

"Then why are there more vampires in here now than before?"

He glanced over his shoulder. His expression was curious. Wary. "And how can you tell that?"

"Werewolves tend to have sensitive noses."

He said "Ah" in a way that suggested he hadn't known I was part wolf. Which was unusual, because vamps usually had no trouble differentiating between a human and a were. But then, I was only half were, so maybe that was screwing with his internal radar. Especially if he didn't have a great deal to do with werewolves in the first place.

He went through another door—one that led into a small foyer containing two elevators—before he answered the actual question. "The feeding rooms are flushed out after every session. The vampires within return to the bar when this happens."

"Flushed out?"

He punched the DOWN button. "Cleaned and fumigated. If you are a wolf, you would have smelled the state of some of our customers. We may cater to the less fortunate among the vampire ranks, but that does not mean we can let our standards slip."

And I was betting that the flushing had little to do

with disease and pest control, and more to do with literal flushing. As in, the feedings often got a little more messy than what he was admitting.

The elevator doors opened with a soft *ping*, revealing a dark wood interior and minimal light. It was only thanks to the fact that Azriel remained steadfastly at my back that I walked inside it.

"I'll take you down to the whores' quarters first. By the time you've finished there, the cleanup will be done and you can look through the feeding rooms."

I nodded, although I wasn't looking forward to either prospect. The doors closed and the elevator ground into action. As I watched the numbers tick slowly down, I asked, "How many whores are there currently living here?"

"We keep a stock of about twenty in the rooms at all times."

Stock. It was a word that suggested the whores were little more than cattle to these vampires. My anger swirled. No wonder Hunter wanted this kept hushed up. "I wouldn't have thought that would be a sufficient number for a club this size."

"It's not. We rotate them every couple of days. We have about one hundred whores in all."

That was a hell of a lot of whores, especially when this was not the only club catering to addicted vampires. Surely it wasn't possible for that many whores to go missing and absolutely no one notice? "So where do you send them once they've finished their shifts here?"

He shrugged as the elevator came to a bouncing stop on level six and the doors opened. The smell of humanity and hopelessness was so strong, my stomach began to churn.

"They're taken to the recovery wards."

The color scheme in the hall was back to the black and red of the entrance, although the matting underfoot was thicker, and oddly spongy. I half expected water to come oozing out of it every time I took a step. Or something worse.

I crossed my arms and shoved my imagination back into its box. "I take it the recovery rooms are not in this building?"

Marshall glanced over his shoulder again. "What makes you say that?"

"The fact that I can't smell a great mass of humans." And the fact that Azriel had sensed only twenty of them.

"Ah," Marshall said. Obviously I was guessing a whole lot more than he'd wanted me to. "No, they are not. But they can be accessed from various levels here."

"Accessed how?"

He stopped at a gated doorway and punched in a code. "Via tunnels. As I said earlier, we have no wish for humanity at large to know about the existence of these clubs."

The doorway opened, revealing another long corridor. Doors lined either side, the spacing between each suggesting the rooms weren't all that large. Maybe prison-cell size, if that. And I wouldn't have called that well-maintained, generous accommodations.

He stopped at the first doorway and said, "How about we start here."

"How about we don't," I said, not trusting that Marshall

hadn't prepared the whore within to be questioned before we'd arrived. I pointed to one of the doors farther down on the opposite side. "Let's try that one instead."

Something flickered in his eyes. Annoyance, or something darker. Either way, it again reminded me of Hunter. I half wondered if there was more of a connection between them than just being friends. "It does not matter which—"

"Then it won't matter if I prefer the person behind door number seven."

He studied me for several seconds, his face impassive even though the air suddenly seemed filled with tension. Enough so that Valdis's fire began casting fiery blue shadows across the dark walls again. Then he shrugged and walked over to the indicated door, punching in several numbers.

As the door swished open, he turned to face me again. "I suppose you'd like me to remain outside, also?"

"Yes, actually, I would." I hesitated, nostrils flaring, smelling soap, woman, and need. "What's her name?"

"Amanda."

No last name. But then, that was to be expected given that these people were being treated as little more than cattle. I guess they had to be thankful that they got a name rather than just a number.

I stepped into the room. The walls, floor, and bedding were all a soft green—a color that was renowned for enhancing the feeling of tranquillity and calm. The only splashes of color came in the form of a white bedside table and a bookcase filled with old books. There was no TV, no radio—in fact, nothing that would give this woman access to what was happening in the world beyond her cell.

As the door swished shut behind us, my gaze met Amanda's. She was a generously built woman with thick brown hair, ruddy cheeks, and several chins. Marshall might not be giving his whores access to the outside world, but he obviously provided a bountiful table—which I guess made sense, considering how often the whores were fed from.

She was clothed in a checked cotton dress and lying on the bed, a book in one hand and a Coke sitting on the bedside table. Her eyes—which were an odd shade of green-gray—showed little in the way of interest.

"Amanda?" I spoke softly, though I wasn't sure why. Marshall might not be able to hear me, but I had no doubt he was monitoring our every move, even if I couldn't see any cameras. "I'm Risa Jones. I need to ask you a few questions."

She didn't respond, just returned her attention to her book. Obviously it was more interesting than I was. I glanced at it briefly. A romance—one I'd read and enjoyed.

I walked across the room—it took only three steps—and squatted beside the bed. "How long have you been here, Amanda?"

She shrugged and continued reading.

"Have you ever experienced any problems when you feed the vampires? Or witnessed such events?"

This time she didn't even bother shrugging. Maybe I should have questioned the whore Marshall had been pointing me toward. Maybe he'd simply picked a more talkative one.

I made a frustrated sound and glanced at Azriel as he squatted beside me. "Well, this was a great idea."

"Let me try," he said, and lightly touched two fingers to Amanda's forehead.

Her face went slack. Azriel closed his eyes and, for several minutes, there was little noise other than the sound of both my and Amanda's breathing.

Then Azriel opened his eyes again. *She cannot answer you,* he said, his mind voice grim. *Because she does not know.*

How can she not know the answer to such basic questions? I asked, confused. *I mean, even if Marshall has placed some sort of restriction on her ability to speak about her experiences here, it'd be right there in her memories, wouldn't it?*

It should be, but it's not.

My gaze went to Amanda. *So her memories have been cleansed?*

Recent memories, yes. The touch is deft, but it was nevertheless there. It has Marshall's taint.

His use of the word "taint" suggested he had no liking for Marshall, even if he showed no hint of it in any other way. *What about her past? Has that been erased, as well?*

He frowned, glancing at her. Valdis flickered with an odd purple-red fire. I wondered if it was anger or distaste.

Anger, Azriel said, *and the woman's past has not been erased. It simply does not exist.*

I raised my eyebrows. *How can her past not have been erased if she has no memory of it?*

That I do not know. He rose and held out a hand. *But you will get no answers from her, because she has none.*

I placed my hand in his and let him pull me upright. He didn't release me immediately and I can't say I was upset about that. *Something strange goes on here.*

Which was definitely an understatement. *Do you think it's worth attempting to talk to any of the others?*

He shrugged. *We could try. I suspect the result would be the same.*

So did I. Still, we had to try, if only to tell Hunter that we had. I pulled my hand from his, but curled my fingers to retain the heat of his touch a little bit longer as I walked across to the door and knocked on it. It opened immediately.

"So," Marshall said, "find out anything useful?"

"You knew we wouldn't." I paused. "How long have you been erasing their memories? And why are you doing it?"

Again that oddly familiar darkness stirred in his eyes. "It is not common practice." He hesitated. "Although most of our current stock have experienced it at one time or another. I'm afraid it is easier to treat physical wounds than mental ones."

"So you simply erase the memory of the physical trauma and push them back into the feeding pen?" I kept the anger out of my voice, but only barely.

Azriel rested his hand in the middle of my back. Energy flowed from it, somehow calming me.

"These people are junkies. They will do anything— agree to anything—in order to get their next fix. What we do, we do with consent."

I wasn't believing that. Not after what I'd seen in the room behind us. How could anyone who had no real idea what was going on from one hour to the next consent to anything? I glanced down the hall. "Can we talk to the person in the room second from the end?"

"If you want," Marshall said.

Meaning we wouldn't find anything different. And we didn't. Like Amanda, the thickset man in room eighteen—who, oddly, possessed the same green-gray eyes as Amanda but otherwise looked nothing like her—had no immediate or past memories. Although he did have a games console rather than books.

Marshall glanced at his watch as we came back out. "The feeding rooms will be available if you'd like to view them now."

I nodded, although I seriously doubted we'd find anything of interest there, either. We headed back to the elevators and up two levels. As the doors opened, the scent of antiseptic hit and my stomach began to churn again.

"God," I said, blocking my nostrils with my hand but not really succeeding in blocking the smell. It clung to the back of my throat and burned into my lungs. "How bad do things get here that you have to wash the rooms down so completely?"

"It is not that bad," Marshall said. "You just have an overly sensitive nose."

That might be true, but it didn't change the fact that the smell was hideously strong. He stepped out of the elevator and motioned to the long corridor before us. It was basically the same size and length as the one below, although the red and black color scheme had been replaced by basic metal walls, ceiling, and floors. Easier to wash down, I guessed.

"All the rooms are the same size and shape," he said.

"Do you want to inspect them all, or would you rather have a random viewing?"

I studied the closed metal doors ahead. I wasn't exactly sure what I was hoping to find, and I was more than a little convinced that I'd actually find nothing. But my sense of trepidation was increasing, and I knew from long experience that generally meant my psychic radar had picked something up. Whether there actually *was* something here that would help our quest, or what I sensed was nothing more than extreme distaste over what happened here, I wasn't exactly sure. Yet.

I glanced at Marshall. "Right now, I just need to walk down the corridor and get a feel for the place."

He raised an eyebrow, but waved a hand to indicate I should go right ahead. With Azriel as my shadow, I walked slowly down the center of the hall, my footsteps echoing across the silence as I studied the rooms on either side. My senses—psychic and not—were on high alert, trying to find something—anything—out of the ordinary. Or rather, out of the ordinary for a place that catered to whore-addicted vampires.

There is much pain and sorrow in this place, Azriel commented as we passed the third set of doors. *And much anger.*

I can't imagine that being so addicted to pleasure that you'd allow yourself to be treated like cattle would be a happy situation to find yourself in, I replied.

The whores have no memories, past or present, he said softly. *What I sense does not come from the living who serve in these rooms.*

We walked by the fourth set of doors, and something teased the edges of my awareness. It was a sensation of something not quite right. Something that existed in this world and yet not.

I frowned, my gaze searching the doorways ahead before settling on one that was set slightly apart from the others. Whatever it was, it was coming from there.

I stopped and half turned to look back at Marshall. "What's that room down at the end? The one that's separated from the others?"

"Just another feeding room."

"Why is it not in line with the others?"

"It's bigger, that's all." He shrugged, like it wasn't important, but I had an odd sense that it was.

"Why is it bigger?"

He hesitated, and I knew that if I'd been closer, I would have seen that flash of darkness in his eyes again. "Sometimes our clients prefer joint feedings."

I frowned. "I thought you said that vampires watching each other feed can get dangerous."

"It can."

I stared at him as the realization of what was happening in that room sank in. *That's* why the antiseptic was so strong. They were cleaning, all right, only it wasn't for the dirt, blood, and bugs that might come off their clients. It was the bloody remnants of humanity they were washing away.

I turned my back on him, my fists clenched against the sudden rise of anger. I hated what this place was doing to people. Hated that I couldn't do anything about it. Because of Hunter, because of the threat she represented—not just to me but to all those I cared for. And even to those I didn't, like Jak.

Azriel touched my back again, but this time the

surge of warmth failed to calm. I took a deep breath that did just as little, then walked toward that room.

The closer I got, the more my skin crawled.

I reached out and gripped the handle. The metal felt cold under my touch. Cold and somehow otherworldly.

There are ghosts within, Azriel said. *Many, many ghosts*.

I wasn't afraid of ghosts. I never had been. Until now. I licked my lips and pushed the door open.

It hit me. Not the ghosts themselves, but rather their anger. The force of it was so strong it thrust me back into Azriel. He grabbed my waist, holding me upright as I battled to breathe against the sheer force of emotion that was battering us.

It wasn't ordinary anger. It was *murderous*.

These ghosts were angry enough to kill.

And maybe even had.

Chapter 4

"Holy shit," I muttered, staring into the room with wide eyes. The ghosts were filmy wisps, but there were so many of them that their presence made the room appear fog-bound. "Can you feel that?"

"They are not pleased about something," Azriel agreed. His body was pressed against mine, an oddly comforting sensation.

"That is an understatement," I muttered, knowing I should move and yet reluctant to do so. He didn't seem inclined to move, either. "Can ghosts actually muster the energy to kill?"

"No. As many as there are here, they would never hold enough power to take one life, let alone five. Besides, the victims were poisoned and then eaten. That is not the behavior of ghosts."

"Ghosts?" Marshall said, suddenly appearing beside us. He'd moved so silently I hadn't even heard his approach.

I nodded toward the room. "There's at least twenty in there, which suggests to me you've been understating what actually goes on in this room."

"I haven't understated anything. The joint feedings

are dangerous. I told you that." He peered into the room. "I can't see any ghosts."

"If you're not psychic, you wouldn't." I somewhat reluctantly pulled away from the comfort of Azriel's support. "Did any of our victims use this room?"

His gaze met mine. "Yes."

"All of them?"

He hesitated. "Yes."

Which meant this room—and these ghosts—was the connection. But why the depth of anger? I frowned at the swirling, ethereal mass. If I wanted answers, I really had no other option but to go in there and try to talk to them.

Whether they'd be willing to talk to *me* was another matter entirely. I wasn't my mother, and talking to the souls of those who'd refused—or been unable—to move on from this world wasn't something I'd ever tried before. My strength lay in talking to the souls of those who still lived but were close to the next world—the sick, the dying, the comatose.

Although Tao's soul had remained elusive to even me.

I flexed my fingers, suddenly aware of Amaya's hissing again. Her energy swarmed down my spine, pinpricks of power that tickled and burned. She wanted in that room. Maybe demons weren't the only thing she liked to eat.

I shivered, though I wasn't sure whether the cause was my sword's apparently insatiable hunger or the waves of emotion continuing to roll out of the feeding room. I glanced Marshall's way again. "I want a list of everyone who died in here."

"That is not—"

"Do it for me, or do it for Hunter. Your choice." And we both knew Hunter wouldn't take no for an answer, so there really wasn't any choice in the matter. "I don't know if the dead in here *are* the connection, but it's a possibility we need to follow."

He nodded, though his expression suggested he was far from happy. Not that I really gave a damn about that. I took a deep, steadying breath, then stepped into the room. The energy of the ghosts crawled across my skin and the air felt like molasses with the intensity of their anger. Amaya's hissing intensified, and the sound met the fury of the ghosts head-on and countered it. Enough that I could breathe a little more easily, anyway.

I studied the vaporous forms flitting around me. I could see them, feel them, and if I concentrated hard enough, I could hear them. But it was a very distant thunder, unclear but nevertheless threatening.

"Are you seeking revenge?" I asked them.

The rhythm of their murmuring neither increased nor decreased. Either they couldn't hear me or they were simply ignoring me.

I frowned, but tried again. "Are you responsible for the deaths of five addicted vampires?"

Still nothing in the way of any discernible response. Frustrated, I glanced at Azriel, but he merely shrugged. "As I have said before, I am neither able nor allowed to communicate with the lost ones."

Which left us with little more than we'd already had. I glanced around the metal emptiness of the room, trying not to visualize how they'd all died, then spun on my heel and walked out. To say Amaya was unhappy with this was another one of those understatements. And her pissed-off hissing was giving me a damn headache.

As the door slammed shut behind me and the sound echoed down the long hall, I said to Marshall, "I suggest you stop using that room. It wouldn't be wise to introduce any more anger into it."

"It's not like I planned such deaths," he said. My instinct said it was another lie. "But even if I *had*, what the hell do any of us have to fear from ghosts? They're not likely to be the cause of our current troubles, given that they have no flesh, let alone teeth."

"They may not be responsible," Azriel said, before I could reply, "but the depth of their anger and grief is certainly enough to attract other entities."

As Marshall's gaze swept Azriel, it narrowed a little. Trying to read him, I thought, and knew he'd have more luck trying to read the metal walls around us. After a moment, he must have realized this himself, for he said, "What other sorts of entities might we be talking about? Demons?"

"That is always possible, given what is going on elsewhere," Azriel replied. "But we should not limit our search to just demons. There are spirits more than capable of this type of kill. Wendigos and Rakshasa would be two of them."

"Rakshasa? I've never heard of them," Marshall said.

Neither had I, but I wasn't about to mention that.

Azriel glanced at me, amusement briefly creasing the corners of his eyes. "Rakshasa are unrighteous spirits— always female—able to take on various physical forms.

Like Wendigos, they are malevolent and cannibalistic, and their fingernails are venomous."

"Well, both of those certainly fit what's happened to our victims." I crossed my arms and tried to ignore the rising sense of dread. I really, *really* didn't want to face a spirit that could take on human form and eat me, but I had a growing suspicion that such a confrontation lay in my future. "How do we go about catching and killing this thing, whatever it is?"

"It has found the perfect hunting ground in this place," Azriel said. "It will be back."

"Unfortunately, it's not exactly a place I can hang around very easily."

"In flesh form, no," Azriel agreed. "But you have other options."

Options I wasn't going to discuss with Marshall earwigging. I glanced at my watch and grimaced. It was nearly four. I had to be at the café in two hours—so much for my relaxing afternoon. "We need to check out the home of the last vamp who died before I have to go to work."

"Meaning I can open the feeding rooms now?" Marshall asked.

I studied him distastefully, wondering why nature had paired an uncaring heart with such a merry countenance. But I guess that could be said about a lot of successful businessmen, and that's all Marshall was. And the people who had died were nothing more than stock. "Yeah," I said, my voice barely civil. "Just not this one."

He didn't look pleased, but I guessed if he feared Hunter enough, he'd obey. And if not, he'd open the room again once I left, and bugger the consequences.

"Excellent," was all he said.

He motioned us toward the elevator. It bounced us up to the lower ground floor and we stepped once more into the stinking morass of needy vampires.

I crossed my arms and followed Marshall through the darkness. The flickering light of the two swords cast eerie shadows across the gaunt faces of the nearest vampires, and it was all I could do to keep walking at a steady pace.

It was a huge relief to reenter the little foyer and watch the double doors close securely behind us.

"We'll be in contact if we need anything else," I said, clasping Marshall's offered hand. This time his grip was much stronger. "What was the name of the last victim, by the way?"

Hunter may have sent me his name and address, but it never hurt to double-check. She liked her games.

Marshall seemed amused, and I suspected its cause was Hunter's aversion to information giving. Obviously, he was well acquainted with it. "Jake Green. What about the ghosts?"

I shrugged. "I'll tell Hunter. She'll probably know someone who can disperse them for you."

Which wouldn't solve anything if he just kept on creating more of them, but that really wasn't my problem right now.

Although it might be in the future.

Azriel touched a hand lightly to my back, guiding me out the front door and into the black and red hall. Valdis gave me enough light to see by, although her flames still held a tinge of red. Thankfully, Amaya had calmed somewhat, though I think it was going to take hospital-strength painkillers to get rid of the headache she'd given me. To be fair, though, that could just as much have been caused by the situation we'd been in as by her song.

"Where to next?" Azriel asked, as he began climbing the steps.

The street-level door opened as we approached and the sudden rush of sunlight had me blinking back tears. "According to Hunter, Jake Green lived about five minutes away, on Little Miller Street. Flat one-twelve. I'll meet you there." I looked around, wondering where the Cazador was.

"He awaits near your motorbike," Azriel said and winked out of existence.

I grimaced and made my way back to my bike. It was tempting to look around to see if I could pinpoint our shadow's position, but that might only give the game away. He might be invisible, but I doubted he was dumb. I climbed onto my bike and rode across to Little Miller Street.

It turned out Green's flat wasn't actually a flat, but an old redbrick warehouse that had been turned into accommodations for the homeless. I studied the building for a moment, then turned the bike around and parked farther down the street, near another—cleaner—factory. Maybe I was doing the homeless a great injustice, but I'd rather be safe than sorry when it came to my bike. Azriel was waiting out in the front. I opened the somewhat grubby-looking door and stepped into the carpeted foyer. Inside were two people; the woman behind the desk was tall, thin, and blond, and she looked somewhat harassed. The man standing in front of the desk was older, grimier, and smelled of dirt, urine, and booze. And he didn't sound happy—although it was hard to say since he wasn't actually speaking English.

The woman's gaze landed on us. "I don't suppose either of you speak German, do you? I only know a couple of phrases."

I shook my head, but Azriel stepped forward and touched the man on the shoulder. He said something in the same guttural tones that the man was using, got a reply, then turned to the woman. "His name is Hans Klein and he is seeking accommodation for the night. He has fourteen dollars."

As Azriel said this, Hans dumped his money on the counter. It was grubbier than he was. The blonde didn't bat an eyelid—she was obviously used to it. "Could you explain that he has to fill out these forms? Can he write?"

Azriel asked, then nodded and said, "We are here to view room one-twelve."

"Jake Green's room?" Her gaze came to me. "Are you Risa Jones? If you are, we were told to expect you."

Obviously, Hunter had been in contact with her. Either that, or she was psychic. I showed her my driver's license and, once she'd checked it, she put a key on the desk. "Up the stairs, second to last door on the right."

"Thanks." I swept up the key and headed for the stairs. The hall above was basic but clean, and I suspected the same would apply to the rooms themselves. But to the homeless, basic was probably like five-star to us. I glanced at Azriel. "How come you know German?"

"Reapers do not only collect English-speaking souls."

"I know, but isn't it against the rules for reapers to communicate with the souls they collect?"

"There is no rule against it, but generally most souls have no desire to speak. However, there are always one or two who like to talk." His amusement crinkled the corners of his eyes. "You would be one of them, I think."

"Are you suggesting I talk too much?"

"I would never suggest anything like that," he said, the gravity in his voice belied by the twinkle in his eyes, "even if it is true."

I laughed, though the sound died on my lips as the smell of death began to invade the air. I stopped in front of room one-twelve, staring at the police tape that barred our entrance. Even though I wasn't squeamish, I really didn't want to go in there. I'd been in the presence of death far too much today.

"I can view it alone, if you prefer," Azriel said.

I shook my head. "The Directorate sets up mobile recording units at crime scenes. Hunter will know if I don't go in there."

"But this is not a Directorate investigation."

"Not officially, but that doesn't mean she won't follow protocol when it comes to keeping a record of everything—and everyone—that goes in or out of that room." Even if no one else ever saw the recordings.

I opened the door, then ducked under the tape. A soft whirring greeted my appearance, and I looked up to see the black, oval-shaped recording device hovering about a foot or so above our heads. I gave it a cheery wave, showed it my driver's license, then turned my attention to the room.

And I really wished I hadn't.

The room itself was basic—a bed, a dresser, an old TV, and a small bathroom that contained all the necessary facilities—shower, basin, and toilet.

But the walls were smeared with dried blood, and there were recent stains on the brown carpet—stains that hinted at human body parts. One was in the shape of a leg, another a foot, then part of an arm, and god knows what else. Thankfully, all the bits had been gathered up and, from the smell, now lay under plastic sheeting on the bed. Oddly enough, I couldn't smell putrefaction, just death and aged meat. Maybe vampires didn't rot like the rest of us when they died.

What I couldn't sense was Green's ghost. Maybe this death had been ordained, which meant a reaper had been here at the time of his death to guide his soul onward. I glanced at Azriel and he nodded in confirmation.

"And unfortunately, too much time has lapsed since his death for there to be any lingering sense of the creature who caused it."

"If it is a spirit rather than a demon, would you still have been able to sense it?"

"If we'd been early enough, yes."

Well, that was something of a relief, if only because it meant that if this thing decided to attack us, he'd sense its approach before it actually got to us. My gaze fell on the black plastic mound and my stomach turned. As much as I didn't want to look at the remnants of Jake Green, I knew that I had to. Because of Hunter, and because I needed to see if there was anything that might give us a clue as to what had done this. Hunter may have had guardians in here and might already know the answer to that particular question—especially if this was just another test to prove my worth—but that only meant it was more important than ever that I do whatever I needed to do to see an end to this case.

I stepped closer and tried not to breathe too deeply. Jake Green might not be rotting, but he was still dead, and that was never a pleasant thing, not even at the best of times. I reached back for Amaya and carefully slid her point under the nearest edge of plastic. She spat yellow sparks that suggested her distaste was as great as mine, but thankfully she *didn't* set anything alight.

I folded back the plastic. Jake Green was little more than a mound of parts. One leg, several arm parts, bits of bone and torso and trailing innards, and finally, his head. Thankfully, *that* was facing away from me. I had no desire to move around to check it out.

"God," I muttered, revulsion giving my voice a harsher edge. "This thing didn't just eat him. It tore him apart."

"The state of the body does suggest there was a feeding frenzy." Azriel moved around me to squat in front of the head. "Which is not the usual modus operandi for a Wendigo."

I sheathed Amaya, then rubbed my arms, trying to chase away the gathering chill. "What about a Rakshasa?"

He shrugged. "I do not know enough about them to confirm or deny the probability. But given the anger of the ghosts, it is always possible that the creature who did this is merely echoing how the whores all died in that room."

"So they *did* die in a vampire feeding frenzy?"

His gaze met mine. "You know they did."

"No, I *suspected* they did. There's a difference."

"As you often say to me, only by a matter of degrees." He reached out and pressed his fingers on either side of the severed head.

"Oh god," I said, the revulsion curling through me suddenly getting stronger. "You're not going to try to capture his last memories, are you?"

He glanced at me, one eyebrow raised. "You have seen me do this before. Why the distaste now?"

I waved a hand at the remnants. "Because of this—the way he died. I really don't want to see it in all its gory detail."

"Then do not look." His gaze flicked past me, and I knew without looking that he was studying the recording device that hovered just above my right shoulder. He added silently, *I do this for you—to help solve this case quickly so that we can get back to more urgent matters—rather than possessing any real interest in knowing the details of this death.*

The problem is, the more urgent matter is at a standstill until my father contacts me or Jak comes up with something.

Which does not alter the need to get this task over with just in case either event happens.

I acknowledged the truth of this with a half shrug, and he returned his attention to Green's head. Valdis's sides began to run with blue fire as Azriel closed his eyes. Energy surged, sharp and almost bitter in the small room, and in the space between Azriel's hands pictures began to flow—flickering images that didn't move quite fast enough to blur—meaning the gist of his death, all the blood and gore and body bits flying, was there to see in living color.

I bit my lip, swallowing heavily against the bile that rose in my throat. When the images finally died, I sighed in silent relief. Azriel removed his hands but didn't immediately get up. He bowed his head for a moment and spoke, the words musical and oddly captivating. Saying a prayer for the soul that had already moved on.

Finally, he rose. "It is definitely a Rakshasa, and that really is not good news."

Considering the way fate had been treating us of late, it wasn't like I was expecting good news. "Why?"

"Because as shape-shifters, they are notoriously hard to track down and even more difficult to kill."

"Fabulous." Not. *What about Valdis and Amaya?* I added silently, not wanting Hunter to know about the swords.

In theory, demons and spirits are of a similar nature, he said. *If the swords can destroy one, they should be able to destroy the other.*

But you've never had reason to test it?

Spirits are of this world, and therefore generally not the concern of Mijai.

What if they venture onto the fields between the worlds?

Then maybe. But they rarely do and, even then, it is only ever onto the paene.

Which was the shadowy divide between this world

and the next. "So is there anything that kills them for sure?"

He hesitated. "Most dark spirits are dispelled by sunlight, which is why they hunt by night."

"Meaning we have to capture the fucking thing before we can kill it? How the hell are we going to do that?"

"White ash and silver hold dangerous energies to the spirit kind. It might be possible to cage the Rakshasa with either until the morning comes."

"Unfortunately, I'm part were. I can't handle silver without it burning me."

"White ash, then."

I wrinkled my nose. It'd be my luck that white ash would do jack squat and I'd be left wishing I had silver. I studied the body for a moment, then frowned. "There's one thing I don't get. I can understand the Rakshasa going after the vampires who caused the deaths of those in the large feeding room, but why now? These deaths have been happening for years."

He shrugged. "I can't answer that because I do not know enough about the Rakshasa. But it is possible the anger and need for revenge were not strong enough to be a serious draw to dark energies until now."

An unsettling thought stirred. I studied him for a moment, then said, "So does that mean you and I could be serious draws for darker energies? I mean, you've tasted revenge, and I'm currently chasing it."

He hesitated. "Darker energies, no. Darker fates, perhaps."

Trepidation tripped through me. "Meaning what?"

"Meaning, my fate was decided the moment I was assigned this task. Yours, however, is not so clear."

"I thought your becoming a Mijai was the end result of your revenge. Are you suggesting there's more to it?"

Again he hesitated. "I will never be as I was, thanks to my actions on this plane."

For some odd reason, I had the feeling he was talking about a future action rather than a past one, but his expression—or lack of it—told me I wasn't about to get any more information out of him.

"Then why is my fate so unclear? And does it mean I might or might not be punished, even if I do get my revenge?"

"It means I do not always have the answers you need. This is one of those times, simply because there are still too many variables."

And that, I thought, might not have been a lie, but it wasn't the whole truth, either. He knew far more than he was letting on when it came to my fate.

Something flickered in his eyes—surprise or acknowledgment; I wasn't sure which. It was frustrating, to say the least, but it was also pointless to challenge him. He'd tell me more when he was ready, not before.

I sighed and glanced at my watch. If I didn't leave soon, I'd be late for work. "I don't think there's anything else we can do here."

I said it more for the benefit of the hovering crime scene recorder than Azriel, but he nodded anyway. "You go to work now?"

"Yes." I studied him for a moment. "Why?"

"Because I will use the time to research the Rakshasa."

And leave me unguarded? Interesting, given the attack only this morning.

I do not—would not—leave you unguarded. I will simply request help with this matter. He walked around the bed and touched a hand to my elbow, lightly guiding me to the door. *This distrust of yours grows old, Risa.*

I guess it would, but I just couldn't help it. We both knew that no matter what he said or did, in the end, his mission was the only thing that mattered. Right now, that mission and I were intimately connected, but if something happened to alter that situation, then I'd more than likely find myself unguarded and alone.

He didn't say anything to that, even though he would have heard the thought as clearly as if I'd said it out loud. Maybe, despite all his declarations, he knew it to be the ultimate truth.

I returned the key, then headed back down the street to my bike. The ride to work cleared my head a little, as did getting lost in the mad rush of food and alcohol service that the next eight hours at the café brought. Business was still booming, and if it continued at this rate, we were going to have lines of people waiting to get in that rivaled anything the Blue Moon—which was only several doors up the road—had. Which was amazing, considering the Blue Moon was one of the most popular wolf clubs in Melbourne, and we were only one of many cafés catering to the hungry hordes that spilled over from it.

The night went by fast, and once the next shift had rolled in and the changeover was completed, I counted the takings, then ran upstairs to have a shower, washing the grime of the shift and the lingering smell of ghostly deaths—a smell that was in my mind rather than on my skin—away.

It was nearly four by the time I got home and I barely had the energy to even strip. I was fast asleep almost as soon as my head hit the pillow.

The play of fingertips across my bare back stirred me hours later. I murmured sleepily, not ready to wake yet. The gentle caress paused, as if waiting for sleep to claim me again. *Dream,* I thought wistfully. Only the dream smelled of lemongrass, suede, and musky, powerful male. I smiled. *Lucian.*

The play of fingertips began again, sweeping slowly down my spine, the movements teasing, erotic. I became aware of his weight resting gently on my legs, of the heat of desire that swam all around me. The force of it burned my skin.

His big hands briefly cupped my butt and pressed my cheeks together. He kissed each one, the touch so light I barely felt it, yet it sent a tremor that was all anticipation shooting through my core. His touch moved on, down to my thighs, then slowly between them, until his fingers slid through waking slickness and found my clit.

A moan escaped and he chuckled softly. "It seems my plan to take you when you sleep isn't quite going as I'd envisioned."

He continued to stroke me, sending little shudders of pleasure skating through me, making it difficult to think, let alone talk. I licked my lips and croaked, "And what fun is there to be had in loving an unresponsive body?"

"Oh, none at all." He pressed two of his fingers into

me, sliding them in and out. I shuddered and raised my butt a little, allowing him greater access. He chuckled again, but his movements remained deliberate and painstakingly slow. "The fun comes with wakefulness, in feeling your surprise when—a heartbeat before your orgasm hits you—you realize that I've been fucking you senseless."

His words had my pulse racing. God, I wanted that. All of that. *Now*. "I'm a wolf," I said, my voice becoming more than a little breathless as those shudders of pleasure got ever stronger. "I'm always going to wake way before either of those moments."

"As I've sadly discovered. It does not, however, alter my plan."

And of that, I was glad. "Trouble is, all I'm feeling is finger fucking. When does the real action start?"

"Wolves," he said with a chuckle. "Always impatient."

And with that, he pulled my hips upward into doggie position and slowly thrust into me. I moaned as my body clenched around him, wanting his heat deeper, wanting him to go faster. He did neither, keeping the rhythm of his movements slow and steady, even though I could feel the tremble of desire that rode him where our flesh connected.

Then, with a suddenness that made me growl in frustration, that connection was gone. He chuckled again. "Patience, little wolf, patience."

He shifted his position, then flipped me over onto my back. Before I could even squawk a protest, his body was pressed against my length and his lips were claiming mine. And this was no ordinary kiss—the kiss of an Aedh is like no other. It's designed to enthrall, to not only captivate but sweep aside all objections and allow the Aedh to bed and impregnate the woman of his choice. Aedh usually did this only when they were nearing the end of their life span, and with human females only when they could find no female Aedh to mate with. Their lovemaking never actually lived up to the power and magic of their kiss, but it was still pretty damn fine.

Of course, Lucian was no ordinary Aedh. Not only had his wings been ripped off as punishment for murder—he'd taken revenge against the man who'd killed his half sister—but he'd been confined to human form for many, many centuries. In that time, he'd come to appreciate some of the finer aspects of holding human form, and making love was definitely one of them. To say he had an insatiable need to indulge in the pastime *without* impregnating his partner was something of an understatement.

Just as saying he was kissing me senseless was something of an understatement. He kissed me until my head spun and desire became a burn that would surely consume me if it wasn't quenched. Then he released me and moved down my neck, the butterfly kisses he trailed along my skin making me tremble and groan. He kissed both breasts, then closed his mouth over one, alternating between sucking and swirling his tongue around the edge of the areola as he pinched and squeezed the other. My fingers clenched the bedsheets, and it was all I could do not to scream against the force of the sensations crashing through me.

As the shudders of pleasure assaulting my body

threatened to become a quake, he continued his journey downward, kissing my stomach and belly button.

Then he reached my lower lips and began to slowly trace the edges, tantalizing me with possibilities. My breath hitched as his tongue passed briefly over my clit, but he moved on quickly. *Too* quickly. I moaned, and he laughed softly, his breath a teasing coolness that felt almost as good as his tongue's caress.

He explored further, each thrust of his tongue delving deeper. It was an intimate yet gentle assault that left me delirious with pleasure, and I was torn between wanting it to go on and on yet not sure I could actually stand such torture for too much longer.

Then his tongue swirled around my clit again. I screamed as my body bucked and my orgasm crashed through me with a suddenness and intensity that left me trembling but still wanting more. Of him. *All* of him.

I grabbed his arms and swiftly switched our positions, straddling him quickly and thrusting him deep inside.

His hands moved to either side of my hips, holding me steady and still. "Wolves," he said, the disappointment in his expression somewhat destroyed by the mirth so evident in his powerful, jade green eyes. "No stamina whatsoever."

"Oh, really?" I said, more than a little amused. "I somehow doubt you'd last long under a similar assault of pleasure."

"I disagree. You forget I've had centuries to practice restraint and delay pleasure."

I raised a somewhat mocking eyebrow. "Shall we test that theory out?"

"I'm sure I'll thoroughly enjoy such an experiment, but do be prepared to fail, my dear."

I grinned. "I'm going to enjoy watching you beg."

"Hell will freeze over before that happens."

I snorted softly and began to rock back and forth, riding him gently, enjoying the feel of his flesh so deep inside and the sensations that flowed from such an intimate and basic connection. Slowly but surely our movements became stronger and his thrusts more urgent, but as the point of no return approached, I withdrew, coming down on all fours, straddling him as I claimed his lips and kissed him long and hard. A dangerous play, given just what his kiss could do to me, but right then, the need to prove he could be made as delirious and needy by our lovemaking as I was just that little bit stronger.

When that sense of urgency finally eased, I repeated the process, riding him until desire and the need for release began throbbing through his flesh and mine. Once more I retreated, and this time he groaned, just as I'd groaned. But that was still a long, *long* way from begging.

So I began an exploration of his body, kissing and tasting his chest, his abs, his stomach, taking my time but moving ever so slowly downward. When I took him in my mouth, he shuddered and tangled his hand in my hair, gently encouraging me to continue. I swirled my tongue around the tip of his cock, then down the length of his shaft, tasting myself on him as I licked and teased, never lingering in one place for very long. It wasn't long before his breathing became harsh again and that gentle pressure on my head became more and more insistent, encouraging me without words to take him fully.

I did, and he moaned again, his body thrusting instinctively upward, his cock filling my mouth completely. I sucked him, teased him, played with him, until his shaft was throbbing with the need for release and the salty taste of come was thick and strong and threatening to explode.

Once again, I retreated. He shuddered, then laughed, his voice hoarse as he said, "No retreat, no surrender, and certainly no begging. That's the motto I've lived by and I see no reason to change that now."

"We'll see," I murmured, as I moved back up his body to repeat the whole process again.

By the third time around I think we were both close to breaking point. I was drenched in sweat and aching so fiercely I was half convinced Tao wasn't the only one who had a fire elemental burning inside of him. God, if one of us didn't give in soon, we'd both expire.

As the taste of him grew ever saltier, I once again withdrew, but this time he growled "enough"—the sound almost animal in its intensity—and flipped our positions, kneeling between my legs as he dragged me forward and up. Holding me steady, he drove into me, and it was no gentle mating. It was all animal, all desperate need. He pumped furiously, his cock driving so deep it felt as if he was trying to spear himself right through every inch of me. And I was right there with him in that desperation, meeting him thrust for thrust, needing, aching, for release.

It came in an explosion that was unlike anything else we'd shared so far, so deep and intense I actually blacked out for several seconds. When I regained my senses, he was lying along my length, taking most of his weight on his arms and his body still in mine. The Aedh, despite the intensity that had just consumed us, was not finished yet.

But I think I was.

I raised my head a little and kissed his lips. "You begged."

He smiled and wiped the sweaty strands of hair out of my eyes. "I growled 'enough.' That's different."

"Only by a matter of degree. I win. You lose."

He grinned. "Actually, I rather think I won even if I did technically lose."

I chuckled softly, and let my gaze run over the planes of his face, half wondering how nature could be so cruel as to give such perfection so little real emotions. I could have happily settled down with Lucian if he'd been anything other than an Aedh, with no want or need for anything beyond fulfilling the desires of his body. "So what are you doing here at this hour of the morning? And how did you even get in?"

Not only did we have one of the best security systems installed in our converted warehouse home, but Ilianna had finally figured out the magic used in the wards—which were basically stones that could repel magic, spirits, or evil, depending on the spell infused within them—that my father had left behind the last time he'd talked to me, and she'd used that magic to install wards of her own around our home. Which meant no Aedh—or even reaper—could get in. And I knew for sure Azriel couldn't, because he'd apparently tried more than once—and it was something of a blessing given this morning's session. The thought of his witnessing such a wanton display had embarrassment stirring in me, although I wasn't entirely sure why. I was wolf—or part wolf—and lovemaking in full view of others wasn't exactly a new experience to me.

Lucian nuzzled the side of my neck. "Ilianna let me in as she went out, and I thought it was pretty obvious what I'm doing here."

"And I thought you said you had several important meetings to attend today and that I wouldn't see you until later tonight."

"Something came up."

"Yeah." My tone was sarcastic. "And I'm still feeling that something."

He chuckled softly. "What can I say? Your body drives me insane."

And his avoidance of questions was driving *me* insane. "Seriously, I saw your schedule. You had meetings starting at eight thirty, then rolling right through until almost seven tonight. They can't all have canceled."

"You snooped through my appointments calendar?" He nipped my earlobe just a little harder than necessary and I flinched. But even so, my treacherous hormones began to stir and hum. "That's not polite."

"Neither is reading my mind during sex," I replied testily, as his teeth caught my lobe again and gently gnawed it. A shiver that was half expectation, half apprehension rolled through me. "But that doesn't seem to stop you from doing it."

"Speaking of which, who the hell is Jak?"

I growled low in my throat and thrust him off me. "No one."

I swung my legs off the bed and stalked across to my rather opulent bathroom. Every bedroom had its own and, like all the other rooms in this place, the bathrooms were huge, each one containing a massive spa bath, a double walk-in shower, a toilet, and a big hand basin. In mine, the oversized white wall tiles contrasted sharply against the heated black slate under my feet, and the lighting was warm and muted. Thankfully, Lucian didn't immediately follow me in. There were some things a girl liked privacy for, and peeing was definitely one of them.

He said, "And yet your actions just now would suggest otherwise."

The toilet flushed as I padded over to the shower. When I stepped in, the water automatically came on at just the right temperature. I might not flaunt the fact that I was insanely rich, but there were definite benefits to being so, and one of those was being able to afford a system designed to ensure that you never had to battle with water temperature again.

"My actions," I snapped back, "are related to annoyance at you rather than any need not to talk about Jak."

"Then tell me who he is."

I swung around and watched him enter the bathroom. He walked like a cat. A big, golden, beautiful cat.

"I'll start answering questions when you do."

He walked into the shower cubicle and the second showerhead came on, covering him in water. The beads glistened in the warm light as they rolled almost reverently down his muscular body.

I held my ground and he stopped in front of me, his arms coming to either side of mine, effectively penning me. "I told you, I had several cancellations."

I pushed my hands between us and tried to shove him away. I might as well have tried to knock down a skyscraper. I might be part wolf, and might therefore be a whole lot stronger than an average female, but he wasn't human, either. And he was bigger and stronger in almost every way imaginable.

"Damn it, you're lying. I know it; you know it."

His gaze swept mine, though what he was searching for I couldn't say. After a moment he grunted, and if I hadn't known better, I'd have sworn it was an almost frustrated sound.

"My eight thirty meeting finished earlier than expected, and my ten o'clock had to cancel because his wife went into labor. Satisfied?"

I didn't answer. I couldn't. I tasted no lie in his words and yet I had an odd feeling it wasn't exactly the truth. And while I did trust Lucian, there was that growing niggle in the back of my mind that kept suggesting he wasn't being honest with me, that he'd *never* been entirely honest with me. Oh, his much-stated desire to seek revenge on those who'd ripped his wings from his flesh was real enough—and understandable, given that the process also robbed him of his ability to take Aedh form—but I wasn't so sure that anything else was.

Of course, that niggle might also be nothing more than Azriel's distrust worming its way into my thoughts.

"Your turn," he added, a touch of impatience coloring his voice.

I snorted softly. "Why should I have to tell you? Why don't you just pluck the answer from my thoughts like you usually do?"

He growled low in his throat and pressed against me, pinning me hard against the cool white tiles. The water that streamed down on us did little to ease the heat and awareness that surged between us.

"Once I might have. Now, that is not so much an option."

I frowned, my gaze searching his, seeing frustration mingling with growing arousal. He wasn't lying—not about this. Curiosity mingled with relief. "Why not? You've had no trouble before now."

"I know." He pressed one knee between my legs. I tried to shove him back again, but with as little success as before.

"Then what's changed?"

"I suspected the reaper might have had something to do with it, but this has not got his imprint."

Alarm stirred. Reading my mind was one thing, but if Azriel was also altering the direction of my thoughts . . . "Meaning you've felt him before?"

"I've sometimes felt his echo. He reads your mind far more than you think, Risa."

The alarm abated. I was well aware of just how often he was reading me. It was the thought of him actually doing more that had me worried. But even as that thought crossed my mind, I swiped it away. Azriel wouldn't do that. He was a man—a being—of more integrity than that. Lucian, on the other hand, was an entirely different matter.

He nudged my knees farther apart, obviously preparing to claim me more intimately. I ducked under his arms and retreated, but I was nowhere near fast enough. He grabbed my hands, pinning them behind my back as he pressed me belly first against the wall.

"Damn it, Lucian, this has gone far enough."

"Then tell me who Jak is," he murmured, his words little more than a heated breeze near my left ear.

I shivered, torn between desire and growing anger. "Why do you need to know? It's not as if you're jealous or anything."

"At first, it was nothing more than curiosity." He shifted his grip so that both of my hands were held in one of his, then he pulled me back just enough to slip his free hand between the wall and me. He cupped my breasts, pinching and rolling my nipples, playing me like a master played his favorite instrument—with ease and assurance. He added, "Now, however, it is something of a challenge."

"And yet another one you won't win."

"Oh, have no doubt that I'll win this one," he said softly. He continued to knead and press and tease my flesh, until I was trembling to the tune of his fingers and beginning to hunger for a whole lot more. It was frustrating—*truly* frustrating—that I just couldn't seem to say no to this man and actually mean it. It was almost as if he'd become an addiction. "When I mentioned a moment ago that I wasn't able to read your thoughts as much as I used to, I did leave a little information out of the equation."

"There's a surprise," I muttered, my body still quivering under the delicious assault.

He chuckled softly and once again gently prized my

legs apart with his knee. Then he claimed me from behind, his cock thick and hard and oh-so-heated as it thrust up into me. I made a sound that was a confused mix of annoyed growl and moan of pleasure. He chuckled again, his lips brushing my ear before he whispered, "I can read you when I fuck you. And right now, I intend to fuck you so completely that protecting the elusive Jak's identity will be the very last thing on your mind."

And that's exactly what he did. Until the water went cold and the shower automatically shut down, until my body was trembling with exhaustion and the repeated waves of orgasm. Until, I guess, he'd finally mined the information from my mind. Only then did he allow himself to come, and finally end the ordeal.

For several minutes neither of us moved. His hands were still wrapped around mine, and my legs were so wobbly that his grip was the only thing keeping me upright.

He released me, then blew out a breath, the breeze of it whispering past my cheek. "So," he said, and for the first time there was weariness in his voice. The legendary Aedh stamina had finally hit a wall. "Jak is an ex-lover you met up with yesterday morning."

If I'd had the energy I would have pushed him away from me. As it was, it was all I could do to turn around and glare at him.

"Yes."

"Why?"

"He's in town and wanted to catch up. Nothing more, nothing less."

His gaze swept mine, as if he was trying to work out

whether I was telling the truth or not. And that surely meant he *hadn't* dragged all the information about Jak out of my mind during the marathon session. Though whether the relief that followed this realization stemmed from Azriel's distrust or my own lingering sense that something wasn't quite right, I couldn't honestly say.

"So you won't be meeting him again?"

"I might. I might not." I hesitated, then added in a more biting tone, "Which right now is exactly what I'm thinking when it comes to seeing you again."

He chuckled softly. "As if you could give up what we share so easily. Do not fool yourself, Risa. Roughhouse or not, you enjoyed every inch of what we did here today."

"I did, but that isn't the point." I ran my fingers through my sweaty, matted hair, then added, "Just go. I don't want to see you, I don't want to smell you, and I certainly don't want to feel you. Not now, and not in the foreseeable future."

He raised an eyebrow. "And just how am I to get out, given the wards and the security system you have installed in this place?"

"Easy," I muttered. "I'll let you out."

I slipped past him and walked naked to the front door, waiting impatiently as he unhurriedly dressed and sauntered out.

He stopped in the doorway, his expression still amused. "I give this anger two nights, at the most."

"Yet another bet you'll lose," I snapped back, and slammed the door on his retreating butt.

But as I stalked back into my bathroom to see if the water had reheated enough to grab a quick shower, I had a sneaking suspicion that lasting even one day without feeling his touch was going to be a whole lot harder than I might wish.

Jak called as I was preparing my breakfast. I slid the huge pile of eggs and bacon onto the plate, then grabbed my coffee and walked over to the dining table. After pressing the vid-button, I propped the phone up against the vase of roses in the middle of the table, and sat down.

"You're just eating breakfast?" Jak said, by way of greeting as his dark features popped onto the phone's screen. "It's four in the afternoon—it's closer to dinner than breakfast."

"I worked late at the café last night." And I'd fallen back into bed after my second shower, catching another three hours of much-needed sleep.

"So why not prepare dinner?"

"Because I felt like bacon and eggs." I dove into my meal as I spoke. Jak had seen the best and worst of me during our time together, and I saw no reason for politeness now. "I gather you're not phoning to discuss my breakfast times."

"You gathered right."

I looked up and saw that laughter crinkled the corners of his ebony eyes. And I was reminded of the times we'd shared similar late-afternoon breakfasts, of the fun, and the loving that had followed.

I tore my gaze away from the screen and tried to concentrate on eating. Those times were gone. Remembering them would do nothing more than remind me just how empty my current love life was. Sex—no matter how fantastic—could never replace the intimacy of a real relationship. Not long term. And ultimately, that was what I really wanted.

Of course, that was exactly what I *wasn't* going to get from Lucian, or even Azriel. Although I guess Azriel did appear to have the capacity for emotions, which made him one step up the ladder from Lucian, but still not a great option. Hell, as much as part of me still hungered for what Jak and I had shared, he wasn't Mr. Long Term, either, no matter what I might have thought or how much I'd loved him when we'd been an item. He was married to his work, and everything and everyone else came second to that.

"Then tell me what you want."

"Risa," he chided softly, "you know I don't like talking over the phone. One never knows just who is listening in."

"Nice to see you're still paranoid about people stealing your scoops," I said. "Although I'd like to know when that has ever happened."

"Actually, it happened several months ago. You remember that piece the *Age* ran on the rat gangs running the old sewers?"

I scooped up several pieces of bacon and munched on them contemplatively, then eventually said, "No."

He snorted. "Nice to see *you're* still keeping up with world events."

"Hey, I don't get enough spare time these days to waste it reading newspapers." Especially since *he* was often featured in my favorite one.

"Well, take it from me, that scoop was mine—and the bastard only got it half right."

"Well, I doubt the half-right bit would have annoyed you too much."

"Sweetheart, you really need to get over this whole resentment thing and move on."

I did my best to ignore the ache that washed through me at his use of the endearment. "I have. I'm just having a little trouble resisting the urge to needle. Where do you want to meet, and when?"

He shifted position, and I recognized the lighthouse print behind him. He was home rather than at work. "Look, this story you've handed me is a little tricky given not only the Directorate's involvement but a definite unwillingness on the street to discuss the buy-up. I think it would be better if we appear to meet accidentally rather than on purpose. Might be safer for us both."

Alarm swam through me. "Meaning you've been threatened?"

"Not in so many words, but I got the distinct impression it might be better to leave this one alone." He laughed, and his face came alive. "Which of course only stirred my curiosity all the more."

I snorted softly. He hadn't changed, not one little bit. "So where do you want to meet? And don't say the Blue Moon because I don't go there anymore, and I'm certainly not dancing with you."

"Ah, Risa, that's such a shame." His voice was almost wistful. "We were so good together."

"*We were* being the correct phrase there."

"Perhaps." He shrugged lightly. "What about Chrome? Do you and that gang of yours still hang out there?"

Chrome was a trendy bar in Brunswick that Ilianna,

Tao, and I had all but lived in as university students. The booze was cheap, the atmosphere fantastic, and on a Friday night, it was still the only place in that area to be seen. "Yeah, once or twice a month, just for old times' sake."

"Good. Shall we say seven?"

Seven would still leave me time to see Tao. "Okay. Save me a barstool."

"Naturally." He hesitated, then added softly, "I love the new hair color. Makes your eyes stand out more."

And with that, he disconnected. I swore softly and wished that he—and the past—would just leave me alone. Which was a stupid desire, since I was the one responsible for bringing him back into my life. The past was always going to come as accompanying baggage.

I finished my breakfast, then went back into my bedroom, swapping my dress for a summer top and jeans. Although the jeans I found myself reaching for were the Kevlar-infused ones, and that had me wondering if my sometimes unreliable clairvoyance ability sensed a bike fall in the near future. I hoped not—I didn't want the Ducati damaged.

It was close to five by the time I locked up and headed down the side steps to the garage. Azriel was waiting near my bike, his expression as remote as I'd ever seen it. Not happy about something, that was for sure.

"What's happening?" he asked, his voice as neutral as his expression.

I raised an eyebrow as I plucked my helmet free of its stand. "What, you haven't been following every single thought I've had since I woke up?"

Yellow fire flicked up Valdis's side, although Azriel's

expression remained stony. "You know that's not possible when Ilianna's wards are powered up. She has placed far more restrictions than your father did."

"How is that something I'm supposed to know when you've never bothered to tell me before now?"

He ignored the sarcasm in my voice and simply said, "I take it Jak called?"

"Yes." I sat astride my bike and half wondered if he was annoyed because Lucian was allowed into the warehouse and he wasn't. "He refuses to discuss anything on the phone, so I'm meeting him at seven."

"But you're going to see Tao first?"

"Yes." I eyed him for a moment, wondering again why he'd reverted back to the stiff and unyielding Azriel I'd first met. It couldn't *just* be annoyance over Lucian, surely. I added silently, *Is our watcher still near?*

Yes.

Which meant I'd better act like I'd been investigating the case rather than sleeping and fucking. "Did you manage to scope out any information about the Rakshasa?"

"Some. I'm told the best way to kill them is to smash the heart of their dark god, which is usually to be found in a sacred urn within their lair. This will make the Rakshasa stay in flesh, and render them easier to kill."

"*Their* lair?"

He nodded. "Apparently they are found in packs of six or more."

Fabulous. *Not*. "If there's six or more of them, I can't say I fancy the idea of tracking them back to their lair. Surely there's another way to kill them . . ."

"If you can trap it when it's about to consume its

next victim, then white ash, silver, or even sunlight might destroy it."

Might. Not a good word choice. "What about the others in the lair?"

"There is usually only one hunter per pack. Take out the hunter, and you probably destroy the others."

"Which means we need to be there when it selects its next victim, then track it home if the trap doesn't work." I stared at him as dread settled into the pit of my stomach. "And *that* means keeping watch at Dark Earth. That's not something I want to do."

"Then do not." *But remember, you do this because you fear Hunter and her council.* He paused, then added, with a little more emphasis than was needed, *How do you think she would react if you backed out of this investigation now?*

Badly. And with much venom. I sighed. "Dark Earth is not a place I want to go near again—especially at night."

"I'll be there."

And he would protect me as much as he could. I knew that. But I also knew he was just one against a possible frenzy.

"You do not have to be there in the flesh."

I frowned. "But you warned me against taking Aedh form too much because it might attract the wrong sort of attention."

"It might, but if you do not want to physically wait at Dark Earth, then we are left with Aedh form or watching from the gray fields."

"In the gray fields we'd at least have the Dušan to guard us."

He nodded. "But the Raziq prowl there. There is a

greater chance of discovery if we step onto the fields for any great length of time."

"We risk that no matter what we do," I muttered. "Any idea how long it might be before the Rakshasa feeds again?"

"The five victims have all died within a week. From what I have been told, their feeding cycle lasts a month, and then they will go into hibernation again."

"Spirits hibernate? That's a new one."

He ignored my comment. "After the initial frenzy, the hunter will space her kills more evenly. We may have a couple of days before the agony and fury of the lost ones call to her again."

"I really don't want to be hanging around that club night after night waiting for a spirit that may or may not appear."

"No." He hesitated. "I am attempting to get more information. It might also be helpful if we had greater details about the time and date of the deaths. There might be a pattern we could use."

If there was a pattern, surely Hunter and the Directorate would have seen it. "I'll ask Hunter to send the information to me."

He nodded. "Once we get that, we can decide the best way to proceed."

The best way to proceed—or rather, the sanest way to proceed—would be to run a mile in the other direction. I mean, a flesh-eating, shape-changing spirit with poisonous talons wasn't exactly something anyone with an iota of sense would want to tangle with. But it wasn't like I had any real choice, because right now I was stuck with two millstones hanging around my neck—the agreement to help Hunter and a vampire council still debating whether or not it would be better to kill me. A wrong step might be fatal in more ways than one.

"I'll see you at the Brindle." I didn't bother waiting for an answer. I just shoved my helmet on, fired up the bike, and raced into the street.

Unfortunately, it was peak hour and all the main roads were playing parking lots again. Frustrated, I swung into a side street and took the more roundabout but better-flowing route to the Brindle.

Only trouble was, I didn't get there.

Chapter 5

One moment I was cruising down the street behind a belching truck; the next I was hit side-on. The force of the impact ripped me from my bike and sent me flying toward a light pole. It happened so fast I didn't even have time to try to protect myself—I just hit the pole and wrapped around it like an old bit of rubbish.

Then I slumped to the ground, battling to breathe and struggling to ignore the pain stabbing into my brain as well as the gathering tide of blackness that threatened to wash away consciousness.

I couldn't let go. I just *couldn't*.

It was a thought that made no sense, but one that had me struggling to rise nevertheless. I made it to my knees—the pain was too great to go any farther. Although getting even that far meant I hadn't broken anything major. *Yay for the strength of werewolf bones*, I thought fuzzily.

Something warm and sticky gushed down the side of my cheek. I swiped at it and hit the visor instead. It was half hanging off, and swinging back and forth with my movements. I swore and wrenched it off completely. It clattered to the ground, though oddly made no sound. In fact, the whole world seemed to be silent. Or maybe I just couldn't hear through the roar that seemed to be filling my head.

I blinked and looked around. Saw my bike lying on her side, hydrogen leaking from her tanks. It looked surreal, like blood, and I hoped like hell her wound wasn't fatal.

That odd roaring got louder and I suddenly realized what it was. It was Amaya, screaming a warning, screaming for blood.

It was then that I saw them—Ania. And this time, there weren't only six or so. This time, there were so many that it looked like an ethereal tower of white speeding toward me.

A hand wrapped around my arm and yanked me upright. My heart just about jumped out of my chest, even though instinct and something else—something that was infinitely deeper and decidedly scarier—told me it was Azriel.

Power surged as he pulled me close and wrapped his other arm around my waist. Valdis blazed at his back, as eager as Amaya to fight, but neither sword was getting its wish today. Azriel's power burned around me—through me—sweeping us both from flesh to energy. A second later we were on the gray fields, but they weren't the fields that I knew. My gray fields were a place of shadows, a place where things not sighted in the real world suddenly gained substance. But in Azriel's arms, the fields were vast and beautiful, filled with structures and life that were delicate and unworldly.

Then the brightness and warmth of his world was

gone, replaced by a darkness that felt damp and smelled faintly of rot and excrement. The sewers, I thought dazedly. Why the hell were we in the sewers?

"Because this is the last place the Ania or the Raziq will think to look for us," Azriel said.

He shifted his grip and guided me down onto a chair. Which was a smart move, because if he'd simply let go I think I would have fallen. My legs were like jelly and my whole body was shaking.

I looked around. Wherever we were, it didn't actually *look* like a sewer. It actually resembled a small control room of some sort, filled with computers and what looked to be some kind of projector . . .

Memory stirred, and I suddenly realized that this was the control room where Ike Foreman had held me and questioned me about the keys for the portals of hell—although we still had no clear idea for whom he'd been working. He'd died in the sewer just beyond the main doorway, shot by Lucian. The image of Foreman's face—and the surprise that had flitted across it a second before he died—rose, and I suddenly found myself wondering *why* he'd been so shocked. It wasn't the fact that death had found him; of that I was sure.

"We'll just be here long enough to stop this bleeding," Azriel continued, drawing me out of my thoughts. But his attention was focused on the helmet that had saved me, and after a moment he unsheathed Valdis. "Stay still."

I tightened my fingers around the arms of the chair, suddenly fighting the urge to flee. "What the hell are you intending to do?"

"Your helmet shattered when you hit the pole, and there are several pieces embedded in your head."

Well, that would certainly explain the pain in my head and the blood on my cheek. "So just take them out and then remove the helmet. There's no need to try to cut it off—"

"I suspect moving the shards will cause greater bleeding. Valdis will obliterate the shards and heal the wound at the same time." He paused, and his gaze met mine. There was something unyielding in his eyes, almost as if he were drawing a line in the sand. "You said you trusted me."

I licked my lips. "I do, but using Valdis to dig them out seems a little like using a jackhammer to hit home a nail."

"Valdis would never harm you. She can't."

I raised my eyebrows at that. "Why not?"

His expression became closed again. "Do you trust me?"

That was a question I'd answered more than once. He was connected to me on a chi level—and far more strongly than he was admitting—and he knew just how much I *did* trust him, even if the occasional doubt raised its ugly head. I motioned for him to proceed.

Valdis's fire was a strange green-gold as he brought her close. Droplets of fire splattered across my skin, hissing as they touched, yet not hurting. Warmth flushed upward from my neck and face, until even the ends of my hair felt like they were on fire. There was a brief retort, and a bitter smell—which was a mix of melting fiberglass and burning carbon fiber—filled the air.

Then it was gone, and with it the stabbing pain in the side of my head.

Azriel sheathed Valdis, then slowly—carefully— removed the helmet. The shards digging into my skull might have been eliminated, but it still hurt like shit. I blinked back tears, and gripped the chair arms so damn tightly that my fingernails tore into the leather.

"You were extremely lucky," Azriel said, and held the helmet so I could see it.

The whole left side was broken, much of it dented inward toward what was now a jagged and somewhat melted hole in the center. It was destroyed—but it had undoubtedly saved my life.

My gaze rose and met Azriel's. The anger that burned in the mismatched blue depths just about snatched my breath away. "The Ania could have killed me."

"By mistake, yes, but if they'd actually wanted to kill you, they could have easily done so by now. And remember, it wasn't so much an attack in the café as an attempt to capture you." He tossed the helmet aside. It clattered against the old stones and rolled limply into the shadows. "It would also appear that changing your hair made little difference. They obviously know more about your habits than I presumed."

I didn't have the energy to say "I told you so," and simply leaned back in the chair and closed my eyes. While the pain in my head had all but gone, the rest of me felt more than a little pulverized. But I guess feeling that way was better than actually being so, and that had very nearly been the reality.

"I can't step away from everything and go into hiding, Azriel," I said, after a moment. "That won't find the Rakshasa and it certainly won't find us the keys."

"No, but staying away from the things they are aware of—like your bike, the café, and your apartment— would be a good start until we figure out a way to stop these attacks."

I opened my eyes again. "Do you really think we can stop them? I don't."

"We *can* stop them." He said it firmly, like he was trying to convince himself as much as me. Which was an odd thought, since he generally saw these things in black-and-white—*will* or *won't*. "But until we do, we should do all that we can to avoid them."

"I won't stop visiting Tao. I can't." Ilianna might send me regular updates, but that wasn't the same as being there.

He grimaced. "That could be dangerous, not just to you but to Ilianna and Tao."

Fear slithered through me. "The Ania couldn't mount an attack inside the Brindle. Her magic wouldn't let them."

"The Ania couldn't, no, but the Raziq might well attempt it if these ambushes keep failing."

And the witches had already warned us that the Brindle had no defenses against the Raziq. "That's only if they *are* the ones behind them."

"They are. I felt their touch behind the Ania this time."

Well, *fuck*. I swiped angrily at the blood still dribbling down my cheek. Valdis might have healed the worst head wound when she melted the helmet shards, but there were obviously several smaller ones if the blood was anything to go by. "I guess this means I'm staying at the Langham again—"

"Not the Langham," he cut in. "You've stayed there before, so it would be wise not to risk it."

I grimaced. Being hunted by minor demons wasn't half as annoying as missing out on staying at my favorite five-star hotel.

Azriel wrapped his hand around mine and gently pulled me to my feet. "You, Risa Jones," he said softly, "have a strange way of looking at things."

He was standing so close that his breath teased my lips as he spoke, and his scent—a scent that was man and musk and sharply electric—filled every breath. And all I had to do was lean forward, just a little, and I'd be kissing him. But as much as I wanted to do just that, I also feared it could forever change our relationship— and maybe not in a good way. So I simply said, "This, coming from a man who can describe lovemaking only as enlightening."

How my voice came out even I had no idea, given the tumultuous push-pull being waged inside me.

"It is an apt word when one has never experienced it before." His gaze was steady on mine and he showed no inclination to release me. Maybe he simply figured I wasn't steady enough after the accident, but something inside me whispered *no*. Azriel knew exactly what he was doing—and what it was doing to me. And that, in turn, implied intent.

"Tell me what you want, Risa." He said it so softly it was little more than a whisper that ran through my mind.

What did I want? *I don't fucking know,* I thought, my gaze searching his. Or rather, I *did* know, but I just didn't have the courage to reach for it when he was the one person who had my back no matter what I did. And right now, that was more valuable to me than whatever this was between us.

I took a deep, somewhat shuddery breath, and said, "Right now, I really want a shower and fresh clothes. Then I need to meet Jak."

He didn't say anything for several heartbeats—which wasn't that long given just how fast my heart was beating—then he inclined his head slightly. Conceding to what lay unspoken rather than what had been said.

"What hotel?"

I shrugged. "I'm known for my five-star tastes, so we're probably better off going to someplace like the BreakFree on Little Bourke Street."

The words were barely out of my mouth when his power surged around us, sweeping us quickly through the gray fields before re-forming us inside a bathroom. Two women were standing at the washbasins, but neither paid any attention to us. He was obviously taking care of that, too.

He released me and stepped back, and something deep inside mourned the loss of his closeness. "I thought you might like to wash the blood away before you check in."

I glanced at the mirror and saw the blood streaking my face and matting one side of my hair. I grimaced, turned on the taps, and ducked my head under the water, rinsing my hair, then scrubbing my face and neck. As the two women walked out, I hit the dryer button, flicked the nozzle upward, and finger-dried my hair—wincing several times in the process as my fingertips caught the smaller cuts on my head. At least short dark hair had its good points—it didn't take long to dry, and you couldn't see the blood that was still weeping from the other wounds.

"I don't suppose you want to do me a favor?" I said, as I turned around. He merely raised an eyebrow, so I added, "I have a bag of spare clothes and basic toiletries sitting in my locker at the café. Could you go grab it?"

He nodded, and disappeared so quickly I was tempted to think he'd been looking for an excuse to distance himself. I rang my mechanic to pick up the Ducati as I walked over to the reception desk, then booked a room for a couple of nights and headed up to it. A long hot shower didn't do a whole lot to ease the aches, and if the bruises already beginning to appear were anything to go by, I was going to have a rainbow adorning the left side of my body come tomorrow.

My bag was waiting for me on the floor near the towels once I'd finished. I frowned, wondering how he'd gotten in here without my sensing him, then shrugged and got dressed.

He was standing at the room's one window, his hands clasped behind his back and Valdis burning with a muted reddish yellow fire. He didn't say anything or turn around, so I walked across to the bed, grabbed my phone out of my purse—which thankfully had survived the crash relatively unscathed—and rang Ilianna.

"Hey there," she said. "I was getting worried about you."

The vid-screen wasn't showing a picture. I frowned and pressed the MODE button, figuring it might have somehow gotten switched in the accident, but it made no difference. Which meant I'd be looking for a new phone in the near future—just what I needed on top of everything else.

"Yeah, sorry, but it looks like I won't make it there tonight."

"I had a feeling there was trouble."

"There was. And I think I need to step away from things until we sort out what the hell is going on."

"Damn," she muttered. "I gather you're okay? What about the Ducati?"

Obviously, she'd had more than a feeling if she knew I'd been on the Ducati when trouble hit. "I'm okay, but I have no idea if the same can be said about the bike, as we had to abandon her."

"Abandon the Ducati?" Her tone was one of mock horror. "Good god, how will you cope?"

I snorted softly. "I'm not actually sure. Lonny's going to pick it up for me and send me a report once he's checked out the damage."

"You want me to take over your shift tonight?"

"Only if you feel up to it. If not, they'll just have to manage. I'll arrange for a temp to cover the rest of the week."

"I'll head in and cover the busiest hours. And don't worry about a temp—Margie has been asking for more hours, so this will make her happy."

Margie was one of our newer waitresses, but she was doing a business course and seemed to have a really sensible head on her shoulders. Ilianna had already pinned her as a potential manager, so this would be a good chance to see how she handled things.

"How's Tao?"

"Much, much better," she said, relief briefly lifting the tiredness in her voice. "The sunnier room has done wonders to stabilize his internal temperature, and though he's not yet awake, we're getting more gruel into him and he no longer looks so gaunt."

Thank god, I thought, and briefly closed my eyes against the sting of tears. "Any idea when he's likely to wake up?"

"No. His body still appears to be adjusting to the presence of the fire elemental. I doubt he'll wake until the merging is finished."

And until he did, we wouldn't know what the end result of that merging was. It was a very real possibility that Tao might not even know us once he woke up. It just depended which nature was stronger—the werewolf or the elemental.

"Ring me the minute anything happens," I said. "And in the meantime, you and Mirri be careful."

"Oh, trust me, if we were any more cautious, we'd be dangerous."

I laughed softly. "Give Tao a kiss for me."

"I'll give Mirri one for you, too," she said, somewhat primly.

"You'll use any excuse to kiss that girl of yours," I said, amused. "So give her two. Might as well make it worthwhile."

She laughed again, but the sound died a little too quickly. "You need to be careful, particularly tomorrow night."

Unease prickled across my skin. "More omens of trouble?"

"You, or someone near you. I can't define it more than that, so just keep an eye out, okay?"

"I will."

"Good. Keep in contact, Ris, or I'll be calling in the cavalry."

Meaning Aunt Riley and Uncle Rhoan—two people I did *not* want involved right now. Mainly because they'd lock me up, throw away the key, and attempt to investigate this whole mess themselves—and that would only end up with them getting hurt. Because no matter how good the pair of them were, this was far beyond their experience and capabilities. Hell, it was beyond mine, but at least I could see the reapers and walk the gray fields.

I shoved the phone away and looked at the time. It was six thirty—time to get moving if I was going to make my appointment with Jak.

I studied the still silent Azriel and frowned. "Are you okay?"

He turned, his expression carefully neutral but his body language hinting at tension. "Of course. How will you get to this café without your bike?"

"I'll catch a cab." I tilted my head slightly, continuing to watch him through slightly narrowed eyes. "You've retreated."

"I do what I am here to do. Nothing more, nothing less."

Which no doubt was a direct result of what I'd said. Or rather, what I *hadn't* said—that I wanted him. Though *why* he wanted it voiced when our chi connection gave him all manner of insight into my thoughts and emotions, I had no idea. But I could hardly complain about his retreat when it was a result of my own. "Then I'll see you at Chrome."

"You won't see me," he countered. "But I will be there."

And with that he disappeared again. I grimaced and grabbed my purse, slinging it over my shoulder as I headed down to the lobby to catch a cab.

I arrived at Chrome a couple of minutes past seven. The place was packed even though it was Wednesday, the music pumping and the air rich with the warm scent of alcohol and humanity. I squeezed my way toward the long chrome bar that ran the length of the rough brick wall to the left of the door and found Jak perched on one of the red-cushioned stools down the far end.

He turned as I approached, but his quick smile of greeting faded abruptly. "You look like shit," he said, catching my hand to steady me as I perched on the stool next to him. "Are you okay?"

"It's nothing a gallon of beer won't fix." I ignored the reminiscent side of me that wanted to enjoy his touch and gently pulled my fingers from his.

"Already done," he said, sliding a tankard my way. "What happened?"

"Fell off my bike." I shrugged and took a drink.

He watched me, eyes slightly narrowed, obviously

suspecting there was more to the story than what I was saying. "And the Ducati?"

"Alive but dented. What did you want to see me about?"

His wry smile made my insides twist. God, how I just wished that part of me would get over it. But that, it seemed, was not to be.

"Straight down to business, huh?"

"It's the only reason I'm here, Jak."

He snorted softly. "Well, I'm afraid there's more bad news than good."

Of course there was. Fate wasn't likely to give me only good news now, was it? "So hit me with it."

"As you are aware, John Nadler is an extremely elusive man. He has an office in Collins Street, but is rarely ever there, and while he owns a house in Brighton, none of his neighbors can tell me the last time they saw him."

"Well, he's not a ghost, because the heirs of both James Trilby and Gavin Appleby are suing the consortium for a bigger piece of the money pie, and a ghost generally can't hire lawyers or appear in court."

"Ah, but he hasn't yet appeared in court—and won't, because the case settled out of court yesterday."

I frowned. "Even if the lawyer handled the settlement, surely Nadler has to appear to sign the papers."

"He may have to sign the papers, but he didn't actually have to appear at the meeting to do that. Apparently Frank Logan—the lawyer in question—was meeting Nadler at two today to do all the official stuff, but the meet wasn't at the office."

I raised my eyebrows. "And you know this how?"

"Because I talked to the secretary."

And no doubt raided her mind in the process. It was the only way he'd get that sort of information. I couldn't imagine someone who had Nadler as a client employing anyone who gave out confidential information, however minor.

"So we have nothing."

"Not exactly nothing." A waiter went past and filled up the nearby nut bowl. Jak snagged it and pushed it between us. "We still have the lawyer."

I scooped up some peanuts. "You've made an appointment to talk to him?"

Jak snorted. "The man charges like a wounded bull. On my salary, I can't even afford his first-appointment rates."

"So you want me to go talk to him?"

"Well, yes and no—and this is where the good news comes in. He's apparently going to be at the Financial Markets Foundation for Children gala tomorrow night. I want you to get us tickets."

Go to a ball with Jak? I wasn't sure that was a good idea—not when he looked so damn good in black tie. "Mom supported a lot of charities, but I can't recall the foundation being one of them. And I doubt I could ring up at the last moment and get tickets."

"You can't. I've already checked, and they're sold out."

Which was good for the foundation but not so good for us. "So what do you expect me to do? Beat someone over the head and steal their ticket?"

He grinned, and it lit up his entire face, making that stubbornly stupid bit of me ache. "Well, as a last resort, maybe. But I figure that maybe you should try some of your mom's contacts first. Surely with all the work she did for charities, someone somewhere would owe her—or her daughter—a favor or two."

"Nice of you to remember how many charities she supported. Shame it didn't reach the damn article."

He patted my hand lightly. "Now, now, you know that's not true. I did mention it, if only in the introduction."

"Generous of you," I muttered, and once again slipped my hand from under his.

Amusement glittered in his dark eyes. He knew *exactly* what he was doing to me, the bastard. A thought confirmed by his next statement.

"The spark is still there, Ris."

"That spark is nothing more than werewolf nature," I said with determination. "And it's not something I'm about to give in to, so stop playing games."

"That's hard when—bruises aside—you look so damn good."

I was half tempted to look down just to see how hard it was, but I resisted. That sort of action would only encourage him—and was no doubt precisely *why* he'd chosen those words. "Then maybe you should have thought a little more about that story you wrote."

He was shaking his head before I'd even finished. "We both know I'd sell my soul mate for the right story, and we certainly weren't soul mates."

And that one sentence encapsulated why I—even if I could forget about the past—wasn't about to revive my relationship with Jak. I didn't need another relationship with a direct line to nowhereville.

And yet, even as that thought crossed my mind, a voice deep inside was whispering, *Liar*.

He added, "So, do you know anyone who might be able to wrangle some tickets? Otherwise, I'll have to resort to trying to interview him outside the venue, and given that I normally report on paranormal oddities rather than galas, that might raise suspicions in the wrong quarters."

I opened my mouth to say he was out of luck, that I didn't know anyone, but then I paused. Mike—the accountant who looked after the financial side of the café as well as having been my mom's financial adviser and now mine—had said a few days ago that if I ever needed help with anything outside of financial matters to give him a call. And while I'm sure he wasn't actually referring to tickets to a gala fund-raiser, it was worth a shot.

"I might." I slipped off the barstool. "Wait here while I go call him."

I made my way to the front of Chrome and stood to one side of the entrance, where it was less noisy, to make the call.

"Risa," a plummy, feminine voice said, "What can I do you for?"

"Hi, Beatrice," I said. "I'd like to speak to Mike if he's available."

"Just a moment, and I'll check."

Music came on the line as she switched over, but a second later Mike's low and pleasant voice replaced the music. "Risa, is there a problem? I wasn't expecting to hear from you until the next business activity statement was due."

"There's no problem. I just wondered if you could do me a small favor."

"You already know I will if I can. It's the least I can do in honor of your mother."

He and Mom had been lovers for more years than I could remember, although they were never seen together and seemed content to keep the relationship totally secret. So secret, in fact, that until Mike had all but confirmed it last week by his unusual offer to help me any way he could, I wasn't entirely sure their relationship wasn't a figment of my imagination.

"It's nothing major, as I said. I'm just looking for tickets to the FMFFC ball tomorrow night."

"The gala?" he said, surprise evident in his voice. "I wouldn't have thought that sort of thing was your style. Your mother's, certainly, but not yours."

"It's not," I admitted. "But I have a friend who is doing a story on several people who'll be there, and he can't get tickets."

I felt bad about lying—or half lying—but giving him the truth might be dangerous, and I'd endangered enough people as it was.

"So why is this your problem?" he asked.

"I owe him a favor and he's called it in." I shrugged, then remembered the vid-screen wasn't working. "This will make us even and get him off my back."

He grunted. "I haven't got tickets this year, but I'll ring around and see what I can do. Give me a few hours."

"Thanks, Mike. I really appreciate it."

"No promises," he said and hung up. I shoved my phone into my purse and went back inside.

Jak raised his eyebrows. "Success or failure?"

"Neither. He's ringing around and will let me know." I reclaimed my stool, then my drink, taking several sips of the cool amber liquid.

"Huh." He munched contemplatively on peanuts for a few seconds. "I've got a friend of mine keeping an electronic eye out on Nadler's house. He'll let me know who's coming and going."

"Well, it obviously won't be Nadler if the neighbors haven't sighted him for months."

"No." He paused again, munching on more peanuts before adding, "I've also been researching his family. Seems rather convenient to me that all his next of kin are listed as dead."

I raised my eyebrows. "Why has that snagged your interest? It happens. Hell—me, for example."

He gave me a wry look. "But you and your mother are somewhat special cases, and we both know it."

We did. Only *he* didn't know just how special. Mom had been created in a madman's lab, and while I was the result of a more conventional mating, my father was about as far from conventional as you could get.

"It still doesn't make his lack of siblings or relations that unusual."

"If he was a much older man, I'd agree. But he isn't and it just feels wrong."

"So you think he's been bumping off his relatives?"

He grinned again. "What I suspect is something far more exciting than just a spot of family bloodletting."

I couldn't help smiling at the excitement lighting his features and churning the air. He really did get turned on by this sort of intrigue—and it was damnably hard *not* to react to it.

"So, hit me with it," I said in a wry voice. "Or are you intending to drag out the suspense as punishment for me not submitting to your werewolf wiles?"

"Well, damn, I hadn't actually thought of that—"

I punched his shoulder lightly and he laughed. Just for a moment, it felt like old times.

"What I suspect," he said, softly and rather melodramatically, "is that while our John Nadler might not be a ghost, he could be the next best thing."

I gave him a deadpan look. "I *will* resort to greater violence if you don't get on with it."

He laughed again, and the sound ran across my senses like a summer rain, warm and inviting. "I think what we're looking for is not just a man but rather something a whole lot more. John Nadler, I suspect, is a face-shifter."

Chapter 6

I blinked in surprise. "But they test DNA at birth. If he wasn't human, then it would have been discovered. Mistakes like that just aren't made."

"Helki werewolves are not the only ones capable of face-shifting," he said. "I know for a fact the military has human face-shifters. Did a story on it quite a few years ago."

"But from what I've heard, they're rare."

"Rare doesn't mean impossible. But I rather suspect that the Nadler who was born fifty-six years ago is dead, and that a face-shifter has taken over his face and his life, and *that's* who is now running the consortium."

I frowned. I certainly knew how easy it would be to assume someone else's appearance, having done it myself. But stepping fully into their life was a whole different matter. "What makes you suspicious? The lack-of-relatives factor?"

"In a way, yes. Nadler was an only child, as was his mother. But his father had two brothers and one sister, and they provided Nadler with a total of five cousins."

"And they're all dead?" That *did* raise my eyebrows. You'd think at least a couple of the cousins would still be alive, considering that some of them had to be younger.

"All dead, and all within a three-year time span."

My frown deepened. "Something like that would have raised suspicions with the police or at the coroner's office."

"Not if each and every one was classified as either an accident or natural causes."

"And were they?"

"Yep."

At least that explained why Stane hadn't picked up on this. He didn't have Jak's naturally suspicious nature. "So if your suspicions are right, and a face-shifter *was* cleaning Nadler's house in preparation for a takeover, what about business partners and the like? They're often more familiar with someone than relatives are, simply because they spend more time with them."

He grinned and raised a hand, signaling to the waiter for two more beers. I finished the remnants of my first and slid the glass toward the waiter as he appeared with the second one.

"Ah, now this is where it gets *really* interesting." Jak's excitement ramped up another notch. I took several gulps of beer, but it didn't do a whole lot to quench the rising flame of desire. Damn it, I would *not* go there. He continued. "Nadler supposedly had a partial breakdown when his parents died in a car accident. He took six months off work, and when he came back, his colleagues noticed a change in him, but put it down to the recent trauma. Interestingly, he left that business two weeks later to run the newly formed consortium."

"A consortium with a paper trail so convoluted it's almost impossible to track down its true beginnings."

"Exactly." He raised his glass and clicked it lightly against mine. "All roads point to the man we know as Nadler being a face-shifter."

"You've made a case for it," I agreed. "But it's no certainty, and it's not something his lawyer can tell us. Hell, if a face-shifter *has* taken over Nadler's life, then there's no saying that the Nadler the lawyer sees is the one everyone else involved in his day-to-day life does. He's a face-shifter, remember."

He frowned slightly. "Hadn't actually thought of that."

I grinned. "Sorry to burst your excited little bubble."

"Oh, you haven't." His expression held altogether too much warmth and a whole lot of sexual hunger. And that, I suspected, wasn't so much about the desire that raged between us as it was about the thrill of a case that had him intrigued. Which wasn't saying he didn't want me; it was just that I wasn't the prime motivator of said hunger.

Which didn't make the desire surging through *me* any easier to ignore. I dropped my gaze back to my beer and took several slow, deep breaths. They helped about as much as the cold beer.

"Thing is," he continued, "the lawyer will at least be able to describe the Nadler *he* knows well enough for me to work up a sketch, and we can go from there."

"That's a good idea."

"Oh, I'm full of them."

"There's no denying you're full of something," I said dryly. "But I'm not sure I'd call it ideas."

His soft laugh shivered across my senses enticingly. Damn, damn, *damn*.

"Well, I'd offer to show you exactly what is filling me at the moment, but I rather suspect you'll refuse."

"Don't you know it." Thankfully, my phone chose that moment to ring, cutting off any other comments he might make along those lines. It was Mike. "I'm guessing it's bad news, seeing not much time has passed."

"On the contrary," he said. "The tickets will be dropped off at the office tomorrow at nine, and you can pick them up anytime after that."

"Excellent." I gave Jak the thumbs-up. "Thanks heaps, Mike."

"Glad to help," he said, and hung up again.

"Fantastic," Jak said as I put the phone away. "What time do you want me to pick you up?"

"It's supposed to be a chance meeting, remember? I'll meet you there." Besides, he and I confined in a car was not a good idea if he was going to continue radiating desire so strongly. My brain and emotions might want to keep their distance, but my hormones remembered the good times, and they were more than willing to take the chance and dance with him again.

"Not because of any ruse, but because you don't trust me," he commented, amusement crinkling the corners of his dark eyes.

"Not one iota. You, my friend, have seduction on your mind." I finished my drink and stood. "I'll see you tomorrow night."

"Bring your dancing shoes," he said.

I snorted in disgust, and his laughter followed me out the door. *Damn him to hell,* I thought, and fleetingly wished I hadn't argued with Lucian. It would have been nice to ease the ache of desire in his arms. I could always go to Franklin's, a discreet up-market wolf club I often used at times like this, but even as that thought crossed my mind, my nose was wrinkling. The club had lost some of its appeal lately—mainly because Lucian had a sexual repertoire my usual partner at Franklin's had no hope of competing with.

Azriel appeared beside me as I walked up the road to the taxi stand. "The face-shifter theory is an interesting one."

His voice was still very formal, and irritation swirled. But did I really want the easygoing, warm version when desire raged so badly inside me? *Yes*, that insane part of me whispered. *Most definitely*. I ignored it and said, "It would certainly explain why no one can find Nadler."

"If he is being so cautious with who sees him, it is also probable that he is not only keeping an eye on his lawyer's movements, but he would have ensured that the lawyer could not actually describe him."

I stopped and looked at him. "Mind tampering?"

He nodded. "It's possible."

"But that implies our fake Nadler is more powerful than we'd thought." And probably more dangerous, although his actions with the soul stealer gave more than enough warning about the lengths to which he was willing to go.

"Exactly," Azriel said. "I do not think it wise for Jak to accompany you to this ball."

"There's no way in hell he's going to remain behind. He wants this story, Azriel."

"Maybe so, but that is neither here nor there. Do you agree that it would be better for him not to appear?"

I frowned. "Yes, but if we stop him, he'll be furious." And knowing Jak as well as I did, I had no doubt he'd pursue the story without us, and that, ultimately, could be even more dangerous. At least this way we had some control over his actions.

"He can be stopped and yet still think he was there," Azriel commented.

My gaze searched his for a moment—although why, I have no idea, given that he was still in retreat mode. "So you'll keep him at home somehow, but feed him false memories afterward?"

"Yes."

"Won't work. He's a reporter, and reporters talk. He'll discover soon enough that no one can remember seeing him there and he'll suspect I've done something."

Azriel raised his eyebrows. "But what if—as far as everyone was concerned—he did appear?"

Meaning *he'd* become Jak? "How is that going to keep him safe? I mean, for all intents and purposes, everyone will think he was there."

"True. But remember, Ilianna warned you that more trouble could be headed your way tomorrow night, and the timing coincides with this gala. It's possible the face-shifter we know as Nadler is ready to react at the slightest hint of a problem."

A taxi pulled into the rank up ahead, and I started walking again. "I'm not sure you could pull something like that off convincingly."

He fell in step beside me again, his hands clasped

lightly behind his back and the warmth of his presence doing more damage to my breathing than Jak's excitement had. "Why not?"

"Because—" *Because he's warm and real, and you're not.* Not in a flesh-and-blood sense, anyway—even if he felt altogether *too* real right now. "You can't inhabit the personality of a person you hardly know."

"I am as real as you, Risa," he said softly. "And you'd be surprised at just what I can do."

No doubt. I took a deep breath and blew it out slowly. "If you think you can be convincing, then it's worth the chance. As much as I hate what Jak did to me and my mom, I don't want to see him hurt."

"This will at least keep him safe from whatever trouble Ilianna has seen coming tomorrow night." He hesitated, then added, "But it has a second benefit."

I glanced at him. "That being?"

"He doesn't get to dance with you." And with that he winked out of existence again.

Goddamn you, Azriel. You can't keep running like that.

Why not? his thought came back. *You do.*

Which was not something I could argue with. I grabbed the cab, gave the cabbie the hotel's address, then dragged out my phone again and called Hunter.

"This is not what I would term a timely phone call," she commented, and though her voice was mild, I was suddenly glad the vid-screen was broken. "Yeah, sorry, but I had an accident and fell off my bike."

"I am aware of that fact," she said crisply. "Just as I am aware that you're planning to be at the FMFFC ball tomorrow night. I do hope you were intending to include that in your report."

I closed my eyes and swore internally. I'd forgotten all about our damn watcher. "If I'd gotten the chance to make a report, I would have."

"And I, of course, believe that implicitly." Her voice was dry. "I have the information you requested, but with the privacy requirements of this investigation, I will not be sending it to you, electronically or otherwise."

Meaning I'd have to meet the bitch. Great. I rubbed my aching head wearily. "Where and when?"

"Dark Earth. Half an hour."

She hung up before I could answer. I swore again, this time out loud, then leaned forward and gave the driver the new address.

Unfortunately, it didn't take long to get there. Azriel appeared the minute the cab stopped, catching my hand and holding me steady as I climbed out, then just as quickly releasing me. Even so, the memory of his fingers against my skin seemed to linger, teasing imagination and desire.

Damn it, this avoidance—on *both* our parts—just couldn't go on. I might not want to confront whatever it was that was actually happening between us, but it was getting clearer and clearer that I would *have* to. For the sake of my sanity, if nothing else.

But not yet, that voice inside whispered. *Not yet.*

It seemed my inner voice was very much a coward.

Barkley Street was a hive of activity. Half of Brunswick had apparently decided to shop here tonight, which surely meant that getting into the club via its secret entrance without anyone seeing us would be that much harder. I couldn't wrap the shadows around me like a vampire, after all, and I sure as hell wasn't going to take Aedh form. Not when the Raziq were actively hunting me.

But as we neared the nook, the buzz of magic began to crawl across my skin and the shadows within seemed dense and forbidding. It was a place that repelled inspection rather than inviting it. I couldn't even see the door, although it was little more than an arm's length away.

Hunter suddenly appeared out the darkness. She looked me up and down, then said, "Nice to see you're prompt about some things."

Her voice gave as little away as her expression, but that still didn't stop the tremor that ran down my spine. I was entering a club that catered to vampires with a blood whore addiction, and I was doing so with one of the most powerful vampires in Australia. I was insane.

Thank god I wasn't alone.

Her gaze went to Azriel. "You're allowing me to see your true form. Why?"

"Those I hunt always see my true form," he replied evenly.

A comment that briefly made me wonder if he was, in some way, hunting me, despite his assurances to the contrary. It would certainly explain why I saw his real form when generally I only saw whatever form the reapers took on.

Hunter raised dark eyebrows, amusement glowing in her green eyes but not actually altering her otherwise remote expression. "Are you suggesting my mortal soul is in danger?"

"What you do not possess cannot be in danger."

She laughed. It was a rich, warm sound that nevertheless sent another round of chills down my spine. "I like you, reaper. Very much."

With that, she turned and walked back into the nook, becoming one with the shadows. I hesitated, glancing up and down the street to see if anyone was paying any attention. No one was—unfortunately. As Azriel's fingers touched my spine and urged me forward, I took a deep breath and followed the bitch inside.

The dual fire of the swords peeled back the darkness and provided glimpses of Hunter ahead. Amaya was hissing again, the sound a constant static in the background of my mind. She didn't like this place any more than I did.

The heavy door at the end of the corridor swung open as we approached—Hunter and Azriel silently, me with more of a clatter—and Brett Marshall himself appeared to greet us. Or rather, to greet Hunter.

"Mistress," he said softly, kneeling before her, head bowed. "All is ready."

I blinked. Mistress? Was Marshall one of Hunter's fledglings? It would certainly explain their similar mannerisms. And why he'd been trusted to run an establishment like this.

Then the rest of his words registered. *All is ready?* What the hell did that mean?

I didn't know, and I suddenly had a bad feeling that I *didn't* want to find out.

Hunter touched Marshall's head lightly as she swept past him, and he shuddered in what almost looked like orgasmic pleasure. Then he was up and following her, not even bothering to look at us. In the scheme of things, I guess we were not that important.

The woman at the desk looked almost identical to the woman who'd been there earlier. Only her shoes were different—red instead of black. I wondered if they were twins, or whether Marshall simply preferred a certain look.

The next set of doors opened and the stink of vampire, booze, and lust hit like a hammer, snatching my breath and sending me stumbling. Azriel caught me again, his grip gentle yet strong, filled with a heat that leapt from his skin to mine. It chased away the fear, chased away the aches, and this time I didn't immediately pull away from the sensation. I very much suspected I'd need that inflow of strength if I was going to make it through the hours ahead.

We moved deeper into the club, heading not toward Marshall's office but rather toward the elevators. The blue and purple fire of the swords pierced the shadows, briefly illuminating the gaunt faces and haunted, glowing eyes of the vampires closest to us. Hunger was rife in the room, so thick I could have carved it with a knife. I edged a little closer to Azriel and wondered why Hunter had chosen this place, of all damn places, to meet. She was the one who'd warned it would be dangerous for me to be here at night, and yet here she was, risking the life of someone she supposedly valued.

It is merely another form of warning, Azriel said.

I glanced at him. *Of what? Behave, or you'll be vampire meat?*

Yes. His gaze met mine. *She does not like your offhand manner in dealing with her.*

I snorted softly. *She can read my thoughts—she has to know I'm scared shitless by her, and that my manner is nothing more than false bravado.*

She can read some thoughts, but not all. He half shrugged. *She has been alive a very long time. It becomes very easy for the old ones not only to lose humanity, but to expect certain levels of deference.*

Subservience, you mean.

If she expected subservience, you would be dead.

I half smiled—an expression that quickly died as I followed Hunter and Marshall into the elevator. Being stuck in a small metal box with those two and going down into the bowels of what had become little more than an abattoir was not my idea of a good time. But if I edged any closer to Azriel, I'd be crawling into his pockets. *What did you mean, some thoughts, not all?*

Just that.

So the nano cells are working? I knew they were, but I still needed reassurance—at least when it came to Hunter.

Yes. She is only picking up minor bits and pieces.

My gaze searched his for a moment. *How the hell do you know this? I mean, Hunter's no slouch when it comes to telepathy, and I can't imagine you'd have easy access into her mind.*

I'm a reaper. The human—and non-human—mind is open to us in all its chaotic glory.

So what can you tell me about Marshall's comment?

We go to meet others.

The elevator doors opened, revealing the basic metal corridor of the feeding rooms. *Others?* I asked silently, then glanced at Hunter. "Why the hell are we here?"

"I wish to see this room of ghosts," she said, as she stepped out of the elevator. "And it is as good a place as any to discuss what you need to know."

The others wait in that room. There are three—all vampires.

I hardly expected them to be anything else, given the place we were in, but the point was, why the hell were they there?

They are there to see you. To talk to you.

Oh god, I thought with sudden clarity. *It's the council. Or part of the council.*

Was it a trap? It couldn't be. Hunter wanted to use me; she didn't want me dead.

But Hunter wasn't the council. She didn't control it. Not yet.

I licked my lips and reluctantly trailed after her.

"Going to that room isn't a good idea." In more ways than one. And yet I couldn't retreat, couldn't run. Hunter might be striding purposefully toward the feeding room, but there was a coiled readiness in every moment. She would react—fast and brutally—if I ran. "The fact that they're ghosts doesn't mean they're incapable of understanding everything that goes on in that room. If we discuss anything there, they might just pass the information on to whatever is causing this."

She glanced over her shoulder at me. "I know."

I blinked. That wasn't exactly the answer I'd been expecting. "Maybe I'm a little slow, but wouldn't the ghosts passing on the information mean the killer may run?"

"If it is a Rakshasa, as your reaper suspects, then I

doubt it. They are creatures drawn to the dark energies of death, despair, and revenge, and there are few places in Melbourne that hold those in great abundance. It will continue to be drawn here while it is in its feeding stage, regardless of the threat we pose."

I studied her curiously as we stopped near the doors to the bigger feeding room and the three people who waited inside. "You've come across them before?"

She looked down her nose at me—no mean feat when she was actually shorter than me. "I have lived a very long time, and I've hunted far greater nightmares than a Rakshasa."

And she'd *be right at the top of any sane person's nightmare list,* I thought grimly, and saw her green eyes flash dangerously. With the way my luck had been running of late, it was no surprise she caught *that* particular thought.

Marshall opened the door for us. The room was the same sterile, ghost-filled place it had been before, only this time the smell of antiseptic wasn't as strong. Marshall *had* stopped the use of this room.

But this time the ghosts were not the only beings in the room.

All three were long, thin strips of humanity. There were two men and one woman, different in looks and nationalities, but all sharing two common traits—a fierce, cold-blooded glow in their eyes and a cruel twist to their mouths.

I'd thought Hunter was the most dangerous person on earth. Seemed I was wrong.

"Marshall, close the door, please," Hunter commanded. As he obeyed, she joined the three in the center of the room, then swung around to face me. If she sensed the ghosts, she had no reaction to them.

"I have the list of those who have died in this room," she said without preamble. "But the Cazadors will chase that avenue. What else do you want to know?"

She made no effort to introduce her companions, and they remained silent, studying me with cold intent. Chills raced up and down my spine, and Amaya hissed in useless fury. I flexed my fingers, and tried to concentrate on the business at hand. I had a bad feeling that I would find out what was going on soon enough.

"In other words, you have no intention of telling me how many died in this room." I took one step closer to her and the ghosts, then stopped. The bitter, bloody anger that surged around me struck as sharply as any whip. My flesh shuddered under the impact of it, and I half wondered if my already battered body would gain yet another rainbow of bruises to add to its collection.

"That is not something you need to know."

My gaze flicked to the vampires on either side of her. The energy that poured off them felt dark and coiled. I licked my lips and said, "What about the autopsy reports? Can I see them?"

"There is nothing in those reports that disagrees with what you already know. All five victims were torn apart and half consumed, and the poison used could not be identified."

Frustration and fear swirled through me. "I wanted to see the reports so I can read them myself. If I'd simply needed questions answered, I would have asked them."

Step warily, Risa, Azriel warned. *I do not think it wise to be too antagonistic toward Hunter in front of her peers.*

Once again my gaze flicked across the three, and I had the sudden sensation of snakes about to strike. I shivered.

"There are no files, Risa. Every report comes to me verbally. As I've said, I will not risk this investigation—or these clubs—becoming a matter of public knowledge."

I crossed my arms, but resisted the urge to rub the chill from them. "Okay, did all five victims come from a similar social and economic background?"

"No."

I waited, but she wasn't forthcoming with any further information. Which was damn annoying given that they supposedly wanted this case solved, and wanted my help to do it.

A slight smile teased her lips. The bitch might not be reading my mind, but she was certainly reading my reactions to this whole situation *and* enjoying them. And while she wanted my help to find the keys and—to a lesser extent, it seemed—to hunt down this killer, she was also very much a cat toying with a mouse it might yet decide to eat.

If the three council members didn't devour me first.

"The first two victims had high-profile jobs in the advertising industry," she drawled eventually. "The third was little more than a pen pusher in the local government's vampire affairs department. The last two were living off charity."

"If the first two victims were high profile, why did

they come to a place like this? You've inferred this is not one of your more up-market blood whore clubs."

"It isn't," Marshall said. "But there are some who do not wish their addiction to be known in the wider vampire community, and so they attend clubs that they would otherwise consider beneath them."

Vamps like the first two victims might not want their addiction known, but in coming to *this* particular club, they'd served that information up to Hunter on a silver platter. And I had no doubt that she would use it to her own advantage. "How long has each of the victims been addicted?"

"All five were long-term addictives."

"Define 'long-term.'"

"Centuries rather than years."

That raised my eyebrows. For some reason I'd been thinking blood whores were a modern phenomenon, but I guess it made sense that they'd been around almost as long as vampires. After all, addictions had been alive as long as humanity—it was just the substances that had changed over time.

"Meaning the Rakshasa could be specifically targeting those who have caused the most suffering."

"It is a possibility." Her tone suggested it was one they'd already thought of.

"So maybe all you have to do is tell longtime addictives to avoid the club until this thing is either caught or goes away."

"That," she said heavily, "is extremely naive thinking."

"Yeah, well, that's what you get when you expect a restaurateur to become a hunter."

Her green eyes flashed again, and Amaya's hissing suddenly sharpened—one bitch wanting to taste another's blood.

I shivered again, suddenly realizing I was beginning to understand the static language of my demon sword. *That* was almost as scary as the four people who stood so elegantly in front of me.

"You are far more than just a restaurateur, Risa, and we both know it. Although your current level of questioning is more than a little disappointing."

I wasn't so worried about disappointing *her* right now—which was probably proof of my insanity—but rather the three silent council members. The tightly coiled energy radiating off them seemed to be getting stronger—even the ghosts were reacting to it. The moaning and wailing had sharpened to a continuous shriek that vibrated through every part of my being. Between it and Amaya, I felt like I was being torn apart by sound.

I took a deep breath and tried to ignore the assault on my senses, tried to think more like Aunt Riley. There *had* to be some similarities in all five murders besides this room and the manner of their deaths. If there was one thing I'd gleaned over the years from hanging around two guardians, it was the fact that most killings had a particular pattern, even if it wasn't immediately evident.

"Okay, then, what about the times of their deaths?"

Hunter paused. "All between the hours of two and three. An exact time of death could not be determined due to the extensive damage done to the bodies."

I frowned. "Does that mean you also have no idea

when the inhibitor was introduced via the scratches? Or where it was applied?"

Marshall said, "I checked the security footage. All the victims bore scratches when they left this club, but this is not entirely unusual."

They had good cameras installed if they could pick up minor scratches. "No, but in this situation, it's definitely another link. What time did they all leave the club?"

"All five left at different times."

I frowned. "So had they been here feeding beforehand for very long?"

"Yes," Marshall said. "As has been noted, they were long-term addictives. Unfortunately, the longer the term, the greater the need."

That wasn't unusual when it came to any sort of addiction, but we weren't talking about an inanimate substance here; we were talking about human life. I couldn't help asking, "But surely there comes a time when such an addiction becomes too dangerous for both the abuser and the vampire population in general?"

"It does," Hunter said, her expression impassive yet cold. "And when that happens, it is dealt with appropriately."

Meaning good-bye addictive. I rubbed my arms. "So what time did they all stop using these rooms?"

"All four were stopped from using the facilities just after one a.m."

And the hour between midnight and one was witching hour—the hour when all things dark and dangerous came out to play.

"That," Azriel said softly, "is a possible link."

Hunter's eyebrows rose delicately. "Why?"

He regarded her steadily, and I suddenly wished I could read his thoughts. I had the distinct impression they'd be very interesting right now.

He ignored her question and asked instead, "Were blood whores killed in this room the nights the addicted vampires were murdered?"

Marshall glanced at Hunter and, at her nod, said, "Yes. In each case there were fatalities."

So much for the whores being well looked after, I thought, as anger surged. My gaze flicked to the silent three, and I felt an answering rise of emotion in them—anger or hunger, I wasn't entirely sure which. But in this situation, one was as deadly as the other. I returned my attention to Hunter and fought for calm.

Azriel stepped closer, his shoulder pressing against mine. I didn't know if it was for my benefit or theirs, and I didn't really care.

"Then that is the link," he said. "The hour between midnight and one is a very powerful time. When bloodshed is combined with anger and the desperation for revenge, it becomes a call few dark ones could resist. I'm surprised only the Rakshasa has answered."

I looked at him. "So if the bloodshed stopped, the Rakshasa would be less likely to appear?"

"That," Hunter said immediately, "is never going to happen."

"Not even to save lives?"

"The object here is not to save the lives of people I care less than zero about, but to find this thing and stop it. As your reaper will no doubt confirm, the Rakshasa will just move on to less tasty hunting fields if we are not successful here. Such is the nature of a killer."

And the five of them would know all about *that*. "So what do you expect me to do?"

She smiled, and it was the smile of a predator whose prey had just stepped neatly into a trap.

But she didn't answer. The tallest of the three councillors, a thin man with dark auburn hair and muddy, empty eyes, stepped forward.

"What we expect"—his voice was like silk, smooth and sensuous—"is for you to be here every night from midnight to dawn to wait for this thing to appear."

Horror spread through me. Spend half the night here? Every night? With a room filled with blood-addicted vampires above me and a bloodbath around me?

"Are you insane?" The words were out before I'd really thought about them, and that coiled sense of darkness sharpened abruptly. For several seconds I couldn't even breathe.

"The sanity of the council may be a debatable point, but it is not the question we seek to answer here," he said softly. "You and your pet reaper *will* wait here for this thing, and then you will stop it by whatever means necessary."

I felt Azriel's move before he even made it, and pressed a hand against the flat of his stomach, stopping him. But his anger surged past me, churning the ghosts into a frenzied dance of horror.

The councillors seemed unmoved.

"Why?" I asked bluntly. "I thought the keys were the priority, not this thing. If I die here, those keys will remain out of your reach forever."

"And if you do not stop this thing within the next seventy-two hours, the end result will be the same."

I frowned, confused. "What result?"

"The keys. If you do not find this killer, then the keys will slip away from our grasp regardless."

Fear slithered through the confusion. "And, why, exactly, would you think that?"

He smiled, but there was nothing pleasant about it. "Because the council recently took a vote on your situation. The decision was deadlocked, three for killing, three against, three undecided."

My gaze swept them. These three. I swallowed heavily.

"And?"

"And," he said flatly, "you have precisely seventy-two hours to prove your worth as a hunter to us, or an execution order will be issued."

Chapter 7

"Touch her, and you die," Azriel said, his voice as flat as the councillor's, but somehow far more deadly.

The councillor merely smiled. "I know enough about reapers to understand that would not be a wise choice on your part."

"*I* am not strictly a reaper, and I am not bound by all their rules."

The councillor raised an eyebrow and looked somewhat disbelieving, but Hunter touched his hand, then said, "Killing Odale will only sway opinion further against you. After all, you are apparently the one person who can find these keys—and there is some belief among the council that it would be better to leave the keys lost than to have anyone else gain them."

An opinion I actually agreed with, except for the fact that in *their* version, it meant me dying. That bit I wasn't so keen on.

"I thought you were on my side."

"Oh, I am." She shrugged lightly. "I believe it would be to our benefit to keep you alive *and* find those keys, but votes ebb and flow, as does power. Right now—thanks to the fear and uncertainty these keys have raised—the tide of opinion has swung many against my belief of your usefulness. You need to prove otherwise."

Or die. Fantastic options, I had to say. "Three days is hardly long enough. I mean, what if this thing doesn't front?"

"It will. It may have taken five victims within a week, but its hunger will still be great. Track it to its lair, Risa, and kill it. Prove to these three—and to the council at large—that I'm right. Prove that you can be the asset I have said you will be."

Great. Now she was using me to cement *her* power. I thrust a hand through my hair. "I can't stay in this room. Not while vamps are feeding."

"You won't. Marshall?"

He turned and moved to the far side of the room. A keypad sat there, looking oddly out of place in the sterile whiteness of the room. He pressed in a code, and beside him a door slid open. Beyond it was a small boxshaped room.

"It is fully shielded," Marshall said. "No vampire will sense your presence in there, no matter how strong their telepathic skills might be."

Meaning I was safe from Hunter's intrusions? Somehow I doubted that. "And why would you have a room like that installed in a place like this?"

She smiled. It wasn't pleasant. "Because there are some who like to watch."

Horror crawled through me. *She* liked to watch. God. I licked my lips and tried to ignore the thickening sensation of fear. "How do I get out of this place once dawn rises?"

"There is a door-release button within. Use that if the Rakshasa appears. Otherwise, Marshall will retrieve you." She took a step forward, the movement fluid and elegant. "Watch carefully, dear Risa, and pass the tests. I really *would* prefer for you to remain alive for a while yet."

Her warning suggested there would be more than just one test. I glanced at the man she'd identified as Odale, and saw the anticipation flicker through the dead space of his eyes. Whatever else they had in mind, it would be bloody. I swallowed heavily, shoved intuition back into its box, and said, "Yeah, so would I."

She nodded, and swept rather regally from the room, the three councillors following silently in her wake. The dark energy of their presence seemed to linger long after they'd gone.

"Risa," Marshall said, the sudden sound of his voice making me jump. "You need to step inside. Our first customer will arrive in a few minutes."

Oh *god*. I closed my eyes for a moment, then, with Amaya spitting fire all over the place, I forced my feet forward and entered the box-room. It was even smaller than it looked, barely big enough to hold two chairs. Interestingly, there was a camera discreetly placed in one corner, and the back wall was not only padded, but had hand grips. I didn't want to know why. I really didn't—but that didn't stop my imagination throwing up all sorts of sick possibilities.

The door whooshed shut and the darkness closed in. As did fear.

"Are you all right?" Azriel asked.

"No, I'm fucking *not*," I snapped. Amaya's hissing

increased, buzzing through my brain like a saw, sharp and hungry. Her fire spilled across the darkness, giving it a creepy glow. I took a deep breath and exhaled it slowly. It didn't do a whole lot to ease either her noise or the tension and dread roiling around inside me. "Sorry. This isn't your fault."

"No," he agreed. "But that does not mean I cannot help you."

I eyed him for a minute, then said, "How?"

"You do not need to be here to watch. I can do that."

"Nice thought, but there's one problem." I pointed at the camera. "We're not the only ones watching. And we have no idea whether it's Marshall, Hunter, or those fucking councillors behind that camera." Hell, for all I knew, they could be recording everything we said, as well.

"I could find out."

"And what good would knowing do? It doesn't alter the fact that I have to stay here for the entire evening."

He fell silent, but the room beyond suddenly wasn't. The ghosts began to moan, the sound one of agitation and horror. It crawled across my skin like a rash, making me itch. Making me shiver.

Then came the sound of footsteps. Two pairs entering, one leaving. A blood whore being delivered. My stomach began to churn. I couldn't listen to this. I really couldn't.

"Then don't," Azriel said, and touched two fingers to my forehead lightly. "Sleep, Risa. I will guard this night."

"I can't—" But the protest died on my lips. Sleep closed in and I knew no more.

I woke hours later, feeling stiff and less than refreshed. The scent of blood was heavy in the air, mingling with the stench of antiseptic. In the other room, someone whistled tunelessly, the sound grating across waking nerves.

I stretched, trying to work the kinks out of my body, and realized I was lying across the two chairs, my back against the padded wall and my coat under my head. I opened my eyes. Azriel leaned against the far wall, underneath the camera. His arms were crossed and his eyes were hooded. But a strange red-purple fire flickered along Valdis's sharp sides.

"I should be angry at you for knocking me out like that," I said. "But all I want to know is, can you force me to do things other than making me sleep?"

His gaze met mine briefly, then pulled away. "If I could, you can be assured that I would have by now."

I could hear no lie in his words, and relief slithered through me. I pushed rather stiffly upright and said, "I'm gathering nothing happened?"

"Plenty happened," he said, his voice harsh. "But it wasn't the sort of action we seek."

I glanced at him sharply. "You're angry."

"Obviously."

"Why?"

He flicked a hand toward the other room. "What happens in that room is beyond an abomination. Yet there is nothing I can do about it."

"Reaper rules?"

"Reaper rules," he agreed grimly. "Sometimes, I wish—" He stopped, then shrugged. "But I cannot. This perversity is one of human nature, and therefore it is something I am not able to stop."

I swung my feet off the other chair, wincing a little as stiff muscles protested the movement. "Why the anger now? Why not before, when we first discovered the truth about this room?"

"Before there were merely words and ghosts. Tonight, there was death, and a soul being set free by the brutal death of her body. Blood whores may be well aware of the risks involved in their addiction, but those who work here are not. It goes against every instinct to simply stand here and listen to that happen, Risa."

I studied him for a moment, wishing I could comfort him but not exactly sure he would welcome it. "I'm sorry—"

"Don't be," he interrupted. "This atrocity was not of your doing."

No, but I was the reason he was here to witness it. I sighed. "I'm gathering the Rakshasa didn't appear?"

"No. But Hunter is right—it is still in its feeding stage. It will appear sooner or later."

Great, except I didn't have much of a later, thanks to the council threatening to kill me if I didn't catch this thing within the next seventy-two hours. And six of those hours had already slipped by. "What will we do if it doesn't appear tomorrow night?"

"I don't know." He hesitated. "But the council will not kill you. I will ensure that."

I smiled. "Because you need me alive to find the keys, right?"

I said it teasingly, but his only response was a flash of annoyance. He pushed away from the wall and said sharply, "Marshall comes."

"Azriel—"

The door opened before I was entirely sure what I'd been about to say. Marshall appeared, smelling and looking a whole lot fresher than I did. "I take it our Rakshasa did not make an appearance?"

He said it testily, as if it were our fault. "If it had," I retorted, standing up, "we wouldn't still be fucking here."

His eyebrows rose at my tone. "My, my, a little irritable this morning, aren't we?"

"I'm stiff, sore, and tired, and I just want to get out of this house of horrors before I'm tempted to violence."

Amusement touched his thin lips. "That would not be wise in this place. Not if you wish to leave it alive."

"Marshall, you have no idea just what I'm capable of. Now, can we cut this dance and just get out of here?"

His gaze skimmed me before it slipped to Azriel. He might not be worried about me, but the same could not be said when it came to my reaper. He shrugged and said, "This way."

The smell of antiseptic was stronger out in the main room, but it wasn't fully cleaned. I tried to ignore the broken bits of humanity that still lay scattered about the floor, but I could hardly ignore the stench of blood and the horrified moaning of the ghosts. Not when I was forced to walk through them. It was a wall of misery and fierce anger, and it cloaked me like a shroud, suffocating me.

Somehow, I controlled the urge to run. Somehow, I got out of that hellhole without giving in to the desire to draw Amaya and shed some blood and body parts myself.

I glanced at my watch when we got to the street above. It was barely six, far too early to go get those tickets from Mike.

"I think I'll go back to the hotel and grab a shower, and then I'll need to shop for tonight." I glanced at Azriel. "Do you need to visit Jak to assume his identity?"

"Yes." His expression was back to giving little away. "But I can do that later, once you are safely back at the hotel."

I nodded and dragged out my phone to call a cab. Amazingly, it arrived within a couple of minutes and in no time at all I was back at the hotel and washing the stink of death from my body.

The rest of the day went by quickly. I shopped for clothes and shoes, purchasing not only items for the gala, but enough to see me through several more days. Then I bought a new cell phone and headed to Mike's to grab the tickets. He wasn't in, so the stay wasn't long. I rang Jak on the way back to the hotel.

"Okay, I have the tickets in hand," I said.

"Good." He hesitated. "I did a little more research on Mr. Elusive. It appears the real Nadler was married fifteen years ago. It only lasted a couple of months, but she might be the one person who can give us some decent information."

"Meaning she's still alive?"

"Surprisingly, yes. Obviously, if we are dealing with a face-shifter, then he either didn't know about her or didn't think she was enough of a threat to his takeover of Nadler's life."

"So she may not be able to tell us much."

He snorted softly. "Are you kidding me? You're a

prime example of just how well you women can hold a grudge against a lover who has spurned you in some way."

"If I was holding a grudge, I wouldn't have come to you in the first place."

"Lie," he said equably. "You came to me because you needed me, and no grudge, no matter how well cherished, was going to get in your way. Simple as that."

I couldn't exactly deny that statement when it was the complete truth. So I simply said, "Have you managed to track down the wife's current location?"

"Certainly have," he said cheerfully. "Want to meet me there?"

"Maybe. If you'll share where 'there' is."

"Oh. Yeah." He paused, and in the background, paper rustled, meaning he was flipping through his notebook. He'd never really taken to the electronic kind—he'd always said they were too easy to steal. Although if his rat-gang story *had* been stolen, then his scribbling barely legible notes in a book wasn't exactly foolproof, either. "Okay, she's a waitress at Dino-Bar over on Swan Street. She works the morning shift and takes a break about one, so our timing should be perfect if we both head there now."

"The divorce obviously didn't go well if she's forced to waitress for a living."

"Yeah, it was nasty, from all the reports. He got the better lawyers, and they really did a number on her."

And a bitter woman was more likely to tell tales. "I'll see you in about twenty, then."

"Righto."

He hung up. I told the taxi to wait as we drew up

beside the hotel, then dashed inside to dump my purchases. Within minutes I was on my way again, heading to Swan Street.

Jak was waiting for me outside the Dino-Bar. Which was, I noted with some annoyance, a male strip club. Just what I needed when my hormones were so primed for action. Obviously, my annoyance showed in my expression, because he held up his hands. "It's not a deliberate choice on my part. I had no idea it was a male strip club until I got here."

"This is a general pissed-off look, not one specifically aimed at you." I studied the plain, yet oddly gaudy facade. The Dino-Bar was obviously not one of your more up-market strip clubs. "Are you going to have a problem getting inside?"

"No—all sexual orientations are welcome, from what I've briefly seen."

"Then let's get inside."

He touched my back, guiding me. Heat crawled from the epicenter of that light touch, spreading through me in wicked waves.

I swallowed heavily and did my best to ignore the sensation. The interior was dark, and smelled of humanity, booze, and arousal. The building was wider than it was long, the bar along the left wall and a high stage dominating the back. Two men in cages were gyrating to a slow, heavy beat, their movements mechanical and about as far from sexy as you could get—at least to *this* half werewolf's eyes. But apparently I was the only one who thought that, because the crowd gathered beneath them was whistling and catcalling.

Jak guided me to the bar, ordered two beers, then

put down some extra cash. "We need to speak to Jacinta Nadler."

The barman studied him for several moments, then nodded and swept up the notes. "She's on a break. I'll call her out for you."

"We'll be at that table over there," Jak said, pointing with his chin toward the far corner.

The barman nodded and ambled over to the phone. We picked up our drinks and took them to our table. He studied me for several seconds over the rim of his glass, then said, "Why is a wolf as hot as you so damn frustrated?"

"That," I said heavily, "is none of your damn business."

He grinned. "I'm a reporter. Puzzles are my business."

"Not this one. Not any longer."

I glanced up as a woman approached our table. She was small and shapely, with ample breasts and thick blond hair. She was also almost naked—paisley flowers covered her nipples, and the only other thing she wore was a glittery G-string. As Jak had said earlier, the club seemed to cater to all sexual orientations. Both sexes worked the floor, and the scantily clad females got as much attention as the males.

"You wanted to see me?" she said, her voice raspy and her brown gaze jumping warily between the two of us.

"Yes." Jak drew out his wallet and showed her his press pass.

She grimaced. "Fucking press. Man, I've done enough talking to you lot."

She turned to go, but I reached out and stopped her. "We're doing a story on your ex. We want to out him for the bastard he is."

She sneered, obviously unimpressed by this bit of news. "He'll wipe the floor with you. And then he'll get his press buddies to complete the hatchet job." She eyed Jak. "You, my friend, won't even be able to get a job at McDonald's afterwards."

"Oh, I doubt that'll happen," Jak said calmly. "I've got more than a few friends of my own."

She studied him for several more seconds, then drew up a chair and sat down. "I haven't talked to you. Understand?"

We both nodded, and she relaxed slightly. "What do you want to know?"

"Everything you can tell us about your brief time with him. Who he associated with, what companies he had at the time, who his friends were, and what he really did to you and your family."

Her smile was bitter. "That could take more time than I get for a break. *And* I know squat about his businesses."

"Just tell us what you can." I hesitated. "I'll make it worth your while."

She eyed me, distrust obvious, then shrugged and began talking. Her story proved to be more than a little harrowing—she'd barely been eighteen when she'd met Nadler, and had been attracted to both his power and his money—the same power and money that had all but destroyed her. Even Jak looked a little sickened by the end of it all.

"If you hated him so much, why not change your

name?" I asked curiously. It'd be one of the first things I would have done had I been in her position.

Of course, if I'd been in her position, I probably would have shoved a hand into his chest and ripped his black heart out.

Jacinta grimaced. "Because 'Nadler' is easier to say than my maiden name—Gutierrez."

"We're talking about a man who did everything he could to ruin your life. Even if you hated your maiden name, you could have changed it to something else. Why keep his?"

Something flickered in her eyes. Shame, perhaps. "I kept it because it annoyed him."

There was more to it than that, I thought, studying her. "Money."

She glanced at me sharply. Jacinta Nadler, I suspected, had *never* been the innocent she portrayed herself to be.

"He paid you to keep it, didn't he?" It was a guess, but I knew it was right.

She looked away. "I deserved it after what he put me through. And if keeping his name meant I got it, what harm is there?"

"But why would *he* want you to keep it?"

She snorted. "Why do you think? Men like that never like losing their possessions. At least this way, he retained the illusion of ownership."

I wondered what other terms she'd agreed to. Wondered what had happened to the money. Surely she wouldn't be working in a place like this if she still possessed it.

Jak said, "What about Nadler personally?"

She frowned. "What do you mean?"

"Well, did he have any particular habits—"

She snorted. "Aside from smacking the shit out of me, you mean?"

He grimaced. "Yes."

She frowned. "Not really. Although he did love polo. Used to play it every week."

"Used to?"

"Yeah. He stopped after the accident. His horse slipped in the mud and came down on top of him. Broke his arm and gashed his ankle pretty bad. He was lucky, though—the only scar he got out of it was from the ankle wound. It would probably be barely noticeable by now."

Jak smiled at me. If it was barely noticeable, our face-shifter might not have bothered with it. We finally had an identifying mark.

Now all we had to do was actually find him.

I said, "Have you got any photos of him that we could borrow?"

She snorted softly. "I burned every single one of them. Wouldn't you?"

"Hell, yes."

She eyed me for a moment, then added, "He's become something of a recluse of late, but if you want photos you should track down James Blake. He took the wedding photos—you never know, he might have kept them."

I glanced at Jak. He was already writing the name in his notebook.

"Thanks for your help, Jacinta. We do appreciate it." I slipped her some cash, and she palmed it with practiced ease.

"Just make sure you burn the bastard good and proper."

With that, she got up and left. I finished the last of my beer, then handed Jak one of the tickets for the ball. Azriel might be intending to take his place, but I needed to keep up the pretense and not make him suspicious. "We're at the same table, so I'll meet you inside around eight."

He nodded. "Until then, I'll run a search on the names Jacinta mentioned, and try to uncover some photos of the polo accident."

"Have fun," I said dryly as I rose.

He gave me a smile that just about blinded me. "Oh, the fun will happen tonight. I intend to dance your shoes off, my girl."

And "dancing" just happened to be a wolf euphemism for sex. I snorted softly. "You're as hopeless as ever."

"Nothing ventured, nothing gained," he said. "Don't forget to pay the bartender on the way out."

I did, then headed back to the hotel, where I promptly undressed, crawled into bed, and went to sleep.

The awareness of being watched woke me sometime later. For several minutes I didn't stir, letting my body wake and my senses capture the warmth of that sensation. It flowed through me like a river, teasingly sensuous.

But before I could fully react to it, it disappeared. Azriel knew I was awake.

Frustration swirled, deeper and stronger than before,

but again, I squashed it and simply said, "Did you catch all that info at the bar?"

"Yes."

His voice was as distant as ever. I sighed. "Thoughts?"

"The information will only prove worthwhile once we pin down the face-shifter inhabiting Nadler's life. Until then, it does not help."

"Well, no, but at least it's more than what we had."

"True."

"Have you visited Jak yet?"

"No. He is not home yet."

I twisted around to look at him. He was standing over near the window again—a favorite spot, it seemed— and despite what I'd sensed when waking, his back was to me. For once, Valdis was as quiet as her master.

"How do you know he's not home?"

"Because I checked five minutes ago."

"Oh." I studied him a few moments longer, then sighed again and climbed out of the bed. He didn't look at me, though the awareness in the air seemed to sharpen. "I guess I'd better go get ready."

He didn't answer, but there was no need to, either. By the time I'd showered, changed my hair color to auburn, and tweaked my facial features enough so that anyone who knew me wouldn't recognize me, then got dressed and done my makeup—which included body makeup to hide some of the bruises—he'd left.

I grabbed my purse and ticket and went downstairs to catch a taxi. The Central Pier function center, situated behind Etihad Stadium, was little more than a gigantic shed. A long line of taxis and limos waited in front of it, each taking its turn in dropping off passengers dressed to the nines and dripping in jewelry. A thief would have a field day, I thought, though it would be a bold thief who operated where several high-ranking members of the police force were present.

I climbed out of the taxi when it was my turn. The heated evening breeze whisked around me, playing with my dress and revealing teasing glimpses of my legs. The dress was demure by my standards—and positively nunlike compared to Aunt Riley's—but the bruises that littered my left side and back had forced more of a cover-up than normal. Not even body makeup was adequate to hide some of them. My right leg was the one place that wasn't rainbow-colored, and the long split up the side of the shimmery dark green dress made the most of that.

I made it inside without a problem and was escorted to my table. Azriel had already arrived and, for the first time, he was fully dressed. But the dark suit emphasized rather than downplayed his lean, muscular body, and he looked fantastic.

"Thank you," he said, rising as I approached the table.

Heat colored my cheeks and I had no idea why. It wasn't like he hadn't caught errant thoughts before—and generally far worse than that. "Why bother with the pretense, though?"

"Because I am actively projecting Jak's image to all in this room. Wearing his suit lessens the depth of detail I have to transmit, and makes it easier to maintain over a longer period."

He pulled out the chair for me, his fingers brushing my spine as I sat, just as Jak's would have. A tremor ran through me. This was *dangerous*. Possibly more so than if it *had* been the real Jak.

I placed my purse on the table, then picked up the water jug and poured a drink. Wine was not a good idea. I might not get drunk on the stuff, thanks to my werewolf constitution, but enough of it could certainly dull common sense, if only for the briefest time. Right now, with Azriel looking so good, I needed all the good sense I could get.

"Have you seen Frank Logan yet?" I hadn't seen our lawyer on the way in, but that didn't mean he wasn't here.

"Not as yet. But I walked around when I first arrived. He's been placed two tables across to your left, next to the man wearing the odd toupee."

I looked around and restrained a laugh. The hair-piece in question sat on the gentleman's head like a scraggly gray cat ready to pounce on the next unfortunate person to pass by.

"That cannot possibly be the height of fashion," Azriel continued blandly.

I turned back and met his gaze. Just for a moment, humor and warmth teased his lips and crinkled the corners of his mismatched blue eyes, and my breath caught somewhere in my throat.

If I got through this evening without giving in to temptation, it was going to be a goddamn miracle.

I gulped down some water, then said, "What about our Cazador watcher? Is he still around?"

Azriel's gaze flicked past me for a moment. "Yes."

I resisted the urge to look over my shoulder. "And does he follow us into the hotel room?"

"No. He generally waits in the lobby."

"Generally" meant not always. Great. Not that there was a lot I could do about it.

I drank some more water and glanced at my watch. Time seemed to be crawling by. I wasn't sure what else to say to Azriel, so I made small talk with the woman sitting on my left, and picked at the various courses as they came and went.

Frank Logan finally made an appearance just as they started the fund-raising auction. He was a big man with dark hair, a roman nose, thin lips, and a sharp chin.

I leaned closer to Azriel and said, "Can you listen to his thoughts from here?"

"Maybe." His expression was closed, giving little away. After several minutes, he said, "Someone has placed major barriers around his mind."

I frowned. "But I thought the human mind was open to you to read, and that not even vampires could block you?"

"They can't. And Logan isn't a vampire."

A point I was well aware of, so I didn't bother reacting to it. "So how come his mind is blocked? Why can't you get past it?"

"I didn't say I couldn't get past it, but the existence and strength of the barriers suggest whoever is behind them is well aware of just how a reaper operates."

I raised my eyebrows. "Are the blocks aimed at reapers specifically? Because that would mean someone is aware that we're targeting Logan."

His gaze came to mine. "Yes."

Shit. I took a deep breath, half listening to the auctioneer chattering on about the signed, framed football jumper they were auctioning. "Does that mean we've wasted our time tonight?"

"No. I can break the barrier, but not without one-on-one contact."

"Meaning we have to catch him alone?"

"Yes."

"That's going to be hard at a function like this."

He shrugged. "Not necessarily. Is it not human nature to want to visit the bathroom after a large intake of alcohol?"

I glanced across at Logan. He'd suddenly started guzzling beer like it was water. I met Azriel's gaze again. It was as impassive as ever, but deep in those blue depths, amusement lurked. "Your doing?"

"His memories may have been blocked, but his control centers have not."

I grinned. "Brilliant idea."

"I do have them occasionally."

I snorted softly. "And you're modest to boot."

"What is the truth is hardly modest."

"But it also suggests you've had more than a few bad ideas."

There was a flicker in his eyes that spoke of regret. "No Mijai is infallible. That is why we are dark angels."

I half wondered what infallibility he was talking about, because I very much suspected it *wasn't* the actions that had made him a Mijai.

The auction finished and music started up. Logan

rose and—looking decidedly unsteady on his feet—grabbed the hand of the blonde sitting next to him and dragged her toward the dance floor.

"Do you think we should keep close to him?" I asked, half fearing the answer would be no, and yet—absurdly—also fearing a yes.

He wasn't looking at me, but rather Logan. "It would be more advantageous if we were close. It will be easier to prevent others from following him into the bathroom."

Damn. I took a deep breath and slowly released it. "Can you dance?"

He glanced at me. "If dancing requires little more than shuffling your feet from one side to the other, as many on that floor are currently doing, then yes."

Relief washed over me. Shuffling from side to side was a whole lot more survivable than the close body contact I'd been half imagining.

He rose and offered me his hand. My hesitation was brief, but nevertheless there, and again that annoyance flashed in his eyes. It made me wonder what energy Valdis was emitting, but for some reason his sword wasn't visible. I wasn't even sure he was wearing it. I *was* wearing Amaya, but she was always shadow-wreathed and therefore invisible.

"I am never without Valdis," he said, one hand against my spine as he guided me toward the floor.

"Then why can't I see her?"

"She hides her form."

"*She* hides it?"

He nodded. "She does not naturally shadow, as

Amaya does, but she can hide her form when I need all of my energy."

We reached the edge of the dance floor. Logan was deep in the center of the crowd, so Azriel's hand slipped from my spine to my fingers, the movement sensual. Delight shivered through me.

As he led the way through the crush of people, the music abruptly changed from pop to a slow waltz. I eyed his broad back suspiciously. "Did you do that?"

He turned around, then pulled me closer. "*Would* I do that?"

Though his expression was still its usual bland self, there was an edge in his voice that had my pulse rate skipping. Or maybe that was simply his closeness, the way his body seemed to fit so well against mine, the play of his muscles against my skin as he moved in time to the music. The gentle caress of his fingers across my back.

He didn't speak. I *couldn't speak*. I couldn't even look at him. If I did . . .

I shivered again, feeling like I was being torn apart, my mind a tumult of conflicting emotions. Desire and fear waged a fierce war inside me and I couldn't predict which one would win. Or which one I *wanted* to win.

The waltz went on, and the dance became more sensual. I'm not entirely sure how that happened, since our actual movement and position remained unchanged. But suddenly it was as if there were no one else in the room—it was just me and him and the intimacy that was building between us.

"Risa," he said softly, "look at me."

I shook my head. My courage had come under attack from many avenues over the past few months, but I'd never expected it to fail in the face of desire. I just *couldn't* meet his gaze. I feared what I would see, what I would have to acknowledge.

What it would lead to.

"*Look* at me."

This time, the demand in his voice was undeniable, and I found my gaze rising almost against my will.

My breath caught somewhere in my throat.

Because there in the blue of his eyes was a desire so stark and raw it burned my very soul.

"You cannot deny this, Risa," he said softly. "You cannot deny *us*."

Oh god, oh god, oh god . . .

It was a litany that tumbled unchecked through my thoughts. I couldn't think any more than that, couldn't react, my brain and body held captive not just by what I saw in his eyes, but what I felt, as well.

Because what I felt was *him*. His energy, his being.

Against my skin and in my mind. He burned me, inside and out, making me tremble and ache and wish for . . . for what? Not sex, not exactly. More a completeness.

As if that made any sense.

I licked my lips and somehow managed to croak, "It could change everything between us, Azriel—and maybe not in a good way."

"That is possible—maybe even probable. But what is acknowledged might also be controlled."

It might not, too. "I think it's a very *bad* idea."

"I tend to agree."

That rawness still burned me, making me ache for something I couldn't even begin to describe. "Then why . . . ?"

"Because," he said, a harsh edge of determination in his tone. "I have no other choice."

"There are always choices," I said, quoting his own words back at him. "And wouldn't seducing me break one of those many rules Mijai have?"

He didn't immediately reply, but his hand slid sensually down my spine and came to rest on my rump. The effect was electric—a firestorm that ripped through my body, making me shudder, making me ache.

"Azriel—" I stopped, not entirely sure what I was about to say. Not sure that I *should* say anything.

"The rules are very clear," he said softly. "But sometimes the gain is worth the punishment."

And with that, his lips met mine.

It wasn't a kiss. Not exactly. It was flesh against flesh, true, but it was a whole lot more. It was energy and spirit and desire all tied up in one gentle motion, and it made me fly and, at the same time, made me weak.

"This will not end here," he said, so softly that his words were little more than a sigh across my lips. "It *cannot* end here."

I still couldn't answer. I just stared at him, seeing the determination deep in those raw depths and wondering why he'd forced the issue now and not before.

He didn't answer those thoughts, but I didn't really expect him to. Instead, he stepped back, breaking the spell of his closeness. Cool air washed between us, and a gasp of surprise escaped my lips.

"Logan moves," was all he said.

But his fingers slipped down to mine, and once again he was leading me through the crowd. I was glad of that light contact. I don't think I could have moved of my own accord.

There were several people between Logan and us in the corridor that led to the bathrooms, but all the men did an abrupt about-face and walked away. Hopefully, I thought with a smile, their bladders would hold.

Logan pushed the bathroom door open, and five seconds later we followed. Logan was in the process of getting the old boy out, and gave me an owlish look as he hastily did himself back up.

"Here now, you can't—" His words cut off and he fell silent.

Azriel glanced at me. "Lock the door."

I did so, then leaned back against it and crossed my arms. Azriel touched two fingers to Logan's forehead, and closed his eyes. For several minutes nothing happened. Then someone bashed on the door behind me, the suddenness of it making me jump.

"The bathroom is closed for cleaning," I yelled. "Give us ten minutes, or use the bathrooms on the other side of the building."

Muttered curses followed this statement, but the footsteps moved away.

Azriel stepped back from Logan, who didn't move or respond in any way. Azriel obviously still held his mind, keeping him unseeing and unhearing. "I have a description of the man Logan knows as Nadler, but I suspect it is not the right one."

I frowned. "Because we're dealing with a face-shifter?"

"No, because Logan's memory centers show signs

of recent intrusion. Whoever Nadler is, he obviously doesn't want the form Logan sees to be known."

"Suggesting he *could* be tracked through it." That is, *if* the description we pulled from Logan's memory was the right one, and not another means of subterfuge. If it wasn't, then all of this had been a waste of time.

"Not necessarily," Azriel commented.

I stared at him for a moment, wondering if he was referring to our dance or our actions with Logan. I wasn't sure I wanted an answer—especially if it referred to the former rather than the latter.

"Meaning what?"

"Well, it is obvious that the person behind the reworking of Logan's memories is extremely powerful. Whoever it is also has enough knowledge about reapers to set up reasonably strong blocks."

"And?" I asked, sensing there was such a block in place.

"It was done sometime today."

I blinked. "They definitely knew we were going after Logan."

"Yes."

He said it flatly, with no emotion in his voice or his expression, but nevertheless, my hackles rose. "If you name Lucian as a possible suspect, I'll—" What? What threat could I possibly make to someone like him?

"Whoever is behind the stealing of the key has been one step ahead of us for a while. Lucian is a suspect, whether you wish to acknowledge it or not." He held up a hand, cutting off the angry reply that was on my lips. "But there are other options. Jak knew we were going after Logan. As did your accountant."

I snorted. "It could hardly be Jak, since he knows nothing about reapers, and Mike only knew I wanted the tickets to get a reporter friend in. Neither of them is a very likely suspect."

"I agree."

Which left us with Lucian. He didn't say the words, but they hung between us all the same.

"I haven't talked to him since I ordered him out of the apartment, Azriel."

"But he *has* formed a telepathic link with you. He may never need to talk to you again."

And that, if his tone was anything to go by, would be an extremely welcome event. "Only trouble is," I retorted, "it's a link that's become somewhat faulty."

He studied me for a moment. Logan was still and silent behind him, and I briefly wondered if he would have any memory of what we were saying.

"No, he will not," Azriel said, then added, "Why is the link faulty? The connection between an Aedh and his lover usually only becomes stronger over the course of their brief time together, not weaker."

"I don't know why it's faulty," I snapped back. "But apparently he can only read me during sex. I haven't had sex with him for over twenty-four hours."

"But you want to."

"Of course I fucking want to. He's a fantastic lover."

"You should not—"

"Don't tell me what I should and shouldn't be doing when it comes to my love life, Azriel!" I exploded. "Because no matter what happens between us, we both know you'll be gone once the keys are found and this mess is all sorted out. You'll never be anything more than a blip—pleasurable or otherwise—on the radar of my life."

He didn't say anything to that. I guess there was nothing he actually *could* say. It was the truth, pure and basic.

He turned around and touched Logan's forehead. The older man blinked several times, then swung around to face me.

"—come in here," he said, his voice hinting at anger.

I blinked, then realized he was finishing the sentence he'd started when we first walked in. "Oh, sorry," I said hastily. "Wrong bathroom."

I unlocked the door and left. Azriel was two steps behind me.

"Now what?" I lightly rubbed my arms—there was a decided chill coming from his direction.

"Now we see what happens when he leaves."

I half frowned, then remembered Ilianna's warning. "Why would anyone go to the trouble of tampering with his mind if they were intending to kill him tonight?"

He shrugged. "Why would anyone fuck a man she does not entirely trust?"

For a moment, I could only stare at him. Then the anger rose, so swift and sharp I had to dig my nails into my clenched fists to resist the urge to smack him.

"Because," I all but hissed, "despite all that is sane, I find myself wanting you."

And with that, I stalked away from him. He didn't follow. He didn't need to. He was connected to my chi and he could find me whenever he wanted.

Still, I was grateful for the brief respite. Once I'd

reached my table, I grabbed the wine bottle, filled a glass, and drank it swiftly. It didn't do a whole lot for the fury boiling inside me, and I half wondered just how many bottles it would take before it did. Probably more than the bar had in stock.

After five minutes or so, Logan approached his table, looking a little green around the gills. Obviously, his enforced consumption of alcohol was not sitting well.

He picked up his jacket, said good-bye to the blonde sitting next to him, then staggered toward the exit. I picked up my purse and followed.

The air outside was cool and thick with the scent of the nearby ocean. I shivered a little as I trailed after Logan, and I wasn't completely certain whether the cause was the chill in the air or the rising tide of my trepidation. Logan was taking more steps sideways than forward, but he was still moving at a decent pace, and in no time at all he'd passed from the bright protection of the venue's entrance to the deeper street shadows.

The sense that something was about to happen grew. I scanned the streets around me, seeing nothing out of place. But in this darkness, would I?

And then it happened. A shot rang out.

Logan staggered and fell to his knees, just as a second shot sliced through the night. Something hit me from behind, and I found myself on the concrete, my heart racing and a fiercely warm body covering me.

"Azriel?"

"The second shot was aimed at us," he said. "Stay here."

His weight lifted from mine as he winked out of existence. I studied the buildings around me for a moment, then pushed to my feet. If someone was going to shoot me, then they could hit me as easily lying down as standing up.

"Mr. Logan?" I flared my nostrils, taking in the scents of the night.

Blood ran on it, thick and fresh.

He was dead. I knew he was dead, even though I couldn't see a reaper waiting to claim his soul. Still, I had to check. I approached slowly, but stopped several feet away. Logan had twisted as he'd crumpled and his dead eyes were staring at me balefully. The bullet had entered his forehead and blasted its way through his head, leaving an exit wound bigger than my fist. Blood and bone and brain matter had splattered onto all the nearby surfaces.

Someone had wanted to make very sure that even in death, Logan's mind couldn't be read—which all but confirmed that someone had been aware that we'd been intending to speak to him. But how? And who?

Frowning, knowing they were questions I wasn't likely to get answers to anytime soon, I took out my phone and rang the cops. I should have rung Uncle Rhoan, but I really wasn't up to answering the questions that would undoubtedly follow.

Azriel reappeared as I hung up, his fierce expression suggesting things had not gone well.

"You didn't find the shooter?"

"I did. He was stationed on top of the stadium roof, but by the time I got there, he'd thrown himself off it."

"He *killed* himself?"

"Yes." He glanced behind us. "People are approaching. We should leave before we are seen."

"Azriel, I'm a witness. I have to—"

"Have you forgotten the councillors' edict?"

I had. I closed my eyes, breathed deep, then glanced at my watch. It was close to twelve. *Shit*. "I need to change," I said wearily. "I'm not going to that place dressed like this."

He didn't answer, just stepped close, took me in his arms, and whisked us both out of there. But the minute we were back in the hotel room, he stepped back. It didn't stop the awareness that trembled across my skin, nor did it ease the heat of desire shimmering between us. I might be angry with him, but that didn't stop me from wanting him.

"Azriel—"

"Get changed," he said curtly. "Or we'll be late— and I suspect that would not be wise."

"There's lots of things that wouldn't be wise," I muttered as I headed for the bathroom. "But *I* suspect that's not going to stop them from happening."

"Some things are destined and can never be changed," he agreed flatly. "No matter how much we might wish otherwise."

I changed quickly into my jeans and sweater. "And here I was thinking destiny was a fluid thing."

"Destiny *is* fluid," he said. "And sometimes so is death. Logan was not destined to die this night, so his soul will roam."

"Shame you won't break *that* particular rule and talk to his soul." I glanced in the mirror, studying the not-me image. After a moment, I imagined my face with dark golden hair and a smattering of golden freckles across my nose, then reached down for the face-shifting energy and made it happen. Then I turned and walked out.

Azriel's gaze swept my face, and he nodded minutely. Meaning, I guessed, that he approved. "Why would we need to talk to his soul when we already have all the information he could give us?"

"Well, he actually didn't give us everything, since someone had tampered with his memories. But would those blocks hold after death?"

"I do not know," he said slowly. "It is not something any of us have needed to discover."

I picked up my purse and slung it over my shoulder. "Do you think it would be worth trying to find out?"

"As I said, I cannot speak to the lost ones. It's not a matter of breaking some rule. We are physically not capable of speaking to them. They are lost—to rebirth, and to us." He paused. "But you could most certainly attempt it."

I frowned. "But I haven't the training—"

"No," he agreed. "But the witch Adeline Greenfield suggested you had more of your mother's talents than you thought. Was not one of her specialties talking to the lost ones?"

What he called lost ones—people who died before their time—I called ghosts. And no matter what Adeline had said, I'd certainly had no luck trying to communicate with the ghosts at the club. "Mom talked to souls, yes, but I never got the impression she targeted ghosts."

"Who else could she target?" He said it gently, as if

he were talking to a simpleton. "Souls who die at their given time move on to either the light or dark path. There is no communicating with them once they have gone through the respective portals."

"Well, how was I to know that?" I grumbled. I glanced at my watch. "We'd better get moving—"

I'd barely said it when he stepped close, caught me in his arms, and whisked me through the glorious brightness that was *his* gray fields. We re-formed in the small dark chamber next to the feeding room. The smell of antiseptic was thick in the air, catching in my throat and making me cough. They'd obviously just cleaned up after a session. I closed my eyes for a moment, grateful to have at least missed that, then turned to face the camera and held up my watch.

"Here on time, as ordered," I said, though I wasn't sure if they would hear me or were even watching. I turned around and faced Azriel. "You'd better go release Jak, hadn't you?"

"Will you be all right in this place alone?"

"I'm hardly alone. I have Amaya, remember."

"True." He still looked doubtful, however.

I sighed. "I'll be fine. Just don't forget to give Jak *all* the appropriate memories."

"He will get what he requires."

I snorted softly. "We were seen dancing, Azriel. Include that—all of that."

He just gave me his inscrutable face. Which meant, I was beginning to suspect, *Screw you. I'll do what I want.* "We still need his help, Azriel, whether you like it or not."

He inclined his head slightly, but again, I couldn't really tell whether it was agreement. "I won't be long," he said, and disappeared again.

I plopped down on the chair, and after a few minutes of twiddling my thumbs, dug out my phone and rang Ilianna.

"Do you know what fucking time it is?" she mumbled by way of hello.

"Yep," I said cheerfully. "But I figure if I'm up, you should be, too."

"Karma will bite your ass for this," she muttered.

"Karma already has," I said. "Trust me, sleep and I haven't exactly been steady companions over the last couple of days. How's Tao?"

"Improving," she said. "His core temperature continues to come down, and he's finally starting to put weight back on."

"But he hasn't woken yet?"

"No." She paused, and soft steps echoed. I was being taken into the bathroom, I suspected. Guess that's what I got for waking her at an ungodly hour. "But we don't think it'll be too long before he does."

"Fabulous. But I didn't only ring for that."

"I'm glad," she said dryly. "Or I would have had to clip you around the ears next time I see you."

I grinned. "Even with the threefold rule?"

The threefold rule was a witch belief that whatever you put out into the world—be it positive or negative—would return to you threefold. Very few witches chanced doing the latter, and with good reason. I'd seen what happened to a witch who cast evil, and it hadn't been pretty. Of course, I'd played a part in her downfall, but then, she *had* been trying to kill me, and it was thanks to one of her creatures that Tao lay unconscious.

"That rule doesn't apply when it involves those who maliciously wake their friends in the wee hours of the morning."

I laughed, but the sound died on my lips as the ghosts in the other room began to moan. I closed my eyes briefly. God, another session was about to start. I swallowed heavily, and somehow said, "Listen, can you give me Adeline Greenfield's number?"

"Sure," she said, worry suddenly in her tone. "But why?"

"Because she said last time I saw her that I had more of Mom's talents than I suspected—"

"Which is something I've been saying for years."

"And," I continued, ignoring her, "I need her to teach me how to contact ghosts."

"But you can already see ghosts. It's part of the reason you hate hospitals."

"Yes, I can see them," I agreed. "But I can't communicate with them. At best, I can hear their moaning."

And the moaning in the other room was getting louder, becoming more agitated.

"Which has never bothered you before now, so why the sudden urgency?"

"Because a man we need information from was killed tonight, but his soul was uncollected. I want to talk to him again, to see if he can tell us anything else. To do that, I'll probably need to step onto the astral field."

She said nothing for a moment, then, "I'm gathering this is Hunter's job?"

"No." I wished it was. It would be a whole lot easier talking to a ghost than having to sit here and listen to the bitter cacophony coming from the other room while I waited for a monster to make an appearance. "He might be able to help us pinpoint John Nadler, the third member of the consortium that's been buying up the land around Stane's shop."

"You know, if this information source is now dead, then it suggests Nadler really doesn't want to be found. Step carefully, Risa."

"Yeah, yeah, I will."

She snorted. In the background water splattered into a sink; then came more footsteps. She'd finally moved out of the bathroom.

"Here's Adeline's phone number." She reeled off the number, and added, "But don't you *dare* ring her now. She'll be asleep, like most normal people."

"Don't worry. I'm only this inconsiderate to my friends." I paused, then said with a grin, "And besides, I'm sure you and Mirri can find a pleasant way to pass the time until sleep arrives again."

"Mirri's on night shift," she reminded me, "so if I play with anyone, it'll be myself."

I grinned. "Flying solo can be fun."

"I'll remind you of that the next time you're whining about the lack of men and sex in your life." Her voice was dry. "Just be careful, Ris. I'm still getting some bad vibes from this whole Hunter deal."

No surprise there, since I had a council execution order hanging over my head. But I didn't say anything— she was worried enough as it was. She didn't need to know the details.

"I'll be fine," I said. "Just make sure you be careful, as well."

"I will. Night."

"Night."

I hung up, shoved the phone away, then leaned back against the wall, listening to the growing wailing and wishing it could cover up the other sounds and smells coming from the room. The scents of hunger, desire, and blood, the moans that were filled with ecstasy rather than anger, the rending of material and the smack of flesh against flesh. The vampire involved to-night was obviously into aggressive sex as well as blood taking.

Normally, sitting here listening to someone else get-ting sexed would have had lust surging through my veins, but in this atmosphere, it was little more than ashes from which no fire could be raised.

As the sounds in the other room began to ramp up to a climax, the howling of the ghosts became so sharp and bitter that I had to cover my ears with my hands. But even that failed to lessen the impact. It was a sound that tore through the fabric of my being, until it felt like I was unraveling.

And then something else began to creep into the at-mosphere. It was an ill wind, dark and twisted, barely there at first, but gathering in strength as the feeding in the room drew closer to culmination and the howls and screams of the ghosts got stronger and louder.

And they weren't the only ones. Amaya was hissing

fiercely, her fury filling my mind, her need to rent and tear so strong, I had to dig my nails into my hands to resist the urge to run out into that room and kill everyone.

Because it wasn't just ghosts, a blood whore, and a vampire out there now.

The Rakshasa had finally answered the desperation of the ghosts.

Chapter 8

Azriel, I thought, *you'd better get your ass back here right now, because I am* not *facing this thing alone.*

But I drew Amaya regardless. She slipped eagerly into my hand, the lilac fire dripping from her black edges sizzling as it splattered across the floor.

Then energy of a different kind swept around me and, a heartbeat later, Azriel appeared. Valdis was drawn, her blade running with blue electricity. The fires of the two blades filled the small room with light and, in the other room, that gathering of dark energy began to fade.

"It has sensed my arrival and retreats to the gray fields," Azriel said. "Quickly."

And with that, he disappeared. I swore, sat down, and closed my eyes. I didn't bother reaching for calm, didn't bother to center myself. I simply wrenched my soul free from my flesh and flung myself onto the fields. For a moment everything spun around me, a whirl of gray that had my stomach churning and my pulse rate shooting through the roof. Or maybe that was simply fear.

The Dušan exploded from my arm, her lilac form quickly gaining flesh and shape, until she seemed so real that I wanted to reach out and touch her. She swirled around me, the wind of her body buffeting mine as her sharp ebony gaze scanned the fields surrounding us. I wondered if she sensed the Rakshasa, or if she was merely reacting to the knot of fear growing in the pit of my stomach.

I spun around, my gaze searching the silvery plains. But there was nothing; no one was here. Then I remembered what Azriel had said—if spirits traversed the fields, it was only via the paene. I'd come too far into the fields.

I dove for the shadowy divide between the fields and the real world, and spotted it. The Rakshasa was a boiling, writhing mass of dark gray that almost merged into the mist that was this part of the fields. And it was quickly receding into the distance.

Azriel was easier to find—he was a blaze of sunlight in this ghostly otherworld, a force whose very presence throbbed through my being. He was closer to the creature than I was, but nowhere near close enough.

I ran forward, Amaya gripped tightly in my right hand and the Dušan's serpentine form swirling around me. Her eyes glittered fiercely as she continued to scan the fields around us—searching for trouble. Searching for a threat.

I hoped like hell she didn't find it.

But even as that thought crossed my mind, trumpets echoed, the sound oddly haunting in the hush of the fields. The last time I'd heard those trumpets, it had meant the Raziq were hunting me.

Fuck, fuck, fuck.

I kept my gaze on the receding forms of Azriel and

the Rakshasa, trying to increase my speed and catch up, but having little success with either. I might walk the fields, but this was not my world, and it seemed that the constraints of my flesh were affecting me here. Speed had never been one of my gifts.

The haunting echo of the horns drew closer. Amaya was a fierce storm battering my thoughts, wanting to stand and fight, and frustrated that we weren't, while the Dušan's movements were getting more and more agitated. My gaze swept the shadows, but I couldn't see anything or anyone.

They were out there, nevertheless. I could feel the ill wind of their presence rushing toward me.

And then, from out of nowhere, they struck.

Only it wasn't the Raziq. It was a writhing mass of sinuous, sluglike forms that had stalks for eyes and seemed to bleed a white substance from all over their bodies.

They rolled out of the shadows like a gigantic bowling ball and came straight at me. The Dušan screamed and dove into their midst, sending gray forms scattering as she bit and slashed. Several rolling lumps reformed out of the main mass, the smaller ones circling me as the larger one—with the Dušan still in its midst—continued rolling toward me. I jumped out of its path and swung Amaya. Purple fire trailed from her blade, splattering the nearest creatures as she sliced through their beings and cut them asunder. Gray muck sprayed from their bodies and the mass seemed to writhe with greater agitation. But it didn't fall apart, didn't seem to be deterred. It simply did a long looping turn and came at me again.

The Dušan rose from its midst, twisted in midair, then dove again, teeth wide, chomping down on gray forms, flinging them left and right. It still didn't seem to have any effect. The writhing forms just drew closer, instantly filling the spaces created by the Dušan.

A wind hit me from behind. I staggered a little, caught my balance, then swung around. One of the smaller masses had broken the circle and was coming straight at me. I swung Amaya. Her blade hit the ball of slugs and came to a shuddering halt—it was as if something had gripped her hard. She screamed her fury, spitting fire that sizzled and flamed out the minute it struck the oozing sides of the slugs. I swore and pulled back with all my might. She came free with a weird sucking sound just as a second small mass of slugs swept in. I swung to face it, but it arced, avoiding the sweep of the blade. As it passed me, the white mucus that bled from its pores exploded, splattering through the air. I twisted away from it, but nowhere near fast enough. The mucus plastered my left side and instantly hardened, pinning my arm to my body and immobilizing my leg.

Glue. It was some form of fucking glue.

There was no fighting this. All the slug balls had to do was keep their distance and spit their glue at me, and I'd be trussed up tighter than a turkey at Thanksgiving in no time. I *had* to get out of here.

Sorry, Azriel, it's too dangerous for me to stay here on the fields. I closed my eyes and flung myself back into my body. The force of it sent me toppling off the chair and onto the floor. And that's where I remained, doing nothing more than sucking in air as pain shuddered through my body and tiny men with hammers went crazy inside my head. After several heartbeats, the shifting magic crawled sluggishly over my face, my body unable to sustain the change when my energy reserves were so low.

And matters weren't being helped by Amaya—she was a continuous scream echoing through the outer reaches of my thoughts, and the Dušan was writhing up and down my arm, the movements somewhat disturbing and definitely furious. Neither of them, it seemed, was happy about my sudden retreat.

Not that I particularly cared. I couldn't fight if I was all glued up, and I had no intention of landing in the hands of the Raziq—I had no doubt that was who'd sent those things. For whatever reason, they didn't seem prepared to get their hands dirty trying to capture me, be it here or on the fields.

I released Amaya, then tried to get up, but with both my left arm and leg out of action, it was decidedly awkward. Eventually, I skewed myself around until my back was pressed against the wall, then did a sideways sit-up. I poked the white substance warily; it had set like rock, and made an odd, almost hollow sound when I tapped it. I dug my fingernails under one end and tried to break it away from my clothes, with little success.

I reached for Amaya and pressed her point lightly against the muck gluing my leg. Her hissing dropped several octaves—becoming more a grumbling sound, as if she was reluctantly obeying my unspoken need— and the flames dancing down her sides ran across the mass of white. The pungent scent of burning flesh began to infuse the air. It wasn't my flesh burning but the white substance. It might look and work like glue, but it obviously wasn't.

After several more minutes, the glue had disappeared, leaving only a powdery white stain on my jeans. I repeated the process on my arm, but this time, the powdery substance had chewed through my sweater and the skin underneath had a pink sheen, almost as if it had been burned.

I pushed myself to my feet, but the room spun and I had to grab at the wall to stop myself from falling. Heat shimmered around me; then Azriel appeared, quickly catching my other arm and holding me steady.

"You need to sit," he said.

"No," I replied, swallowing bile as sweat broke out on my brow. "I need to stay right here. Otherwise, I'm going to throw up all over your boots."

"These boots are part of the illusion I wear, so it would not matter."

"Which doesn't mean they won't get ruined when I vomit all over them."

It was a nonsense conversation, but right then I just needed to get my mind off the pain and dizziness. Slamming my soul in and out of my body like that had *not* been one of my brightest decisions, and I doubted I would repeat it anytime soon.

"Well, yes," he said equably, "but the point is, I can regenerate the boots—and the body."

"Does that mean you don't scar?"

"Do you see the wound from the silver bullet I took?"

My gaze swept over him, although I knew all I'd see was warm, suntanned flesh. "That's a skill I need."

"What you need is to get back to the hotel and wash that powder from your arm—otherwise the rash may well get worse and scar."

"Damn." I took another slow, deep breath, then carefully pushed away from the wall. The room only did a minor dance before it steadied.

Despite stating that I needed to take a shower, Azriel righted the chair, then sat me down. "I did not catch the Rakshasa."

"I gathered that." I ran a hand through my sweaty hair. "And unfortunately, it now knows we're here waiting for it."

"Yes." He squatted in front of me, taking my left hand in his and rubbing it gently. Up until that moment, I hadn't realized just how cold it was. "But I do not think that will stop it from coming. Its hunger is great."

I frowned. "Why wouldn't it just seek out a safer hunting ground?"

"Because, as I said, it is drawn by great anger and despair. There is much of those emotions in this place."

My fingertips were beginning to tingle with heat, a sharp sensation that wasn't exactly pleasant. And while part of me wondered why he didn't just flush heat and healing through me like he usually did, the sensation of his hands rubbing mine felt too good to complain. "But there are other dark clubs—why wouldn't it just choose one of those?"

"I suspect because of the ghosts. It is their need, their anguish, that is the draw here."

"Does that mean the other places don't have ghosts?"

He shrugged. "They undoubtedly do, but for whatever reason, they are not as vocal or as angry."

"But why? I mean, they're all in the same situation—why would these ghosts be more vocal than the others?"

"Perhaps they aren't. Perhaps the Rakshasa—for reasons we cannot understand—simply chose this club over the others."

"So now that it knows we're here, it may hunt in the other clubs?"

"Possibly."

Wouldn't that make Hunter a happy woman? I closed my eyes as the warm, prickly sensation began to spread through the rest of my hand, but I resisted the urge to pull it from his. I wanted to enjoy the press of his fingers just a little bit longer. "Do you think we should remain here until dawn?"

"No. The Rakshasa may be hungry, but it isn't stupid. It won't return tonight."

I sighed in relief. "I'm glad, because I really don't want to be here when those ghosts start up again."

"We won't be." He rose, pulling me upright with him, then encircling my waist with his other arm. His face was its usual inscrutable self, but there was an odd tension in his body and Valdis flowed with a muted red fire. "Ready?"

I nodded. Energy swept around me, through me, tearing us apart and flinging us through the fields so quickly it was little more than a blur.

I gasped as we re-formed inside the hotel room. "Sorry," he said, his hand sliding almost sensually around my waist before he stepped back. "I did not want to risk being on the fields for long. Not with the Raziq's creatures still loose."

I frowned. "Why aren't they being hunted?"

"They are, but our resources are still stretched thin." He paused. "Go shower, Risa."

I studied him for a moment, knowing there was more to it than that, but also knowing he wouldn't share until he was good and ready. With a half shrug of my own, I grabbed a shirt and some fresh panties and headed for the bathroom to clean up.

Twenty minutes later I felt somewhat refreshed, and though my arm was still red from the remnants of the slug glue, it didn't look bad enough to scar. I got dressed, then finger-dried my hair, suddenly glad to be wearing my own face once more, even though I'd probably have to face-shift again when we left the hotel. The Raziq might have attacked me on the gray fields, but they hadn't yet managed another attack on this plane. The subterfuge, as tiring as it was, appeared to be working.

I sighed softly, then jumped a little as my cell phone rang.

I dug it out of the pocket of my discarded jeans, and said, "Hello?"

"I must say," a familiar voice drawled, "I am very disappointed."

Lucian. Damn it, he was the *last* person I wanted to talk to right now, even if my hormones were suddenly saying otherwise. And what was it about this man that got to me so quickly? I hadn't thought about him all fucking day, and yet the minute I heard his voice, I became a seething mass of need.

If I hadn't known otherwise, I'd have said he'd put some sort of spell on me—except that Ilianna would have spotted anything like that.

"What do you want, Lucian?"

It was tersely said, but he didn't seem to notice. His soft laugh ran across my senses as sweetly as a caress.

"What do you think I want? You, on me, under me. I want to feel your supple body, want to caress your silken skin, want to lose myself in the wonder of loving you."

Each word had visions of our tangled bodies rising, and sweat prickled across my skin. I closed my eyes and sagged back against the bathroom wall. I could resist this. I could resist *him*.

"Only trouble is," I said, the anger in my voice aimed more at myself than at him, "I don't want to see or feel you. I've already told you that."

"I may not be able to feel your need, but I can hear the lie in your words, Risa."

"I don't care. I said at least forty-eight hours and I meant it. Maybe next time you'll reconsider the roughhouse tactics and try a little more respect."

And with that, I hung up, and turned my phone off for good measure. It would piss him off even more, but I really needed to make the point.

Although what I *really* needed— I stopped the thought and frowned. Because if I was honest, what I *needed* and what I *wanted* were two entirely different things. I might need Lucian's brand of loving with a fierceness that was indescribable, but the person I *wanted* was Azriel.

And yet, I still feared taking that step. Still feared

where it would lead, and what would happen when all this was over and he left for good.

Because I had a suspicion that if I let Azriel in, he could lay waste to my emotional being far more easily than Jak ever had.

I took a deep breath and slowly released it.

I couldn't risk it. I *shouldn't* risk it.

I closed my eyes and knew that more than likely I *would* risk it.

I shook my head at my own recklessness and walked into the main room. Where I stopped. Azriel was standing in his usual spot at the window, but his arms were crossed and tension rode his shoulders. Valdis was oddly silent. Neither of them was giving me any clue as to what he was feeling or thinking.

But in many ways, that was clue enough. After all, he knew precisely what I'd been thinking.

"Just because I can read your thoughts does not mean I always do," he said softly.

"And yet you are right now."

"Yes."

"And?"

"And what?"

I scanned his broad back, willing him to turn around and face me. He didn't. Meaning he wasn't about to make this easy. This step, if I took it, would be my decision and my decision alone. Despite his words earlier, he wouldn't do anything further to influence me. "You have no thoughts? No desires?"

"I have plenty of both, but ideally, none of them are ones that I should act upon."

I forced my feet forward, closing the distance between us. Even though the heat radiating off him burned across my skin, making my breath catch and my pulse race, the few inches that now separated us still felt like a mile or more.

"And realistically?"

"Realistically, I wish to plunge Valdis's screaming heart into the Aedh's flesh and rip him asunder."

Though there was no emotion in his voice, I felt it nonetheless. It burned inside me, bright and fierce. I licked my lips, wondering why I was suddenly so attuned to him. "Why do you want to kill him?"

He didn't answer, but just for a moment, flames flickered down Valdis's side, rich and red. The color of anger. The color of desire. It stirred through the threads of my being as sweetly as a caress.

"I didn't think reapers were capable of an emotion as strong as jealousy." I was standing so close to him that my breath washed across his shoulders as I spoke. His skin twitched so sharply it was almost as if I were flaying him.

"It is not jealousy," he retorted. "I simply do not trust him. And I do not like the timing of that phone call, so soon after Logan was killed."

"Lucian didn't kill Logan. You found the shooter."

"Yes, but who controlled the shooter? He was a Razan, Risa. Maybe he was Lucian's Razan."

"Lucian hasn't got Razan."

"How can you be sure of that? He has been on this earth for a long, long time. He may now revel in pleasure, but have no doubt he has also become proficient at lying."

"You and I know it's more a guess than a certainty."

I raised a hand and brushed my fingertips across the back of his neck, following the swirling tribal patterns inked into his skin. A dark fire seemed to ignite deep in the heart of them. "Lucian said he'd been stripped of most Aedh powers—how then could he possibly create human slaves *and* sustain them?"

"I am sure he can do more than what he says."

"So you have proof of this? Or is it merely distrust and dislike?"

He didn't say anything. He didn't need to. I let my fingers slide down to the stylized black Dušan that dominated the left half of his back. It, too, seemed to gleam with a dark fire when I touched it. But then, it was alive, even if it couldn't gain form on this plane.

"That distrust," I continued softly, "isn't the only reason for your sudden need to kill Lucian, is it?"

"No."

"Then why the change?"

Even as I asked the question I had my doubts that he would answer it. But once again he surprised me.

"Because," he said, his voice even though the air around us suddenly seemed to crackle with anger and tension—the same sort of tension that rode his powerful body. "He is the reason you are standing where you are, contemplating what you are."

"No, he isn't."

"Do you deny the desire he raised when he called?"

"No." I ran my fingers back up the tribal patterns. A tremor moved through him as I touched the one that resembled a comet trailing fire. "But he is not the reason I'm standing here, Azriel. He's not the one I want right now."

"But you will want him in the future?"

I hesitated, but there was no denying the reality of the situation. I would have sex with Lucian in the future—partly because I generally enjoyed being with him and partly because it was a means of self-preservation. If Jak had taught me anything, it was never to invest too much of myself in a relationship unless I was absolutely certain it was that "forever" one. And neither Lucian nor Azriel could be that, no matter how much I might enjoy being with Lucian or how strong the pull toward Azriel.

"Yes," I said eventually, and let my hand drop back to my side. "I will continue seeing Lucian. But that does not mean I cannot also be with you. Werewolves are by nature—"

"Do not," he interrupted sharply, "use your werewolf heritage as an excuse. It is fear that governs your actions on this, nothing more, nothing less."

"I prefer to call it self-preservation." I stepped back from him, though it was the last thing I wanted to do. "You said I couldn't continue to deny what is between us. Well, I'm not. But I will not commit wholly to something that must end when all this is over. If you want otherwise, then I'm sorry, but I just can't do it."

"And I do not know if I—" He cut the words off and took a deep breath. Then, finally, he turned around to face me. His mismatched blue eyes were turbulent and dark, but the emotions moved through them too quickly to identify. "You once wondered what it would be like to make love to a reaper. That is not something I can share with you. You are not ready for it."

I raised my eyebrows, but said nothing, simply because I sensed a "but" coming.

The smile that twisted his lips was a brief acknowledgment that he was still following my thoughts.

"But," he said softly, lightly pressing his palm against my cheek, "I *can* share what it is like to be with a reaper in human form. And perhaps in the end that will be less dangerous for us both."

He didn't mean physically dangerous. He meant emotionally. And he was wrong on both counts. He was breaking all reaper rules, and I was risking my heart yet again—how could any form of relationship between us not be considered dangerous?

And yet, as he'd noted earlier, sometimes the gain was worth the punishment—or the broken heart, as I suspected might be the case for me if I wasn't very, very careful.

"I don't care what form you're in, Azriel," I said, meeting his gaze steadily. "I just want you. Here. Now."

His hand slid from my cheek to the back of my neck, then gently tugged me closer.

"Well, then," he said, his words a warm caress that made my lips tingle, "I guess I have no choice."

And with that, he kissed me. Gently and sweetly, as if this moment was something so very rare and precious, and he was intent on enjoying it for as long as he could.

But it was also a whole lot more than just a kiss, because the minute our lips met, energy swept through me, until my nerve endings were more alive than they had ever been, and quivering with . . . with what? It wasn't desire, not really. It was more than that. *Bigger* than that. It was as if I stood on the edge of a precipice reaching for something far beyond my understanding.

As the kiss deepened, I wrapped my arms around his neck and pressed against him, until the only thing separating us was the thin layers of our clothing. Yet it still felt like heated flesh against heated flesh, need against need. His hand slipped down my spine, his touch light but devastating, making me tremble in a way I'd never trembled before. Because it wasn't just his touch—it was the press of his body against mine, the flow of energy around us, the gentle dance of awareness that seemed to ebb and flow with every breath, as if somehow more than just our physical selves was involved in this dance.

Then his lips left mine and lightly brushed my chin. I raised my face and sighed in pleasure as his kisses moved down my neck. When he reached the collar of my shirt, he pulled back slightly and undid the first button, then kissed the skin he'd exposed. I closed my eyes and shuddered in delight. He moved down to the next button, slowly undoing it, pressing the shirt farther apart, then kissing the newly exposed skin.

Too slow, I thought. *Far too damn slow.*

I raised my hands and ran them across the muscular planes of his chest. His breath hitched; then he caught my hands and pulled them away.

"This," he said gently, though his gaze burned with determination and something else, something that made me quiver with expectation and just a tiny bit of fear, "is for you. I want to explore you, worship you. Just feel, Risa. Just enjoy."

"I don't—" *know if I could survive that.* Which was

silly, and yet I couldn't ignore that niggle of fear that continued to burn within the desire.

But I'd made the decision, taken the step, and I would not back out. I doubted I could have even if I'd wanted to—the connection between us was far too strong to ignore now.

"Please," he said softly, "let me give you this, if nothing else."

I nodded. There was nothing else I could do. Nothing else I could say.

He undid the next button, spreading the shirt wider and kissing the exposed skin. Then he repeated the process, one button at a time, down my body. I quivered every time his lips touched my flesh, until it felt like I was floating on a growing haze of desire, need, and expectation.

Finally, when all the buttons were undone, he trailed his kisses back up my body, then briefly claimed my lips as he slid the shirt from my shoulders. As it fell around my feet, he stepped back a little, his heated gaze roaming across my breasts and stomach as if he'd never seen me naked before. Then, with a slight groan, he bent and captured one hard nipple in his mouth. I gasped, gripping his shoulders as he licked, and nipped, and teased, my body so assaulted with sensation that my knees felt weak. When he moved to my other breast, I whimpered, unable to stand the torture of being touched and yet not being able to touch. God, I so wanted—

No. The soft word flowed into my mind, a command I could not disobey.

And he continued the sweet torture, until it was all I could do not to scream in pleasure and frustration.

Finally, he relented, and his kisses moved back down my belly again. He ran his tongue along the edge of my panty line and it felt like he was branding me. I shivered; then my breath caught somewhere in the back of my throat as he hooked his fingers under the top elastic and drew them down my legs. Once I'd stepped out of them, he tossed them to one side, then quickly rose, catching my hand and leading me to the bed.

Where, once I was lying down, he kissed me again, heated and hard, with all the desperation of a man at the edge of his tether. And the kiss . . . it was so much more. It was heat and desire and need, yes, but it was also a dance of beings, of souls, as if in this one moment, we were almost one, not two.

Almost.

He pulled back with a suddenness that had me gasping and, for a moment, simply stared at me. Then he closed his eyes and took a deep breath, as if he were battling for control.

Once again, he began his slow and torturous journey down my stomach, assailing me with his kisses. As my body twitched and burned, I wondered how the hell I was going to stand much more without giving in to the need to take what I wanted—him. In me, loving me. Hard.

Then his tongue flicked over my clit and my breath escaped in a whoosh as delight exploded through me. I groaned, arching up against him, urging him on, wanting him to explore further, deeper. His tongue swirled around my outer lips as he gripped my hips, holding me steady as he tasted and teased, until I couldn't think, couldn't breathe, could only feel. And I felt as if I were about to explode.

And then, as his tongue teased my clit yet again, I *did* explode, and I was little more than a whimpering, moaning mess as my body rocked and shook in pleasure.

"Risa," he said softly, as the tremors began to ease. "Look at me."

I opened my eyes. He was straddling me, his body quivering with need, his cock thick and hard and deliciously ready. And I was ready for him. Oh so ready.

But as my gaze met his, something within me stilled. Just for a moment, everything felt perfect, everything felt right.

And that scared the hell out of me.

But as much as I wanted to look away, I couldn't. All I could do was stare into the turbulent, powerful blue depths as he slowly, carefully, entered me.

And then all I could do was groan in pleasure.

Because again, it wasn't just our flesh connecting. It was deeper than that, richer than that. Scarier than that.

Then he began to move, and there was no thought, no fear, only sensation. Within and without, as if this moment, and this man, were everything that was ever meant to be. On and on it went, until it felt as if the threads of my being were unraveling.

And then everything *did* unravel, and I was shuddering, shaking, and screaming in pleasure as his body stiffened against mine and his essence filled me, body and soul.

For several minutes afterward, neither of us moved. When I could finally breathe—think—I cleared my throat and said, "Well, I'm kind of glad you could only make love to me as a reaper in human form."

He shifted enough to transfer his weight from me onto his elbows, and stared down at me with an odd sort of half smile. "Why is that?"

"Because if that's an indication of what it would be like to have sex with you in reaper form, I don't actually think I could survive it."

He laughed softly, then bent and kissed my lips. It was soft and gentle, but nevertheless the connection between us stirred to life, shivering through me like a curtain of silver. Part of me wanted to step through it and see what lay on the other side, but most of me simply wasn't willing to take that risk. So I just kept on kissing him. Hunger stirred between us, gathering speed and strength.

"You know what else I think?" I said after a while. Then I scowled. "Well, of *course* you do."

He smiled. "No, I don't. I was occupied with your lips, not your thoughts."

I raised an eyebrow. "So to stop your following every thought, I simply have to kiss you?"

"It does raise interesting possibilities."

"That," I murmured, as I tensed myself around his erection, "is certainly true."

His smile grew as he began to move inside me. "And this thought you had?"

"Ah yes," I said, running my fingers down his back, enjoying the reaction of his body, the slight hitching of his breath. "I was thinking that the woman you used to catch your friend's killer was a very fine teacher when it came to the art of lovemaking."

"As I said, it was very enlightening."

I snorted softly. "Enlightening? That really doesn't seem an adequate word."

"For this, it isn't," he agreed.

"And what would you call this?"

"This," he said softly, his gaze holding mine, burning with an intensity I didn't quite understand, "is everything that matters, and I intend to enjoy every second of it while it lasts."

Just for a moment, that silver curtain parted, and I knew *exactly* what he was thinking—that it wouldn't last beyond this day. Because he was determined to control the uncontrollable. "Azriel—"

"Don't," he said.

So I didn't. I just enjoyed.

The sharp ringing of the phone woke me many hours later. I groaned and groped the bedside table blindly, but couldn't find the damn phone.

It said a lot about both my mental state and my overall tiredness that it took me several more minutes to remember I'd left it in the bathroom.

"Here," Azriel said.

I opened one eye and looked at him, my vision rather bleary. *He* seemed disgustingly refreshed. "It's totally unfair that you look like you can go another six rounds and I feel exhausted."

"It's one of the benefits of being a reaper rather than a humanoid." His face was back to being its usual unreadable self, and while I'd expected it, I still hated it. He held out the phone. "Do you wish to answer this?"

"Who is it?"

He glanced down at the phone. "Jak."

I groaned, but raised a hand, made a "give me" motion, then hit the RECEIVE button and said, "You'd better have a good reason for ringing me at this hour, otherwise I *will* have to kill you."

His laugh was soft and teasing, but my hormones were too sated to react. "And here I was thinking I was the only one who woke up with a hangover."

Hangover? I glanced at Azriel and he shrugged. I guess it was one way of getting around the whole memory problem—you simply gave them a reason not to remember every little detail.

"Well, it was a long night."

"It sounds like you didn't enjoy yourself," Jak said. "I'm totally hurt."

"Oh, I enjoyed myself." More than he could ever imagine—only *he'd* had nothing to do with it. I glanced at Azriel as that thought crossed my mind, and caught the half smile that flirted briefly with his lips. "But I'm not enjoying this conversation. What do you want, Jak?"

He sighed dramatically. "And here I was thinking that after our dance, you might be a little less business, and a little more pleasure."

"Yeah, well, you thought wrong."

"Sadly, yes."

"Jak, the reason you're calling is . . . ?"

He laughed. "Damn, but it's fun baiting you. The

reason I'm calling is that I found James Blake, the photographer Jacinta mentioned."

"I'm surprised he's not dead, like Logan and everyone else who could identify Nadler."

"Yes—although it does lend weight to the theory that our face-shifter doesn't believe his past is much of a threat to his future."

"Which makes me wonder why we're even bothering to follow up on these things."

"Hey, we gleaned one vital fact yesterday—the real Nadler had a scar. Who knows what we may gain today?"

"I'm breathless with anticipation."

My voice was dry and he chuckled softly. "I hope you remain that way until we meet. I'd love a repeat performance of last night."

I ignored his comment and looked at the clock on the bedside table. It was nearly eleven, which meant I'd had a whole two hours' sleep. No wonder I felt like crap. "Where is his studio located?"

"He's retired, so no studio. But he lives in Williamstown and he's expecting us around lunchtime."

If he was living in Williamstown, he had to have made a lot as a photographer, because that area—thanks to its proximity to both the sea and the city—wasn't cheap. "I've got to hire a car, so it'll probably be at least an hour before I can get there."

"I'm already on my way, but I'll grab some lunch to waste some time."

"Don't go question him without me."

"Wouldn't dream of it," he said blandly. "I've sent you the address, too. I'll be waiting in a—"

"Red Honda Accord," I finished for him. He'd been driving them since he'd gotten his license, and I very much doubted it had changed.

He laughed again. "Yeah. See you soon."

I tossed the phone back onto the bedside table, then sat up and hugged my knees close to my chest. "Just what sort of memory did you give Jak, exactly?"

Azriel shrugged. "You said to give him all the appropriate memories."

"Meaning not just the dance, but the kiss?"

He eyed me. "Yes. That is what you wanted; is it not?"

"Well, yes. I mean, no." I frowned. "I hadn't actually expected you to go that far."

"Then say what you actually mean."

I snorted softly and climbed off the bed. "You're a fine one to be telling me that, Azriel."

He shrugged again, and walked across to the window to resume his usual position. The intimacies of the last few hours would have seemed like a distant memory if not for the ache in my body.

I studied the muscular planes of his back—planes I knew intimately now—for several minutes, then said, "So, we're back to being formal, are we?"

"It is safer."

"Safer for who?"

He glanced at me, blue eyes calm. Yet there was turbulence in him—I could feel it. "For you. If I am distracted, it could prove fatal—to both yourself and to my quest."

"And the quest is all-important," I snapped. Which wasn't fair, but it wasn't exactly fair of him to retreat like this, either.

Though why I was getting upset when I *had* been expecting it, I had no idea.

He didn't answer. No surprise there. I grabbed some clothes and headed into the bathroom to shower. Once I was dressed, I closed my eyes and imagined a face with freckles and brown hair, but left my eyes their natural color. The magic swirled around me with far less enthusiasm than ever before, which could only mean that I was near the end of my reserves. I needed a break from it, and I needed some decent sleep—not that I regretted the lack of it last night, even if this morning's remoteness took some of the shine off it. Grimacing, I headed out of the bathroom, picked up my phone and purse, and said, "I'm guessing I'll meet you there?"

"You will."

He didn't turn around. Didn't kiss me good-bye. I flexed my fingers, resisting the urge to smack some sense into his thick head, then swung around and headed downstairs to arrange for a rental car.

In less than twenty minutes I was on the road. There wasn't that much traffic around, so it didn't take me long to get to Williamstown. Once there, I parked the little Daihatsu on one of the side streets just down from Blake's and climbed out.

The day was hot, and the sun shining with a ferocity that had me sweating in an instant. I pulled off my light sweater and shoved it back into the car, suddenly glad I'd put on a tank top underneath it. It didn't take me long to find Jak—the red Honda stood out like a sore thumb on a street lined with demurely colored Mercs, Volvos, and Audis. While the relatively small size of the surrounding houses gave no hint that this wasn't one of your more run-of-the-mill neighborhoods, the lineup of cars on the street certainly did.

Jak climbed out of the Honda and gave me a decidedly leisurely once-over. His gaze, when it finally rose to meet mine, was heated and hungry. My hormones thought about doing a little quickstep, then decided it involved too much effort.

"You," he said softly, his voice a low rumble that was easy on the ears, "look mighty damn fine. I do prefer your normal hair color, though."

"I'm only wearing blue jeans and a white tank," I said dryly, stopping several feet away from him. Even so, his hunger washed over me, warm and enticing. "And what you prefer is not something I ever consider when I change my look."

"A sad but true statement. But just to let you know, a tank with no bra underneath is eminently exciting to *any* male."

Except if he's a reaper, I thought snippily. I motioned to the white weatherboard house a few doors down from where he'd parked. "Shall we proceed?"

"If you're intent on being all business, then I guess I have no choice." He stepped back and waved me forward. "Which does not mean I cannot enjoy the view from behind. Those jeans are fetchingly tight around your ass."

I snorted softly and just kept on walking. The picket gate creaked as I opened it, and the garden beyond was filled with ornamental grasses and purple flax plants rather than flowers—what I'd call a man's garden rather than a woman's.

I walked up the steps, scanning the entrance for

some sort of doorbell. There was nothing, so I rapped my knuckles on the glass door.

Only when I did, it opened slightly. And the minute it did, I smelled the blood.

Fuck.

"The source of *that*," Jak said grimly, "is more than just a paper cut."

"Yeah." I pushed the door all the way open. Several rooms ran off the long central hallway, but the door at the far end was closed. The blood scent seemed to be coming from that direction—certainly there was nothing out of place in the hall itself.

"Should we go in or call the cops?" Jak said.

I glanced at him, eyebrow raised, and he grinned. "Okay, okay, we both know I want to go in and investigate, but I thought you might prefer to call the cops."

"Given that we don't know yet what we're dealing with, I think investigating is a better option."

His grin grew. "I've always loved the way your mind works. And the body isn't half bad, either."

"Umm, blood? Possible dead body and front-page article?" I reminded him.

"Oh, yeah. Right." He became all business in an instant.

I shook my head and stepped forward cautiously. Sunlight filtered through the open doorways on either side, crisscrossing the hall and lending the honey-colored floorboards a richness they might not otherwise have had. The first room was a living room, but there was nothing out of place in it, or in the two bedrooms that followed. Every room was as neat as a pin—there weren't even dust motes dancing in the sunbeams.

But the blood scent was getting stronger the closer we got to the closed door at the far end of the hall, and tension slithered through my body.

If that scent was anything to go by, whatever awaited in the room beyond was bad. Real bad.

I licked my lips, then carefully pushed the door open with the tip of my shoe. The scene that greeted me froze me on the spot.

Because the room beyond was a kitchen that was a smaller version of my mum's.

And just like my mum, James Blake had been totally and absolutely ripped apart.

Chapter 9

"Oh my *god*," Jak whispered, horror in his voice. "That can't possibly be—"

I flung out an arm to stop him from moving into the room. The gesture was automatic. My gaze had locked on the gore and blood scattered around the room, and a sick sense of déjà vu crawled across my skin. Though this murder—and my mom's—were similar to the MO of the Rakshasa, this wasn't her work. She fed off her victims. Whoever was responsible for this simply tore their victims apart. Somehow I managed to say, "It can and it is. We need to call the Directorate."

He glanced at me sharply. "Why? This is gruesome, no doubt about it, but there's no indication it's the work of a non-human. I mean, not even a vampire could tear someone apart this completely. Some kind of power tool *must* have been used."

"It wasn't. Trust me." I took a deep, shuddering breath and closed my eyes. Bad mistake, because the minute I did, I saw Mum bits, Mum's head . . . Bile rose and I swallowed heavily, then grabbed Jak's hand and dragged him out of there.

"What the fuck?" he said, trying to wrench himself free. "Risa, there's one hell of a story in there—"

"And it's not one you'll ever be allowed to print," I said. I stopped in the garden and sucked in several deep breaths. It didn't do a lot to ease the churning in my stomach, but it at least cleared the scent of blood from my lungs.

"Why not?"

"Because I've seen this before."

He studied me for a moment, frowning. "Where?"

"When my mum died." I waved a hand toward the house. "That's precisely the way she was killed."

"Oh, *fuck*," he said, his face going white. "I didn't know. I'm so sorry—"

"Don't," I cut in. "No one knew outside the Directorate and me, so you have nothing to apologize for."

"And that's the reason you want the Directorate called in? Because they're the ones that investigated your mom's death?"

Azriel? Are you near? I thought, then said out loud, "Yes. Only there were no clues and, until now, the killer hadn't resurfaced."

Azriel appeared behind Jak and lightly touched his neck. Jak froze, his eyes going suddenly blank.

"Are you okay?" Azriel asked.

"Mostly." I wrapped my arms around my body, and wished they were his arms, not mine. "I guess you've already been inside?"

"Yes. As before, there is nothing to suggest who is behind this murder."

As before . . . I shivered, and again tried to ignore the images that rose.

"No scent or spiritual essence—or whatever it is that you Mijai track by—whatsoever? How in the hell is something like that even possible?"

"The lack of scent is understandable," he said calmly. "Humans have had scent-erasing soap for many years now."

I waved a hand in acknowledgment. "But how can the killer not leave any other trace of himself behind?"

"Anything is possible if one is extremely careful, and our killer obviously is."

I took a deep breath and released it slowly. "Then what the hell is the link between my mum's murder and this man's?"

"That is obvious." His voice was grim. "*You* are the connection."

I blinked. "Why would I be the link when it comes to a retired photographer I didn't even know?"

"You might not have known James Blake, but you were intending to question him about Nadler. You were also investigating Nadler and his consortium when your mother was killed. I doubt it is a coincidence."

"But—" I paused. Pain and guilt rose like a ghost, but I pushed them back down and added, "I can understand someone killing Blake to keep him quiet, but Mom didn't really know much about my investigation."

"She was a very strong psychic," he replied, his voice soft. "You do not know what she might or might not have known."

And now never would, I thought bleakly. "Do you think they'll go after Nadler's ex, as well?"

"It is possible."

I swore, dug my phone out of my purse, and said, "Uncle Rhoan." The psychedelic patterns ran across the screen as the auto connect sprang into action.

Then Uncle Rhoan appeared. "If you're ringing to tell me you've discovered another dead body, I will not be happy. You know I wanted you off these investigations."

Fortunately, there was a resigned weariness in his voice rather than anger. I had a suspicion that either Aunt Riley had talked to him or he'd simply come to accept that I wouldn't stop sticking my nose into events. "I'm afraid there *is* another body and his name is—was—James Blake. He was a retired photographer who happened to be the attending photographer at John Nadler's wedding. He was killed the same way as Mom."

He was silent for a long moment, then said, "Are you okay?"

My attempt at a smile came out more of a grimace. "Queasy as hell, but holding up. You need to get people out here, but I also need you to check on Jacinta Nadler—we talked to her yesterday, and it just might have placed her in danger."

He paused, and barked out orders to whoever was in the room with him, meaning he was at the Directorate rather than at home, then said, "Who's we?"

I hesitated. "Myself and Jak Talbott."

"Jak Talbott?" His voice was incredulous. "The reporter who used his relationship with you to do that hatchet job on your mother?"

I winced. "Yeah, that very one."

"Why the *hell* are you working with him?"

"Because I'm trying to track down John Nadler, and Jak's got a lot of useful street contacts."

His sigh was one of exasperation. "Riley's right. You're not only pigheaded but determined to see this through no matter what you have to do, or who you have to use."

It was no surprise she'd said that—she knew me better than most. "If it was Riley who'd been murdered," I said softly, "wouldn't you react the same?"

"The difference is," he snapped, "I'm a trained guardian. You're not."

"No, but I've been taught to fight by two of the best, I'm not without means of protecting myself aside from that, and I have a reaper following me about who needs to keep me alive."

He grunted. Whether that meant he was finally accepting my continuing pursuit of both Nadler and my mom's murderer was anyone's guess. "Okay, I've pinpointed your location. I'll be there in fifteen minutes." He hesitated, then added, "Do not go back into that house until I arrive."

"I won't." I hung up and glanced at Azriel. "No matter what you think of Lucian, he can't have been involved in this. I haven't seen him, haven't talked to him since last night, and even if he could read my thoughts, he wouldn't have had time to get down here before Jak or me."

"All of which is true," Azriel commented. "That does not, however, change my opinion that he is involved in all this somehow."

"You," I said flatly, "are annoyingly pigheaded."

"Perhaps it is the company I keep that makes me so."

I snorted and waved a hand at Jak. "You'd better release him."

"Do you wish me to update his memories to include your ringing the Directorate?"

I nodded. Azriel touched Jak lightly and energy swirled, whispering through me like a sweet autumn breeze.

Then he dropped his hand and met my gaze again. "And just to be clear," he said, his voice even but a teasing light suddenly gleaming in his eyes, "I am not as immune to the virtues of that top as you believe."

And with that, he disappeared again, leaving me shaking my head and smiling like an idiot.

"Care to share the joke?" Jak said dryly.

I glanced at him. "Sorry, just something my uncle said."

"Your uncle the guardian, I gather we're talking about?"

"Yeah." I put my phone away. "To say he was rather surprised to discover I'm working with you on this is something of an understatement."

Worry crossed his face. "He didn't threaten violence, did he?"

"No." I studied him for a moment. "Has he before?"

Jak cleared his throat and looked a little uncomfortable. "You could say that."

"Really? When?"

"The first time when I wrote that story on your mom; the second when we broke up. He can be a very scary man, you know."

"He *is* a guardian." I said that a little too cheerfully,

if Jak's darkening expression was anything to go by. "But the threats can't have been too bad. I mean, not only are you still alive, but you walked away from them intact."

"Only because I swore on my mother's grave not to do another report on your mother, and to keep well away from you. The latter of which I am obviously not doing."

I patted his arm comfortingly. "Because we all know the story means more to you than the threat. And don't worry—Uncle Rhoan knows I contacted you, not the other way around."

"Doesn't mean he won't be pissed," he muttered, then plopped down on the step. "How long will they be?"

I sat down beside him and glanced at my watch. "About thirteen minutes."

As it turned out, they arrived in eight. Or at least Uncle Rhoan did—it seemed he'd beaten all land speed records to get here.

He came through the gate, a crime scene kit slung over one shoulder. His gray eyes swept the two of us critically. "You haven't been inside?"

I shook my head. "Other than the initial entry when we found the body, no."

"At least you can obey *some* orders." He glanced at Jak, his gaze narrowing a little. "You will *not* report anything you see inside. Not until we give you clearance. Is that clear?"

Surprise flitted across Jak's face as he nodded. He'd obviously been expecting to be banned from the proceedings.

Rhoan opened the kit and handed us both gloves

and plastic booties. "Put those on, and don't touch anything without asking."

We both obeyed. Once Rhoan had the floating crime
scene recorders up and operating, and was similarly
kitted out in gloves and booties, we headed down to
the kitchen.

"Jesus, it *is* similar," he said, as he entered. Then he
glanced over his shoulder at us. "Stay at the doorway,
you two."

He moved deeper into the room, carefully avoiding
the bits of blood and gore. James Blake's torso was only
half hidden behind the island, his entrails streaming
out from his ruptured body like fat sausages.

"Arms have been ripped off." Rhoan's gaze met
mine as he added softly, "Head separated."

I swallowed grimly. I'd been expecting it, but the
knowledge still clawed my stomach. "Any idea what
time he was killed?"

"The cleanup team will give us a more accurate
time, but I'd say within the last half hour. The blood
hasn't really begun to coagulate, and there's no sign of
rigor mortis."

"Can't have been," Jak said. "I was parked outside
for half an hour while I was waiting for Risa to arrive.
No one came in or out."

"You couldn't have seen the back door if you were
parked out front," Rhoan said.

"True, but the front door was unlatched when we
got here. That's why we entered in the first place."

Rhoan glanced at me—as if for confirmation—then
rose and walked to the end of the room. He disappeared through another doorway, but after a few min-

utes came back. "Okay, the back door is locked and the security chain is still in place. They didn't enter that way. You two want to check the other rooms for an entry point?"

I glanced briefly at Jak and, in unspoken agreement, he checked the rooms on the right, and I checked the ones on the left. Crime scene recorders floated along after each of us, making a note of everything we did. In the rooms I checked there were no windows open, no windows unlocked, and no sign of any other sort of disturbance.

I said as much to Rhoan, as did Jak when he returned a few minutes later.

"Well," Rhoan said, his voice grim, "that leaves us with three options—he knew his killer, there's magic or some form of demon involved, or it was an Aedh."

"Demons?" Jak said in an incredulous tone. "And what the hell is an Aedh?"

"That's one I'll let you field, Ris," Rhoan murmured, bending back down to examine torso remnants.

Jak's gaze came to mine expectantly. I grimaced. "You know how in many religious drawings angels are depicted as powerful and luminescent beings with wings?"

He raised an eyebrow. "You're saying they're angels?"

"No, I'm saying they're the reason religion depicts angels as they do. They're the template. The reapers are actually the real angels—they're the ones who guide the souls to heaven or hell, and they're also the warriors who protect us."

He blinked. "Reapers?"

"Yeah." I paused. "I've been able to see them all my life."

"Huh," he said. Then, "Weren't you scared out of your mind as a kid?"

"A sensible person would be," Rhoan commented without looking up. "But, as we all know, sensible and Risa do not have a whole lot in common."

"I love you, too," I said dryly, and he flashed me a grin. I glanced back at Jak. "And no, I wasn't scared. How could I be? I've always seen them, even if I didn't always know who or what they were."

"Could your mom see them?" he asked.

"No, although she could see and talk to ghosts." I paused, studying him. "I thought you didn't believe in my mom's gifts."

"No, I didn't believe the history she told everyone— a history I all but debunked, as we know. I never refuted the fact she possessed some psychic skill."

I snorted softly. "Some? You have no idea just how powerful my mom was."

"If your skills are any indication, I'm guessing that's true."

And he'd reached that conclusion without ever seeing *half* of my skills. Especially not my Aedh side— which is why I'd sidestepped mentioning it.

"What about demons, then?" he continued. "Can you see them, too?"

I hesitated. "Yes. But they're not that commonplace— hell is a pretty efficient prison."

At least until the keys had been created.

Jak scraped a hand across his bristly jawline. "I've learned more about this weird and wonderful world of ours in the last ten minutes than I did the last twenty-nine years."

"And it's information you will never repeat." Rhoan gave Jak his guardian expression—the one that held no emotion and yet still spoke of all kinds of hell waiting for you if you dared disobey. "None of this is information we want known by the general population. We couldn't afford the panic."

"But they have a right—"

"And *I* have the right," Rhoan interrupted, voice terse, "to call in a telepath and erase your memories if you do not agree to keep this silent."

Jak glanced at me, his expression disbelieving. I could only smile grimly. "I've seen it done. And the fact that you possess mild telepathy skills yourself won't save you."

"Well, this *sucks*." He blew out a frustrated breath. "What about the Nadler story? Will I be allowed to print any of that, or am I wasting my time?"

"You can report it, within reason," Rhoan said. "Once the case is solved."

"That I can agree to." He eyed Rhoan warily, then added, "Is that deal solid, or is it more a 'have to check with my superiors first' arrangement?"

"It's solid. I'm second in command in the guardian division."

Jak grunted. "Good."

A phone rang sharply into the brief silence. I jumped slightly, then reached for my phone—only to discover it was Rhoan's. He answered it, and his expression got progressively grimmer.

"Get another team out there," he said eventually,

"and tell them to report in as soon as they have prelim results."

"Oh no," I breathed. "Don't tell me—"

"Yeah," he said, as he shoved his phone away. "Jacinta Nadler is dead."

"Fuck," Jak said. "Nadler really *is* clearing the remnants of the past, isn't he?"

I closed my eyes and took a slow, deep breath. And wondered if Azriel was right—that Mom's murder, and these, might be connected. But if Mom had known something about Nadler, how had Nadler known she did? As far as I knew, she'd never met him.

Did that mean Azriel was also right in suspecting there was a rat in the ranks?

It wasn't a thought I was willing to entertain, yet I couldn't entirely ignore it, either.

"It would appear that he is," Rhoan said. "Although she wasn't murdered like this. It's been made to look like a home invasion—she was raped, brutalized, and then her throat was cut."

I closed my eyes. God. We'd done that. We were responsible for that. If we hadn't talked to her—

"Risa," Rhoan said gently, obviously guessing the direction of my thoughts. "We've also talked to both her and Blake. The only person to blame for these deaths is the monster behind all this."

He was right. I knew that, but it didn't make me feel any less responsible. Because they hadn't died when the Directorate had talked to them; they'd died when *I* had talked to them. But I didn't say anything, watching as he ran a gloved finger around the bloody separation wound just below the victim's belly button. "You know, it's almost as if someone has thrust a hand into Blake's stomach and somehow ripped him apart from there."

"Aedh," I said, rubbing arms suddenly chilled. "The Aedh can do that."

"So can demons," Rhoan said, standing up. "Let's not discount anything or anyone until we have forensic results." He glanced at his watch. "They should be here any minute. In the meantime, why don't we start going through Blake's belongings and see if we can find anything that relates back to Nadler. Or anything else that seems out of place."

He must have seen the surprise cross my face, because he added wryly, "I have officially given up trying to keep you out of this investigation, so I might as well make use of you. And I hate paperwork of any kind, even if it is simply going through it to find clues."

I snorted softly. "Where do you want to start?"

"Let's start with the first bedroom, and work our way through the house from there."

Which is precisely what we did. It was a long, boring process and by the time we'd gone through every room—except the kitchen, which now held the cleanup team—I was tired, hungry, and more than a little over it. Which was probably the whole reason Rhoan had agreed to let us help. It wasn't so much that he hated this sort of paperwork search; it was that he was hoping it would act as a deterrent and stop me from sticking my nose in any further.

There was zero chance of that happening.

I leaned my shoulder against a doorway and averted my gaze from the goings-on in the kitchen. "What about a storage shed? Did you see one outside when you checked the back door?"

Rhoan nodded. "You two can look at that while I get an update from the team. Use the side gate."

As one, Jak and I spun and headed out. "Phew," Jak said, "it's nice to breathe air untainted by blood."

"Yeah," I agreed, although in all honesty, I'd stopped smelling it after the first half hour. What did that say about me?

Jak unlatched the side gate and waved me through. I walked down the concrete path, then around the back of the house. Two small garden sheds sat in the far corner.

I opened the door of the first one and looked inside. It was all garden tools and whatnot. "Any luck with that one?" I asked Jak as I relocked the door.

"Yeah," he said, disappearing inside. "There's lots of plastic tubs."

I stopped just behind him. "Plastic tubs containing micro disks, no less."

"Hundreds of them. We could be here for months." He flashed me a grin. "Not that I'd mind being stuck in a tiny room with you for that long. I reckon I could break down your resistance to my obvious charms by the end of it."

I nudged him with my elbow. "You start at that end, I'll start at this."

He nodded and walked to the end of the shed, pulling down the first of the tubs and quickly breaking the seal. It didn't take all that long to find disks dated the day Nadler was married—all the tubs were categorized by year and month, so it was simply a matter of check-ing the dates of the first couple.

"Five disks for Saturday the eighteenth," Jak said, pulling them out and handing them to me. "You got somewhere we can check them? I really don't want to hand them over to the Directorate without at least see-ing what we have."

"I have at work." I hesitated, biting my lip. I had no doubt that Rhoan would claim these disks the minute we left the shed, but I really needed to know why Ja-cinta and Blake had died, and these things just might hold the answer.

"Well, that's going to do us a fat lot of good when it's there and we're here," Jak said sarcastically.

"I know." Silently, I added, *Azriel, would you mind freezing him again?*

Azriel appeared behind him and did precisely that. "What do you plan to do?"

I dropped my purse on the shelf near Jak, then wrapped my fingers tight around the small disks. "I'm going to Stane's in Aedh form, and get him to do a quick copy."

Azriel frowned. "It is dangerous to take Aedh form—"

"And it's even more dangerous to be on the gray fields at the moment. We have to take some chances if we're ever to solve this mess."

He studied me for a moment, then nodded. "I will meet you at Stane's."

I nodded, closed my eyes, and called to the Aedh within. The magic responded slowly, almost sluggishly, which meant that I was still pushing my limits strength-wise. I needed to eat and I needed to sleep, and I very much suspected the latter of those wasn't going to be on my agenda for a while yet.

Eventually, though, the heat and energy that was my Aedh half surged, numbing pain and dulling sensation as it invaded every muscle, every cell, breaking them down and tearing them apart, until my flesh no longer existed and I became one with the air. Until I held no substance, no form, and could not be seen or heard or felt by anyone or anything.

Except reapers and undoubtedly the Aedh, if they were close enough.

I flowed out of the shed and into the sky, zooming quickly across the city, my form buffeted by the gentle breeze beginning to stir the heated afternoon. Stane lived on West Street in Clifton Hill, in one of the two buildings not purchased by the consortium. The Phoenix club—a twenty-four-hour bar that was situated several doors down from Stane's—was the other. It was also the reason Stane's place was covered with graffiti and had thick grates over the windows and door. Apparently the Phoenix's patrons didn't mind engaging in a bit of drunken destruction as they made their way home.

I swept under the front door and into the small space zoned off by the containment field, then re-formed shape. But my legs were jelly and I dropped like a stone to my knees, red-hot needles jabbing into my brain and every breath feeling like it was tearing at my lungs. It was so bad this time that I couldn't even maintain the face-shift. Its energy crawled across my skin as I resumed my regular form, and there was nothing I could do to stop it. Just as there was nothing I could do about the pain, the shaking, and the sweeping bouts of dizziness and nausea other than wait until they all eased.

The camera above the doorway buzzed into action, and a voice said, "Fuck, Risa, are you all right?"

"No," I whispered. "But give me a minute or three, and I will be. And turn off the field."

Energy flowed through my mind, a sweet caress that did little to ease the pain. A heartbeat later, Azriel appeared, the heat of his presence flowing over me, chasing the chill from my flesh.

"Do you need help?" he asked, as he knelt beside me.

Yes. "No." I took a shuddering breath. "You can't keep siphoning your strength to me, Azriel. Sooner or later it's going to turn around and bite us on the ass."

"Which is a rather illogical expression when you think about it."

I half laughed, but it came out a groan as the pain sharpened abruptly. "God, don't make me do that again."

"What I won't let you do is take Aedh form to return," he said, his voice still soft but edged with steel. "You are at your limits now."

I nodded. To be honest, I wasn't even sure I *could* take Aedh form again. Not until I'd regained some strength, anyway.

Footsteps clattered down the stairs and a second later Stane appeared. For once, he wasn't covered with dust and cobwebs, although his brown hair was still unruly and his jeans still wrinkled. But his short-sleeved white shirt had been ironed and he was actually wearing shoes rather than going about in bare feet.

"Liking the new look." I pushed into a more upright

position and winced as the needles in my head went into another stabbing frenzy. "I'm gathering you've got a hot date?"

Stane gave Azriel a nod of greeting, and knelt in front of me. "Actually, Mom's coming for a visit. I thought I'd better clean up."

My gaze swept the downstairs area. It was small, cluttered, and smelled of dust and mold. There were shelves everywhere, all packed with boxes, old and new computer parts, and ancient-looking monitors of varying sizes.

Of course, mold and dust weren't exactly good for computers or the various other bits of electronic equipment scattered about, but I'd learned a while ago that this area was little more than a ruse. The expensive items were all kept upstairs.

"I wouldn't have bothered," I said. "She's going to take one look at this area and have a heart attack. Your normal state is positively pristine compared to all this."

"Oh, she knows *exactly* what I'm like, but she likes me to make an effort on a personal level when she's visiting." His gaze scanned me pensively. "You look as if you need Coke, painkillers, and food—and not necessarily in that order."

"One and two would be good," I said. "We haven't got time for the third."

"Then I shall run ahead and get them ready." He paused, his gaze falling on the disks I still clenched in my hands. "They for me?"

I nodded. "I need them copied quickly so I can return them before they're missed." And before *I* was missed. Rhoan might have said he'd given up resisting the inevitable, but I suspected that wasn't entirely true—not when it came to my chasing down leads without his input.

Stane took the disks and gave them the once-over. "You're lucky I never throw anything out. They stopped production of these disks at least ten years ago."

"Not surprised. I just hope they're okay—they've been stored in a shed for a while."

"As long as the container was airtight and out of direct sunlight, they should be all right. They have a long life span." He pushed to his feet. "I'll see you both up there."

I watched him bound back up the stairs and wished I had half his energy.

"You could," Azriel commented, "if you didn't push yourself so much."

I gave him a somewhat wry look. "The lack of sleep isn't entirely my fault, buddy boy."

He nodded in agreement. "But I was not aware it would affect you so. Next time I shall be more cautious."

I raised my eyebrows and tried to ignore the sudden jump in my pulse rate. "I thought you said there would be no next time."

He studied me, his face giving as little away as usual. "It was merely a figure of speech, not an indication of intent."

In other words, what he wanted and what he intended were two totally different things.

He rose, the movement abrupt. "Do you want help to get up?"

I put my hand in his and let him haul me upright. For several seconds the room did a drunken dance around me, and it was only his grip that kept me upright. Eventually, the pain and dizziness eased. I took a deep, somewhat shaky breath, and glanced down. My clothes, as usual, hadn't exactly come through the Aedh shift in one piece.

My jeans had fared the best, with only a couple of small holes dotting the calf area. The dust from the missing patches clung to the skin visible underneath, giving my leg a weird blue sheen. My tank top was rather ragged around the edges and now had ventilation across my belly button, but it was at least still wearable. The same could not be said about my panties, which were little more than annoying bits caught in unmentionable places. One of these days I was going to learn to keep a change of clothes in my purse—although it wouldn't have done me any good in this instance, because my purse was back in the shed.

"Ready to move?" Azriel asked.

I took another deep breath, then nodded and walked forward carefully. The needles in my head reacted, but not as fiercely as before, and by the time we reached the top of the stairs, I felt a little more normal. Or at least as normal as I ever got lately.

Stepping into Stane's inner sanctum was like stepping into another world—a world that was clean, shiny, and filled with the latest in computer technology. In fact, Stane's system dominated the main living area and wouldn't have looked out of place on a spaceship. There was a bathroom to our immediate left, and a bedroom farther down, although I doubt he used it much—he seemed to spend much of his life stationed at his bridge.

I grabbed one of the spare chairs near the computer and plunked down rather inelegantly. Stane came out of the kitchen area in the living room and handed me some painkillers and an open can of Coke.

"Thanks." I quickly downed both the pills and several large mouthfuls of fizzy soda, then swallowed a burp and added, "How long will the transfer take?"

He shrugged. "A couple of minutes. What are we looking for?"

"These disks came from the man who photographed Nadler's wedding. We're hoping that if we have a youngish picture of Mr. Elusive, we might be able to figure out what he should look like these days."

"Clever thinking." Stane pressed several buttons on the left console screen. On the right, thumbnail images flashed up. "And there's no maybe about it. I have a program that can age any facial image fed into it."

"Excellent." I wheeled the chair closer and indicated the thumbnails on the screen. "They from the first disk?"

"First and second," Stane confirmed. "How are we going to know which one is Nadler?"

"I was talking to his wife yesterday. It should be easy enough to pick her out." I leaned forward a little, scanning the images that were loaded onto the screen. "None of these is her."

He grunted and scrolled the screen over to the next page. "These are the third and fourth disks."

The first lot of images was a continuation of the previous ones, but a buxom blonde began appearing in the latter half. "That's Jacinta Nadler," I said, pointing.

"And a rather well-endowed lass she is," Stane said as he enlarged one of the pics. "Let me guess—she's a stripper or works as a topless waitress in a strip club."

"Not every woman who has large tits works in a strip club," I said dryly.

"Oh, I know, but she has the look."

"There's a look?"

He nodded. "It's mainly reserved for those who have been in the business for a while—there's a world-weariness evident in their eyes." He indicated her picture. "She's young here, but she's got it, which suggests she'd been working at the game for quite a few years before she married Nadler."

I remembered the impression I'd had that Jacinta Nadler had never been the innocent she made out to be—even at eighteen. "So how do you know so much about strippers and their game?"

He grinned. "Hacking into strip club security cams is an entertaining way to keep the skills up, not to mention have a bit of fun."

I snorted softly. "Why would a well-to-do business-man risk his reputation by marrying a stripper?"

Stane laughed. "Are you kidding? Look at her. I'm betting Nadler was in his forties when the two of them were hitched. She's blond and big-breasted—the classic type of woman men like him seem to go for when their midlife crisis happens."

"Yeah, but they don't often marry them." And I'd never thought to ask her how she'd met Nadler, which was stupid because it might have given us another means to find him. I frowned. "Don't suppose you could do a search on her, and see if you can pull up a bit of history?"

"Tax file records are probably our best bet if we want to know where she worked."

That had me raising my eyebrows. "You can get into the tax office records?"

He gave me the sort of look a teacher might bestow on a bright but inattentive student. "If I can get into the Directorate records, why would you think I couldn't get anywhere else? Trust me, the Directorate has the latest and greatest anti-hacking features."

"But it hasn't stopped you from accessing their system."

"Well, no. But it does take me longer these days." He wheeled across to the other screen and typed for several minutes.

I leaned forward and hit another of the images loading onto the screen. And there, standing beside a glowing Jacinta, was the man who had to be John Nadler.

He wasn't what I'd expected. He was tall, with thick black hair, an arrogant sort of nose, and lips that were little more than pale slashes in his thin face. His eyes were a cold, hard gray, and his body slender but wiry. He looked mean, I thought, and I wondered what the hell Jacinta had seen in him. Or was he merely a way out of a life she'd hated—a life she'd been forced to return to after he'd all but destroyed her?

"Okay," Stane said, wheeling back to my side of his bridge. "Search under way. It shouldn't take that long."

I indicated the picture on the screen. "Meet Mr. Elusive himself."

"If his eyes are any indication, he's not the sort of man you'd want to run into on a dark night."

"You don't need to see his eyes to guess that," I murmured. "Anyone who'd set a soul stealer onto a little girl is someone with very little in the way of compassion or humanity."

He grunted, flashed the photo onto another screen, then opened it in an app and began to work on it. Within a couple of minutes, we had several different photos of just what Nadler might look like now.

"That one," Azriel said, pointing at the third image on the screen, "is the Nadler Logan saw. Only he had a small scar near his left temple."

The image he pointed to was basically a more lined, silver-haired version of the younger Nadler. "Jacinta didn't mention a temple scar, so Nadler must have acquired that after he'd divorced her."

Stane glanced at us. "I gather the Logan you're talking about is Nadler's lawyer?"

I nodded. "He was murdered last night."

"Shit." Stane scraped a hand across his jaw. "This fucker means business."

"We already knew that."

"Yeah, but to kill off someone so closely involved in his current business dealings could make a bit of a mess of said dealings."

"Not necessarily. Logan's practice wasn't a solo one, was it?"

"Well, no—"

"So I'm betting one of the other partners knows enough to take over the reins. Our fake Nadler wouldn't risk jeopardizing his plans by having no one else up-to-date on the lay of the land, so to speak."

"I guess." He studied the image for a moment, then pointed to the scar on Nadler's forehead. "That looks fairly serious. Might be worth checking to see how it was acquired."

I frowned. "If he *is* a face-shifter, it wouldn't matter. He can simply make it disappear when he reverts to his regular self."

"Yeah, but there're certain wounds that are impossible for *any* shifter to heal. Those made with silver, for instance, will always leave a scar, and sometimes the wound can be so deep that scarring is inevitable." He looked at me. "You should know that, given how many scars your Aunt Riley has."

Good point. "Can you do a disk print of those for me? And send a copy of the younger and older Nadler to my phone? I'll need to give the disks to Uncle Rhoan, but I want some images to work with myself." And at least if I gave him the disk, he wouldn't be as shitty with me when he realized I'd already copied them. And he would—the tattered state of my clothes would be enough of a giveaway to someone who knew what I was.

Stane nodded, clicked a button, then flicked the pictures into another program on the other side of the desk. "I'll run a search on all the photos and see if I can find a match on any system."

"He has to exist somewhere." He couldn't disappear off everyone's radar once he'd left the office—not if he wanted to maintain credibility as Nadler. And he could hardly kill off every single person who currently knew him. That would only make it easier for the Directorate to connect the dots.

Stane rose and walked across to the printer sitting on the coffee table—although just why it was there rather than closer to his bridge was anyone's guess. He came back with a disk. "All possibilities are recorded on this."

"Thanks." I shoved the minute disk into my jeans pocket—there was just enough fabric left to hold it in place. I finished my drink, then pushed to my feet. "We'd better get back."

He gathered Blake's disks and handed them to me. "I'll let you know if we get any hits."

I leaned forward and kissed him on the cheek. "Thanks, Stane."

He grinned. "My pleasure. As I keep saying, the black market is positively boring after you lot."

"Well, I'd rather have *your* boring life than my exciting one at the moment."

"Everyone always thinks the other person has it better," was his somewhat philosophical comment. "It's the way of humanity."

It might be the way of humanity, but in this case, he was very wrong. I glanced at Azriel. "I'm ready to go."

He wrapped his arms around me, nodded a goodbye to Stane, and then his energy surged, flooding through me, sweeter and sharper than before. As were the gray fields in the few brief moments between leaving Stane's and reappearing in Blake's shed.

"Whoa." I grabbed Azriel's arm tightly as the shed reeled around me. I waited until everything settled, then added, "Why did the fields appear so much clearer this time?"

He half shrugged. "Perhaps you're merely getting used to traveling with me, and therefore are more able to understand what you see."

Which was totally logical, yet not the real answer—but why I was so certain about this I couldn't say.

"I usually see delicate-looking structures, but this time they just seemed more solid." I hesitated. "And there were beings—or at least, wisps of them. Sort of like souls."

"They could have been souls under escort." He shrugged again and walked over to Jak. "We've lost our watcher, by the way."

I glanced around—a pointless action when I'd never been able to see our Cazador follower in astral form. "Really?"

"Yes. It would appear he loses the connection when we take alternate form."

"Then it's a shame I haven't the strength to take it more often." It would have been nice to be able to follow up on leads without Hunter knowing our every move.

Azriel touched Jak on the neck, and disappeared. Jak blinked; then his gaze focused on me and he said, "I guess making a run for it with the disks is out of the question?"

It took me a moment to realize he was continuing the conversation we'd been having before Azriel froze him. "You can try, but that will only lead to the access we've been given to the crime site being abruptly withdrawn. Besides, Uncle Rhoan isn't only half wolf; he's half vampire, too. You wouldn't have any hope of outrunning him."

"So we lose the information we came here to get?" he said, frustration evident in his voice.

"No, we won't. Just trust me, okay?"

He frowned, and then his gaze swept me. "How come your clothes are suddenly tatty? And how the hell did your hair change color?"

"Long story. Let's get these back to Uncle Rhoan before he comes looking for us."

I grabbed my purse and walked out. He was very quickly beside me. "You're avoiding the question."

"Too right."

"Why? What are you hiding?"

"Secrets, of course." I gave him a somewhat wry glance. "Secrets I'm not about to reveal to a reporter, let alone the one who besmirched my mom's name."

He was silent for a moment, then said slowly, "Nadler's not the only one who's a face-shifter, is he?"

I didn't say anything. He grinned. "That's it. *That's* the secret. Or at least one of them. I suspect you have a whole lot more, because from what I understand of face-shifting, it doesn't destroy clothes like shifting into wolf form can."

"And you've talked to lots of face-shifters to confirm this, have you?" I asked.

"Ha. Confirmation of my guess. Where'd the skill come from—your mom?"

I glanced at him. "You're the one who did the extensive background check on my mom. You tell me."

He grimaced. "Pack background wasn't something I could pin down. But if she *was* a face-shifter, she had to be a Helki. No other pack has that skill."

"You know I'm not going to confirm or deny anything, so give it up."

"And you know I won't. I'm afraid you've become something of a challenge to me."

I shook my head and pushed the gate open. Uncle Rhoan was just stepping around the side of the house. His gaze swept down and came to rest briefly on the disks I held before continuing on, taking in the state of my clothing. His gaze had narrowed by the time it met mine, but all he said was, "Any luck?"

"These disks are the ones Blake took on the day Nadler was married." I slipped the smaller one into his hand, as well. "That last one could prove useful when it comes to looking for the current Nadler."

He nodded and pocketed the disks. "Where are you two off to now?"

"What, now we have to report our every move to you?" Jak said.

"If you want to remain out of jail and on this case, yes," Rhoan said, rather mildly considering the spark of annoyance that flared in his eyes.

I touched Jak's arm, stopping him from saying anything else, and said, "Nadler's lawyer was murdered last night. We might go talk to his secretary, and see if it was somehow connected to Nadler, or if he was working on anything else that might have warranted his death."

Rhoan continued to eye me dubiously. He knew me well enough to understand that I was planning a whole lot more than that. "I don't suppose you were at that fund-raiser last night, were you?"

"Yes. We found the body and called the cops, in fact." There was no sense denying it, because he could easily enough trace the call back to my phone.

"And the murder? Did you also witness it?"

"We would have hung around if we had."

His expression was somewhat disbelieving. "You should have hung around anyway."

I grimaced. "I had somewhere else I had to be. I couldn't."

"Doesn't explain why Jak didn't hang around."

Jak just shrugged. Truth be told, he was probably wondering why he hadn't hung around also.

Rhoan grunted. It wasn't a happy sound. "I won't tell you not to talk to Logan's secretary, because you'll just go ahead and do it anyway. But I do expect you to keep me up-to-date with what—if anything—you discover. Because believe me, if I find out you're keeping stuff back, I will throw your asses in jail until this is all over. And not even my sister will get you out of it."

I knew an ultimatum when I heard one, so I simply nodded. He continued to eye me for several seconds, then stepped to one side and allowed us to pass.

"Well," Jak said, once we were clear of the house and walking back to our cars, "that was intense."

"Yep. And he was deadly serious about throwing us in jail."

"I gathered that, so keep the man updated, for Christ's sake."

I flashed him a grin. "What? You don't fancy cooling your heels in jail with me?"

"Sorry, no. I've been in jail once when I ignored a judge's 'no-print' order." He shuddered briefly. "I don't care to repeat the experience—even with you."

I snorted softly. "Do you think you can use your wily press ways to uncover where the secretary lives?"

"*That* isn't even a challenge for a reporter as good as me."

I rolled my eyes and leaned my butt against the side of his car while he made several phone calls. Eventually he turned and said, "Okay, she lives in a town house in Doncaster—you want to come with me?"

I shook my head. "It'll save you driving me back here."

"I wouldn't mind—"

"I would. You and me trapped in a small car is not a good idea."

"You don't trust me? I'm mortified."

"A statement that would be more believable if you didn't have that smirk on your face." I pushed away from the car. "Just give me the address and I'll meet you there."

He did. "Better not be late—I just might start questioning her without you."

"Better not. I'm all that's standing between you and jail, remember."

He snorted. "The way things are going, you'll be the reason I'm thrown in jail."

I grinned, but couldn't deny it. As I headed for my car, my phone rang. I dug it out of my purse and hit the ANSWER button. "Hello?"

"Well, hello," a familiar voice said. "Are we over our snit yet?"

I ignored the jibe. "What can I do for you, Lucian?"

"Oh, I can think of lots of things, but I'll settle for a simple dinner date."

There was nothing simple about dinner dates with him—that I knew from long experience. "I'm afraid the snit lingers on, so the answer is no."

He sighed. "Risa, we both know that you could have stopped me anytime you wanted. You simply didn't want."

That was possibly true—if I'd had Amaya on me and had forced him back at sword point. I doubted I'd have had the strength—or rather, the willpower—to do it otherwise. Which, again, struck me as odd because up until now I'd never been a pushover when it came to men and sex. But then, up until now I'd never been involved with a full Aedh, either.

"That's not the point, Lucian."

"What if I swear on bended knees not to push against your desire like that again?"

"Then I might forgive you," I said with a half smile. "Just not today. After all, you did bet that I'd only last two nights without you."

"I will hold my tongue in the future," he said, with a laugh. "So, what have you been up to without me? I'm guessing your father hasn't been in contact with you about finding the next key?"

"No. Life has been the same old, same old, I'm afraid."

"Meaning you're at work?" he inquired. "Against the reaper's wishes?"

"Azriel doesn't run my life any more than you do," I said mildly—and, hopefully, sidestepped the question of where I was.

"Perhaps, but he does have a point when it comes to your restaurant. It's too easy for the Raziq to find you there."

"Except, as I keep telling him, they're hardly going to attack me somewhere where there's lots of people." But even as I said that, I remembered the Ania attack in the café and shivered. And I had a bad feeling I'd just tempted fate.

"If it proves easier for the Raziq to net you in a public space, then they will do so. For an Aedh, the end goal is all and nothing else matters."

"And what is your end goal, Lucian?"

"Revenge," he said flatly. "Whatever it takes, whatever I have to do. But I've never hidden that from you."

No, he hadn't. But I was beginning to wonder just how big a part I was playing in his end goal. It was certainly bigger than what he was admitting, and *that* was making me more and more nervous.

And yet I still didn't want to walk away from him. Maybe I really *was* addicted to the damn man.

"Well, this little piece of your revenge pie isn't ready to play nice just yet." I dug my keys out of my pocket and clicked the UNLOCK button. Lights flashed as the car opened.

"You know, that background noise isn't sounding like you're in the restaurant."

"I never said I was."

"So, the bored and horny investment adviser isn't even allowed to live vicariously through your eventful day-to-day life?"

I snorted softly. "Good-bye, Lucian. Talk to you soon."

"Hopefully, sooner than you—"

I cut him off in midsentence, tossed the phone and purse over onto the passenger seat, then climbed into the car.

And only then realized I wasn't alone in the car.

Chapter 10

For a moment, fear froze me to the spot. And that's all it took for the Ania to wrap tightly around me and prevent movement. Amaya was screaming inside my head, her fury burning through my body and her flames flickering across my skin like angry fireflies.

"Azriel!" I screamed, physically and mentally, even as the Ania ripped me free of the seat and the car. I felt the heat of his approach. Then power exploded and there was no Azriel, no world, only darkness and an uneasy sense of movement.

It stopped with a suddenness that made my stomach lurch, and then I was dropped rather unceremoniously onto a surface that was cool and dry. Dirt, I thought, spitting it out of my mouth in between groans. I drew Amaya, then rolled onto my back. Her purple light spread across the black, parting it like glue. Rock surrounded me—above and around. I was in a cavern of some sort, and there didn't seem to be either an entry or an exit point. My tomb—for that's what it suddenly felt like—was about four feet wide and about the same height. I could kneel, but I couldn't fully stand. But a breeze stirred sluggishly across my skin, which meant there *was* a link to the surface here somewhere, even if the air had a stale, somewhat old scent. And that in itself suggested not only that there wasn't a whole lot of fresh air getting down here, but also that I was deep underground.

And if I *was*, it meant Azriel wouldn't find me. My being underground restricted our chi connection, and the deeper I was, the worse it became—although apparently such restrictions *didn't* apply when reapers collected the souls of miners and others who died underground. Not that I was making any immediate plans for him to find me *that* way. What the Raziq planned was anyone's guess.

I glanced up at the ceiling again, and this time noticed a faint, multicolored shimmer that reminded me of oil on water. I swore softly. *That* shimmer was a field of magic designed to prevent me from reaching for the Aedh—something I'd discovered the hard way the last time the Raziq trapped me underground. I guess I had to be thankful that at least *this* time their prison wasn't a sewer.

I sat up. As I did so, an oddly dark surge of electricity ran across my skin, making the little hairs at the back of my neck stand on end and my soul shiver away in fear.

The Aedh were near.

Fear slammed into my heart and for several seconds I struggled to breathe. I closed my eyes and battled for calm. I couldn't give in to fear—not when I needed all my wits about me to survive whatever it was the Raziq had planned. Although what good mere survival would do me in this place deep underground I had no idea. It wasn't like I could run anywhere, even if I'd wanted to. With that shimmer in place, my tomb had no exit point.

"I know you're there." My voice was croaky with fear but sounded oddly flat in the thick atmosphere of the little cavern.

"Sheathe your weapon. It will do you no good."

The disembodied male voice held no threat, but it nevertheless sent a chill down my spine. This was the Raziq I'd spoken to last time—the Raziq that had invaded my brain and made it seem like every part of me was being torn apart.

I licked my lips and somehow said, "Then you shouldn't be worried about me holding it."

The lilac-lit shadows showed no hint of them—not surprising, I suppose. It wasn't like they'd shown a propensity to reveal themselves in our previous encounters.

"Why do human always have to make things difficult for themselves?" he asked, almost philosophically.

I raised Amaya. The sword howled inside my head, a scream that was part anger, part frustration. Her fire spat through the thick darkness and, just for a moment, I saw him—or rather, saw the shimmer of his energy, because he was little more than a pulsating mass of quicksilver. Then it disappeared and all that was left was a sensation of power—power that was amplifying, growing stronger, burning my skin as it skimmed around my arms and snapped tight.

The minute it did, it felt like my arms were on fire. They burned and burned, until it felt like flesh and muscle were being peeled away layer by layer, until all that was left was bone. Bone that fissured and cracked as the flames continued to eat down. I screamed until my throat was raw and no sound came out, but somehow, through it all, I still managed to hold on to Amaya. Energy flowed from her, fueling my body, feeding my will to resist.

But the flames grew stronger, and one by one my fingers began to shatter, until there was nothing left to hold the sword. She fell to the floor, her scream an echo of my own. The power eating my flesh slithered from my arms and wrapped around her. She slid across the floor, well away from both me and the Aedh, and was suddenly silenced. It made the thick atmosphere within the tomb even more frightening and, for a moment, I feared the worst. Then I noticed firefly flickers down her bright edges. They might have silenced the spirit within the sword, but they certainly hadn't killed her.

Relief surged, but for several minutes I could do nothing more than rock back and forth, nursing the broken remnants of my arms as tears streamed down my face. Eventually, the pain eased, and when I finally gathered the courage to look down at my hands, they were whole and unburned.

It had been an illusion. A painful, all-too-real illusion.

"Bastards," I said, scrubbing an arm across my tear-stained face and silently rejoicing for the fact that I could do it.

"We desire your help," the disembodied voice said, "and we will get it, whether you wish to cooperate with us or not."

"You can guess which end of that spectrum I'm going to fall on," I said resolutely and no doubt stupidly.

But I just couldn't give these beings what they wanted, because, in the end, what they wanted was the permanent closure of the portals to heaven and hell. And that, in turn, meant no souls ever being reborn. Not only would the world become filled with the ghosts of those unable to move on, but many of the babies born would be without their assigned souls, and therefore they would be little more than lifeless flesh.

"You would be wise to reconsider your options," he said. "It would be easier for you if you willingly comply."

I snorted softly. "Since when has my welfare been a consideration in any of our dealings?"

"It isn't. It is merely practicality."

"Well, you can take your practicality and shove it where the sun don't shine."

"You do not wish to acquiesce?" His energy began to build again, a maelstrom of power that rumbled like distant thunder across the outer edges of my senses.

Amaya flared brighter, her flames a furious swirl. I could've sworn that just for a moment she moved.

I hugged my arms a little tighter. I knew what was coming. Knew, and feared it. And part of me needed to delay it for as long as I could. Maybe if I did, Azriel might find me. Save me.

A false hope was better than no hope.

I swallowed heavily and said, "What is it you want?"

He paused, as if that was a question he hadn't been expecting. "We wish your help in finding your father."

"That's not exactly true. You want the keys."

"That is our ultimate objective, yes. To achieve it, we need Hieu."

"My father might know the general direction of the keys, but he can't actually find them for you. Which means you need me, as well."

And that meant that no matter what they did to me, they couldn't actually kill me. It wasn't much comfort, however—not given what they'd already done.

"Your father knows the location of the keys, so actually finding them should not present a problem for him. You are not so much of a concern."

"I beg to differ—if he could find the keys himself, he would have done so by now. But only one of his flesh can find the keys and, thanks to you guys, he can no longer take on flesh. So, logically, that leaves me."

Of course, it was a statement that presumed he was actually telling the truth when it came to the keys, and I had a vague suspicion he wasn't. Not entirely, anyway.

"What has been undone can be redone," the disembodied voice said evenly. "That is not a concern."

I was betting it was, because otherwise I'd have been dead. "You held my father prisoner, so why didn't you force him to help you then?"

A slight shimmer of energy snagged my attention, simply because it *wasn't* the darker energy belonging to the Raziq. I frowned, my gaze scanning the little cavern before coming to rest on Amaya.

She was definitely *closer*.

I had no idea how the hell she was achieving it, but I wasn't about to question it. Having her in my hand probably wouldn't make any difference to my situation, considering how the Raziq had divested me of her in the first place, but my fingers still itched to wrap around her hilt. She gave me strength and made me feel safer—something I'd never thought possible when Azriel had first produced her.

"That," the Raziq said, his voice no different and yet suddenly so filled with menace, "is knowledge you do not require."

I licked my lips and said, "How am I supposed to find my father when he's always been the one who's contacted me?"

"We will give you a device that will notify us when you are in his presence."

"Exactly what sort of device?" Amaya was almost within reach of a sideways lunge. I shivered and resisted the temptation to move. "And how does it work?"

"It is attuned to Hieu's life force and will react when he is near. We will be notified."

"My father is smart enough to realize what the device is the minute he sees it." She was close, so close. My fingers twitched and tension began to wind through my muscles. "He'll get the hell out of there before you lot ever make an appearance."

"We do not agree."

I snorted. "Of course you wouldn't. I mean, you've had such great success trying to track him down so far, haven't you?"

"*He* is not so important. The keys are."

If he wasn't so important, they wouldn't be doing their damnedest to find him. "You've got one key— why can't you just make a couple more?"

He didn't answer immediately, but his energy surged around me, singeing the hairs on the back of my neck and making my skin crawl.

Anger. No, not just anger. Fury.

Maybe they weren't as unemotional as everyone believed—at least not when it came to people thwarting their desires.

"We do not have the key for the first portal. Your father has it."

No, he bloody well hasn't. I was pretty sure of that, if nothing else. Whoever *had* stolen the key was someone entrenched in magic—magic that was dark, ungodly, and bitter. And while the Raziq's magic was dark, what I'd felt of my father's wasn't. Not to the same degree, anyway.

But if my father or the Raziq *didn't* have the first key, that meant it *had* to have been a dark practitioner who'd stolen it from under our noses—and, more than likely, it was the same dark practitioner who'd been buying up the land around Stane's—a dark practitioner who was also a face-shifter.

As a general rule, sorcerers weren't able to walk the gray fields, but ley-line intersections were places of great power and could be used not only to manipulate time, reality, or fate, but to create rifts between this world and the next. A powerful enough sorcerer could enter the fields via the intersection and find the gates.

Which is precisely what our thief had done—walked the fields, and permanently opened the first portal to hell.

Still, it must have taken a whole lot of energy . . .

Shit—why hadn't we thought of that before? That might well provide a way of tracking down this bastard . . .

I shoved the thought aside. *That* was an avenue I

could explore later, when every little thought wasn't being listened to by the Raziq.

I flicked a sideways glance at Amaya. Almost there. "So why not make more keys? I mean, you all had a finger in the pie of the first lot, didn't you?"

"If by saying that you mean the Raziq as a whole were involved in their creation, then yes."

"Then why bother with me or my father at all? Why not just make more keys?"

"Because each key was attuned to a specific portal. Unless they are unmade, more cannot be created."

So my father hadn't lied—the keys *could* be destroyed. If nothing else came out of this little session, at least we had that.

Although destroying them would just allow the Raziq to create more—which meant we were damned if we did and damned if we didn't. Personally, I'd rather see the stupid things remain as they were, lost to everyone, but it seemed I was the only one who felt that way. Even Azriel thought it was far too dangerous to leave them undiscovered.

"Are you going to cooperate?" the Raziq added.

I took a deep, shuddering breath. Thought about consequences. Knew I had no choice.

"No."

As I said it, I lunged for Amaya. I never got there.

The pain hit like a sledgehammer, knocking me sideways and damn near senseless in the process. I lay on the dirt in a quivering heap, battling to breathe as their dark energy tore through every part of me and my brain felt like it was on fire.

Because this wasn't *just* a psychic attack. It went far

deeper than that. It was an attack on my body and soul, and it felt like every fiber of my being screamed in agony. Only I made no noise because the sound seemed to be stuck somewhere inside my throat.

The torture continued, on and on, until I was raw and battered and bruised. My skin ran with rivers of blood that soaked into my clothes and deep into the earth, until the bitter smell of it stung the air and burned my throat. And still it went on, until it felt like they were pulling me apart atom by atom, until there was nothing left of me but a screaming, bloody mass of separated particles.

Eventually—mercifully—I blacked out.

But it was a state that lasted nowhere near long enough. As I climbed backed to consciousness, the dark energy of the Raziq still burned at me. It hurt—god, how it hurt—yet within that energy, something fierce and bright burned, calling to me.

Amaya.

She lay underneath my hand. All I had to do was grasp her . . . and do what?

I had no idea. I was working on pure instinct now, totally incapable of any actual thought processes.

My fingers twitched; felt metal. Somehow, I found the strength to grasp her.

I expected fury. Expected to be hit once again by the illusionary flames that had burned her from my grip the first time. But nothing happened. The dark energy continued to flow through me, this time rebuilding rather than tearing apart. My body continued to shudder, scream, but Amaya burned brighter in my mind, her energy flowing through me, giving me strength.

The dark energy began to ease, trickling away like water down a drain, leaving me a quivering, broken wreck.

Now, an alien voice whispered through my brain.

I didn't think. I just obeyed.

I forced my eyes open. Amaya was dark and ghostly, giving no hint of the fierceness that burned within her—and within me. Beyond her, I saw the shimmer that was the energy of the Raziq who'd attacked me.

I drew Amaya back and threw her. It wasn't a strong throw—it couldn't be, not after everything I'd just been through.

It didn't matter. Amaya flew straight and true, flaring to glorious life just as her black blade buried itself in the heart of that dark shimmer. Purple fire exploded as Amaya's flames wrapped around the Raziq's energy, capturing it, drawing it back into herself. Feeding on him.

He screamed. *Screamed.* As I'd screamed—long and hard—until his voice was raw and he could scream no more. If I'd had the energy I would have danced with joy.

There was another explosion, and the force of it shifted me sideways several inches. The flames and the Raziq were gone, leaving only blessed silence.

Amaya slid across the floor toward me, and almost of their own accord, my fingers wrapped around her again. She felt heavy in my hand. Sated.

Somehow I managed to sheathe her. We might have killed one Raziq, but there were plenty more where he'd come from. I didn't want them forcing me to drop her again, and the fact that they *hadn't* seen her either in my hand or in flight made me suspect that if she was sheathed or cloaked, they couldn't.

I lay there waiting for the hammer to fall, my body on fire, every part of me aching and my clothes wet with blood and god knows what else. I stank of fear and sweat and blood and urine, and I knew it wasn't over yet. Not by a long shot.

That oily, rainbow shimmer still crawled across the roof of my tomb, so the Raziq were still here even if I was no longer capable of sensing them. Not that I would have been able to call to the Aedh even if they *hadn't* been present—I just didn't have the strength or will.

"That," a new voice said, "was unexpected."

Which had to be the understatement of the century.

"But at least," he continued, "the transfer was completed."

"What—" I licked dry lips. It didn't help much, because I had little in the way of saliva. "Transfer?"

"As you would not agree to use the device, we placed it within you."

Well, it won't be there for fucking long, I thought resolutely. I didn't say anything, but then, I didn't need to.

"If you remove it," the Raziq said, voice still amazingly calm considering I'd just killed one of them. But he *was* Aedh—practical, unemotional, cold. As long as their objective had been achieved, I doubted they'd care how many of their number I killed. "You will die."

Fear crawled inside me. "Why?"

"Because it cannot be removed. It *will* cease functioning if you die, but I suspect you would not wish that."

He suspected right. But that didn't actually mean I had to believe him. Aedh might be cold and unemotional, but I had no doubt they weren't above lying if it suited their needs.

"Indeed," the voice agreed. "But in this case, there is no need. The device was interwoven into the fabric of your heart when we re-formed you. To take it out, you must take out your heart."

Oh, *fuck*. Two words that *really* didn't seem adequate enough for the shit I was now in.

"Why would you do something like that?"

"You would not aid us. This way, we know your location at any moment, and we will know when your father nears you."

Meaning they'd have me *and* my father. *Fuck, fuck, fuck!*

Then his words hit me. I might have fallen deeper into the shithole, but it might just have one silver lining . . .

"Does this mean you won't be sending Ania and other assorted demons against me and my friends?"

"We will know where you are at any given moment. There is no need for us to do anything else."

Which at least meant I could sleep in my own bed again. The relief that surged at that thought said a lot about the sorry state of my life at the moment.

The dark energy rose again and I cringed, hating the cowardice even as I did it. But it wasn't *his* energy—it was Ania. They spun around me, blanketing me with their ethereal forms, whisking me into that place of black nothingness and uneasy movement.

Then, suddenly, I was back in the car.

But not for long. Arms gathered me and held me close, and the sensation of movement hit again. This time, instead of darkness there were silver buildings and insubstantial beings. Then they were gone and I was back in the hotel room, cradled against a body that was warm and strong.

I didn't say anything. I *couldn't* say anything. I just wrapped my arms around Azriel's neck and held on tight. Not that he appeared to be in a hurry to release me.

His warm energy spread through me in gentle waves, chasing away the chills, healing the hurt, soothing the aches. After what felt like ages, I took a deep, shuddering breath, and said, "You have no idea how glad I am to see you."

"Actually, I do, because I am reading your thoughts." His voice was calm, yet there was an undercurrent within it that spoke of violence.

I opened my eyes and shifted just enough to look up at him. Even that small movement hurt, but it was more a dull ache than the frenzied needle stabbing I'd been half expecting.

His eyes were dark with the fury barely hinted at in his voice. I raised a still trembling hand and ran my fingertips down his stubble-lined chin. "I'm okay, Azriel. They can't kill me. Not yet."

"They *unmade* you. That is death itself in many ways."

I let my fingers slip down his neck and placed my palm over his heart. Its beat was strong and steady and real, and it somehow made me feel even safer than being cradled in his arms.

"At least they put me back together again," I said eventually.

"But you are not as you were. You are now tied to Raziq and it cannot be undone."

Not unless I die. Fear crawled into my stomach and I swallowed heavily. "I know. But at least I can go home now, and I don't have to worry about Ilianna and Tao falling afoul of them."

"There is that."

He strode toward the bathroom. Once inside, he carefully placed me on my feet, then held me as the bathroom did a brief but dizzy dance around me.

"God," I said, swallowing bile, "I hope that doesn't happen too often."

"You need to rest." He gently began to strip the remnants of my clothing from my body. "And eat."

"I know. But there's also Jak—"

"No." He said it softly, but his tone suggested that in this he would brook no arguments.

"Azriel, we need—"

"No," he repeated. "Do not make me force you to rest, Risa."

"But Jak will be waiting—"

"I will visit Jak and alter his memories. You, for once, will do as you're told."

I half smiled. "Given that I'm in no fit state to argue, I'll obey. But don't expect such easy compliance next time."

"Oh," he said, his gaze coming to mine. Humor crinkled his lips and teased the corners of his eyes. "*That* is one thing I never expect when it comes to you."

"You knew the task was dangerous when you took

it on," I said wryly. "You have no one to blame but yourself."

"Indeed," he agreed. He turned on the shower taps, then slid his fingers down to my elbow. "Can you manage to shower yourself, or do you wish assistance?"

At any other time I would have voted for assistance, simply because it would have led to a whole lot more. But I didn't even have the energy for anything resembling a sexual urge, let alone desire.

"I'll be fine." With my fingers pressed against the glass side of the shower, I stepped in cautiously and raised my face to the water. Its warmth ran down my body, washing away the grit, blood, and whatever else was sticky on my skin.

Azriel didn't release me immediately, his grip still on my elbow, as if he expected me to fall down at any minute. "Are you sure you're all right?"

I opened my eyes and looked at him. "Yes. And thank you."

He raised an eyebrow. "What for?"

"For knowing when to do nothing more than hold me."

"That," he said softly, "will never be a problem."

He reached out and gently ran his fingers up my chin to my lips. It hurt, even though his touch was light. He dropped his hand, his fingers suddenly clenched. "I will order your meal and then go take care of Jak. Call if you need me."

I nodded, my skin still aching from his touch. Once he'd left, I simply stood there, letting the heat of the water chase the chill from my flesh and wishing it could do the same to the odd knot of coldness deep inside of me.

After what seemed like ages, I sighed and washed myself properly, then grabbed a towel and stepped out of the shower. One look in the mirror revealed the reason why Azriel's soft touch had hurt so much. Half my face was bruised, and there were similar blotches all over my body. It was as if in taking me apart so brutally, the Raziq had damaged the very fabric of me. And it made the bruises I'd received when I'd been knocked off my bike seem mild in comparison.

My bike . . . damn, in all the madness I'd forgotten about her. And while a bent and busted Ducati sat pretty low on the scale of immediate problems, it was at least something that had a clear path of action.

Unlike everything else in my goddamn life at the moment.

I swung around and went in search of my phone, then remembered I'd left it in the rear of the rental car. Which was unlocked, with the keys sitting inside. If it hadn't been stolen, it would be a goddamn miracle.

I scanned the room, found the hotel's phone, and rang Lonny to see what the damage was.

"Well, it ain't pretty." His voice held even more of a drawl than usual, and that probably meant bad news. "We can fix her, but it's going to cost. Spare parts for that model are a bitch to find."

"I don't care what it takes. Fix her."

He grunted. "Figured you'd say that, so I've already started ringing my sources. You want an estimate or shall I just go ahead?"

"Just do it." Money wasn't a problem, and even if it

had been, I wouldn't have cared. She was the first thing I'd ever purchased with my own money, and I'd be damned if I let her go. Besides, she was a reminder of the sane, normal life I wanted—a life that seemed to be slipping further and further away from me. "Thanks, Lonny."

"I'll be in contact if we have a problem," he said, then hung up.

I rang Ilianna next, getting an update on Tao—who was still improving but not yet conscious—and asking her to alter the power of her wards so that Azriel could get into our apartment.

The doorbell rang as I said good-bye to her. Figuring it was probably the meal Azriel said he'd order, I shouted, "Hang on a minute," then quickly threw on a shirt and jeans. I grabbed some of the change I'd dumped onto the bedside table the night before and walked across the room to open the door.

"Just put it—" The words froze in my throat.

Because it wasn't *just* a waiter and one of those new hover trays standing outside my door. A grinning Lucian stood behind them.

"Ma'am?" the waiter said politely.

"Oh, yeah, just put that over on the table." I stepped aside and waited until the tray and the waiter had moved past, then quickly raised a hand to stop Lucian. In a heated whisper I added, "How the hell did you find me?"

"I simply phoned hotels asking to speak to you until I found which one you were staying in."

Damn, I should have thought of that. Next time I wanted to hide from the world, I'd better use a false name! "But you didn't leave a message."

"No. I thought you'd have a harder time ignoring me if I simply turned up." His gaze suddenly fixated on my face and his smile faded. "You've been in the hands of the Raziq, haven't you?"

I hesitated, but it was pointless denying it. And I guess if he was going to help us find the remaining keys, he had to know just how much deeper the shit-hole had gotten. "Yes."

He swore softly. "How the hell did that happen? Why didn't the reaper stop it?"

"He couldn't—"

"It's his job to *protect* you."

His voice had sharpened significantly, and the waiter glanced over at us. I gave him what I hoped was a reassuring smile, then met Lucian's angry gaze and added softly, "He *is*. But it's not that simple."

"It fucking *is*—"

"Lucian," I cut in. "Enough. I'll explain."

"Then explain." He glanced down at my hand. "But I would suggest you allow me to come in first."

I dropped my hand and waved him inside. The waiter had finished setting out my meal, and approached with the tray in tow. "Will that be all, ma'am?"

"Yes, thank you." I gave him the change as a tip, then closed the door behind him.

Lucian stood in the middle of the room, his arms crossed and his stance radiating displeasure. "So, explain."

Rather than answering immediately, I walked over to the table and lifted the lid off the various plates. Azriel had ordered steak, vegetables, and pasta, as well as several cream cakes. After a few minutes of dithering,

I picked up the triple-layer chocolate cake and started eating it. The steak and veggies might be the saner choice, but I needed the immediate sugar rush.

Lucian waited. Anger rolled off him, thick and heated. The little hairs on my arms stood on end, even as my pulse rate quickened. It wasn't exactly fear, and it wasn't a more sexual reaction, but rather sat somewhere in between. Which was kind of odd, because up until now I'd always reacted on a purely sexual level to his presence.

"Over the last couple of days," I said eventually, as I finished the cake and licked the cream from my fingertips, "the Raziq have made several attempts to capture me using Ania. We managed to thwart most of them, but we were simply caught off guard this last time."

"If they caught you off guard, then the reaper *isn't* doing his job," Lucian snapped. "He is sensitive to the creatures of hell—there is no known way they should have been able to sneak up on you."

"They didn't. They were transported in magically and were just *there*. There was nothing Azriel could have done to prevent it." I picked up my knife and fork, then glanced at him pointedly. "And *you* wouldn't have been able to do anything, either, so stop giving me attitude and just sit down. Having to look up at you is making my head ache."

He grunted, but pulled out one of the chairs and sat. "What, exactly, did the Raziq do?"

"From what they said, they unmade me and attached some sort of sensor to my heart. It'll inform them when I'm in my father's presence."

"Enabling them to capture him." His voice was

grim. "This is not good news for those of us wanting to keep the keys out of their hands."

"Exactly." Then I frowned and added, "'Those of us'? That's an odd way of putting it, isn't it?"

He shrugged. "Are you sure that's what they've done?"

"That's what they said they've done. And they definitely pulled me apart."

"The bruises are evidence enough of that." He leaned forward and placed a flat hand against my chest. It wasn't a sexual touch by any means, but my pulse still reacted to the warm press of his fingers. After a moment, he swore and sat back. "The dark energy of the tracer definitely beats within you."

I wasn't surprised, but my stomach still sank. I guess a tiny, foolish part of me had hoped the Raziq had been lying. Still, I couldn't help asking, "How can you be so sure?"

"Because I am not unfamiliar with such things. I've seen their use before."

"Where?"

"It was a long time ago, and doesn't matter now."

In other words, mind your own business. He and Azriel were more alike than they thought. "They said it cannot be removed."

His expression was grim. "It can't. Not unless you die."

Having Lucian confirm *that* particular fact made me feel sick. I put the knife and fork down and pushed the dinner plate away. "Which means the minute my father appears, they'll grab us both."

"Unfortunately, yes." He thrust to his feet and began

to pace, every movement reeking of frustration. "Which does not mean it cannot be stopped."

"The only way it can be stopped," Azriel said, appearing in the room in a sudden rush of heat and anger, "is via the use of dark magic. And *that* is never a wise choice."

Lucian swung around, his expression like thunder. The dislike that emanated off the pair of them made me feel like I was a red cape between two bulls.

"Lots of unwise choices have been made over the course of the last few weeks," Lucian spat out. "But we do what we must to reach the endgame, don't we, reaper?"

"Dark magic may be a path you choose to walk, Aedh, but it is not ours."

Lucian snorted and glanced at me. "If you believe he's not willing to do whatever it takes to get what he wants—and remember, what he wants is the same as what the Raziq want—then you are a fool."

"Actually," I said, rubbing my aching head wearily and wishing they'd both just leave me alone, "what I believe is that neither of you is telling me the entire truth when it comes to what you really want. That said, why do you both believe dark magic can null this thing inside me? Why not regular magic?"

"Because the tracker isn't of this time or place," Lucian said. "And regular magic would not combat it. Only dark magic has that chance."

I frowned. "But white magic is strong enough to combat dark, so why wouldn't it work against this?"

"Because what lies inside you is very different from the magic of this world," Azriel said. He stood on the other side of the table, his arms crossed and his face unreadable. But Valdis flickered with blue-black energy and the air around him seemed to shimmer with heat. "But that does not mean we should not explore the option."

Lucian snorted. "My wings may be clipped, reaper, but I am still Aedh. Believe me when I say that the magic of this world will not be strong enough to counter what lies within her."

"Which does not negate the fact that we should at least try it first," Azriel snapped. "Dark magic has a way of staining its users."

"Does that mean this thing inside me is dangerous?" I asked hesitantly.

Azriel glanced at me. "I do not know." Silently, he added, *Has Amaya reacted to it?*

I frowned. *She seems no worse now when it comes to background chatter than she was before the tracer was attached.*

If the tracer in your body does anything more than inform the Raziq of your father's presence, she will react to it. Until she does, you are probably safe.

It was the "probably" bit of that sentence that was worrying. I glanced at Lucian again. "If anyone can counter this tracer, it'll be the witches at the Brindle."

Lucian snorted and crossed his arms. "I do not have your faith in their teachings *or* their power."

"Why? The Brindle may not, in itself, be old, but it still contains eons of witch history and teachings. If there is any way to combat this tracer, then it'll be found there."

"Perhaps."

My annoyance flared brighter. "Why are you so damn sure that dark magic is the only way to go? You're Aedh, not Raziq. What experience have you even had with dark magics?"

His smile was remote and cold. It was a reminder that underneath the "humanized" outer layer, a true Aedh still lay within. "How do you think the keys were made? How do you think the tracer was made? It wasn't the clean, bright power of the fields that was used, but rather the energy that lies between the dark portal itself and blood. Aedh blood."

My father had told me the keys had been made with blood, but for some reason I hadn't made the connection to that and blood magic—and that's what we were talking about here.

I rubbed my temples again and said, "How do you know so much about the creation of the keys, Lucian? And how the hell would you know they're made with Aedh blood?"

He snorted. "I was there when we found the first one, remember? I felt their darkness within it."

"So if you could feel it, why weren't you able to find the key?" I was the one who'd done that, not him.

"Your father disguised the keys. It was only when we were close enough to touch the thing that I could feel the dark energy within it."

He lies, came Azriel's soft thought.

Why would he lie about something like that? I asked. Hell, if he'd wanted the key himself, he could have taken it anytime during the ensuing attack. It wasn't like either of us could have actually stopped him—we were too busy trying to survive. Or at least, *I* was. I hadn't even realized someone else was there—someone other than the creatures who'd attacked us—until it was too late and the key had been taken.

You trust him too much, Risa.

And you distrust him too *much.* I glanced at Lucian. "Even if the Brindle witches couldn't help us, I'm not sure it'd be wise to tempt any sort of blood magic."

"Dark magic isn't always blood magic," Lucian replied. "It may be the strongest form of black magic, but it often also depends on the strength of the practitioner."

"It's a rather moot point, given that none of us is, or knows, a dark practitioner," I said wearily.

And Ilianna would kill me if she discovered I was even discussing the option.

"Remember, I have lived on this earth a very long time," Lucian said. "I may not know or practice dark magic, but I do know how such practitioners might be found. It is not as hard as the witches of this world think."

I pushed to my feet and walked to the coffeepot. Lucian didn't move out of the way, forcing me to brush past him. The musky, powerful scent of him teased my nostrils, stirring the ashes of desire.

And again, that struck me as odd. I might be in a physically wretched state right now, but given the fierceness of our attraction up until now, I'd have thought the stirring of lust would have been stronger.

I poured myself a coffee, then turned around and leaned back against the counter. "If," I said slowly, "the Brindle witches cannot find a way to mute the tracer, then we may have to resort to dark magic. But I draw the line at any sort of blood magic."

This is not a wise move, Azriel commented.

I knew that. I also knew that we might have no other choice—not if we wanted to keep my father, the keys, and me out of Raziq hands.

Lucian nodded. "I will see what I can find out."

"Good." I took a sip of coffee, then added, "In the meantime, get the hell out of here. I need to rest, and I can't do that with you two dumping animosity all over each other."

Lucian scowled. "Evict the reaper, then. I cannot see why—"

"Lucian, go. We both know I probably won't get to rest if you stay, and right now that's what I need above anything else."

His gaze swept over me, and then he nodded. "This time I will comply."

He'd fucking comply next time, too. Otherwise, he and I wouldn't be seeing each other in *any* way. If there was one thing I couldn't abide, it was a man who ran roughshod over his partner—a fact I thought he might have cottoned to after being on the outs these last couple of days.

He sent a less than pleasant glance Azriel's way, then spun and left the room. As the door slammed shut behind him, I walked back to the table and sat down. I pulled the dinner plate toward me and resolutely ate everything on it—more out of the knowledge that I needed the sustenance than any real desire to actually eat.

"You should sleep," Azriel said softly. "You are running at the limits of your strength."

"I know." I leaned back in the chair and drank some coffee. "Tell me honestly—do you think the Brindle witches' magic is going to be strong enough to counter the Raziq's tracer?"

"It is an option we must try."

"That's not what I asked."

"No." He hesitated. "In all honesty, I do not think it will. Aedh magic is strong, and the Raziq have traveled down a path that has twisted and darkened theirs. I doubt we reapers would be able to counter it, let alone human magic."

"But didn't you say reapers aren't particularly well versed in magic anyway?"

"We are soul guides first and foremost, but we were forced to at least gain *some* knowledge about magic and the portals when the Aedh priests all but died out." He half shrugged. "But the dark magic that beats within you is far stronger than anything we have dealt with up until now."

A fact the Raziq had undoubtedly been aware of when they'd shoved the tracer into me. I drank some more coffee, then said, "What are we going to do about the Rakshasa?"

"We will find it and kill it, as the councillors require."

I snorted softly. He made it sound so simple, yet we both knew that was far from the case. "Yeah, but it knows you're hunting it now. Do you really think it will come into that room without first checking that we're not near?"

"If we are not near, we cannot know when it arrives."

There was that. I gnawed my bottom lip for a moment, then said, "There was a camera in the room, and

I'm guessing there's sound, too. Maybe we could use that to our advantage."

"The Rakshasa will not be visible on a monitor. Nor will you hear either her or the ghosts through a microphone."

"No, but doesn't the Rakshasa scratch her victims and follow them home before devouring them?"

"Yes." His eyes gleamed with sudden understanding. "We can watch for such an event from a distance, then arrive at the victim's house and set a trap for the Rakshasa before it arrives."

"The only trouble is, the victim will be a vampire, and will sense my presence before he or she gets near the door."

And given that I felt like shit and it was a state that didn't seem to be improving in any hurry, I very much doubted I'd have the strength to remain in Aedh form for very long.

"I will set the trap and wait for the Rakshasa," Azriel said softly. "You do not need to be near."

I sighed. "Yes, I do. Hunter—and the councillors—want *me* to prove myself, not you. It has to be my sword and actions that kill this creature. Remember, her watcher is a witness to all that we do." I paused. "Or have we permanently lost him?"

"He is downstairs. It appears he returns to our home base—wherever that happens to be—when we take energy form and he loses us."

"Well, it doesn't alter the fact that I need to be involved in the Rakshasa's demise. I need to prove myself useful. Otherwise I'm dead."

"Hunter does not want you dead. Not when you are still of use to her."

"Hunter is *not* the council, even if she has grand plans to become head supremo."

"Do not doubt that if Hunter wants you alive, you will remain alive, no matter what the council might threaten."

I frowned, but before I could say anything, my phone rang. For several seconds I debated whether I should answer it or not, but in the end, the need to at least know who it was won out over the need to retreat from the world and get some sleep.

One glance at the screen told me it was Jak. I hit answer and said, "Hey—"

"No time for small talk," Jak cut in brusquely. "Just get your uncle to the secretary's place quick smart. Three men just busted their way into her house and they obviously *don't* intend to sit down and chat."

Chapter 11

"Oh, fuck," I said, then added, "Don't go in. Wait until we get there."

"Ris, it's three against one woman. I can at least even the odds a little—"

"Jak, you have no idea what you're—"

I didn't get the rest of the sentence out, because the bastard hung up on me. I swore, hit my contacts list, and dialed Uncle Rhoan.

"What is it this time?" he said, his voice resigned.

"Just got a call from Jak. Apparently three men just busted their way into Logan's secretary's place. You need to get someone out there immediately."

"Why the hell is Jak there, and not you?" he snapped.

"Long story, but I'm about to head there now."

"Ris—"

I knew what was coming, so I hung up. It'd piss him off, but right now I was more concerned about Jak's safety than Rhoan's fury. Jak might be a werewolf—and more than capable of handling himself in any normal situation—but this was about as far from normal as you could get. Just because they looked like human males didn't mean they actually were.

"Azriel—"

The rest of the sentence caught in my throat as Azriel's heat and arms wrapped around me. Then we were out of there, zipping through the gray fields so fast they were little more than a blur. My feet touched solid ground a heartbeat later, and the air became thick with the sound of screaming—a scream that stopped all too abruptly. The brief silence that followed was broken by the snarls of a wolf—Jak.

"Stay here," Azriel said, immediately disappearing again.

I snorted and ran for the house. You'd think he'd know by now that I wasn't about to obey an order like that—no matter how sensible it might be.

The snarling had come from a town house at the rear of a block of eight. More than a dozen people had gathered in the driveways of the other houses—all of them peering toward the very last town house in the row— but no one approached it. Which was pretty sensible, given that most of the people watching were either women with children or elderly.

I ran past them all and around the double garage that dominated the front of the town house. The front door had been forced open, with one half left swinging from a hinge that was barely holding on and the other lying in pieces on the white tiled floor. There was no sound coming from inside the town house now. Everything was ominously quiet.

Ignoring the tension that curled through my belly, and hoping like hell that Jak was okay, I drew Amaya and stepped inside cautiously. The purple fire flicking down her length was muted and halfhearted, and her hissing was little more than its usual background noise. If there was danger here, she wasn't sensing it.

Which didn't mean I shouldn't be careful.

I took several wary steps. Bits and pieces of furniture lay scattered everywhere, evidence of a fierce fight. The air was rich with both scent of blood and the musky odor of wolf, and twined within it was the fainter, more odious scent of unknown males. *Human* males.

But three human males—no matter how strong—shouldn't have been able to overwhelm a werewolf unless they'd gotten the drop on him.

Or they'd been armed with silver.

I walked cautiously through the living room and into the dining room. There was less mess here, an indication, perhaps, that more running than fighting had happened.

I stepped into the next room—the kitchen—and saw Jak. He was sitting on the floor leaning back against one of the cabinets, his eyes closed and an expression of pain etched into his face. He was nursing an arm that was bloody and torn, and his clothes were less than decent—although I wasn't sure if that was a result of the shape-shifting or the fight. But he was alive, seemed relatively unhurt—slashed arm and pained expression aside—and relief slithered through me.

Until I looked beyond him. A gray-haired woman lay still and silent on the floor near the small table, her neck twisted at such an odd angle it could only mean it had been broken. Her eyes were open but unseeing, and an expression of terror had been forever frozen onto her face.

Jak hadn't been able to save her. I closed my eyes and cursed the killing efficiency of Nadler's men.

But at least Jak *had* gotten one of them—and the bastard was still alive. He was lying several feet away from the woman, his legs also twisted into odd shapes. He probably would have been screaming had he been conscious, and part of me was tempted to slap him awake just so he could suffer for the death he'd caused.

I resisted the impulse, though, and sheathed Amaya as I walked over to Jak. His nostrils flared; then a slight smile touched his lips—indications that he knew I was close even if he didn't open his eyes.

I knelt wearily beside him. "I thought I told you to stay outside and wait for us."

"Yeah, I'm going to do that when someone is being murdered." He finally opened his eyes and gave me a somewhat annoyed look. "I'm not that much of a bastard, Risa."

"I didn't say you were. I just didn't want you hurt."

I gently pulled away the remnants of his shirt and inspected the wounds underneath. The knife wounds were long and deep, and while some of the bleeding had been slowed by his shift back into human form, the deeper ones were still weeping.

"You didn't?" he said in a surprised voice. "I would have thought the opposite."

I gave him a lopsided smile. "If I'd wanted you hurt, I would have done it myself. Which doesn't mean," I added hastily, as his gaze warmed, "that I am, in any way, ever going to forgive you for what you wrote."

He grimaced. "I sometimes regret what I wrote, but

I'm afraid it never lasts long. It was a good story, Risa, and it was the truth."

"As you saw it."

"Which is the only way I can ever report things." His gaze sharpened. "And now, you'd better tell me about that sword-wielding man who suddenly popped into existence and saved my ass."

I sat back on my heels and wondered why he'd seen Azriel's real form.

In this case, simply because I allowed it. Generally, it is only powerful clairvoyants who see us as we are.

Which Jak isn't, so why reveal your true self?

You trust him.

Yeah, but I trust Lucian, too.

That is totally different.

I wasn't so sure it was, but I glanced back at Jak. "You don't want to shift shape and heal your wounds first?"

"Just answer the damn question, Risa," he snapped. "I'm really not in the mood for games."

I grimaced. "Remember I mentioned that I could see the reapers?"

He stared at me for a moment, then said incredulously, "You're telling me he's one of them?"

I nodded. "Although technically, he's not just a reaper, but a Mijai—he guards the gates to heaven and hell, and hunts down the bad things that come through them."

He studied me for a moment, clearly trying to decide if I was pulling his leg or not. "You're serious, aren't you?"

I tore off my shirtsleeve and used it to bandage the

worst of his wounds. "Does that mean you didn't believe me when I mentioned them before?"

"To be honest, I had no idea what to think. I mean, ghosts and demons I can accept, because there's been enough evidence of both over the years. But reapers? And winged beings that no one has ever seen except in the pages of religious books?" He shook his head. "I'm an investigative reporter. We tend not to believe anything unless there's some form of proof."

I snorted softly. "And when there's no proof, you make it up from half-truths or outright lies."

His black eyes glimmered with sudden anger. "I have *never* concocted a story. You of all people should know that."

I did. I was just being petty and baiting him—not that I was about to admit it. "The secretary obviously knew enough to identify our face-shifter. It's bloody frustrating that his people got here before us."

"Yeah. He seems to know exactly what we're up to. I mean, first Logan, then the photographer, now the secretary—surely it can't be a coincidence that he's killing them in the same damn sequence that we're seeing them."

"We're talking about someone who has shown no hesitation about sending a soul stealer against anyone who opposes his plans to buy up the area around the ley-line intersection. Who knows what other type of dark magic he has at his beck and call?"

"Magic wouldn't reveal our intentions. Not from what I know of it, anyway," Jak said.

I shrugged. I didn't know enough about magic to say whether it was possible or not, but there was definitely some force at work here—even if it *was* human based. Jak was right—the sequence of the murders very likely *wasn't* a coincidence.

Awareness surged across my skin, and I twisted around. Azriel appeared with two men in tow. Both of them were pale and wide-eyed with terror. Obviously, the journey through the gray fields had shocked them.

He dropped them unceremoniously on the floor. They stayed where they fell, breathing but unmoving, meaning he'd restrained them in some way, even if the restraints weren't visible.

His gaze moved from me to Jak. *Do you wish me to render him unconscious?*

No. I've told him about you. It's easier. Out loud I added, "Did either of the men tell you anything?"

"They're not men—they're Razan."

I blinked. *That* was something I hadn't expected. Razan belonged to the Aedh—did that mean our face-shifter was either Aedh or in league with one?

"Can't be," I said automatically, even as instinct suggested it very likely *was*.

"Hate to interrupt," Jak said dryly, "but what the hell is a Razan?"

"Basically, it's the long-lived human slave of an Aedh," I answered, almost absently. To Azriel, I added, "Are they wearing the tattoo?"

In reply, he leaned down and tore the shirt away from the back of one of his captives. Two tattoos were revealed—one of a dragon with two swords crossed above it and, on the right shoulder, a ring of barbed wire.

Confusion swirled through me, and I frowned.

"That barbed-wire tat is the same one the rat-shifter saw on the fellow who'd paid him to deliver the note and the book from my father."

"First," Jak said, exasperation in his voice, "you really need to introduce me to the seminaked, sword-bearing reaper. And second, I thought you didn't know your father."

"I didn't know my father until recently," I said. "And Jak, meet Azriel."

The two men nodded at each other. Azriel said, "The fact that these men are Razan suggests your father could be in league with our fake Nadler—if these men were sent here by Nadler, that is."

"There's no one else who would gain any benefit from the death of Logan, the photographer, and now his secretary, so it has to be Nadler." I paused, chewing absently on my lip. "And it makes no sense for my father to be involved with someone like him. Even if he can no longer attain human form, he's probably more powerful than any human could ever hope to be."

Azriel nodded in agreement. "Even a human involved in dark magic who has control of a ley-line intersection would not be as powerful as your father."

It should have been one hell of a scary thought, but maybe I was simply too damn tired and sore to feel any more scared than I already was. I rubbed my aching head wearily, and said, "None of this is making any sense, is it?"

"Especially not to me," Jak muttered.

I gave him a half smile, but it faded quickly at the sound of approaching steps. I almost reached for Amaya, then relaxed as a voice said, "Risa, it's Harris West from the Directorate of Other Races."

"We're in the kitchen," I answered, a little surprised that Rhoan hadn't come. But then, he *was* head guardian these days, and I guess I couldn't always expect him to show up when I called.

But he'd still sent one of the daytime division's best. While most vamps weren't able to traverse the daylight hours, other nasties could, which meant these days the Directorate had a full complement of specialized non-humans in its ranks. From what Aunt Riley had told me, I knew that Harris wasn't only a powerful werewolf; he was also an extremely strong telekinetic.

He appeared several seconds later, a tall, dark-haired man with handsome features. His eyes were the blue of the ocean, his shoulders broad, and his body lithe as a wolf. He scanned the room quickly, his gaze pausing on Azriel and briefly narrowing—which made me wonder just whom he saw—before finally coming to rest on me. "Up to your neck in it again, I see."

"Afraid so. I gather Rhoan updated you on what has been going on?"

"Yes. He also suggested that I wring your scrawny neck," he said in a wry voice. "But I'll settle for an update."

I gave it to him, suddenly grateful that Rhoan *hadn't* shown up. Harris took statements from Jak and Azriel—although Azriel merely backed up what I'd already said—then, as the cleanup team arrived, told us to leave.

I helped Jak rise and we walked outside. I, for one,

was more than a little relieved to have gotten off so lightly.

"What now?" Jak said, still cradling his bleeding arm.

I grimaced. "I'm going home to catch some sleep. I think you need to stop that arm from bleeding."

"I meant case-wise."

"I know, but I'm all out of ideas right now."

"What about those photo disks you gave your uncle?"

God, I thought irritably, he was like a rat with a tasty morsel—he just wouldn't let it go. "I have copies in the hands of a computer geek who'll contact me the minute he gets any relevant information out of them. Until he does, we're basically at a standstill."

"I'd love to know how you managed to get those photo disks to your friend without me or your uncle realizing it." Jak paused, his gaze moving past me. "Or did your reaper friend have a hand in that? I'm thinking if he can pop into existence to chase bad guys, it probably means he can transport himself around invisibly."

"He can."

The fact that *I* could—when I was fit enough, anyway—was something I kept to myself. I trusted Jak, but only to a point. If this whole scenario with Nadler didn't pan out into a decent story, I didn't want him suddenly deciding to do a follow-up piece on me.

"So until your friend comes through, we have nothing, as I said." He rubbed a somewhat bloodied hand across his bristly chin. "I hate it when a story stalls. I might contact a few people and see if there's any whispers on the streets about these murders."

"Let me know me if you uncover anything interesting."

He gave me a wry sort of grin. "I'm hardly likely to do anything else, given the threat your uncle has left hanging over our heads."

If that threat prevented Jak from chasing leads without first informing me, then I couldn't be sorry about it—even if I wasn't exactly intending to obey it myself.

"I'll ring you tomorrow if I don't hear anything before then."

He nodded, gave me a sketchy wave good-bye with his good hand, then headed off down the street, dripping blood as he went. Obviously he had no intention of shifting shape to heal himself just yet. But then, he'd always been somewhat reluctant to shift shape in public—mainly, I think, because he never liked to remind people he was a werewolf. Humans might have accepted non-humans as a whole, but that didn't mean there weren't pockets who feared all things supernatural—especially at the very low levels of society, where suspicion of anything bigger and stronger tended to be entrenched. Jak might have the skill to relax people and make them talk, but that skill couldn't always override a base-level apprehension of non-humans.

I watched him walk away for several seconds, then turned to face Azriel. "I need to sleep."

He snorted softly. "I believe I suggested *that* some time ago."

"Well, I'm finally giving in to the inevitable—if you'll zap me back home, that is."

"You're abandoning the hotel?"

I nodded. "I want to sleep in my own bed, seeing as the Raziq aren't such an immediate threat."

"And the things you left at the hotel?"

"I can get them later." When I was rested and able to think logically again.

"Then home we shall go."

He stepped close and wrapped his arms around me once more. I rested my head against his shoulder and closed my eyes, enjoying the sensation of his physical presence as his heat and energy tore through me like a storm, sweeping me from that place to mine in a heartbeat.

As my feet touched the wooden floors of our building, I sighed in pleasure. The huge industrial fans hanging from the vaulted ceilings whirled, gently moving air that was cool and still smelled faintly of roses and lilac—the scents lingering from potions Ilianna had been making earlier in the week. But there was dust on the dining table and over all the other bits and pieces scattered about, and there was an odd sense of abandonment in the way everything lay where it had last fallen. But I guess that was to be expected, since Tao was still unconscious and Ilianna was dividing her time between the Brindle and Mirri's.

"Are you okay?" Azriel asked softly.

His breath tickled the top of my head and stirred a sense of well-being deep inside. Or maybe well-being wasn't the right word—it was more a sense of safety. Of being right.

Which was dangerous thinking—things would never be safe or right while the Aedh, the reapers, and Hunter were all such fixtures in my life.

I pulled out of his warm embrace and took a step back. The big living room felt so much colder without the cocoon of his warmth.

"I'm going to bed."

"Once you are safely asleep, I will return to the fields and see what additional information I can uncover about ensnaring the Rakshasa."

I frowned. "I thought they were best caught in their lair."

"Yes, but to trace this Rakshasa back to her lair, we first have to watch her dismember and eat her chosen victim. I don't think either of us could sit through that nightmare easily."

He had *that* right. I hesitated, then leaned forward and dropped a kiss on his lips. "Night, then."

Surprise and something deeper—something that was desire and yet a whole lot more—flitted across his expression before he got control of himself again. "What was that for?"

"A kiss good night is something of a custom here on earth," I said, my lips still tingling with the warmth of his. "Don't tell me the woman who showed you the delights of human procreation never kissed you good night like that?"

"No." His expression gave little away, but there was a decidedly devilish twinkle in his eyes. "It is, however, a custom I could grow used to."

I smiled, but resisted the temptation to kiss him again, and backed away instead. I might be bone-weary and aching, but I had a suspicion if I did it again, the desire to rest would be overwhelmed by another sort of desire entirely.

"Night, Azriel."

He nodded and winked out of existence. He was still near; I knew that because his heat swirled around me. I resolutely turned and made my way to the bedroom, stripping off clothes and letting them drop to the floor as I went. I'd pick them up later, when I had more energy. I pulled back the covers, crawled underneath them, and was asleep before I could even smile in pleasure.

The sharp ringing of the telephone woke me sometime later. I opened an eye and glared blearily at the object making all the noise, but it didn't catch the hint and stop. After several more seconds of the incessant sound, I groped blindly for the handset and croaked, "Hello?"

"Well, you sound like crap," Stane said, all too cheerfully.

"That's how I feel, so it's really no surprise." I rubbed my free hand across gritty eyes, then glanced at the clock. It was just after six, meaning I'd had a whole five and a half hours' sleep. "You'd better have a good reason for waking me, because otherwise I'm going to send Azriel over there to beat you up."

Stane laughed. "No, you wouldn't. You're too much of a softie to do something like that to your friends. Besides, you need my hacking skills."

His hacking skills wouldn't be impaired by a little beating or two, I thought grumpily. "Stane, what do you want?"

"A night out at the Red Iris, no expense spared."

I sat up abruptly, and bit back a groan as my head just about exploded. "You found Nadler?" I said, the words little more than a hiss through gritted teeth.

"Well, I've found the version currently striding around as Nadler. He has a little beach house down at Portsea. I've just sent you the address."

Portsea being the sort of place where even the littlest of houses meant big prices. "Don't suppose there's any way you can check if he's down there?"

After all, according to his neighbors, he hadn't been sighted at his Brighton home for some time, so there was no guarantee he'd be in Portsea, either.

"There's no handy-dandy traffic cameras nearby, so I had to resort to more underhanded tactics. In this case, that meant digging up his cell phone number. Which, I might add, was not an easy thing to do. Phone companies are fierce when it comes to protecting the private numbers of their customers."

But not fierce enough, obviously. Although it did have to be said that Stane was one of the best when it came to hacking.

"So, the dinner will include the finest bottle of champagne the Red Iris has," I replied dryly. "Just get on with it."

He chuckled softly. "Our Mr. Elusive is, according to the GPS tracker on his phone, at his Portsea house right this moment."

Finally, we'd caught a break. I closed my eyes in relief. "For that, you can have two bottles of their finest."

"Excellent," he said. "Let me know how it goes."

"Will do." I hung up, then twisted around as the surge of energy told me Azriel had appeared. "You heard?"

He dropped my purse and bag of clothes onto the bed—obviously he'd been back to the hotel room to collect them. For a reaper, he was pretty damn considerate. Sometimes, anyway.

"Yes," he said, his voice flat. "But you should—"

"Azriel—" I said, cutting him off before he could finish that sentence. "Give it up. I'm not going to be left out of this chase in *any* way. And if you leave without me, I'll just chase you in Aedh form."

I pushed the blankets off me, clambered out of bed, and went over to my huge walk-in wardrobe.

"I know all that," he said, his tone still flat and yet oddly hitting at the annoyance that swirled like a distant storm somewhere deep inside me. "But I continue to hope you will eventually do the sensible thing. I *know* there is sensible in you somewhere."

I gave him a grin as I pulled on some clothes. "I'm afraid it doesn't appear all that often."

"So I've noticed." He'd crossed his arms and was watching me somewhat grimly, but Valdis flickered with red-gold fire and the energy that surrounded him became more heated than usual. And it echoed through me, stronger than that distant storm and far, far more alluring.

Which was *not* what either of us needed right now. I resolutely ignored him and concentrated on the business of getting dressed. Once I was, I walked back to the bed to grab my phone, checked the address Stane had sent me, then shoved it and my wallet into my pockets before finally turning around to meet his gaze again.

Heat still shimmered between us, and if Valdis was any indication, he seemed no more able to control or deny it than I could.

"Ready?" he asked softly.

I couldn't help a slight smile. "Always."

Amusement touched his lips and warmed the edges of his eyes. "I have noticed that about you."

Then his energy swept through the two of us, and as one, we surged across the incandescent fields before finding shape once more in the shadows of a two-story building.

Still far too aware of him for my own good, I stepped quickly away from his embrace, but the sharp movement had the world doing a crazy dance around me. I locked my knees against the wobble in my legs, determined *not* to fall. Azriel held out a hand, not quite touching me, but obviously ready to catch me. I think it was only stubbornness that kept me upright.

After a moment I said, "Where are we?"

"We are in the front yard of the house across the road from Nadler's," Azriel said. "There is no one home, so there is no immediate hurry to move."

Thankfully. I looked around, trying to get my bearings. The area we'd appeared in wasn't what I'd expected. When Stane had said Portsea, I'd been imagining the Port Phillip Bay side near the golf club and the peninsula. This looked to be the back beach area—which meant the houses were a fraction cheaper and often older.

"What about Nadler's? Is he—or anyone else—home?"

His house wasn't much to look at—in fact, it was pretty much typical of the beach houses that could be found up and down the bay. It was flat-roofed, with the ground floor being brick and the first floor weatherboard, and it featured a wide balcony that jutted out from the first floor, supported on either side by steel poles. A flat-roofed carport stood on the left side, and in it sat a Toyota Land Cruiser.

"I cannot sense life inside," Azriel commented.

I frowned. "Surely he couldn't have up and disappeared in the few seconds it took us to get here."

"I wouldn't have thought so," Azriel said. "And his vehicle is still there."

"Maybe he's visiting a neighbor." I studied the houses on either side—which didn't tell me a whole lot—then dug my phone out and called Stane.

"Hey, that was quick," he said.

"We haven't caught our man yet, so don't get excited."

"Well, damn."

I smiled. "Can you check his location for us again?"

"Hang on." A slight *whoosh* sound told me he was rolling from one desk to the other, and then he said, "He's still at the house. Why?"

"Because Azriel's not picking up any sign of life inside the house, that's why."

"Maybe he's just left his phone there."

"Maybe." But somehow, I didn't think so. Instinct was suddenly suggesting the reason was a whole lot darker than that. "Thanks, Stane. I'll get back to you."

I shoved the phone away and met Azriel's gaze. "I guess we should go in there and check it out."

He nodded, caught my hand, and tugged me toward him again. We reappeared in what looked like some sort of rumpus room. It ran the width of the house and was very shadowed, thanks to the fact that all the blinds had been pulled down. A large TV and several sofas dominated one end, while on the other, there was a Ping-Pong table, and on the wall a much-used dartboard. The faint aroma of toast lingered in the air, but there was no kitchen in this room, so it was obviously drifting down from somewhere else. But there was something else underneath that scent—something odd and unpleasant.

Frowning, I pulled away from Azriel again and somewhat cautiously stepped toward a door that led into a short corridor. My legs didn't wobble, but that one step still had a somewhat disastrous effect—it set off an alarm, the sound shrill and ear-piercing.

"Fuck," I said, running into the corridor and hoping like hell it led to the front door. "I didn't even think of the place being alarmed."

"You wish to leave?" Azriel said, his footsteps silent as he followed me.

"No, I wish to turn the damn alarm off."

Immediately ahead were stairs leading upward, but the corridor made a sharp turn to the right and, as I'd hoped, led to the front door. And right beside it was the alarm control box. It was very old technology, but it still featured a handprint scanner and that was something I couldn't get around. So I did the next best thing—drew Amaya and shoved her sharp point into the heart of the box. The box exploded spectacularly, throwing sparks everywhere, but at least it shut the damn alarm off.

Although it still seemed to be sounding in my head.

"Right," I said, sheathing Amaya and looking around. I couldn't see any cameras—one thing to be thankful for, I supposed—and I doubted they'd be hidden, given both the age of the house and the alarm. Hiding them would be more trouble than the old house was worth—it was the land that was the prize with this place. "We probably have five to ten minutes to look around before either security or the police arrive."

"Then we had better proceed with our search."

Azriel stepped aside and let me lead. I walked into the first bedroom, my footsteps echoing on the polished boards, the sound beating in time to the pounding in my head. The room, small but neat, contained little more than a double bed and a chest of drawers. The other three bedrooms were much the same, and the bathroom possessed a double shower and a sink. There was no sign of everyday use in any of the rooms, which meant that if our fake Nadler lived here full-time, he had to be doing so upstairs.

We went up to the next floor. And there, in the living room, discovered the source of that strange scent.

It was a body.

Nadler's body, to be precise.

"Well," I said, frustration heavy in my voice, "this fucks everything up."

I stopped near Nadler and stared at him grimly. He lay on the floor in front of the large, L-shaped leather sofa, and he was on his side, his knees tucked up toward his chest and his arms crossed. The pose was childlike, and there was an almost serene expression frozen onto his face—as if this death was one he'd welcomed. There was no blood, no apparent trauma on his body, nothing to indicate how he'd died—although his skin was extremely pale and looked decidedly strange.

Almost like meat that had been left in a freezer for too long. My gaze drifted to his feet—they were bare, and on one leg I saw the faded remnants of a scar. This was the *real* Nadler, if what Jacinta had told us was true—in death, a face-shifter couldn't hold on to any physical alterations he might have made in life.

Somewhat reluctantly, I stepped forward and touched him. His skin was cold—almost icy—and his muscles taut. It had to be rigor mortis, which meant he'd been dead for at least twelve hours.

"This death is nowhere near *that* fresh," Azriel said, voice grim as he knelt beside Nadler.

I frowned. "If it was a lot older, he'd be smelling more than he is."

"Yes, but the natural decomposition process has somehow been restricted."

Being stuck in a freezer would do that—and it would also explain his icy skin and the freezer-burn look. I looked over at the open-plan kitchen. There was a refrigerator-freezer at the end of the counter, but the freezer section wasn't anywhere near large enough to hold a body—even one curled up like Nadler was.

Azriel added, "His soul does not linger in this room."

Good. I'd *really* had enough of ghosts for the moment. "Meaning he died when he was meant to?"

Azriel shrugged. "That is hard to say. Just because his soul isn't here doesn't mean this death was written. Souls tend to haunt the place where death found them—if Nadler was not killed here, then his soul would not be here."

I frowned. "Can you read the last moments of his life?"

He shook his head. "As I said, this is not a fresh death. Memories do not linger for more than a day once the flesh is dead."

That they lingered at all was amazing. "Then is there any way you can tell how long ago he was killed?"

"Reapers escort souls. We do not analyze the method of their deaths."

I crossed my arms and leaned a hip against the high back of the sofa. My muscles were still quivery, and even that minor bit of support felt good. "Yeah, but *you* hunt and kill demons who prey on humanity and destroy said souls—surely that has given you some knowledge of when a death might have occurred."

"Sometimes, yes. In this case, no. His body composition is not usual."

If he wasn't fully thawed, then I guess it would seem unusual. "If his death is a lot older than a day, it means he was probably already dead when both the secretary and the photographer were murdered."

Azriel glanced up at me. "Yes."

I frowned. "So why would our face-shifter order them killed if he was ditching his Nadler identity anyway?"

"That is a question I cannot answer."

"I know—I'm just venting." Damn it, this *didn't* make sense.

He studied me for a second—no doubt noting the way I leaned against the sofa and knowing full well why—then said, "There is one possible reason."

"What?"

He swept aside Nadler's dark hair to reveal his left temple. "There's no scar here."

"And the version Logan knew had a scar," I said, suddenly understanding.

"Yes," Azriel said. "And no doubt the one his secretary knew, as well. With them dead, there would be few left who dealt with him regularly and therefore few who could mention differences between the shapeshifter *they* knew as Nadler and this one, who is the real Nadler, given what Jacinta told us."

That made sense—and it said a lot about my overall state that *he* was the one making these observations, not me. I mean, I'd been around guardians all my life and over the years had learned a fair bit about the inner goings-on of the Directorate and the law. "Then why kill Blake? He certainly couldn't have identified the recent version of Nadler."

Azriel shrugged. "Humanity often suffers from illogical patterns of thinking."

It was a somewhat harsh observation, but sadly, more true than not. I scrubbed a hand through my hair, then glanced out the windows as the wail of sirens suddenly seemed to sharpen. "We'd better get out of here. Can you take me back to Stane's?"

Surprise flitted briefly across his features, but once again I found myself in the cocoon of his arms as he shifted us. I have to say, it was a nice place to be.

"Well, *fuck*," Stane said, as we appeared next to his bridge. "You guys could at least give a little warning before you do that—it's enough to give someone a heart attack!"

"You are not destined to die via a heart attack," Azriel said, his voice mild. "So I would not be concerned."

Stane gave him a somewhat uncertain look. "I don't

know whether to be relieved or worried by that statement."

Azriel offered nothing further, which only sharpened Stane's uncertainty. I smiled and walked into the kitchen to help myself to coffee.

"Our hunt for Nadler hit a dead end. Literally."

"He's *dead*?" Stane's voice was incredulous.

"The real Nadler is, yes. The fake has scarpered, it seems." I took a sip of coffee, blanched a little at its bitter taste, and threw several extra heaping teaspoons of sugar into it. It didn't help much, but I drank it anyway. I needed something to keep me upright.

"Well, *that* puts a fucking spanner in the works."

"Maybe." I walked back and sat down on the spare chair near his bridge.

Stane raised his eyebrows. "You have thoughts?"

"Decidedly muddled ones at the moment." I half grinned. "But it occurred to me that whoever has been impersonating Nadler for the last ten years or so wouldn't have killed him off without a backup identity in place. He went to a whole lot of trouble to buy the buildings in this area, and I doubt he'd relinquish control that easily. So there's either a fourth member of the consortium in place that we haven't yet uncovered, or Nadler's last wishes will ensure that our face-shifter still has control of all the land around here."

Stane frowned. "If there was a fourth member of the consortium, I would have uncovered him by now."

"Then our only other hope is digging up the will to see who was the main beneficiary."

He nodded thoughtfully. "I can do a search through the trustees office and see what I can find."

The public trustees office was a government department that offered professional help when it came to wills, asset management, and estate management services. I sipped my coffee and thought about Nadler's body. "We do have another option. Maybe."

"And that is?" Stane asked, when I didn't immediately go on.

"Well, when we saw Nadler's body, two things became obvious. One, he'd been held in captivity for a while. He had an almost ghostly tone to his skin—it was almost as if he hadn't seen any sun for a very long time. And two, I think he was frozen."

Stane blinked. "Frozen?"

I nodded. "He had a freezer-burn look about him."

"God." Stane rubbed a hand across his chin. "Well, most decent-sized box freezers will hold a human body, and they could be put anywhere with power. But searching for it would be the proverbial needle in a haystack."

"Yes, but you couldn't keep a body in a freezer just anywhere, could you?"

"Well, no, but any storage facility with power would be suitable." He gave me a somewhat wry look. "Do you know how many of those there are in this city?"

"Hundreds, if not thousands. But we can still do a search for one under the name of Nadler, just on the off chance that we find it."

"It seems unlikely he'd be so stupid, but I guess it can't hurt—and if we do find one, maybe I can raid the security tapes and see who has been accessing the unit."

"My thinking exactly." I finished the rest of the bitter

coffee and stood. "As ever, let me know if you find something."

"As long as you don't forget the dinner you owe me."

"When this is all over—"

"Forgive me if I'm being a little picky, but this might not be over for months. Years, even. A wolf could starve in that time."

I grinned. "So, next week then."

If, I added silently—and somewhat grimly—I was still alive in a week's time.

"Date," he said.

I glanced at Azriel. He took the hint and whisked us out of there. Once we'd reappeared at home, I walked into the kitchen. Stane's bitter coffee had woken me up, but I really needed something to eat if I was going to get through the rest of the evening.

I zapped a large helping of leftover lasagna in the microwave, then grabbed a fork and headed into the living room. Azriel was standing in the middle of it, his arms crossed and his pose watchful. Ever the guard, I thought, and wondered if reapers even knew how to relax.

"Not in the sense that humanity does," he answered.

I dropped onto the nearest sofa. "As usual, that reply is not very informative."

He half smiled. It sent a hum of delight swirling through me. "In very simple terms, we mingle energies and recharge."

"Mingle energies? That sounds almost sexual."

"There is no 'almost' about it."

So in their free time, reapers basically ran around having sex? And they called werewolves horny bastards. "How different is it from human sex?"

This time the smile was full-blown and sexy, and it didn't just swirl, it stormed, leaving me breathless and aching.

"It's as different as night from day."

A statement that did *nothing* to relieve the desire raging within me. I licked my lips and tried to concentrate on eating. However much my hormones might rage, now was *not* a good time for that sort of action. Christ, I was barely even capable of standing.

You don't have to stand to make love, my treacherous inner voice whispered.

I studiously ignored it and continued to shovel food in until the lasagna was almost gone and I was sure I could speak with some semblance of normalcy. Not that he'd be fooled—there was that damn chi link, after all.

"Is this mingling what you meant when you said you couldn't make love to me as a reaper, because I wasn't ready for it?"

His expression closed up again. "In a sense, yes."

I sighed in frustration. Getting *any* sort of information out of him was like squeezing blood from a stone, but it was far worse when it came to questions about his life as a reaper.

Before I could say anything else, my phone rang, the sound sharp in the brief silence. The ringtone told me it was Hunter.

I briefly considered not answering it, but that wasn't likely to do much. The bitch would just track me down and confront me in person. At least if she was on the other end of the phone, she didn't have access to my thoughts.

"The reason I didn't ring with an update," I said without preamble, "is because there isn't a whole lot to tell you. The Rakshasa sensed our presence in that room and made a run for it. Azriel wasn't able to track it back to its lair."

"That is extremely unfortunate given that the deadline clock is counting down." Hunter's voice was cool. "I do not wish to lose a good resource, Risa, so I suggest you do your utmost to catch this thing."

I snorted softly. If she considered me a good resource, then her other resources obviously sucked big-time. My mother I was not.

"Trust me—I have no intention of getting dead just yet, but we do have a problem. I can't stand guard in the viewing room tonight. The Rakshasa knows we are waiting for it now, so it'll be overly cautious. We need to try something else."

"Such as?"

I hesitated, thinking fast—not an easy task at the moment. "There are cameras installed in the ghosts' feeding room, so would I be wrong in thinking there are some who get off on watching others feed and kill?"

"Yes." She paused. "The camera feed goes down to several side rooms in the main bar."

"What sort of side rooms?"

"The sort you find in werewolf bars," she said, her voice dry. "The kind that allows participants privacy if they prefer."

The image of a blood whore–addicted vampire jerking off while he watched another feed and kill made my stomach flip-flop, and I was suddenly glad I'd just about finished the lasagna. "Surely we could snag one of those to use."

"Only if your reaper remains ready to fight. Marshall cannot remain with you for that long, and it is only his presence by your side that gets you through the bar safely."

I was betting Azriel had a whole lot more to do with that than she was giving him credit for. Every vampire might see him as something different, but reapers had a natural ability to see and take on whatever form a soul would most accept, so it was natural that they could also see what souls feared. Given the reaction of the nearby vamps, I was betting the latter was what he'd been projecting.

Still, being in such close proximity to that many hungry vamps wasn't something I was keen on. "There have to be monitors elsewhere, surely. What about the security area?"

"The security area is not situated on-site—and the cameras in the feeding rooms do not transmit to the main system. We do not wish to risk anyone hacking into them."

I wondered if Stane could, then erased the thought. That would only put him in unnecessary danger, and I refused to do that any more than I already was.

"But surely someone is keeping an eye on what goes on down there. I mean, you haven't got an endless supply of whores—have you?"

"Of course not." Hunter's voice was cool. "That would be absurd—and illegal."

My heart began to pound a little harder. It may have

been absurd and illegal, but my intuition was prickling, suggesting that's *exactly* what they had.

An endless supply of blood whores could mean only one thing—they were being created *and* farmed. They *had* to be—how else could the vamps guarantee supply? And it would certainly explain the strange lack of memories in the two whores Azriel had tried to read, and their oddly identical eyes.

Fuck, this situation was getting deeper and shittier by the moment. And the worst thing was, I couldn't *do* anything about it. I couldn't even tell anyone. We'd all be dead in an instant if I did.

"Surely Marshall has monitors in his office."

"He does not," she replied coolly. "It is either the viewing room or one of the side rooms. Your choice."

If I'd had a real choice, I would have gone back in time and recanted the words that had led me into this impossible situation. I'd known when I'd said them that it was stupid and dangerous, but I'd been so desperate for revenge that I think I would have agreed to enter hell itself if it meant finding Mom's killer.

Working for Hunter, and being under threat from the vampire council, wasn't exactly hell, but it wasn't far off it, either. Especially considering that Hunter and the Cazadors were no closer to finding Mom's killer than we were.

"Tell Marshall we'll take one of the side rooms." We simply couldn't risk staying in the viewing room again. The Rakshasa's hunger might force her to return, but I doubted that she would simply appear like she had the last time. After all, she now knew we were here and, at the very least, would be more cautious.

"That is very brave of you," Hunter said. "The council will be impressed."

And that, I suddenly realized, was the whole point of this exercise. Impressing the council, making them believe that keeping me alive was a far better option than killing me. This *wasn't* about the Rakshasa or the vampire killings. This was about Hunter strengthening her power base.

And I was one of the foundation stones.

I rubbed my head wearily. If I'd had the energy I would have cursed long and fluently. But the truth of the matter was, I'd brought this on myself by agreeing to her terms back in that forest, and now I had no option but to deal with it.

"I don't give a fuck whether the council are impressed or not. I just want to find this thing so I can concentrate on the business of finding the remaining keys."

And with that I hung up. It might not have been wise, but I was way past tired and beyond caring.

"Then get some sleep," Azriel suggested. "I will wake you when it is time to return to the club."

My gaze rose to meet his. That thick sense of heat and desire still swirled within me, but stronger than that was the need to be held. Just held.

He took half a step forward, then stopped and clenched his fists. "Go," he said, his voice holding a rough edge. "Rest."

I briefly closed my eyes, and half wished Lucian was here. He, at least, would have understood the need for contact and comfort that wasn't sexual—although truth be known, while he might have held me, it wouldn't have been for long. He was a sexual being, and that's where it would have ended.

What I needed, I thought bitterly, was a straightforward relationship with a normal everyday man.

Someone like Jak—only less work oriented and more trustworthy.

But an ordinary man was *not* something I was likely to find anytime soon. Nor was it wise to bring such a man into my current situation.

Which meant, like it or not, I was going to bed alone. I forced my feet into action and walked into the bedroom, where I stripped and climbed under the sheets. It wasn't long before sleep caught me, but it was far from peaceful. Visions haunted me—blood and death and needle-sharp talons that sliced flesh to the bone.

It was only when arms wrapped around me and pulled me close to a heated body that somehow made me feel safer than I'd ever felt that the dreams dissipated and I was finally able to sleep.

I followed Azriel into the bowels of Dark Earth, carefully watching where I placed each foot. It was pissing down outside, and although the hidden entrance looked solid, water seeped underneath it, making the steps slick and treacherous. The last thing I really needed right now was to break a leg.

Mind you, if there had been the slightest chance that a broken bone or two could have saved me from the high council's edict, I might have considered the option.

We reached the long corridor and walked down to the door. It opened to reveal an impatient-looking Marshall.

He glanced at his watch when he saw us, then all but spat, "What the hell time do you think this is?"

"It's five to twelve," I said, somehow keeping my voice even, though all I really wanted to do was hit him one and then spin on my heel and walk out. I was working for *Hunter*, not her fucking lackey. "And it's the same time we normally arrive, so why the carrying on?"

"Hunter told you—"

"Nothing," I snapped. "As usual."

Of course, I *had* hung up on the bitch. Maybe she'd hung me out to dry information-wise because of it.

Or maybe she'd never intended to tell me, especially if this was another bloody test.

Marshall's grunt didn't sound pleased. "Well, the place is fucking packed tonight, which is why I wanted you here earlier. I wanted to get you into the side room before the main rush."

"Would it matter? Everyone in the main bar will know I'm there. They'll hear my heartbeat."

"Yeah, but without really seeing you, they'll just presume you're one of the thralls entertaining a client. Now they'll know otherwise." He glanced at Azriel. "Hope your friend has come prepared to fight, because if things get nasty—and I suspect they will, given the wait we have for the feeding rooms—I won't be able to control it. Not with the size crowd we have."

I stared at him for a moment, then said, with a touch of exasperation in my voice, "You can cut the act. I know the council intends to test me."

"They want you tested, yes," he spat back. "But I'm not entirely sure they want a bloodbath in this facility—which is exactly what they might get by introducing fresh meat and inciting trouble at this hour of the evening."

Dread rolled through me. "Fresh meat?"

He gave me a look that hovered between annoyance and concern. "We're talking junkies here, remember? For most of them, any female in this club who *isn't* a vampire has two purposes—to feed from or to provide sexual service. The thralls do the latter, the blood whores the former."

And if this *did* all end up in a bloody fight, it would just make the whole situation worse. Fresh-flowing blood and hungry vampires were never a good mix. "Will you step in if things get bad?"

The look he gave me was answer enough. He'd been ordered not to.

"This way," he all but growled, and turned, leading the way into the main room.

The doors closed silently behind us, and the darkness felt thicker, more oppressive, than before. I walked down the steps, my gaze sweeping the room, searching for the many vampires I could smell but not see. The stench of their hunger sharpened as we moved through them, until it seemed so thick that I could reach out and touch it. Fresh meat indeed.

I reached back and drew Amaya. She flared to life at my touch, her blade shadowed but dripping lilac rain across the floor. This time, her hissing was audible rather than just in my head. She was giving the nearby vamps a verbal warning not to come close—even though that's exactly what she wanted. Her hunger and excitement ran like electricity through my mind, and I knew if I concentrated hard enough I'd understand *exactly* what she was saying—as I had when I'd been the Raziq's prisoner. It might have been only one word, but it had been clear and it had helped me kill one of the bastards.

But I didn't concentrate. To be honest, I wasn't really ready to understand the language of my sword, and fear had a whole lot to do with it. I couldn't escape the notion that understanding her might somehow make me more like her and less like me.

Which might seem silly in the cold light of day, but right now, with darkness and danger all around us and her hunger beating a drum inside my brain, making me itchy to react, it seemed a very real threat.

So I clenched her hilt tight and edged a little closer to Azriel as we trailed Marshall through the darkness. Sullen, hungry faces were briefly illuminated in the fire of Amaya's brightness, then faded away, but the farther we moved into the room, the thicker and more danger-ous the atmosphere became.

Azriel drew Valdis and swept her lightly from left to right. She hit nothing, but her blue fire lifted the dark-ness even further, and gave the gaunt figures that flirted briefly with the light a surreal glow.

A glow that spoke of hunger and need.

I shivered and hoped like hell the Rakshasa made an early appearance. I wasn't sure if the swords would keep the vampires at bay once Marshall left us.

They will not, Azriel said, *because that is not what the council wish. They aim to test or kill, and they would be happy with either outcome.*

Since Hunter doesn't want me dead, this test makes no sense. My gaze darted sideways as a shadow moved. A vampire bared his fangs at me, madness in his eyes. I raised Amaya and he withdrew, but there was a light in his eyes that suggested it wouldn't be for long.

As you have noted, Hunter is not the council, even if she is one of the most powerful vampires in its ranks.

So why doesn't she put that power to use and save me from idiotic situations like this? It doesn't make sense.

Hunter plays for more than just your life. And remember, she is not constrained by human sensibilities.

But she was human once.

Near-immortality has a way of cleansing the soul of any semblance of humanity. It is rare for anyone—human or otherwise—to live for many centuries without time washing away all that they once were.

That's not always the case, I said, thinking of Uncle Quinn, who was only a hundred or so years younger than Hunter.

As I said, it is rare.

We continued to walk through the room. By the time we swept into a narrow corridor, sweat beaded my forehead and ran down my spine. I flexed my fingers, but it didn't do a whole lot to ease the tension thrumming through me. We may have made it out of the main room, but we were far from safe, and the ever-growing tide of hunger that trailed us only confirmed that.

The glow from the swords revealed a dozen doors leading off the corridor. Each one had a light above it, some red, some green. The sounds coming from inside the red-lit ones suggested there was some heavy-duty lovemaking going on—some solo but mostly partnered, if the scents were anything to go by.

And suddenly the reason for all the thralls we'd sensed earlier became obvious—they might have been here to provide sex, but they were also more able to withstand harsh punishment, and healed far faster than regular humans, thanks to their blood link to the vampire who had created them. Which wasn't saying they couldn't be killed—they weren't immortal, just as vamps weren't immortal—but short of cutting off their heads or gutting their internals, they were capable of surviving events that would have killed them in the pre-thrall era.

Marshall stopped at the second-to-last door on the right and opened it. As he did, the light above went from green to red. "I don't recommend moving out of here without me."

"It's not like we're going to be any safer inside than outside now, is it?" I commented grimly.

"No." He stood to one side to let us pass. "Not given what the council desires. But I will do my best to limit the damage, both to my club and to my customers."

Meaning we could go to hell in a handbasket for all he cared. Fabulous.

"However," he continued, "this is the only door into this room, so if you remain here, you should be able to handle all but an insane rush."

Which *he'd* all but implied might be in the cards. And the hunger so evident in the larger room certainly backed that up. "The council might not care either way, but I don't think Hunter will be pleased if I end up dead, and I suggest you remember that."

"I think I have more knowledge than you *ever* will on just what will and won't please Hunter." His voice was dry, but there was an undercurrent that spoke of anger. Resentment, even. Which was odd if he *was* her creation. "The viewing screen is to the right, and the control panel to your left. Ensure that the door is locked."

"Like a lock is going to stop any of the vampires out there."

He half shrugged. "No, but I would still recommend it."

Though I couldn't see the point, I locked the door as requested, then turned and looked around. The room was little more than a small white box, with no furniture other than the bed and the light screen. I walked across to the touch panel and slid a finger across the appropriate app. The TV came to life. The scene it revealed was one man viciously fucking another as he sucked the life from the poor fellow. The only sounds to be heard were the slapping of flesh against flesh and the occasional slurp.

I shivered and turned my back to the screen. I might have to listen, but I didn't have to watch. Not the whole sick performance, anyway.

Azriel still stood near to the door, Valdis held by his side. She gleamed with an ugly blue-black fire.

I raised an eyebrow in silent query, and he said, "There is much unrest outside."

I know. Fear sharpened within me. Amaya responded immediately, her noise adding to the ache in my still-tired brain. "When do you think they'll attack?"

"We are not dealing with sensible vampires in this place." He paused, then added, "We're not even dealing with *your* kind of sensible."

The comment drew a smile, as he'd no doubt intended. "Then we could be in *big* trouble."

"And it means you will have to watch the screen to see when the Rakshasa appears. I will deal with what comes."

My gaze flicked to the light screen. The vampire was reaching his climax and the whore was intact, and alive. "I will, when I have to."

He nodded. His attention obviously wasn't on me, but rather on the danger that lurked beyond the closed door.

"How many do you think they'll send at us?" I asked quietly.

"There are at least a dozen, by the feel of it."

Twelve against two weren't great odds by any stretch of the imagination, but they weren't insurmountable given that we had not only Azriel's skills but the two swords, as well. It could have been a whole lot worse. It could have been half the damn room.

I flexed my fingers and glanced briefly at the screen. The room was being cleaned and the blood whore escorted away. "I still can't see the point of testing me like this if they'd rather see me dead."

"As I said, we are not dealing with any rational mode of thinking." He paused. "We could leave. We have that option."

"But it's not one we can take. However crazy this whole setup is, proving I can protect myself against a horde of crazy vamps might just be enough to save me from the council's death edict—especially if the Rakshasa doesn't turn up tonight."

"Then prepare to fight." His gaze came to mine, the blue depths storm lit. "It's not going to be pleasant."

My stomach began to churn. I stepped back and raised Amaya. Her fire burned over the hilt and crawled across my skin, as sharp and as electric as the hissing in my mind. Hissing that said, *Come, come, come* . . .

I shivered, and wished I couldn't hear the beat of those words, or feel the answering echo of anticipation deep inside me. Wished the vamps that were crowding closer and closer down the hall would just leave us alone.

But all the wishes in the world wouldn't change the reality. Not this time.

Then Azriel said the two words I'd been dreading.

"They come."

And they did.

Only not just through the door, but from the ceiling itself.

Chapter 12

There was little warning, just a crack of sound as half the damn ceiling fell on our heads and spewed a seething mass of hissing, hungry vampires onto the floor—at the exact same time the first lot hit the door and crashed it open.

Back to back, Azriel said.

I pressed against him and ignored the plaster still falling around us, Amaya held at the ready and her *die, die, die* chant a scream inside my head.

Azriel entered the fray and Valdis screamed. It was a sound of defiance, a call for blood. I shivered and swung Amaya as the first of the vampires scrambled to their feet. Her fire rained through the air, the droplets hitting floor and flesh with equal deadliness, burning whatever it touched but having little impact on either. Then her sharp point met flesh, but there was no jolt, nothing to indicate I'd hit anything at all. An arm plopped to the floor and blood sprayed, covering all of us. The scent of it filled the air, fueling the hunger already rampant in the room. The nearest vampires turned and attacked the injured vampire, sinking their teeth into his flesh and tearing him apart. They reminded me of dogs fighting over a bone, and again I wondered at the council's willingness to destroy their own just to test my worthiness.

But then again, they weren't exactly sacrificing the cream of vampire society here.

More vampires scrambled to their feet and came at us. I swung Amaya left and right, the movements so fast her fiery edges were little more than a blur. Blood and gore and flesh flew everywhere, the stench of it so thick that bile rose up in my throat and threatened to choke me. And still they came at us, the tide seeming to have no end and certainly no hesitation.

Claws slashed and tore, teeth gleamed. I dodged one blow, barely rocked back against another. Fingernails as sharp as steel sliced across my chin, peeling it open. I cursed, swung my sword viciously, and cut the offending talon off at the elbow. The vampire's scream was one of rage rather than pain, and I had to wonder just what sort of drugs they were all on, because this was more than just blood hunger. It had to be.

Then, with a thunderlike crack, more of the ceiling came down, bringing with it more vampires. I dodged, but not fast enough, and hit the floor with enough force to see stars and lose my grip on Amaya. The vamp on top of me knocked her farther away, and she screamed furiously, the noise cutting through the din the vampires were making. Then another weight joined the first, pressing my face into the floor, squashing my nose and making it difficult for me to breathe. I punched wildly but ineffectively, and the vamp holding my head chuckled. His breath washed over me, and even though I could barely breathe, his odor crawled into my body through my pores, leaving me with the bitter scent of rancid meat.

Then he tore into my left shoulder blade, biting deep. I yelped in pain and bucked, trying to dislodge his teeth and get both vampires off me, but they rode me like cowboys and wouldn't budge. Again the first vamp tore into me, this time my back. I choked back another cry and twisted around, throwing my elbow backward as hard as I could. The vamp riding my shoulders was too intent on sucking up the blood to register the movement, and my elbow smashed into the side of his face, caving in his cheek and throwing him off sideways. I twisted violently to one side and half dislodged the second vampire. He lunged forward, canines bared and bloody and madness in his eyes. I tried to roll away, couldn't, so I threw up a hand in a vain attempt to batter him away. Then, suddenly, Azriel was there, wrapping a fist around the vamp's neck and flinging him back hard.

He reached down and pulled me upright. There was a cut above his left eye and fury in his expression, but he wasted no energy on words, simply turned and dove back into the attack.

I lunged for Amaya, but she was already slithering toward me. I swept her up, then dove sideways as a vamp leapt over one of the fallen and came at me. I swung my sword but he checked his speed, leaned out of her way, then dove straight at me. I dropped, hitting the floor hard enough to knock the wind out, and pulled my sword onto my stomach. This time he couldn't check. The blade pierced his flesh, and his momentum drove her dark metal right through his body and out the other side.

I let him fall, then scrambled to my feet, pulled Amaya free, and swung around to face the next threat.

But it was over, and I'd been proven right. The odds *hadn't* been insurmountable.

More than sixteen vampires lay dead or near dead in the small room, and there were at least another three or four out in the corridor if the bits I could see were any indication. Blood and gore and body parts lay everywhere, and suddenly I was shaking. But it was anger, not fear, not reaction.

Azriel stepped over the bodies and came toward me. "Are you all right?"

"No, I'm fucking *not*." My fists were clenched so tight that Amaya's hilt cut into my hand. I glanced at the ceiling, looking for the cameras I couldn't see but had no doubt were there. "Enough! Do you hear me? *Enough!* No more fucking tests. Either use me or kill me, but stop this stupid waste of life."

"Impressive," Marshall said from the doorway. "I don't believe the council expected you to win so easily."

My fury suddenly had a focus point, and I took a step forward. Azriel threw out a hand and stopped me from going any farther.

It would not be wise to kill him at this time, came his soft warning into my thoughts. *This is not his doing.*

I gave Azriel a somewhat dark glance, then returned my gaze to Marshall. "I hope they realize this circus might well have caused us to miss the arrival of the

Rakshasa—and wasn't killing her our actual reason for being here?"

"It is the reason you are in this club, yes," Marshall agreed, "but not the reason you are on this floor. And trust me, I am no more happy about this waste than you are."

"Then why the *fuck* didn't you do something to stop it? You run the damn place."

His expression darkened. "I may run it, but that doesn't mean I have free rein to do as I wish. And I am beholden to the council for certain supplies."

The blood whores, I thought wearily, and scrubbed a bloody hand across my face.

Marshall added, "And the Rakshasa would not have made an appearance as yet, simply because there has been no killing in that room."

I stared at him for a moment, his words echoing through my brain. "Meaning you know exactly when someone is going to be killed?"

He seemed surprised by the question. "Of course."

"So you send men and women in there to feed the vampires, knowing they're going to die?" I said it flatly, without emotion, even though anger boiled through me, a silent scream of anger that reminded me of Amaya.

"The blood whores in our employ know and understand the risks—and sign a document stating as much." He shrugged. "We do not, however, waste valuable stock. Only the older ones who are reaching the point where it is not economically feasible to keep repairing them."

Economically feasible. God, they really *were* treating the whores like cattle.

And that whole document-signing thing was a farce, because we weren't talking about regular blood whores here, but people who'd been born *and* bred for this life. I very much doubted they'd have any understanding at all of what they'd signed.

The fury continued to build in me, and Amaya's *kill* chant began inside my head again. The urge to do just that was so strong that my legs quivered with the need to move. I didn't, but it was such a close-run thing that it scared the hell out of me.

"I won't stay in this room," I said, through gritted teeth. "Give me another—preferably one with a sink so I can clean up."

He nodded and stepped back, waving us into the hall. I stepped over the bodies and various body parts, noting that the few vampires who were alive were quiet, and showing little of their previous almost insane hunger. Suggesting, perhaps, that it had been ramped up for the occasion by an outside force—either some sort of drug or another vampire.

Again fury swept me, but I somehow kept my sword by my side as I walked past Marshall.

"Take the second door on the right," he said, his expression wary, suggesting he knew exactly what was going through my mind—although I guess that wouldn't have been hard given the expression I was no doubt wearing. It certainly *felt* dark from my side of things.

I walked into the indicated room. It was much the same as the first one, only this one had a small sink area, a medical kit, and a couple of towels sitting to one side of it. Obviously, he'd had this room prepared for us.

I swung around as he came into the room behind us. "Have we your guarantee that this is the end of the tests?"

"There will be no more tests, no more disturbances in this place," he said. "I guarantee it."

"What about the dead? Won't that cause problems given the highly charged atmosphere in the main bar?"

His smile was cool, almost arrogant. "There will be no further trouble from *any* vampire in this place."

Meaning he *could* have stopped the onslaught if he'd so desired. Which also meant he was far more powerful than I'd been suspecting. But then, if he was Hunter's creature, I shouldn't have expected anything else.

"Good," I grumbled. "Now, if you could turn on the TV on your way out, I'd very much appreciate it."

He gave me a somewhat sardonic bow, then hit the control panel to the left of the door and left. The light screen came to life; the room was being mopped out, readied for its next customers.

I took a deep breath and released it slowly. It didn't do much to ease the churning in my stomach or the anger still trembling through my muscles.

Azriel sheathed Valdis and walked toward me. "How is your back?"

I shrugged. It hurt like a bitch but there wasn't a whole lot I could do about it, so there was little point in complaining. And hey, in comparison to what the Raziq had done, it was hardly more than a scratch.

He touched my bleeding chin, studying it for a moment, then motioned me to turn around. I stood my ground. "You can't heal me, Azriel. Any use of energy might just warn the Rakshasa of our presence."

"I'm well aware of that." Though there was little in his expression, his tone was somewhat annoyed. "I merely wish to see how bad the wounds are."

I grimaced, but turned around. He sucked in a breath, and, a minute later his fingers brushed my spine, the touch light, but nevertheless filled with a heat that sparked something deep inside me.

I shivered and crossed my arms, warding myself against the reaction as much as the instinct to turn around and reach for him.

"These are deep," he said, "and I'm afraid they will scar."

The first of many, if I continued to work for Hunter—and it's not like I had another option. And to be honest, scars were the least of my worries right now.

"Just clean them up the best you can. There's a medical kit near the sink."

He walked across to the sink. It was then that I noticed the cuts up both of his arms and a nasty-looking wound that ran the length of his left thigh. It was bleeding quite badly, if the amount of blood gleaming wetly on his dark jeans was any indication.

"Blood loss does not present the same danger to me that it does to you." He wet one of the towels, then opened the medical kit and pulled out an antiseptic sealer spray.

"Why not? I mean, you *can* find death in flesh form."

"Yes, but my life force is energy, not blood. I may bleed, but it does not drain me." He treated my chin, then said, "Take your shirt off."

I did so, then turned my back to him, my eyes on the

screen as he carefully cleaned the wounds. To say it hurt would be an understatement, but at least the pain gave me something to think about other than what was now happening on the TV. Another whore and customer had come into the room. The woman had to be in her mid-forties, with drawn features and scars littering her body—evidence that suggested a long history of feeding vampires. It was a history about to come to an end. Because the vampire who followed her into the room was long, lean, and vicious-looking.

And there was death in his flat brown eyes.

I rubbed my arms and wished I could stop what was about to happen. I didn't want to watch it, either, but I forced myself to witness the unfolding brutality on the screen. She deserved acknowledgment of her death, at the very least, and I doubted the vampires would even care, much less give her any sort of funeral. After all, to them she was little more than another piece of meat. Cattle to be used and abused.

Again anger rose, but I thrust it aside and continued to watch the screen. There was nothing pleasant about this feeding, and certainly nothing that remotely resembled pleasure for the woman. The vampire battered her, fed on her, and tore at her, until her body was slick with blood and all that seemed to be holding her upright was the vampire's brutal grasp. In my head, the keening of the ghosts echoed, getting stronger and more desperate with every sickening blow.

Yet the woman said nothing. Maybe she couldn't. I wouldn't put it past Marshall to somehow restrict the vocal capacity of those whores destined to die.

The feeding seemed to last forever, but in reality it took little more than ten minutes. The vampire ended the woman's torment by driving his teeth into her neck and ripping it open. Blood sprayed across the white walls, and the spark of life in her odd green eyes slowly died as her head lolled back and she stared up at the camera.

And in my head, the ghosts grieved and wept and raged at a world that wasn't capable of hearing.

Then it happened.

As the vampire sucked the last droplets of life from the woman, three bloody rents appeared on his back, stretching from his left shoulder to his right butt cheek. He snarled in fury and spun, but this foe was not one someone like him could see.

But the ghosts could, and they were screaming for murder, not just blood.

The Rakshasa obviously wasn't about to change the pattern of her hunt just to appease the ghosts, though, and nothing further happened. After a few minutes of somewhat confused searching, the vampire stepped over the broken body at his feet and left the room.

"The Rakshasa has also left," Azriel said. "But she waits outside for her victim."

I frowned as I pulled my shirt back on. "Will she sense us leaving?"

"I do not know how sensitive the Rakshasa is to those of us who guide and guard, so I cannot answer that."

It was a risk we would have to take if we were to have any chance of killing this thing. I walked over to the panel, found the intercom, and swiped my hand across it. "Marshall? You there?"

He didn't answer immediately, which suggested he hadn't been keeping an eye on us—although that didn't mean the council wasn't. When he finally came online, his blue eyes were bright and somewhat annoyed. I wondered what we'd interrupted. "What do you want?"

"I want the address of the vamp that's just left the ghost's room," I said without preamble. "The Rakshasa just marked him."

Marshall sucked in a breath. "So kill her."

I snorted. "If it was that easy, I wouldn't be here."

He grunted in acknowledgment of my point. "Jerry Harcourt was the vamp just in there. He rents a room in Lyle Place boardinghouse—it's only a few minutes down the road."

Which meant we'd better hurry if we wanted to set our trap. "Thanks."

"Do you need me to do anything?" Marshall asked.

If he could have done anything, I very much doubted we'd have been called in. But I just said, "No. Just ensure that he leaves, and we'll do the rest."

"Righto."

As the screen returned to the image of the blood-stained room, I swung around to face Azriel. "Will this work?"

He shrugged. "As I have said before, I've never hunted a Rakshasa. I'm told they can be extremely difficult kills."

And this one was killing people who deserved to die—a fact that didn't make going after her any easier.

But since it was my life or hers, there was really no other choice.

"Then we'd better get over there and set our trap." And if the trap didn't work, then we hunted it back to its lair. I shivered, and hoped like hell it didn't come to that. Not if the Rakshasa was feeding more than just herself.

Azriel held out a hand. I placed my hand in his and let him pull me into his embrace. It felt so warm and safe that I wanted to cry. Or maybe that was just a reaction of the bitter anguish that still echoed inside my head.

His energy surged, and in an instant the room disappeared and we were zipping through the gray fields. The room we reappeared in was dark and smelled faintly of urine and booze. Obviously, vampire Jerry did not live in one of your more up-market boarding establishments.

Azriel immediately stepped away and moved to one corner of the room. He raised his hands and paced the walls, murmuring softly. The words were lyrical and easy on the ear, but there was a dark undercurrent to the energy that swirled around and through his voice, and foreboding crawled down my spine. It somehow seemed wrong for such darkness to be coming from beings who were warmth and light.

He continued walking around the room. Mist formed behind him, becoming luminous tendrils that crawled up the walls and across the ceiling, until the soft, glowing, ethereal net of silver covered every compass point as well as the floor and ceiling. When the circuit was complete, the net locked together, then faded. But the power of it remained, making the tiny hairs on the back of my neck stand on end.

"Won't the Rakshasa feel the energy and run?" I asked, rubbing my arms and trying to ignore my growing sense of unease.

Azriel shook his head. "The vampire, however, will sense your presence in this room, so you cannot remain here."

I frowned. "I'm supposed to bring the Rakshasa down, not you."

He smiled and drew Valdis. She glowed with a fierceness that lit the sparse room. "The end result will be the same. Besides, how is the council to know who actually killed the creature? We don't have our follower when we shift via the fields, remember."

That was true. I bit my lip, but for once did the sensible thing—if only because I really didn't have the skill, the knowledge, or the desire to actually fight a spirit creature. "Is there an apartment nearby where I can wait?"

He hesitated, then nodded. "The room across the hall has no one in it."

"That's where I'll wait." I half turned, then hesitated. "Be careful, Azriel. Enough blood has been spilled already tonight."

He smiled, suddenly closer even though I hadn't seen him move. "I have Valdis, and I am well used to dealing with dark creatures." He raised a hand and cupped my cheek. "But I appreciate the concern."

Then he kissed me. It was little more than lips brushing, but it resonated through every part of my being, stirring me in ways I couldn't even begin to describe.

"Go," he said eventually, his voice tight. As if he'd been as affected as I was.

I forced myself to move away, although all I really wanted to do was step into his arms and chase the promise in that kiss.

I closed the door behind me, but hesitated in the hallway, listening to the silence and drawing in the air, trying to get a feel for who or what lived in this complex. I had no idea what Azriel's net would do, but the last thing we needed was one of Jerry's neighbors deciding to run to the rescue. Though to be honest, it looked like the sort of complex where the inhabitants were more likely to help themselves than one another.

The air out here was as unpleasant as it was in Jerry's room. The aromas of booze, age, and urine were entrenched, as were the threads of unwashed humanity. If there were other non-humans in this complex, they didn't live on this floor. I couldn't hear much in the way of activity in any of the nearby rooms, either, but that could have been a result of the late hour rather than no one being home.

Which meant, hopefully, I could break into the room opposite and no one would notice. Or care. I did just that, and caught the door with my fingertips before it could crash back against the wall. I stood there for several heartbeats, my breath caught in my throat as I listened for any sign that someone had heard and intended to investigate.

No one did. I sighed in relief, then shut the door and turned to study the room. It was fresher—and cleaner—than Jerry's, and possessed more in the way of furniture. The room's inhabitant was obviously intent on making himself comfortable, whereas Jerry seemed only to have the basics. But then, the addicted rarely cared for anything other than their next hit.

I double-checked the bathroom and bedroom just to ensure that no one was here, then moved back to the kitchenette and propped myself against the small table. Despite the fact that the worst of my wounds had been sealed by the antiseptic spray, blood still trickled down my back. I wondered briefly if Jerry would smell it and decide to investigate. It would mess things up if he did.

After what seemed an eternity, the creak of floor-boards and heavy—almost drunken—steps eventually began to invade the silence. They drew closer and closer, then paused just outside the doorway. Tension crawled through me. I held my breath, waiting for the moment when our plan went to hell and Jerry either ran or came at me.

For several seconds, nothing happened. I had the image of him standing there, nostrils flaring as he drew in the scent of blood and listened to the rapid beating of a heart. Mine, to be exact.

Whether he was actually doing that I couldn't say, and after several minutes of inaction, his door creaked and he stepped inside.

I reached for Amaya, then stopped. Would the Rak-shasa be able to sense her energy? I had no idea, so I left her sheathed. In this sort of situation, it was better to be safe than sorry. The decision, however, did not please my sword, and she hissed and grumbled in the back of my mind.

I padded across to the door and opened it slightly. There wasn't anything to see in the hall or anything to hear in the room opposite. But as I stood there, an ill wind began to gather. It stirred the hairs on the back of my neck, making them stand on end. I shivered, my fists clenched so tightly against the need to draw my sword that my fingernails were digging into my palms. I might have felt stronger—safer—when she was in my hand, but the energy that dripped off her surely wouldn't go unnoticed by a creature born to the world of spirits rather than flesh.

The wind gathered strength, filling the air with such darkness that it became harder and harder to breathe. And the desire to rush into the room opposite to see what was happening warred with the need to remain safe, but I knew I would only hinder rather than help. I had to let Azriel do what he'd been trained to do.

I opened the door a little farther. No sound came from the room opposite. Jerry might have entered, but he was no longer moving around. Maybe the poison the Rakshasa had administered when she'd slashed his back had taken full effect, and he simply lay there, waiting for the approach of his doom.

And it was certainly coming.

The sense of menace in the air was so sharp it felt like a knife cutting through my soul.

Then, down at the far end of the hall, something moved.

I froze, breathing labored and Amaya screaming furiously in my head. The movement wasn't repeated. My gaze darted through the shadows, but I couldn't see the threat that every sense—and my sword—said was there.

And then I realized why.

The threat *wasn't* in the hall.

It was behind me.

I swung, but it was already far too late.

A smothering blanket of darkness fell around me, and pain exploded. Then there was nothing, simply nothing.

Chapter 13

Waking was an exercise in agony. Every muscle, bone, and fiber ached with a fierceness that had my head spinning and my heart racing. Even my hair felt like it was on fire.

For a minute I wondered if I'd somehow ended up in the hands of the Aedh again, but this pain was different from the torture they'd put me through. This wasn't the pain that came from a spirit being pulled apart. Rather, it was from something more mundane—like a body that had been beaten and abused to the nth degree.

But the blood that rode the air suggested I wasn't any more hurt now than when the Rakshasa had captured me. She obviously hadn't had me for dinner, and while I was naturally grateful for that, it was a fact that only ratcheted up the levels of fear. She was saving me for something, and I had a bad, bad feeling I really *didn't* want to know what.

As my mind crawled toward greater awareness, I realized I was lying on something cold and uneven. Stone rather than concrete. My breathing was labored, suggesting there wasn't quite enough oxygen, and the air itself tasted bitter and decayed.

There was also a strange buzzing in my head, and it seemed oddly—darkly—blanketing.

Frowning, I reached down inside and called to the Aedh. Power surged, but so did pain, a warning that I was still too close to my limits. I ignored it, and called to the change regardless. It surged through me, breaking down skin and muscle as it began the shift from human to Aedh. Then that strange buzzing sharpened, becoming so fierce it felt like nails were being slammed into my head, and the energy stumbled, then receded, leaving me bound by flesh rather than a being of energy.

Whatever that strange buzzing was, I couldn't change while it was near.

Fuck, fuck, *fuck*!

I cracked open an eye. Darkness met my gaze, and it held an odd sense of heaviness, as if the weight of the world pressed down upon this place. And if that were true—if we were deep underground somewhere—then yet again Azriel wouldn't find me.

Which meant I was alone.

Fear swarmed, so thick that for several minutes it threatened to choke me. I might have been trained to fight by the best of them, but I'd never been prepared for a situation like this.

Alone not, came the alien voice that was my sword. *Am here*.

The relief that hit was so strong it left me shaking. Though there was no guarantee Amaya could protect me from whatever it was that waited in this darkness, with her in my hand I at least had a chance. And no matter how small that chance might be, it was better than nothing.

I opened both eyes and looked around. Or tried to, because my head wouldn't move. In fact, *nothing* would move. I was all but frozen, able to breathe but little else.

Panic swelled again, but I tried to ignore it, tried to think. There *had* to be a way out of this—had to be! I wasn't going to just lie here and allow the Rakshasa to tear me apart at her leisure. I might be frozen, but the mere fact that I was breathing suggested that either the poison in the Rakshasa's claws hadn't affected me as completely as it had her vampire victims or it was wearing off quickly.

I prayed it was the latter rather than the former. It would give me more of a chance—as long as the Rakshasa didn't decide to eat me immediately now that I was awake. After all, she did seem to prefer to consume her victims when they were aware.

As my eyes began to adjust, I realized the darkness wasn't as complete as I'd thought, thanks in part to the huge weights of stone that hung high above me. The stalactites gleamed with an odd, ghostly glow, and their light filtered through the surrounding ink, alluding to other outcroppings and hinting at fissures in the rock walls. Moisture gleamed and dripped, splashing onto the stony floor close to where I lay. It ran along the cracks and underneath my body, the chill of it contrasting sharply with the warmer moisture saturating my back. One of my wounds had obviously opened, even if the scent of it didn't sting the air.

But there was more than just stone and fissures here. There were shadows—shadows that were as still as the stone and humanoid in shape.

My heart began to beat a whole lot faster.

If those shapes were any indication, there wasn't just one Rakshasa here, but at least another five.

Panic surged anew, but I shoved it back down brutally. Panicking wouldn't achieve anything, and it certainly wouldn't get me out of here.

Something stirred to my left, and my gaze darted that way. One of the shadows peeled away from the wall and came toward me, the movement languid and oddly sensual. Which was fitting, because the woman who approached was one of the most exotic women I'd ever seen. She had the stature of an Amazon, with skin like warm honey and eyes the color of a newly unfurled leaf. Her hair was a fierce red and glowed like fire. But despite her beauty, there was little in the way of humanity in her expression, and her striking eyes were as cold as any monster's.

She stopped several feet away and gazed down at me. My heart beat so fast I could have sworn it was going to burst out of my chest, and sweat trickled down the side of my face.

"So," she said, her voice holding the edge of an accent that was both foreign and somewhat grating. "You are the one who almost caught me. The one who works with the reaper."

I tried to answer, but no sound came out. My vocal cords were as frozen as the rest of me.

"Why does a human work with a soul guide? I wonder. What makes you so special?"

She continued to study me, but the shadows behind her stirred, and harsh whispers rose, then fell away. I couldn't understand what was said, simply because it wasn't any language I'd heard before, but the Rakshasa raised a pale eyebrow and said, "Perhaps. Perhaps not."

She knelt and ran a finger across my chin. It came away bloody, and she raised it to her mouth and licked it clean.

"Your taste is sweet, but it is no different from that of any human," she mused softly. "Why, then, do the reapers run with you?"

She studied me as if she expected an answer, but even if I had been able to speak, I wouldn't have. I wanted her dead, not informed.

She smiled coldly, and it made me wonder if she was following my thoughts. I had the microcell implants, but had no idea whether they'd work against beings that were essentially spirit rather than flesh. They certainly didn't appear to work against either Azriel or Lucian.

She walked around to my other side, a slight frown marring her face. "There is something about you, however. Something not of this world, and powerful."

God, she was sensing Amaya.

No see, came her response, and with it a heat so fierce it burned into my spine. She was readying herself for battle, but it wouldn't do me a whole lot of good if I couldn't actually grip her.

I frowned, and forced every ounce of energy into trying to move something—anything. After a moment, my right hand twitched. Exhilaration surged. A twitch might not save me, but it was a definite sign that whatever it was that had frozen me was wearing off.

And maybe, just maybe, Amaya was helping. Until her heat had surged, my muscles had been totally unresponsive. As the thought crossed my mind, Amaya's heat increased, storming through my body like wildfire. Sweat began to drip from every pore. It smelled like fear and poison.

"I do not like this," the Rakshasa said, and raised her gaze to the shadows.

Again that murmur rose, the sound uneasy but vehement. The other Rakshasa wanted a kill, needed to taste flesh.

Fear threatened to choke me again. I took several deep breaths in an effort to remain calm, and kept my gaze on the Rakshasa. She was the immediate danger, not the ones who whispered from the shadows.

Her gaze came to mine again. She smiled, and in that instant I saw death.

My death.

Amaya's heat became even fiercer, soaking through every pore and muscle, until it seemed that she was becoming a part of me.

And I suddenly realized that was *exactly* what she was doing. Her energy wasn't just consuming me, it was shifting *through* me. She was moving through my flesh from her position at my back and, in the process, freeing me from the poison that held me immobile.

I twitched my fingers, my toes. Felt elation curl through me, and swiped down on it. *Hard*. Moving a few digits didn't mean I was out of the woods. I needed full movement to have any hope—and even then, the odds were still stacked against survival.

The Rakshasa knelt beside me again. She gripped my face, her sharp nails digging into my skin but not actually cutting. "Your reaper cannot find you here," she said softly. "You are ours to enjoy."

I swallowed heavily. Urged Amaya to hurry the hell up.

"Our dark god demands a sacrifice during the feeding phase," she continued, "and while the vampire would have sufficed, I believe you will bring us far greater favor."

Meaning they weren't going to eat me? I couldn't exactly be unhappy about that, even though I wasn't terribly keen on being sacrificed to their god instead.

She released me and rose. "Prepare her."

The other Rakshasa peeled away from the shadows. I'd been expecting them to be as beautiful as the first one, but that wasn't the case. Several verged on hideous, with yellowed skin, protruding teeth, long breasts and big bellies, while another had an odd number of limbs and the head of a horse. There was a dwarf with a bald head and a bulbous nose, while the last of them was tall and thin, and had the look of an elf. Except her skin was the color of moss and her hair a tangle of hissing serpents.

According to Azriel, the Rakshasa were shapeshifters, so I had to wonder why they'd chosen these forms over something more pleasant. But then, I guess beauty was in the eye of the beholder, and the Rakshasa were spirit rather than flesh. They weren't likely to be governed by the same ideals of beauty as I was.

They shuffled toward me, eyes alight with an odd sense of expectation. I clenched my fists but could do little else except watch them. Amaya still burned through my body, her energy sitting somewhere in my middle, making my innards quiver and twitch—more from the thought of it than any actual discomfort. The ceremony that had made her a part of me had also ensured that she could never harm me physically. I wasn't so sure about the whole mentally bit—at the very least, her constant hissing could possibly drive me around the bend.

Four Rakshasa moved to compass points around my body and began to chant. The sound resonated across the heavy atmosphere, dark and oddly powerful. From deep within the stones came a response—a heartbeat, slow and ponderous. It was as if the stones around me were coming to life.

The serpent-haired Rakshasa appeared, her chant joining the chorus of her kin as she swooped and tore my clothes from my body. I shivered as the cold, dense air hit my skin, and Amaya surged. She was so close to breaking through that I was surprised that the glow of her wasn't making my skin translucent.

Snakes hissed and slithered as the Rakshasa moved around to my feet. She bent and took off my shoes, then tossed them toward the pile of my clothes. Her serpents kissed my toes, their tongues like little needles, pricking rather than tickling. Blood trickled from each of the wounds, the warmth contrasting sharply with the chill of my skin.

I dug my nails into my palms, and the pain cut through the haze of panic threatening to consume me, allowing some semblance of clarity. But it was all I could do to remain still and resist the temptation to get up and run.

I couldn't move yet—figuratively *or* physically. My body still felt heavy, and Amaya had yet to finish her journey through my flesh.

The serpent-headed Rakshasa rose and disappeared back into the shadows. The other four continued their chant, and the beat of life in the stones around and underneath me got stronger. Whatever it was they were calling into life, it would soon be awake and aware. I had a feeling I didn't want to be here when that happened.

I licked my lips, my gaze darting from side to side, trying to find the position of the other two Rakshasa. I couldn't find the exotic one, but the serpent woman appeared again, an ancient-looking urn held with both hands above her head.

She stopped at my feet and spoke. The words were alien, but they ramped the power gathering in the air, making my hair stand on end and my skin quiver in revulsion.

The heat that was Amaya died within me, and I felt a moment of sheer terror. Then I realized the coolness of steel was pressed against my stomach, and the relief that swept me was so fierce that tears stung my eyes.

The serpent woman tilted the urn, her voice more strident, her words more commanding. Water poured down onto my feet and legs, thick and odorous. She continued to pour the liquid as she moved up my body, until I was completely covered in the goopy substance.

She reached my head, bent, and forced my mouth

open, her sharp talons cutting into my skin as the tongues of her snakes darted across my face, tiny whips that cut and tasted. As she tilted the urn, Amaya screamed, *No!*

I didn't think, I just reacted. I grabbed Amaya's hilt, bought her sharply upward, and sliced through the hand that held me so brutally. The snake-headed Rakshasa screamed, the sound shattering the growing spell of power. The heartbeat in the stone hesitated, and the other Rakshasa roared. It was a sound filled with fury and death.

I threw myself sideways, scuttling the Rakshasa on my left and barely avoiding the urn as it crashed inches from my head. The moisture that ran through the shards of the ruined vessel was thick, gluey, and black. Blood, but not human, not animal. It smelled altogether different and alien.

I threw a punch into the face of the Rakshasa I'd scuttled, crushing her bulbous nose and sending blood and bits of flesh flying, then scrambled to my feet and ran for the nearest fissure. It was six against one and that wasn't great odds in anyone's language. If I could restrict available space—restrict the space they had to come at me—I might have more of a chance.

Air stirred, and the sensation of danger swamped me. I swung around and lashed out with the heel of my foot, sending the nearest Rakshasa flying backward. Another dove at me. I sliced down with Amaya, severing flesh and bone with equal ease. I continued to swing Amaya, using her as a shield as I ran backward, and prayed like hell there was nothing between me and that fissure.

My back hit stone, and pain snatched my breath.

Blood began to pour from the wounds on my back and dots danced before my eyes. I hissed, but somehow remained upright and swinging.

The Rakshasa came at me as one, a hideous mass of flesh that cut and tore. I blocked blows, ducked teeth and claws, and attacked as best I could, until the nearby walls were coated and it was hard to know what blood was mine and what belonged to the Rakshasa. But there was no stopping them, no matter how much flesh I hacked from their bodies, because they didn't die. They just regenerated.

This *wasn't* going to end prettily. Not for me, anyway.

And that meant I had to try something else. *Anything* else.

The fissure was several feet away to my left. It was big and dark, and air stirred sluggishly around it, hinting at a possible escape route. Or, at the very least, another chamber.

Anywhere had to be better than here.

I kicked the nearest Rakshasa in the gut, sending her sprawling into her companions, then swung Amaya viciously from left to right, hamstringing several others. Their attack briefly faltered. I spun and ran into the fissure. The walls closed in around me, slick and uneven. The air still stirred, but it was putrid and dense, and my lungs felt like they were on fire.

As my shoulders began to brush the sharp edges of the walls, I slowed, my heart racing and my breath a harsh rasp. Little sound came from behind me— certainly no sound of pursuit. And yet every sense I had pulsed with the closeness of danger. Whether it was coming from the Rakshasa behind me or something unseen up ahead, I had no idea.

I struggled on, slipping sideways through the rock as the space grew tighter. It was blacker than ink in this foul-smelling place, the light of the stalactites having long since faded. Amaya wasn't emitting any flame, either, but I could hear her static running through my mind, a chant that vacillated between the need to kill and the urge for caution.

The fissure grew even tighter, until the rocks were scraping my breasts and butt. I cursed softly, then jumped as the sensation of movement stirred the air around me. I raised Amaya, holding her in front of me even though I couldn't say whether the movement had come from ahead or behind. I scanned the darkness either way, but there was nothing to see or scent, and certainly no sound of steps.

But the Rakshasa were spirits, and maybe they'd finally shed their human skins. If that were the case, then I *wouldn't* hear anything. And it meant I was in even deeper shit. I could fight flesh, and I could see ghosts, but would I even be able to see the Rakshasa in spirit form, let alone fight them?

I guess I was going to find out, because if the gathering sensation of movement was anything to go by, they were coming after me.

I pushed on, my lungs still burning and my head beginning to spin. I swallowed heavily and kept a fierce grip on Amaya. My skin was slick with blood— both mine and the stuff from the urn—but it didn't make me slip through the rocks any easier.

Sound began to creep across the silence. It was soft

and whispery, and I cocked my head sideways, listening intently. The image of snakes slithering down the body of the Rakshasa and onto the floor rose, and I groaned softly. As if I didn't have enough to deal with.

My hip lodged against a rock and I twisted, trying to move around it, only to find myself stuck fast. Panic surged. With a soft cry, I raised Amaya and hit the obstruction as hard as I could with her hilt. The rock shattered like glass, spraying needle-sharp shards into the darkness and sending me sprawling forward. I landed on my knees—hard—and stayed there for several seconds, ignoring pain and gasping for breath as I scanned the ink and tried to get some idea of where I was. There was a sense of vastness to this place, which suggested the fissure had given way to something a lot bigger than the cavern I'd been in before.

Only trouble was, I wasn't alone.

And there was an odd sort of consciousness in the air, a dark energy that thrummed around me even as the stone under my knees beat with faint life.

The house of their god, I suddenly realized, and wondered if I'd run from the frying pan only to step into the fire.

I swallowed heavily and pushed to my feet. There were no stalactites here to light the way, so I swept Amaya in front of me to feel for obstructions. The knowledge that someone was near grew, until it was so thick and sharp it flayed my skin.

"So," the exotic Rakshasa said, her words soft but seeming to reverberate through the darkness, "you bear a dark sword. This is the power I sensed earlier."

I stopped and raised Amaya. Her chant no longer

raced across the edges of my mind, but her energy still burned within me. "It's a power that will kill you all if you do not let me go."

"No matter what weapon you bear, you are, in the end, flesh and blood. All we have to do is keep attacking. Once your life blood has soaked the stone and fed the god beneath our feet, we will dine on your flesh."

Something hit my right calf, and tiny teeth sliced deep. I yelped and jumped away, and the snake hissed. I swung Amaya, but didn't hit anything. Damn it, I needed to see to be able to fight. I was all but blind, and relying on scent and sound just wasn't good enough. Not when these creatures made little sound and had no scent.

One, came Amaya's whisper, *become*.

I frowned, not sure what she meant. Static rolled through my mind, a sound of frustration if ever I'd heard it.

Open, she growled, *join you*.

Meaning she wanted me to open myself fully to her? Wanted me to allow her—a demon spirit encased in steel—free rein to run through me? Control me?

Not, she said. *One*.

I shivered. The one thing I'd feared from the moment I'd plunged her steel into my flesh and felt the surge of her power was that she would somehow gain a foothold in my mind and make me more like her. And now she was asking me to grant her the freedom to leave the sword and fully become one with me.

Every instinct I had suggested it would be a very bad move.

But if my only chance of survival was to do what I feared the most, then do it I would. That determination was what had driven me to confront Jak and ask for his help, and it still drove me now.

I just had to hope that once I'd given her freedom, Amaya would step back into steel when all this was over.

And that was one thought to which she *didn't* reply.

The air stirred to my left. I swung around, stabbing Amaya in front of me. The exotic Rakshasa laughed softly—from the right, not the left. Something hard and cold hit my back and I jumped away, swearing as I swung around. Again, I hit nothing but air.

Blood was now running freely down the back of my legs, and every drop that hit the stone seemed to make the heartbeat stronger.

"The sleep of our god ends," she whispered, this time in front of me. "Soon he will awaken fully, and then we will bleed you out."

"Not if I can help it." To Amaya, I said, *Let's do it.*

Invite, she whispered, excitement in her tone.

Trepidation shivered through me, but it wasn't like I had a lot of options left. I took a deep breath, then silently said, *Amaya, become one with me.*

For a moment, nothing happened. Then power exploded, thick and heavy, surging through steel and flesh with equal ferocity. It was a storm that tore my core apart, fiber by fiber, then pieced me back together, all within a matter of heartbeats.

Only it was no longer me, but *we.*

Because I wasn't alone. Someone else was in here with me, sharing my body and my thoughts, even as she shared her powers and abilities. It was a strange, unsettling sensation.

We opened my eyes. The darkness fell away, and the Rakshasa appeared. Or rather, the blue shimmer of her energy appeared. She was standing five feet away, and there was a pool of seething, sinewy flesh at her feet. She flicked a finger to the left, and several snakes instantly slithered away. Looping around to get behind me.

Amaya hissed. It sounded weird coming out of my mouth. We didn't move, just held the sword as we studied our surroundings.

The cavern itself was vast and roughly triangular in shape. Blue bolts of energy shot across the walls, the rhythm matching the beat of the heart. It seemed to be originating from a shadowed enclave at the very tip of the triangle, and I suddenly remembered what Azriel had said: *Smash the god's power, and the Rakshasa will be fixed in flesh and more easily killed.*

That was our way out of here.

Fight, Amaya growled and raised the sword, sweeping it from left to right so fast that the steel sang as it cut through the air.

No, I bit back. *We stop the dark god rising first.*

The snakes swept in. We moved, the sword little more than a blur as we struck, killing the snakes in one deadly sweep. The Rakshasa sent more snakes at us, but I had no intention of hanging around, waiting for them to get close.

My one chance of getting out of here alive might lie in reaching that enclave and destroying whatever lay within it, and I wasn't about to waste it.

I forced my limbs into a run, battling Amaya's desire to stand and fight as much as the weakness in my limbs. The Rakshasa's reaction was swift and deadly. She lunged after me, her sharp nails flashing. I twisted away, but she raked my back and a scream tore out of my throat. Not just from the pain, but also from frustration. Her nails were poisonous and I had no idea how quickly it would take effect and render me immobile once again.

Then I thrust that thought aside. All that mattered was reaching the enclave, and right now I could still run. My feet slapped quickly against the cold stone, but there was little sound to be heard other than the harsh rasp of my breathing.

Something hit the back of my legs and I stumbled. I flung out my arms to steady myself, and somehow retained balance. Again something struck at me, this time tearing into flesh. Snake. *Fuck.* The sword swung and there was no more snake, just clear ground between us and the enclave.

The exotic Rakshasa came at us. I heard the wind of her approach, felt the burn of her energy against my skin. We twisted away and swung the sword, the dark point slicing across perfect features, splitting flesh and cutting down to the bone. Her skin from cheek to chin peeled away, the flap hanging loose and giving her a half-skeletal look. She screamed, but it was a sound of fury rather than pain. We twisted again, and lashed out with a heel. It hit her high in the neck, hard enough to crush her larynx. Whether it did or not I had no idea, but the force behind the blow was enough to send her flailing backward.

I ran on. In the shadows that lurked around the cavern's point a simple urn sat on a pedestal of stone.

Power within, Amaya said. *Crush*.

We slid to a stop, raised the sword two-handed, and brought her down on the urn as hard as we could. The dark steel sliced through the urn as easily as it would have through butter, and the contents spewed out, a gluey mess of blood and other matter. In the center of the now shattered urn lay a small heart, its rhythm matching the beat in the stone around us. We raised the sword fractionally and slashed down. The blade shuddered as steel met flesh, then slowly, surely, it sliced through. The beat of life in the stone around us became unsteady, erratic.

Not dead, not yet.

I raised the sword to finish the job, but the Rakshasa's scream swung me around. This time it was more than fury. This time it was devastation.

And this time it wasn't just the exotic Rakshasa who came at me, but every damn one of them.

Fight, Amaya said. *Now*.

We did. With a ferocity and skill that wasn't mine, we charged into the middle of them and tore them apart, piece by piece. It was a bitter, bloody battle that had blood pouring from almost every scrap of my body, but soon five of them were dead and only the exotic Rakshasa was left.

I expected her to attack, but instead she stepped back. I raised the sword, fighting Amaya's urge to attack, my limbs trembling with exhaustion as I watched her warily. The Rakshasa's gaze swept the destruction around us, then moved to the shattered remains of the urn. Something close to grief moved across her ruined features, then her gaze returned to mine.

"It is done," she said softly. "The dark god is dead. I have failed in my duty to her."

She bowed low, then dropped to her knees before me and didn't move.

Waiting for me to step forward and finish what I'd started.

Kill, Amaya said, and my fingers clenched tight against the hilt as I raised the sword.

But I fought Amaya's desire and stared instead at the Rakshasa. She just knelt there, waiting for death. I shivered. My task had always been to kill this spirit, but it didn't seem right to do it like this—in cold blood rather than in the heat of battle.

Kill, Amaya said again. *Will I?*

No. I had a feeling that if I acquiesced to her in this, I'd somehow be handing greater control of my body to the spirit within my sword. Besides, this was my task, not hers, not Azriel's. In the end, I had to be strong enough to do it.

To prove to everyone that if the need arose, I *could* do what was necessary to survive.

I closed my eyes, took a deep breath, then raised the sword to full height and swept it down as hard as I could. The dark blade cut through the Rakshasa's neck with ease, but as her head plopped bloodlessly onto the stone and rolled away from her slumping body, I staggered and lost what little there was in my stomach.

After which I fell to my knees and sucked in great gulps of air. It didn't help the buzzing in my head, the trembling in my limbs, or the burning in my lungs. I needed to get out of here—and get help—quick, or this place might become my tomb, as well.

I sheathed the sword, then said wearily, "Amaya, you need to return to the blade."

Better here.

Fear snaked through me. "No," I said determinedly. "This is my body, not yours. Your place is in steel, not flesh."

One, she retorted. *Here.*

"No," I repeated, and closed my eyes, picturing the dark energy of her, imagining my hands encasing it, forcing it out of my body and back into steel.

She fought me every step of the way, until exhaustion trembled through every part of me and I was all but blacking out. But if I did that, she'd win.

Damn it, this was my body, my life, and no matter how much it sucked at the moment, I wasn't about to give it up easily!

It was that determination that kept me going, and slowly but surely I forced her back into the sword. But as her energy and spirit left me, I felt a glimmer of almost reluctant admiration.

My sword respected my actions, even if she'd fought them.

I didn't know whether to laugh or cry, and in the end, probably did a bit of both.

Time to go home, I thought, before either the Rakshasa's poison took effect or I collapsed from blood loss. And the dizziness sweeping me suggested I was closer to blacking out than I needed or wanted.

But how the hell did I get home?

That odd buzzing heaviness no longer rode the air,

but I was weaker than a pup and I doubted I'd have the strength to become Aedh.

Which left me with only one option—chance the gray fields, and hope like hell Azriel found me there before anyone else did. Not that the Aedh had any reason to be hunting me given the tracker they'd placed on my heart, but my father was still out there somewhere, and it'd be my luck that he would choose a moment like this to hunt me down.

I closed my eyes and took a slow, somewhat shaky breath that didn't seem to contain much in the way of air. As I slowly released it, I released awareness of the battle to breathe, the pain that shook me, and the myriad of wounds that washed blood down my body, and concentrated on nothing more than slowing the beat of my heart. Gradually that beat steadied, amplified, as the dark cavern began to fade and the gray fields gathered close. Warmth throbbed at my neck—Ilianna's magic at work, protecting me as my psyche, my soul, or whatever else people liked to call it, pulled away from the constraints of my flesh and stepped gently into the gray fields that were neither life nor death.

The Dušan exploded from my arm, her energy flowing, buffeting me as her lilac form gained flesh and shape. She swirled around me, her movements sharp, edgy, as her ebony gaze scanned the fields around us. Looking for a threat that came from within me rather than anything the fields might offer. At least for the moment.

Azriel, I whispered, and hoped it was enough. I didn't have the energy for anything louder.

He answered. The storm of his approach quivered

through me, but I didn't wait for him. I couldn't. Blackness was beginning to steal through the gray, and I knew my strength was giving out. I had to get back into my body before that happened, or I might end up stranded here in the fields.

And that could be deadly. A body could survive only so long without its soul on board.

This way, I said, and fled, down through the layers of consciousness and into my flesh. Then the blackness overtook me, and I knew no more.

Chapter 14

Awareness surfaced slowly, as did the knowledge that I was warm and safe and—most important—alive. I smiled, but I couldn't seem to shake sleepiness or force my eyelids open, and soon I drifted back to sleep.

It was the aroma of cooking that eventually woke me. My nostrils flared as I drew in the tantalizing scent of roasting meat more deeply, and my stomach rumbled noisily.

"That," a familiar voice mused, "had better be your stomach and not a fart."

Tao, I thought with a sleepy smile.

Then I sat bolt upright in bed. *Tao!*

I stared at him. Rubbed my eyes and stared at him some more. Reached out and touched him. Lightly, carefully, like he was a mirage that might disappear at the slightest sense of movement.

He wasn't a mirage.

He was warm and real and *here*.

"Oh, god," I said, and flung myself at him.

He grunted as my weight hit him, then laughed softly and held me as fiercely as I held him. "It's good to see you, too," he said softly, his words whispering past my right ear. "You gave us quite a scare, you know."

I snorted softly and drew back a little, my gaze scanning his features. He was pale, and thin, and deep in his warm brown eyes something more than human burned, but none of that mattered right now. He was awake, he was aware, and most important of all, he seemed to have come back to us whole.

"When did you wake up?"

"About the same time that Azriel dragged you half-dead out of that hellhole you were stuck in." He gave me a weary smile and flicked my chin lightly. It still hurt, so the wound hadn't completely healed.

"It was touch and go for a while there, you know. Our reaper tried to heal you, but it didn't fully hold. You were out for days, and *he* was like a bear with a sore head. And the depth of his concern scared the *hell* out of us."

Why wouldn't the healing hold? I glanced around the room, half expecting an answer, even though I knew he wasn't near. "Where is he?"

Tao shrugged. "He said something about needing to inform Hunter that the task was done."

Oh fuck, I thought, and hoped like hell the "informing" didn't involve violence. We didn't need Hunter or the council as enemies right now. I took a deep, somewhat calming breath, and my stomach rumbled again.

Tao laughed. "Sounds like you'd better get something into that belly of yours."

"Only if you do the same." I scanned him critically. "You, my lad, need to put on some weight."

He grimaced. "Ilianna's been feeding me like a horse

for days, and with little effect. The new me, I'm afraid, will probably remain razor thin."

I hesitated, then said softly, "How is the new you?"

"Awake, alive, and damn grateful for both."

"But?" I said, sensing there was one.

"But," he added grimly, "I also fear it."

Given that he'd consumed a fire elemental—and survived, something no one had ever done—he had a right to be scared. We didn't know what the long-term effects were going to be—not even the most powerful witches in the country could tell us that.

Still, I said, "Why?"

"Because I can feel it in me, Risa. Its presence burns constantly at the back of my mind, and though I've won this battle, I'm not sure I've won the war. It could yet take me over."

I cupped a hand to his cheek. His skin burned under my fingertips. "You've made it this far. You can—and will—control it."

"Then you have more faith in my strength than I do," he muttered, and rose. "I better get back to the kitchen, before Ilianna cooks the hell out of those steaks. Do you want to eat in here, or out there?"

"Out there. I feel the need to get out and about."

He nodded. "Know that feeling. I'll give you a yell when they're ready."

I watched him walk out of the room, then carefully climbed out of bed. The room swung around me and my legs felt like water, and it was only a fierce determination that I would *not* fall that kept me upright. As Azriel had noted on numerous occasions, I could be a stubborn bitch when I wanted to be.

I walked a little unsteadily across to my bathroom, then twisted around in front of the mirror to check out my various injuries. My reflection revealed a myriad of half-healed wounds, although the one down my spine was by far the worst. Azriel was right—that one would scar.

No more low-backed evening dresses for me, I thought grimly. Especially if my aunt was around. She would *not* take kindly to discovering that I'd been in situations dangerous enough to get hurt this badly without calling her in.

Heat shimmered across my skin. I turned around as Azriel appeared near my bed. His gaze skimmed me, a critical inspection that nevertheless had delight skittering through me.

"You should not be up," he said eventually. "You look exhausted."

"I need to stretch my legs, and I need to eat." I hesitated. "How did the meeting with Hunter go?"

"She was well aware of your victory. Apparently, the Cazador witnessed your fight with Rakshasa."

And *that* rankled him. Massively. "My getting snatched is not your fault, Azriel. I should have been more aware of what was going on."

"As should I." He practically spat the words. "If I *had* been, I would have stopped the Rakshasa before she dove underground, and you would not be in this state."

"Which is a point we could argue endlessly, and one that really doesn't matter anymore."

I grabbed my dressing gown from the bathroom hook and put it on as I walked across the room. He didn't react when I stopped in front of him, but the connection between us was stronger than ever before. His emotions were a tidal wave that crashed through every fiber of my being, a tumultuous mix of desire, caring, and anger. If I'd had the energy, I would have danced. He might be determined to hold what lay between us at arm's length, but at least he couldn't deny the strength of it. Not when it hummed so fiercely.

"In the end, the only thing that matters is that I did what the council wanted and survived." I paused, then grimaced. "My only regret is that with the Rakshasa gone, the ghosts have no outlet for their fury, and the club has no reason to stop that room from being used."

"The grief of the ghosts is powerful enough that it will attract other dark forces. This will not be the last we hear of that room."

"Unfortunately." I rubbed my arms against the chill of premonition. "We can only hope that *next* time, the council do their own fucking dirty work."

"I doubt they will now that they have your services to call on in such matters."

I raised my eyebrows. "So the vote has gone in my favor?"

"Hunter seems confident it will. The Cazador's report was apparently impressive."

He wrapped an arm around my waist and pulled me close. I sighed contentedly and rested my cheek against his shoulder.

"There is nothing you can do about the club or the council's use of the whores," he continued softly. "Not without endangering yourself or anyone you told."

"I know, and that's what's so frustrating."

His lips brushed the top of my head, the touch so light and yet so electric. I shivered.

"Those behind such an atrocity will in the end pay. Karma is a very real force."

"But a force that in this case is not likely to react soon enough."

"That is true."

"Ris," Tao called from the other room. "Dinner is up!"

I pulled somewhat reluctantly out of Azriel's arms. His grip slipped from my waist to my elbow. "Ready?"

I nodded, and with his help, I made it into the living area. Ilianna appeared out of the kitchen, her smile wide and her expression filled with relief.

"Damn, it's good to have you back." She stopped in front of me and dropped a kiss on my cheek. "I'd hug the hell out of you, but you look rather fragile at the moment."

"I look it because I feel it." With Azriel's help, I eased down onto a chair. "I think I need a mountain of food and Coke, and I don't care which comes first."

"Both are on their way," she said, and headed back to the kitchen.

Tao came out of the kitchen, handed me a large glass of Coke, then pulled out a chair to sit beside me. The doorbell rang, and he hesitated. "You expecting anyone?"

I shook my head.

"Nor me," Ilianna said from the confines of the kitchen.

"A human stands at the door," Azriel noted, then cocked his head sideways a little. "A messenger. He leaves."

Oh god, I thought, trepidation suddenly so thick it practically closed my throat. The last two times a messenger had come to our door it was to deliver a message from my father, and a whole lot of trouble had ensued.

I wasn't ready for that.

I really wasn't.

I licked my lips and looked up at Tao. "We'd better see what's been left this time."

He nodded and walked across the room. I twisted around to watch him. He punched the code on the security panel and the door slid open, revealing a plain brown envelope. He swooped, picked it up, then closed the door and walked back.

My gaze dropped to the envelope and my throat went dry. It was from my father. I recognized the handwriting on the front.

I held out a hand and Tao silently gave it to me. Tension rode his movements and his expression was dark. He knew.

I took a deep breath to gather courage, then slid a fingernail under the edge. Inside was a solitary piece of paper. I pulled it out and opened it. The words inside were brief and to the point.

The time has come to find the second key. Meet me, usual place, two days from now.

I didn't say anything. I closed my eyes and handed the piece of paper to Tao.

"Fuck," he said. "This isn't what we need right now."

No, it wasn't, but there wasn't a whole lot we could do about it, either—except pray that fate would give us a break. I didn't think any of us could stand too much more hardship.

But even as that thought crossed my mind, I knew it was futile. Fate had abandoned us long ago, and everything we'd gone through so far was little more than the initial skirmish. The real war was coming, and if I was still alive at the end of it all, I'd be very fucking surprised.

I didn't have the courage to go on, I thought wearily. Didn't have the strength.

But even as the all-too-familiar doubts crossed my mind, I remembered everything I'd done and everything I'd been through—with the Raziq, the Rakshasa, the battle with my sword. Time and again, I'd done whatever had been needed to survive—sometimes with help, sometimes not.

I *had* the courage. I *could* do what had to be done.

Not matter what the consequences.

No matter what the cost.

"I need to speak to a ghost."

Adeline Greenfield paused in the middle of pouring tea into her expensive china cups and looked at me.

"I was under the impression you already could." Her voice, like her appearance, was unremarkable. With her short gray hair, lined face, and generous curves, she reminded me of the grandmotherly types often seen on TV sitcoms. It was only her blue eyes—or rather, only the power that glowed within them—that gave the game away. Adeline Greenfield was a witch, a very powerful and successful one.

"No. I mean, I *can* hear them, and sometimes I can see them, but they don't seem to hear or acknowledge me." I grimaced. "I thought if I was on the same plane as them—if I astral traveled to them—it might help."

"Possibly." She put the teapot back down and frowned. "But didn't you help relocate a ghost that was causing all sorts of mischief at the Brindle?"

The Brindle was a witch depository located here in Melbourne, and it held within its bowels centuries of knowledge, spells, and other witch-related paraphernalia. "Yes, but it wasn't really a ghost. It was actually a mischievous soul who was undecided about moving on."

"Souls are usually incapable of interaction with this world."

"Yes, but the Brindle is a place of power, and that gave her the ability."

She nodded sagely. "It is still odd that you cannot speak to them the same way your mother did, because I'm sure she said you had the skill."

I raised my eyebrows. "You knew Mom?"

She smiled. "Those of us *truly* capable of hearing the dead are few and far between, so yes, I knew her. We had lunch occasionally."

That was something I hadn't known. "Well, no matter what she may have believed, the dead *won't* speak to me."

"Ghosts *can* be vexing creatures," she agreed. "And they often have no desire to acknowledge their death."

"So how is ignoring me helping them disregard the fact they're dead?"

She placed a couple of sugar cubes into each cup, then gently stirred the tea. "We're talking about the dead here. Their minds are not what they once were, especially those who have been murdered."

"I didn't say he'd been murdered."

"You didn't have to. Trouble, my dear, darkens your steps, and it's not such a leap to think that if you want to speak to a ghost, it's because he died before his time. Otherwise, your reaper would have been able to find out whatever you needed." She handed me a cup of tea, then glanced over my right shoulder. "I would prefer it, by the way, if you'd just show yourself. It's impolite to skulk at the edges of the gray fields like that."

Heat shimmered across my skin as Azriel appeared. Of course, he wasn't strictly a reaper, as they were soul guides. He was something much more—or, if you believed him, something much less—and that was a Mijai: a dark angel who hunted and killed the things that broke free from hell.

But what he hunted now wasn't an escaped demon, daemon, or even a spirit—although we certainly *had* been hunting one of those. We'd gotten it, too, but not before the fucking thing had almost killed me. Which was why I was moving like an old woman right now—everything still hurt. I might be half werewolf, but fast healing was one of the gifts I hadn't inherited enough of. In fact, I couldn't shift into wolf shape *at all*, and the full moon held no sway over me.

Of course, I *could* heal myself via my Aedh heritage, but shifting in and out of Aedh form required energy, and I didn't have enough of that, either.

"That's better," Adeline said, satisfaction in her voice. "Now, would you like a cup of tea, young man?"

"No, thank you."

There was a hint of amusement in Azriel's mellow tones, and it played through my being like the caress of gentle fingers. Longing shivered through me.

Adeline picked up her own cup, a frown once again marring her homely features. "Why do you wear a sword, reaper? There is no threat in this house."

"No, there is not," he agreed.

When it became obvious he didn't intend to say anything else, Adeline's expectant gaze turned to me.

"He wears a sword because he's helping me hunt down some—" I hesitated. For safety's sake, I couldn't tell her everything, yet I couldn't *not* explain, either. Not if I wanted her help. "—rogue priests who seek the keys to the gates of heaven and hell so they can permanently close them."

That raised her eyebrows. "Why on earth would anyone want that?"

"Because they're not *of* earth." They were Aedh, energy beings who lived on the gray fields—the area that divided earth from heaven and hell. Or the light and dark portals, as the reapers tended to say. While the reaper community had flourished, the Aedh had not. They'd all but died out, and only the Raziq—a breakaway group of priests—were left in any great numbers. "And they've decided it would be easier to permanently shut the gates to *all* souls rather than keep guarding against the occasional demon breakout."

She frowned. "But that would mean no soul could move on and be reborn."

"Yes, but they don't care about that. They see just the bigger picture."

"But surely the number of demons who break out of hell is minor when compared to the chaos closing the gates permanently would cause?"

"As I said, I don't think the priests care." Not about the human race in general, and certainly not about babies being born without souls and ending up little more than inanimate lumps of flesh. "They just want their lives of servitude to the gates ended."

Which is how I'd gotten involved in this whole mess in the first place. The Raziq had developed three keys that would permanently open or close the gates. The only trouble was my father had not only stolen the keys but had arranged to have them hidden—so well even *he* knew only the general location. And as he could no longer take on flesh form, he now needed me to do his footwork, as only someone of his bloodline could detect the hidden keys.

In fact, *everyone* needed me—the Raziq, the reapers, the high vampire council. And all of them wanted the keys for very different reasons.

Adeline said, "And this is why you wish to speak so urgently to this ghost? He knows of the keys?"

I hesitated. "About the keys, no. But he might have some information about a dark sorcerer who could be tied up in all this mess. We questioned our ghost when he was alive, but someone very powerful had blocked sections of his memories. We're hoping death might have removed those blocks."

"It's a rather vague hope."

"Which is still better than no hope." I took a sip of tea, then shuddered at the almost bitter taste and put the cup down. Tea had never been my favorite beverage.

"When do you wish to start?" Adeline asked.

"Now, if possible."

She frowned again. "Your energy levels feel extremely low. It's generally not considered a wise—"

"Adeline," I interrupted softly, "I may not get another chance to do this."

Mainly because I'd been ordered by my father to retrieve a note from Southern Cross Station later that morning, and who the hell knew what would happen after *that*. But if past retrievals were any indication, then hell was likely to break loose—at least metaphysically speaking, if not literally.

She studied me for several moments, then sighed. "If you insist, then I must help you, even if it is against my better judgment."

"Must?" I raised my eyebrows. "That almost sounds like you've been ordered to help me."

"Oh, I have been, and by Kiandra herself, no less." She eyed me thoughtfully. "You have some very powerful allies, young woman."

Surprise rippled through me. Kiandra—who was head witch at the Brindle—had helped me on several occasions, but only *after* I'd approached her. That she was now anticipating my needs suggested she knew a whole lot more about what was going on than I'd guessed. "Did she say why?"

"She said only that your quest has grave implications for us all, and that it behooves us to provide assistance where possible."

This suggested that Kiandra *did* know about the existence of the keys and our quest to retrieve them. And I guess that wasn't really surprising—surely you couldn't become the head of all witches without *some* working knowledge of the fields and the beings who inhabited them.

"Which is why I need to do this now, Adeline."

She continued to study me, her expression concerned. "What do you know of astral traveling?"

"Not a lot, though I suspect it won't be that dissimilar to traveling the gray fields."

"It's not. Astral travel is simply your consciousness or spirit traveling through earth's realm, whereas you leave this world and move into the next when you journey to the gray fields. But there are a few rules and dangers you should be aware of before we attempt this."

"There usually are when it comes to anything otherworldly."

"Yes." She hesitated. "Thought is both your magic carpet and your foe on the astral plane. If you want to go somewhere, think of the precise location and you will be projected there. By the same token, if you become afraid, you can create an instant nightmare."

I nodded. She continued. "Be aware that any thought related to your physical body will bring you back to your body. This includes the fear that your physical body may be hurt in some way."

I frowned. "If I can't speak or move, how am I going to question my ghost?"

"I didn't say you can't move, and you think the questions, the same as you think of the location. Clear?"

"As mud."

She eyed me for a moment, the concern in her expression deepening. "The astral plane is inhabited by two types of spirits: those who cannot—for one reason or another—move on spiritually, and other astral travelers.

And just like walking down the street, you cannot control who's on the astral planes. But you *can* be certain that not all will be on the side of the angels."

"So I should watch my metaphysical ass?"

"Yes. At your current energy levels, you could attract energies who are darker in life, and they may cause you problems on the astral plane *or* follow you onto this one."

"I can handle unpleasant energies on *this* plane. And if I can't, Azriel can." I paused. "What of the dangers?"

Her expression darkened. "While you cannot die on the field itself, it is possible to become trapped there. It is also possible to become so enraptured by whatever illusion surrounds you on the plane that what happens there can echo through your physical being."

I frowned. "So if I somehow imagine getting whacked on the plane, my body can be bruised?"

"If the illusion is powerful enough, yes. And if you find yourself trapped there, you risk death."

"Why?"

"Because," Azriel said, before Adeline could, "flesh cannot survive great lengths of time without its soul. And while the astral body is not the entirety of the soul, if you find death when your astral being is not present in your body, then your soul is not complete and cannot move on. You would become one of the lost ones."

"And here I was thinking it would be a walk in the park." I swept a hand through my short hair and wished, just once, that something was. "Let's get this done."

She glanced past me for a moment, then rose. "Come with me, then."

I followed her out of the living room and down the long hall, my footsteps echoing softly on her wooden floors. Azriel made no sound, although the heat of his presence burned into my spine and chased away the chill of apprehension.

Adeline stopped at the last door on the right and opened it. "Please take your shoes off."

I did so as she stepped to one side and motioned for me to enter. The room was dark and smelled faintly of lavender and chamomile, and my bare feet disappeared into a thick layer of mats and silk.

"Lie down and make yourself comfortable."

I glanced over my shoulder at Azriel. Though his face was almost classical in its beauty, it possessed the hard edge of a man who'd won more than his fair share of battles. He was shirtless, his skin a warm, suntanned brown and his abs well defined. The worn leather strap that held his sword in place emphasized the width of his shoulders, and the dark jeans that clung to his legs hinted at their lean strength. His stance was that of a fighter, a warrior— one who not only protected me, but who had saved me more than once. And would continue to do so for as long as I was of use to him.

Still, I couldn't help mentally asking, *You'll be here?*

I'll be here to protect your physical form, yes. His thought ran like sunshine through my mind. I wasn't telepathic in any way, shape, or form, but that didn't matter when it came to Azriel. He could hear my thoughts as clearly as spoken words. Unfortunately, the only time I heard *his* thoughts was at moments such as this, when it was a deliberate act on his part. *But not on the plane. Astral travelers are of this world, not mine, so you are basically little more than a ghost to me. I cannot interact with you in any way.*

Reaper rules?

Reaper rules. He hesitated, and something flashed through the mismatched blue of his eyes. Something so bright and sharp that it made my breath hitch. *Be careful. It would be most . . . inconvenient . . . if you find death on the astral plane.*

Inconvenient? I shucked off my jacket and tossed it to one side with a little more force than was necessary. *Yeah,*

I guess it would be. I mean, who else would find the damn keys for you if something happened to me?

That, he said, an edge riding his mental tone, *is an unfair statement.*

Yeah, it was. But, goddamn it, if *I* was an inconvenience to him, then *he* was a vast source of frustration to me. *And* on more than one level. Was it any wonder that it occasionally got the better of me and resulted in a snippy remark?

That frustration is shared by us both, Risa.

I glanced at him sharply. His expression was its usual noncommittal self, but the slightest hint of a smile played about his lips. I snorted softly. If he *was* implying he was as sexually frustrated as I was, then he had only himself to blame. After all, *he* was the one determined to keep our relationship strictly professional now that desire had been acknowledged and acted upon. Although *how* he could ignore what still burned between us, I had no idea. I was certainly struggling.

"Risa," Adeline said softly, "you must lie down before we can proceed."

I did as she ordered, and the mats wrapped around me, warm and comforting. Adeline closed the door and the darkness engulfed us. The scents sharpened, slipping in with every breath and easing the tension in my limbs.

"Now," she said, her voice at one with the serenity in the room, "to astral travel, you must achieve a sense of complete and utter relaxation."

I closed my eyes and released awareness of everything and everyone around me, concentrating on nothing more than slowing my breathing. As the beat of my heart became more measured, warmth began to throb at my neck as the charm Ilianna—my best friend and housemate—had made me kicked into action. It was little more than a small piece of petrified wood to connect me to the earth, and two small stones—agate and serpentine—for protection, but it had ~~sav~~ed my life when a spirit had attacked me on the gray fields, and I'd been wearing it ever since. That it was glowing now meant it would protect me on the astral plane as fiercely as it did on the gray fields, and I was suddenly glad of that.

Though why I thought I might need that protection, I had no idea.

"Let your mind be the wind," Adeline intoned. "Let it be without thought or direction, free and easy."

A sense of peace settled around me. My breathing slowed even further, until I was on the cusp of sleep.

"A rope hangs above your chest. You cannot see it in the darkness, but it is there. Believe in it. When you are ready, reach for it. Not physically—metaphysically. Feel it in your hands. Feel the roughness of the fibers against your skin. Feel the strength within it."

I reached up with imaginary hands and grasped the rope. It felt thick and real and as strong as steel.

"Ignore physical sensation and use the rope to pull yourself upright. Imagine yourself rising from your body and stepping free of all constraints."

I gripped harder with my imaginary hands and pulled myself upward along the rope. Dizziness swept over me, seeming to come from the center of my chest. I kept pulling myself upright and the pressure grew until my whole body felt heavy. I ignored it as ordered, and every inch of me began to vibrate. Then, with a suddenness that surprised me, I was free and floating in the darkness above my prone form.

Only it wasn't really dark. Adeline's aura lit the room with a deep violet, and Azriel's aura glowed an intense gold. Which surprised me—I'd have placed money that his would be the fierce white I saw on the fields. The dark tats that decorated his skin—the biggest of which resembled half of a dragon, with a wing that swept around his ribs from underneath his arm and brushed the left side of his neck—shimmered in the darkness and seemed to hold no distinct color.

Only that half dragon wasn't actually a tat. It was a Dušan—a darker, more abstract brother to the one that had crawled onto my left arm and now resided within my flesh. They were designed to protect us when we walked the gray fields, and we'd been sent them by person or persons unknown—although Azriel suspected it was probably my father's doing. He was one of the few left in this world—or the next—who had the power to make them.

Valdis, the sword at Azriel's back, dripped the same blue fire on the astral plane as she did in the real world, and it made me wonder whether my own sword Amaya would be visible on this plane given that she was usually little more than a deadly shadow.

I shoved the thought aside, then closed my eyes and conjured the image of the area where our ghost Frank Logan had met his doom.

In an instant I was standing in front of the long, gigantic shed that was the Central Pier function center. On the night Logan had been murdered, this place had been filled with life and sound, and the pavement lined with taxis and limos waiting to pick up passengers. Now it was little more than a vague ghost town—literally *and* figuratively.

I looked around. The first thing I saw was a man watching me. He was tall, with regal features and a body that was as lean as a whip. A fighter, I thought, staring at him.

As our gazes met, humor seemed to touch his lips and he bowed slightly.

I frowned, and thought, *Do I know you?*

No, but I know you rather well. I've been following you around for weeks.

His voice was cool, without inflection, but not unpleasant.

Why would you— I stopped and suddenly realized just who he was. *You're the Cazador who Madeline Hunter has following me?*

I certainly am, ma'am.

I blinked at his politeness, although I wasn't really sure why it surprised me. I *had* grown up hearing tales about the men and women who formed the ranks of the Cazadors—the high vampire council's own personal hit squad—and I supposed I'd just expected them all to be fierce and fearsome.

He gave me another slight bow. *Markel Sanchez, at your service.*

Well, forgive me for saying this, Markel, but you're a pain in my ass and I'd rather not have you following me around, on this plane or in life.

Trust me, ma'am, this is not my desire, either. But it has been ordered and I must obey.

I raised imaginary eyebrows. *Meaning even the Cazadors are wary of Hunter?*

If they are wise and value their lives, yes.

Which said a lot about Hunter's power. She might be the head honcho of the Directorate of Other Races, but she was also a high-ranking member of the high vampire council and, I suspected, plotting to take it over completely.

I need to speak to a ghost. You're not going to interfere, are you?

I'm here to listen and report. Nothing more, nothing less.

I nodded and turned away from him. A grayish figure stood not far away. He was standing sideways to me, looking ahead rather than at me. He was a big man with well-groomed hair, a Roman nose, and a sharp chin. Frank Logan.

I imagined myself standing beside him, and suddenly I was. If only it were this easy to travel in Aedh form.

Mr. Logan, I need to speak with you.

He jumped, then swung around so violently that tendrils of smoke swirled away from his body.

"Who the hell are you?" He wasn't using thought, and his words were crisp and clear, echoing around me like the clap of thunder.

I'm Risa Jones. I was standing nearby when you were murdered.

His expression showed a mix of disbelief and confusion. "I'm dead? How can I be dead? I can *see* you. I can see the buildings around me. I can't be dead. Damn it, where's my limo? I want to go home."

He was never going home. Never moving on. He'd died before his time, and no reaper had been waiting to collect his soul. He was one of the lost ones—doomed to roam the area of death for eternity.

But I suspected that nothing I could say would ever convince him of this, and I wasn't about to even try—that could take far more time than I probably had on this plane. *Mr. Logan, I need to speak to you about John Nadler.*

He frowned. "I'm sorry, young woman, but I can't talk to you about clients—"

Mr. Logan, John Nadler is dead—murdered. I imagined a cop's badge, then showed it to him. If he wanted to believe he was still alive, then I wasn't going to waste time arguing with him. *We'd appreciate your helping us willingly, Mr. Logan, but we will subpoena you if required.*

His confusion deepened. "When was Nadler murdered? I was talking to him only today."

Logan's "today" had actually been several days ago. *Which is why we need to speak with you. We believe you could be the last person to have seen him alive.*

Or, at least, the last person to have seen the face-shifter who'd killed the real Nadler and assumed his identity. The real Nadler had been dead—and frozen—for many, many years, and *that* was the body the cops now had.

The Nadler Logan he had known had used Nadler's money and influence to purchase nearly all the buildings around West Street in Clifton Hill—a street that just happened to cross one of the most powerful ley-line intersections in Melbourne. It was also an intersection that seemed very tied up in the desperate scramble to find the portal keys. According to Azriel, the intersections could be used to manipulate time, reality, or fate, and it was likely that whoever had stolen the first key from us—or, rather, me—had used the intersection to access the gray fields and permanently open the first portal.

Suggesting the face-shifter was either a sorcerer himself or he worked for someone who was. Only those well versed in magic could use the ley lines.

Of course, *why* the hell anyone would want to weaken the only thing that stood between us and the hordes of hell, I had no idea. Not even Azriel could answer that one.

But we'd obviously gotten too close to uncovering who the face-shifter was, so he'd stepped out of Nadler's life and into a new one. Unless Logan could reveal something about the man he'd known as Nadler, our search was going to be right back at the beginning.

"I'm not sure I can help you," Logan said. "He was just a client. I didn't know much about him on a personal level."

We're not interested in his personal life, but rather his business one. I hesitated. *What can you tell me about the deal he made with the heirs of James Trilby and Garvin Appleby?*

Trilby and Appleby were the two other members of the consortium that the fake Nadler had formed to purchase all the land around West Street. Their heirs had decided to sue the consortium—and therefore John Nadler, who had, on their death, become soul owner—for a bigger piece of the land pie. They'd reached an out-of-court settlement the day before Nadler had pulled the plug on his stolen identity.

"I'm not sure how that deal—"

Please, Mr. Logan, just answer the question.

He sighed and thrust a hand through his hair. The action stirred the ghostly strands, making them whirl into the ether before settling back down.

From somewhere in the distance came a gentle vibration, and the sensation crept around me uneasily, making the shadowy world surrounding us tremble. It almost felt like the beginnings of a quake, but was that even possible on the astral plane? Even as I thought about it, the shadows around me began to quiver, and Adeline's warning ran through my mind. I took a deep breath, imagining calmness. The shadowy world around us stilled, but the distant vibration continued. It was a weird sensation— and felt like trouble. I forced myself to ignore it and returned my attention to Logan.

"Nadler agreed to pay them several million dollars each," he said, "in exchange for them signing an agreement to accept the wills as they currently stand."

And will those payments proceed now that Nadler is dead?

He frowned. "Of course. The heirs just won't get the payment as quickly because it'll be tied up until Nadler's estate is sorted."

And who is Nadler's heir? He has no children and he divorced his wife a long time ago. A fact that *hadn't* stopped the fake Nadler from killing her.

"You know, there's a good percentage of men and women who forget to change their wills even after a second marriage, and it's not unknown for the first partner to get the estate over the second." He paused, eyeing me critically. "Have you got a will, young woman? It's never too late to start. I can offer you excellent—"

Thanks, I interrupted quickly, and rubbed my imaginary arms. That vibration was getting stronger, and it was *not* pleasant. *But I'm good, will-wise. Now, Nadler's heir?*

"How am I supposed to remember?" His tone was cross. "I haven't got the paperwork with me, and he's not my only client, you know."

I know. Just think back to the agreement. Imagine you have it in your hand.

He frowned and, a second later, ghostly paper began to

form between his hands. I didn't move, not wanting to startle him and lose the moment.

Who is his heir, Mr. Logan?

He's got three—Mr. Harry Bulter, Mr. Jim O'Reilly, and a Ms. Genevieve Sands.

A woman? One of Nadler's heirs was a woman? *Are any of them related to Mr. Nadler?*

"Not as far as I'm aware." He glanced up. "I still can't see why—"

Mr. Nadler was a very wealthy man, I said easily. *And it's not unknown for heirs to kill their benefactors to get hold of their money.*

"That, unfortunately, is true."

How was Nadler's estate divided between the three?

He glanced at the paperwork again. "All three have equal shares in everything."

I frowned. This wasn't making sense. Why would the face-shifter go to all the trouble of killing off Nadler, then divide the estate for which he'd murdered to fully control between three people?

When was the will drawn up?

His gaze flicked down to the bottom of the paper. "The same day he signed the deal with Trilby's and Appleby's heirs."

Which suggested an on-the-spot decision, but I very much doubted the man we were chasing ever did anything without forethought. *Is there anything else you can tell us about Nadler? Any reason you believe someone might want him dead?*

He frowned. "Not really."

I sighed. Logan hadn't really given us anything we couldn't have found out via a little subversive hacking, so maybe his death had been nothing more than the face-shifter leaving no threads behind, no matter how small.

Thank you very much for your assistance, Mr. Logan.

"You could repay me by finding my limo, you know. It seems to have disappeared."

Just use your phone and call it, Mr. Logan. He wouldn't get anywhere with it, but hey, if it made him happy, then what the hell?

He made the right motions, and a somewhat fuzzy white limousine popped into existence. As Logan happily climbed in, I turned away. Time to return—

The thought was cut short by a scream.

A scream that suggested there was a woman on the astral plane in very big trouble.